Personal Violation

Personal Violation

Scott Winslow Legal Mysteries Book 2

David P. Warren

Many thanks to my wonderful, insightful review team, who help me know when I get it right, and when I miss the mark:
Nancy J. Warren
Wendy L. Aiken
Melanie Sue Prisuta

"Courage is resistance to fear, mastery of fear, not absence of fear"
Mark Twain

Chapter One

At 7:30 a.m., Controller, Sarah Willis, stared at subsidiary financial reports on one of three monitors on her desk. She needed the opportunity to stretch, as well as a few moments away from the financial analysis she was preparing. After a protracted period of staring at her monitor, the numbers were beginning to run together, and turning to mush in her brain. Sarah's blond hair and blue eyes framed a radiant smile. Though not Hollywood model gorgeous, Sarah was attractive and compelling. As she made her way down the hall to the communal coffeemaker, Sarah observed that the offices around her were slowly transitioning from ghostly quiet, to active, as early birds began to arrive. She poured a cup of coffee, and then walked back to her office. One of her two Assistant Controllers, Melissa Carter, was removing her coat and getting settled in the office next door to Sarah's.

"Good morning, Melissa," Sarah said, smiling. Sarah's blue eyes sparkled with intelligence, and something else; self-confidence and enthusiasm. She wore her blonde hair at shoulder length, and was attractive, in an elegant way reminiscent of Kate Beckinsale.

"Morning boss," Melissa replied. She looked at Sarah's coffee cup. "How many so far?" Melissa asked.

"This is only number two, today," Sarah said, lifting the cup.

After quick calculation, Melissa said, "So, you've been here since about 6:00 this morning?"

Sarah stopped at Melissa's office door and shook her head. "It's amazing how you do that. I must be pretty damned predictable."

"Only where your coffee consumption is concerned," Melissa said. "And you were here pretty late last night. I mean, I left at 8:00 o'clock, and you were showing no signs of slowing down."

"Yeah, I got out of here about 10:30. Plenty of time to nap before being back here for a Tuesday morning." She took a deep breath. "We've only got one week to get all the subsidiary reporting complete, so I'm feeling the stress. Especially with the foot-dragging I'm getting from a couple of them. How are you doing?"

"I should have Wilson Pharma prepped for you to review by tomorrow," Melissa said. "Jansing Communications by Thursday."

"Great work. Between us, we will make these financials make sense, and get it done on time."

Coffee in hand, Sarah walked back into her office, where the singular picture of her and John on her desk caught her attention. It had been taken eight years ago, shortly after their honeymoon. The picture made her smile, as she reflected on how happy they had been in a world when spending time with each other was the priority. She had been promoted to Controller for Ellison Corporation three years ago, at about the same time his architectural practice began landing almost every contract they chased. Ever since, they both worked sixty hours a week, and saw each other on the run, or while working on emergencies at home. With the loss of time together they had lost some of the intimacy, as well. After eight years of marriage, she and John no longer talked about having kids. It's not that either had decided against children, they just didn't have the time or the lifestyle that would make it work. Hell, they barely had the time and energy for occasional sex. Over the last few years, the most intimate part of their lives had been slowly drifting away. They were both always tired, and it had become so easy not to talk about anything intimate or challenging. It was literally, a cost of doing business. At thirty-nine years old, Sarah had made it to the upper ranks of a corporate giant. An accounting degree, an MBA, and seven years of experience and she was still a young woman. She considered the irony; it took years to achieve a level of success that would assure that there was never time for a personal life.

Neither Sarah nor Melissa stopped for lunch. The day was a race characterized by salads at their desks and little time for extraneous thought, and barely time for bathroom breaks. Melissa appeared at Sarah's door at 7:00 p.m. "Goodnight boss."

Sarah looked up from her monitor and shook her head. "We didn't even have an opportunity to cover the status of the subsidiary analysis. In the morning, okay?"

"I'll be here," Melissa said. "And judging by the looks of things, you may be here still."

Sarah smiled. "I really am going home soon. I'm seeing double, and my head is so full of numbers that they may start leaking from my ears." She paused and then added, "Thanks for your hard work, Melissa."

Melissa smiled, and said, "Thanks, chief. Goodnight," and then she disappeared from the doorway.

At 7:45 p.m. the world outside her office window the sun was long gone and only the city's ambient light illuminated the streets. Sarah analyzed the data and projections of three subsidiaries on three separate monitors. She had to assure that each of the subsidiaries spoke the same analytical language, compared apples and apples and used generally accepted accounting procedures in their analyses. Her eyes were getting tired and she had intermittent thoughts about something that might pass as dinner.

James Nolan, Ellison Company's CEO, stood at the door and gave a knock. "Mind if I interrupt?" he asked.

"Please, Jim, come in."

He sat down and looked at her paper-covered desk and multiple monitors. "Impressive," he said. "The way you're getting all this together. I know some of the subsidiaries have to be coerced into getting things done."

She nodded. "You could say that."

Nolan was about fifty years old; an outgoing, handsome man, with black hair decorated with highlights of grey. He exuded confidence, and focused keenly on anyone he addressed. He laughed and said, "I know you're busy, so I'll cut to the chase. I am coming to the end of my first year here and the Board likes what the team is doing. You guys are making me look good." He paused and said, "I like to reward those loyal to me and I'm thinking that you are right for the Senior Vice President of Finance position. You've got a great handle on operations, as well as the financial side, so in three or four months from now I'm going to suggest your name to the Board. I don't think I'll get much resistance."

Sarah smiled. "That's great news, Jim. Thank you. And thanks for the acknowledgment of my work."

He paused a moment and then said, "I want you to go to Seattle to attend the Urban Attache acquisition meeting tomorrow night." She was puzzled. That meeting was not her typical turf. Worse, she had so much to accomplish with all of the corporate financial reports that she had no time for someone else's side show. Nolan added, "You're going for the Thursday presentation anyway, right? I understand that you are making a presentation Thursday morning, and I can use your help Wednesday night."

"Okay," Sarah said. "If you need me at the meeting tomorrow night, I'll be there."

"Thanks, Sarah. I knew I could count on you," Nolan said. He was quiet for a moment, and then he said, "You know, Sarah, you are an attractive woman and I'd like to know you better." He grinned widely and added, "We could be really good together."

She furrowed her brow. Groping for words, she said, "We are both married to someone else."

He smiled and said, "Sure, but we could really spice things up." She said nothing. "Let me be straight with you. I want to make love to you." He was still grinning as he added, "And I know that you would love it, too."

"I am not okay with that, Jim," she said as sternly as she could. "I'm not in the market for a relationship, and I don't want to be hit on."

"Okay," Nolan said, "we'll leave it for now, but I'm not giving up. I want you in my bed." He grinned widely and then walked from her office. This was not the first time he flirted with her, but it was the first time that he was so direct in asking for sex. Nolan had made periodic comments about how "good" or how "hot" she looked, and tended to let his eyes fall to her chest, but had never gone further until today. This was something else and it made her feel dirty; like she needed a shower. She stared at her computer for a time, but couldn't get what had just happened out of her mind. It crossed her mind that she should report these comments to Human Resources, but if she did, she might be killing her promised advancement. Maybe, she could just keep Nolan at a distance by letting him know she didn't want to hear it. Maybe then, he would leave her alone. She felt sick to her stomach as she picked up her coat and walked out of the office.

As Sarah drove home, she contemplated telling John about Nolan's comments, but decided that it would needlessly make him angry. She thought again about going to Human Resources, but the very thought of going through a process with the CEO was nauseating. Besides, so many women had tolerated so much more. She told herself that if this was as bad as it got, she could handle it. She would let it go for now.

Wednesday was as crazy as expected. Sarah was avalanched by about forty phone calls, a hundred emails, and two meetings that went on far too long. After running between crises all day long, Sarah raced to the airport and boarded the late afternoon plane to Seattle with only seconds to spare. She sat down on the plane, pulled her laptop and began to review financial reports. Time was ticking faster than ever.

When Sarah left Los Angeles, it was a typical March day. It was cool, a little overcast, with the sun periodically trying to break through and in the low sixties. When she arrived in Seattle, it was raining and, as always, amazingly green. She hired a Lyft car to drive her to the Puget Sound Hotel. She checked into her room on the twelfth floor and made her way to the elevator. When it stopped, she walked the well-lit corridor to room 1221. She waved the electronic key at the door handle and a light turned green to acknowledge her right of access. She dropped her suitcase on the bed and looked over at the blinking light on the phone. She picked it up and retrieved a voicemail from Jim Nolan. "Hey, Sarah, this is Jim. Something has come up and I have to attend another meeting tonight. You're going to have to handle Urban Attache alone, but we can catch up tonight. I should be able to meet you in the hotel lounge about 10:00. Thanks, Sarah. See you later tonight."

She shook her head. Things had just gotten a whole lot weirder. She was now flying solo in a meeting that needed someone else's authority and expertise, with no real preparation and only general knowledge of the intended agenda. Sarah prided herself on being prepared for every meeting, so this did not feel good at all. She wondered why Nolan was suddenly unavailable to attend a meeting that was set up for his schedule. She mindlessly put a few things in drawers, and then checked her appearance. She decided that she made a satisfactory appearance for someone operating on reserve energy. Sarah dialed home and got no answer, so she tried John's cell. It went to voicemail. "Hi John. Just calling to let you know that I'm thinking about you. I'm off to the meeting I told you about in Seattle. I hope you are having a good day." She ended the call, and then picked up her briefcase and made her way downstairs. She summoned another Lyft car as she walked. It would be there in four minutes; a green Nissan. There was no time for dinner.

* * *

It was 7:30 p.m. when Sarah walked into the conference room on the twenty-fourth floor of the Winston Building downtown. She was introduced to Urban Attache's CEO, CFO and in-house attorney. They grabbed coffee from a credenza spanning the width of the room, and seated themselves around the conference table in a manner avoiding the appearance of adversarial sides.

"I am here on behalf of Jim Nolan, who wants us to proceed with this acquisition as quickly as we can get everything completed," Sarah said.

She was met with silence, and some disapproving looks. "I understood that Mr. Nolan was going to be here to finalize everything tonight," the CEO, Preston Langley, said with concern.

"He was going to be," Sarah said, "but an emergency came up and he couldn't make it. I can go through the checklist to make sure that everything is in order, with the exception of two issues."

Langley did not look happy. He said, "We agreed to close this deal and that this meeting was to handle those two issues. Now, we're not going to get it done?"

"Let me address those two issues," she said. "We have the revisions to the financials under discussion, and everything looks good, but we need them audited before we can close."

"We'll have the audited version by Monday," Langley said, unhappily.

"The other item was the pending dispute with Caspian Products, over the patent. Can I get a look at the final due diligence documents we requested?"

The attorney, Gabriel Johns, handed her a file containing about a dozen multi-page documents, some of them a page or two, others twenty pages in length. She looked through the documents, five minutes growing to ten, while they all waited silently.

"I can't make the final decision on this," she said, closing the file. "I need our CEO and our lawyer to review these documents."

Langley leaned back in his chair and shook his head. "Like I said before, I understood that final decisions were the purpose of this meeting."

Sarah took her time responding, demonstrating no intimidation or panic. "I understand, but as I told you, Mr. Nolan had a last minute emergency and couldn't be here. I will take the financials, and the final due diligence documents, with me. You send me the audited version of the financials, and I will recommend that we sign off. Mr. Nolan will need to review these," she said, pointing to the newly received documents. She paused and added, "We should have our review complete by the time we get the auditor's certification next week, so there will be no unnecessary delays." There was a lingering dissatisfied silence in the room, as everyone except Sarah considered whether to complain further about the delay. "Let's go through the checklist," Sarah said, "to make sure everything else is done."

They spent twenty minutes covering a list of items that had been completed before her arrival, and found everything in order. Sarah said, "Thank you all for your courtesy. I'm sorry we couldn't get further tonight."

Langley looked at the lawyer and said, "Evidently, we've gone as far as we are going to get tonight, although I'm a little confused about why we set this evening meeting just to kick finalization down the road. Let's get this signed off by early next week." He extended a hand and Sarah shook it, and then the other hands around the table.

"Thanks, gentlemen," she said and walked from the room. These natives were restless, but at least not yet in open revolt. She wondered why Nolan had dumped this meeting on her knowing that she would be unable to respond to the remaining issues, and she was a little pissed off about it. Carrying the files she had taken for review, along with her briefcase, she made her way to the front of the building. The Seattle rain was coming down, as she stopped in the doorway and dialed Lyft to get her ride back to the hotel. What a day.

* * *

Sarah found a soup and salad restaurant near the hotel. She sat in the window and watched people walk, jog and ride bikes in the rain. The people of Seattle handled rain like it wasn't there. Whatever they planned to do, they did regardless of the weather. It didn't seem to slow them down, and it didn't seem to bother them. She ordered soup that was warm and full of chicken chunks. It was just what she needed. As she finished the soup she decided that the other thing she needed was sleep. It was nine-thirty and she had no desire to wait another hour, and then meet Nolan in the lounge for a drink. She wanted a bath, and to settle for the night. She paid the bill and then walked down the busy street of pavers to the hotel, a block away. She made her way to the elevator and then to her room. The king bed looked great. Maybe she should forego the bath until morning. She put her briefcase and files on the table and began to unbutton her blouse. The phone rang and she looked at it like there was an enemy inside this little, electronic Trojan horse. It was Nolan. She hesitated and then picked it up. She really had no choice.

"Sarah Willis," she said matter-of-factly.

"I'm back, Sarah. Can you meet me in the lounge?"

She hesitated just a moment, and then said, "Okay," wishing she had let the call go to voicemail. "I'll be there, shortly."

She looked around the room, wishing she could stay. She took the two files received at the evening meeting and walked down the hall to the elevator. She rode it to the top, where the City View Lounge boasted a 360 degree view of downtown. The large room was inhabited by four groups in suits, all male, and two couples seated in distant corners and focused on each other.

Sarah sat at a table near a window and ordered a glass of Pinot Noir. She debated with herself about whether to confide in Nolan that he left her out of her element by ditching the meeting. She decided to play it by ear. If the situation was right, she would let him know.

Ten minutes later, Nolan walked in and ordered a Jack Daniels. He sat next to her and asked, "So, how was it?"

"Well," she said, "it was a little unusual."

"How so?" he asked, sipping his Jack.

"Because the group expected us to handle everything today, including the last due diligence items and the Caspian patent dispute issues."

"Yeah, sorry I couldn't be there to close the deal," he said, evenly. "I just had no choice. It was critical." He paused a moment and took a long pull on his drink. The glass was empty and signaled the bartender for another. "So what do you think about the issues?"

"I think the financials work, although I told them we wouldn't sign off until we had the audited versions. They say that will be on Monday. As to the patent issue, entirely outside my area of expertise, but I have a few questions about the due diligence documents they provided."

He grinned. "Nice work, Sarah. I really can depend on you." She smiled, but said nothing. "You have some good things ahead for you in this company," he added.

"Thanks," she said.

They were quiet while he quickly finished his second drink and ordered a third. He drank it down in two pulls, while Sarah had one more sip of her wine. Her glass was still half-full, but she was tired and didn't want any more. "Okay, boss, I have to get some sleep so I can get up for my presentation in the morning."

"Sure," Nolan said, grinning. He dropped thirty dollars on the table and stood up. "Stop by my room long enough to pick up a couple of documents that I want you to get a look at."

It wasn't a question. She felt uncomfortable, but wanted to show him she was part of his critical team, so she said, "Okay."

"I'm in 1474," he said.

Just like the office, he was posted one floor above her, she thought, because this hotel didn't have a thirteenth floor. Somehow, hoteliers believed that if they didn't label the floor as number 13, the consumer wouldn't figure out that number 14 is really the thirteenth floor. They walked silently to the elevator. As the elevator rose rapidly, Nolan said, "I'm really sorry I couldn't be there tonight. I know that must have been difficult, but you carried if off beautifully."

"I guess we'll see about that when you start getting calls from Langley asking why they didn't get the guy at the top."

They stepped out of the elevator and walked half way down the hall until they came to room 1474. Nolan waved his key card and they walked into a suite with a big living room and a bar. "Want a night cap?" he asked.

"No, Jim. I'm okay."

He nodded and then walked to the coffee table and pulled a couple of documents from a file. He walked back to where she waited and handed them to her. As he handed the documents to her, he said, "These are first level financials for a new acquisition under consideration. Debt level seems high, but I want to know what you think about the organization's earnings projections."

She felt a sense of relief that he had documents to give her. "Great," she said. "Happy to give them a once over."

He smiled and said, "Thanks. We can talk about it over the next couple of days."

She nodded and said, "Good night." As she turned to leave, he grabbed her arm, pushed her up against the wall and held her while he kissed her. She was momentarily stunned, and then pulled away. She looked at him angrily and yelled, "No!" and then she found her legs and walked out the door, slamming it behind her. She shivered as she walked down the corridor toward the elevators. "Holy shit," she said. "I can't fucking believe it." She wondered if she had been stern enough in shutting him down. They were going to have a talk about this when they got home. This was not okay. She walked into her room and locked the deadbolt. She leaned against the door, still shaking. Sarah wasn't tired anymore, as she paced the room, playing what had just happened over in her mind. It was just the drinks, she told herself. He would be embarrassed by all of this tomorrow. She began to slow her pulse as she put it in this perspective. She called John and got voicemail again. This time she didn't leave a message. She wished he was with her now to help her see this right and to make her feel better. He had a way of making her comfortable when she was worried. She was glad that her desire to retreat to him for comfort hadn't been a casualty of the distance between them.

Sarah took off her suit and hung it up. She found a hotel robe in the closet and put it on over her bra and panties, and began getting ready for bed. She removed her makeup and brushed her teeth. As she finished, and thought about how good it was going to feel to climb into bed, there was a knock on her door. She said nothing and the knocking came again.

"Who is it?"

"It's me, Sarah," Jim Nolan said through the door.

"What do you want?"

"I just want to talk to you for one minute." There was silence. "Sarah, I want to apologize for what happened in my room. I should not have done that."

"Fine, you can apologize more in the morning, Jim."

"Just one minute of your time."

"Tomorrow, Jim," she said again.

"Please Sarah, I just want one minute. It's really important."

She hesitated again, and then opened the deadbolt and the door. "Can I come in; just for a moment?"

"I'm not okay with what happened, Jim. You know that, right?"

"Yeah, I know that," he said, pushing past her and closing the door behind him as he stepped into the room.

"What are you doing?" she asked. "Please leave. Now!"

He nodded and said, "Okay," but didn't move. He stared at her, causing her to draw her robe around her tighter.

"Get out of my room," she ordered.

"You are one beautiful woman, Sarah. You are so gorgeous." He moved towards her and put his arms around her as she pushed him away. "Stop it, God damn it, stop it."

He grabbed her wrists and pushed her back onto the bed. Then he climbed on top of her. "You and I are a team, Sarah. I can make your life great."

She began yelling, "Get off, you son of a bitch. Get off me."

He pulled the robe open and began tugging at her underwear. She let out a scream and then there was a sudden pain as he slapped her hard across the face. He tore off her underwear and then he was pushing himself into her. "You know that you want this Sarah. I can make you feel great."

"Stop it. Get off. Stop it." She began to scream and he put his hand over her mouth, pushing her hard into the bed. She slapped and pushed at him with everything she had, and he held tighter and pushed into her harder. It was hurting now. She pushed hard at his nose, and then she grabbed at his eyes. He lowered his head and thrust harder and harder into her. Sarah heard herself crying. She was unable to move. She turned her head and tried to yell, but his hand tightly covered her mouth. She pushed and scratched at him, but he thrust harder into her. She punched at him with everything she had, and it made no difference. The punches didn't land.

She could do nothing to stop him. She told herself that she would live through this; that she could survive it. He thrusted harder. He was hurting her so much, and he didn't care. He was taking everything from her; everything she had spent her whole life building. She was suddenly weak. She was a victim he could use and throw away. It crossed her mind that he might even kill her. He yelled out as he came inside her and she cried out, with a clenched hand across her mouth. She punched at him hard, without landing a blow that had any effect. She laid on the bed crying and hurting, as he stood and pulled up his pants, and then moved quickly out the door without speaking a word.

She stayed on the bed crying; shaking uncontrollably for a long, immeasurable time. She wasn't sure if minutes or hours passed before she ran to the door and locked it. Then she found herself beating on the door with her fists. She walked into the bathroom and turned on the shower. She was sobbing, and she was hurt. There was blood on her. Her whole body was shaking hard, and uncontrollably, as she climbed into the shower and tried to scrub him off. She washed again and again, but she couldn't seem to get clean. She had no idea how long she was in the shower, scrubbing and crying. It was a terrible nightmare that would never end. When she stepped from the shower, she left the water running. She put two towels around her, covering herself from shoulders to knees, and then she sat down on the bathroom floor next to the toilet and sobbed aloud. She could not control her crying. The violation was so deep that she thought she would never stop crying, and she would never stand up again. Minutes, and then hours, passed, as Sarah sat on the floor, shivering from deep within her and crying, never stopping the water that ran in the shower. She couldn't move. She felt all that every woman who had been raped felt: anger, sorrow, helplessness and the most abhorrent, intimate violation possible.

At 3:30 a.m., Sarah managed to regain a sense of her surroundings. She packed her bag and left the hotel. She summoned a Lyft and went to the airport to get on the earliest flight home. The Lyft driver watched her in the rear view mirror with compassion, as she cried. He could see the despair, and really wanted to help, but had no idea what to say. Immense sorrow and pain filled her eyes, as she left the Lyft car, and moved slowly toward the terminal pulling her bag.

Chapter Two

The plane landed and Sarah drove home in a fog. She felt alone and isolated. Entirely out of character, she was not going to attend her morning presentation. She hadn't even called anyone to tell them she wouldn't make it. Her part of the presentation just wouldn't happen. She hadn't called John to tell him what had happened. She was afraid to tell him; afraid and ashamed. He would be angry. He would want to kill Nolan. And worse yet, he might start to look at her differently. What had she done to encourage this? How did she let herself get into this situation? She had asked herself countless times why she had opened the door to her room. Why she had let him in after he had forcibly kissed her? She felt foolish and blameworthy. She was partly responsible for this. Sarah had always told herself that she was a strong woman and that something like this could never happen to her. She always thought she could be in control in any situation.

Sarah arrived home at 10:30 a.m. and immediately turned on the shower. She took off her clothes, climbed under the shower-head and began to soap herself, over and over again. The memory and the trauma could not be washed away. She couldn't make herself clean again, and she felt like she was falling from a cliff; no control and no way out. Sarah knew that the rape had taken away parts of her that she could not reclaim. She had been damaged.

Sarah dried off and put on a nightgown. She knew that she should seek medical attention, but she didn't want to tell anyone. She wasn't ready to face what had happened to her, and all that it would mean. She climbed into bed, and cried until she drifted off into a troubled sleep. At 7:00 p.m., John came home and found her in bed. She wanted so badly to tell him what had happened, and how she had been violated, but she couldn't find the words. She heard herself tell him that she was feeling under the weather, even while she was pulling the covers to her chin to conceal the remaining bruise discoloration on her arms, shoulders and neck. He kissed her and tucked the covers over her. He told her that she had been pushing herself too hard and that she needed to give herself a chance to recover. He asked if she needed medicine or food and she said no to everything. She told him that she just needed rest.

He closed the bedroom door, not knowing of the trauma that his wife had endured. It was a second awful day when she didn't get help, and when she kept a terrible secret. A second terrible day when she wasn't sure that she wanted to live anymore. It felt like an eternity.

On Friday morning, John kissed her and asked if he could get breakfast for her. She refused. She was still under the weather, but things would get better. She had to promise him that if she didn't feel better by tomorrow, she would make a doctor's appointment.

Sarah stayed in bed all morning. She drifted off to sleep for short periods and then awoke to the stark reality, rediscovering the nightmare all over again. She sat up in bed and found herself sobbing uncontrollably. After a time, she got up and put on a robe. She made her way into the bathroom and opened up the medicine cabinet. She considered the bottles on the shelf. There was a full bottle of aspirin, and there were a number of Vicodin left over from John's old back injury. She stood staring into the cabinet, wondering whether there were enough pills there to allow her to end the pain that inflicted her every waking moment. She wasn't sure, and she didn't want John to come home and find her. She told herself that there had to be another way through this.

Sarah walked around the house, aimlessly looking for some diversion from the reality that tore her apart. She took a seat in the living room and stared out the living room window, not noticing the sunny day outside. A dark cloud had taken her mind, and seemed to be closing in on her. Her life had been taken away from her, and there seemed to be no point in continuing.

At 1:00 p.m. her phone rang. The caller ID said it was Angie Barnett, her best friend since college. She let it ring three times, and then hit the button. "Angie," she said, tearfully.

"Sarah, what's wrong." There was silence. "Sarah, what is it."

"Angie, I was raped," she cried out, the words pouring out of her, almost involuntarily.

"Are you at home?"

"Yes."

"I'll be there in twenty minutes."

Sarah felt some small measure of relief in telling her friend about the nightmare she had been secreting. She put on coffee and sat at the kitchen table to wait for her friend. She didn't have to wait long. There was a knock at the front door and Angie was calling her name. "Sarah, it's me. Let me in."

Sarah walked to the front door and opened it slowly. Angie threw her arms around Sarah as soon as she stepped inside. "My God, Sarah, are you okay?"

Sarah shook her head. "No, I don't think so."

"What happened? Who did this to you?" Her friend was angry, and ready to fight.

"Thank you for coming, Angie. I don't think I've ever needed a friend like I do today."

They sat down on the couch and Angie took Sarah's hands in hers, and didn't let go for two hours as Sarah told her the story. The kiss in his room, his invasion into her room and what he did to her. She told Angie about her guilt and shame. She should never have let him in. She should never have been in a situation where that could happen.

Angie shook her head. "Right, and people shouldn't be where robberies occur so they don't get robbed or shot. This is not your fault, Sarah. This is that fucking pig you work for and he needs to be held accountable." She took a deep breath, fighting back anger she felt toward the man who attacked her friend. "Are you okay, physically?"

"Not great. The pain isn't what it was, but I'm sore. It's a constant reminder of what he did. Not that I need to be reminded." She drew a breath, and then added, "I had a little bruising on my face from where he slapped me. I put make-up over it when I got home, and now it's pretty much faded."

"Have you seen anyone? I mean a doctor?"

"No."

"Did you call the cops?"

Sarah was quiet and then said. "I thought about it a lot, but I worry about what comes from all that."

"What do you mean?" Angela blurted out excitedly, "You have to turn this sick mother fucker in."

"You know what they do to women who come forward. They say that she wanted it, and now she's had second thoughts because she's married. She's a whore. Let's explore her sexual history and see what we can find to attack. Jesus, Angie, the victim of rape gets to be the victim over and over again."

"I understand," Angie said softly, "but the alternative is to let this shit go on every day; to let him do it again."

Sarah was silent a few moments and then said, "I just don't know if I can face all that."

"Since when?" Angie said. "The Sarah that I know can stand up to any man and demand accountability. There is no way she lets him get away with this." She paused and said, "I know that a large number of women who have been raped or sexually assaulted never come forward because it's so hard, but that only assures two things. The first is that the woman remains a victim for the rest of her life, and the second is that the son of bitch just walks free to do it to someone else."

Sarah nodded. "But how do I escape feeling so ashamed about it all? Part of me just wants to never speak of it again."

"Yeah, that's what your boss wants, too." She reflected a moment and then asked, "Have you told John yet?"

Sarah silently shook her head.

"You need to tell him, Sarah. If you don't it becomes a trust issue between you and John."

Sarah nodded slowly. "I know that you're right. I just haven't wanted to face that conversation. I'll tell him tonight."

"And go see a counselor, and a lawyer, right away."

"A lawyer?"

"Yes, damn it. This is not okay and this asshole needs to know it's not okay."

"What did you tell work about why you're not there?"

"Nothing. I haven't called anyone."

"All right. Ask the lawyer what you should do about that."

"I don't know which lawyer to call."

Angie pulled out her cell and dialed a number. "Justin Evans, please. This is Angela Barnett." There was a slight pause and then Angie said, "Justin, you were telling me about a good employment lawyer on the employee side recently, you remember that?" Angie pulled a pen and paper from her purse during the brief silence that followed. "Yeah, I have a close friend who has a significant employment issue." Angie scratched some information onto the page and then asked, "This is the guy you most recommend?" Another pause. "Great. Thanks, Justin."

She handed Sarah the paper. "You need to call, Scott Winslow at Simmons and Winslow. Here's his info."

"That name is familiar somehow."

"Good employment lawyer. He got a big verdict against Consolidated Energy last year for a whistleblower."

"I think I remember hearing about that case."

"Promise me two things, Sarah. Promise me that after you tell John, you'll see a counselor and that you'll make an appointment to see Scott Winslow." Sarah looked worried, so Angie added, "You don't have to commit to do anything more, but go talk to him."

Sarah was momentarily quiet and then she nodded slowly. "Okay, I will."

"Yeah?"

"Yes." Sarah hugged her friend and said, "Thank you so much, Angie." She was quiet a moment and then asked, "Can you stay with me until John comes home tonight? The world looks a little better when I'm with you."

"You bet. Let's go get some coffee and get down to some real girl talk." She smiled. "We can get through this together."

* * *

At 5:00 p.m., Sarah called John and asked him to come home early. She told him it was important and they needed to talk. He said he would leave right away.

When they hung up, Angie said, "This will be hard for him, too, Sarah, but he's not the victim here, you are. And you do not have a thing to apologize for. You just want everyone on your team to help you. That's what John needs to keep as his priority."

"You are amazing, Angie. I don't know what I would do without you."

"You will never have to know that, my friend."

They hugged each other, holding tight. When they pulled back, Sarah could see that Angie was crying.

As John walked in, Angie hugged him and said, "She needs your help, John."

He looked puzzled as Angie walked out of the house. He turned to Sarah and said, "What is it, sweetheart? What's happening?"

They sat down next to each other on the couch and she said, "I need you to listen carefully and not overreact, because that will make it worse."

"Okay," he said, and waited for her to continue.

"I was raped Wednesday night."

"What? Oh, my God. Are you okay?"

"I'm not great, but I'm doing my best to hang in there."

He threw his arms around her and held her tight. She stayed in his arms for what seemed like minutes. He pulled back and looked into her eyes, keeping his arms around her neck, and trying to suppress his own emotional reaction, knowing he needed to see through the anger. He had to be a calming influence and listen carefully to her.

"Who did this?"

"Jim Nolan."

"Jesus. Your boss raped you?" Anxiety filled his face. "You need a doctor. Did you get checked out?"

"I haven't seen anyone yet. Physically, I'll heal. I'm just sore."

"Jesus Christ, that son of a bitch."

She gave him a moment and then said. "It happened at the hotel on Wednesday night after we both came back from our meetings. He pushed me against a wall and kissed me and I walked away. Then he came to my room and knocked. He told me it was to apologize for his behavior."

"Oh, shit," John muttered, anger getting the better of him. "I'll kill that…"

"John. Just listen to me, please."

"Okay, okay," he said, trying to regain control.

She took him through all of it. Everything that happened.

"I feel so ashamed, John. I shouldn't have opened that door. Maybe I should have done something else differently."

When he saw the hurt and fear in Sarah's eyes, he set aside his anger and put his arms around her. "Sweetheart, you did nothing wrong. Nothing. And together we will make it through all of this, I promise."

She teared up and said, "I'm so sorry, John. And I'm sorry for not telling you sooner. Some crazy part of me thought that you would think less of me for letting it happen."

He held her close and told her, "I love you so much. I'm so sorry for what you're going through." He suppressed flashes of anger that arose in the midst of his overwhelming feelings of sorrow and compassion for the woman he loved. He wanted to protect her. He wanted to cry. He wanted to kill James Nolan.

Chapter Three

On Monday morning, Sarah walked into Scott Winslow's office. Donna greeted her in the lobby. "Ms. Willis?"

"Yes," Sarah said, shaking Donna's extended hand.

"I'm Scott's paralegal, Donna. We talked on the phone." Donna is one of those people that everyone is glad to meet. She has a warm smile, and a disarming manner that puts people at ease.

"Yes, I remember you," Sarah said. "When we talked on the phone, you made me feel less nervous about coming here."

Donna saw the concern in her eyes and said. "You can be sure that Scott and I will keep your confidences. We want to help you if we can."

Sarah nodded, but "I'm not sure if anyone can," were the words that came out.

"Let us try," Donna said. "Do you want some coffee?"

"No, I'm okay," she replied.

"Let's go back to the conference room," Donna said. "Scott will join us there."

They sat down in adjacent chairs around a marble conference room table that seated eight. The room was decorated with warm landscapes. Donna said, "Whatever you elect to do, as a woman I want you to know that I am so sorry. No woman should ever have to face what you did. Not ever."

Scott Winslow appeared at the door. He was over six feet and slender. He had brown hair and blue eyes. He smiled in Sarah's direction and extended a hand. "Good morning, Sarah. I'm so glad you had a chance to talk to Donna. You've probably already figured out why she is my right hand."

"I think I have," Sarah said. "Thanks for fitting me in on short notice. Quite frankly, I was not inclined to come at all, but my best friend and my husband made me promise that I would."

Scott closed the conference room door and sat down directly across the table from Sarah, armed with a yellow legal pad and a pen. Donna was on his left, at the end of the table. "So, Sarah, this is kind of a hard conversation. I have to ask you things that you would rather not discuss, so that I can properly evaluate the situation and assess the terrain for you. Part of my job is to give you my thoughts about a potential case, including any bad news." He smiled at her and added, "Two things I can tell you. First, we are on your team, no one else's. Secondly, regardless of whether we go forward on your behalf, everything you tell us is confidential and will not be shared beyond those who work with this office on your behalf. Okay?"

"I appreciate that," Sarah replied.

"Can you take me through it?" Scott asked. "Tell me about the circumstances that got you to Seattle and then tell me everything that happened while you were there through the time of the attack."

Sarah took them through all of it. The request that she attend a meeting with Nolan in Seattle and his last minute failure to attend, leaving her to go alone to a meeting not within her usual purview. She told them of his request that she meet him in the lounge, and his consumption of three drinks, while she sipped on a glass of wine. She told them of the discussion that occurred and how he asked her to make a stop in his room to pick up documents. Then she told them about being pushed against the wall and kissed and running from his room. Scott observed that discomfort was visible in both her eyes and her body language as she spoke. She told them about Nolan showing up outside her room, saying he wanted to apologize, and she told them that, after he asked a few times, she had foolishly let him into her room to apologize. Then she cried as she discussed what he did to her, and how she tried so helplessly to fight. Scott and Donna nodded understandingly, and both took copious notes. Scott periodically asked questions and reassured her that she should continue. When she completed her story, Scott said, "Do you want some water before we continue?"

She nodded, and he left the room for a minute. He returned with water for all three of them. He sat back down and said, "I have to ask you some tough questions, Sarah."

"You mean it hasn't been tough so far?" she replied.

Scott smiled at her, and said, "I'm glad you still have your sense of humor. That says something about your strength of character." He paused and then said, "I have to ask things that are uncomfortable because I need to know the answers to assess the matter legally, and because others will pose these questions if the matter goes further. Are you okay with that?"

"I am," Sarah said, looking to Scott and then to Donna. "I feel safe here."

"That's good, Sarah, and you should. We asked you to come to this meeting alone today because your husband's presence might make it hard for you to answer sensitive questions. After today, your husband can come along with you to any meeting you want him to attend." He paused and then asked, "Had you ever had any personal relationship with Nolan? Anything sexual?"

"No, absolutely not."

"Even a flirtation?"

"He flirted, telling me how 'hot' I was, but there was no flirting by me."

Sarah's eyes showed fear and worry. Donna touched Sarah on the arm, and when Sarah looked at her, said reassuringly, "You're doing great."

Scott smiled at Sarah and said, "Tell me if you need a break. I know this is hard."

"I'm okay," Sarah said, beginning to feel like she was among people she could trust.

"Take me through what happened from the time Nolan left your room after the rape through today. Everything you have done and all conversations that have happened."

She told them everything. She spoke of sitting on the bathroom floor until she left the hotel. She spoke of her withdrawal and isolation until her friend Angie came to her rescue. Donna took Angie's contact information.

"Did you report this to the police?" Scott asked.

"No," she replied, sounding apologetic.

"When did you first tell your husband?"

"After my friend, Angie, came over and we talked on Friday."

"She was the first one you confided in?"

"So, why not him?"

Sarah shook her head. "It was so hard to tell him that I was attacked by someone. I knew what kind of pain he would feel, and how angry he would be at Nolan."

"Did you have any hesitation that he might not believe you? That he would think there was something between the two of you?"

"No, although at some level maybe I feared he might think I didn't do enough to prevent it. I feel like such an idiot for opening that door."

"And why didn't you go to the police with this?"

Sarah sat back in her chair and drew a deep breath. "At first, I thought I should just live with this; that I was strong enough to get past it alone and never speak of it to anyone. Then, I slowly realized that I was not okay anymore—that I was really damaged. For a time, I wasn't even sure that I wanted to live. Even once Angie broke through and helped me see that I needed to stand up, the idea of going to the police sounded horrible; to live the violation all over again as you get questioned about every detail, and to have cops and everyone who sees it in the media wonder if I'm lying, rather than the victim of a crime. I've seen it happen to women who come forward and it all seems to compound the abominable crime already endured."

"It does, Sarah. There is no doubt about that. But it's the only system we have," Scott said. "Is there any physical evidence of what occurred? Clothing, injuries, anything at all?"

She showed him the remnant of a bruise on her neck and one on her arm."

"Have you photographed the bruises?"

"I did, but not until last night."

"Any other evidence?"

"I still have my torn underwear."

"Good, bag them up and keep them safe." Scott paused and then asked, "Sarah, what do you think that Jim Nolan is going to say when confronted with allegations of rape?"

She shook her head. "He will deny anything ever happened or he will say it was voluntary is my guess. Rapists don't admit that they raped someone, do they? Seems like they never own what they've done."

Scott nodded. "That's right. Even in sexual harassment cases that don't involve acts as horrific as rape, they never admit what they've done. They always say it never happened, or it was consensual, or some combination of those things. In over twenty years of practice, I have never seen anyone stand up and say, "Yep. I did it." So, you can be assured all of this will be a fight and they will make us prove it happened while he goes on pretending he's a nice guy who would never do anything like this." Sarah nodded. "You should know that delayed reporting of the crime will be a point of attack for the defense."

"They are going to say it didn't happen because I didn't report it?"

"Yes. They will twist it. They will say that if you claim it was so awful, why did you stay silent? Is that because you were raped or because you slept with your boss, and then had second thoughts? Maybe, this was a way to keep your husband from finding out about an affair."

"This is going to be awful," Sarah said softly, a tormented expression on her face.

"They will urge that if this had really happened, wouldn't she have gone to the hospital, to the police or at least promptly told her husband?"

"It's a hopeless trap," she said, shaking her head.

"You can deal with it, you just have to know that it is something you will have to face. If you elect to pursue legal action against Nolan and the Company, that's what you are getting into. I don't want you to be surprised and I want to be able to give you time to consider it all."

"So tell me in your words, what caused you to delay reporting this crime?"

She took a moment and then replied, "I have been a successful, independent woman all of my adult life. I have always found a way to handle everything that comes along, and that ability to handle anything has become part of my self-image. Then something happened that I never imagined, and it's tied to the place where I have built my career. So, it feels like everything is on the line." She shook her head and then said, "I thought that I could handle everything that happened in life, and it turns out that I can't. I'm also afraid that if I report this crime, it's his word against mine. I will have to relive all the details of the most horrific hours of my life, and then maybe no one believes me. It feels like a no-win situation."

Scott nodded. "Do you feel like you have blame for what happened to you?"

Sarah teared up and said, "I guess I do."

"Why?"

"I should have been smarter. I never should have opened the door to my hotel room."

"Why did you open the door?"

She shook her head. "I actually believed he was there to apologize for forcing the kiss. I was so dammed stupid."

Scott said, "I want you to know that I believe you." He took a deep breath and asked, "When, if at all, do you plan to go back to work?"

"Maybe, tomorrow."

"Before you do, file a police report. Then go to your Human Resources Department and report what happened. Don't discuss it around the office, but be consistent whenever you describe what happened. This was not your fault, this was all about a rapist. That's what you tell them."

"I've worked with human resources executives a number of times. They know me pretty well, so I hope they can be fair."

Scott gave her a concerned look, and then said, "What you need to know is that dealing with human resources is the ultimate two-edged sword. It's where employees have to go to report harassment, discrimination and a wide variety of problems, right? Most employee handbooks tell you that's where you have to take any concern. They take it even further and point out that employees can be subject to discipline for a failure to report harassment, discrimination or other unlawful conduct."

"Right," Sarah said.

"The problem is," Scott said, "they are also the department charged with protecting the company from liability and their personnel are judged based upon how well they do that. The law says they have to investigate harassment, discrimination and other types of claims. Their people get trained on conducting investigations. But the findings and quality of that investigation often determine whether the company will be held accountable.

As a result, human resource representatives are trained to think in terms of how to protect the company. They protect themselves and their future by protecting the company, and sometimes they protect the company by preparing an investigation report that the company wants to see. If an investigation is successfully used to shield the company from liability, the human resources employee is going to get accolades, and maybe his next raise. If that investigation doesn't protect the company from a verdict, the investigator, and maybe the other human resource reps involved, may not be so popular." She looked concerned, but stayed silent. Scott gave her a smile and said, "So, the reason I tell you all this is that you may be surprised about the extent to which human resources will go to protect the company's interests at your expense. They may choose to believe Nolan or they give too much weight to the fact that this was not reported for a few days. Or they may recite the facts differently than the way they actually happened because it favors the result they want to achieve."

"So, what's the point in going through this process if the deck can be stacked at the outset?"

"Because you have to do it. If you don't, they take you through the employee handbook you signed, pointing out where you are obligated to report such events to human resources. But if you go through the process, you have complied with the requirements, and I can use the results. If they get facts wrong, if they misstate what witnesses say, if they leave out critical details or don't speak to witnesses, then I can go after them for all of those things and challenge whether the investigation is legally adequate."

"Okay, so I go through this and give them every opportunity to get it right, or to screw it up."

"Exactly. When you talk to the investigator, tell him or her about every time Nolan said or did something inappropriate; leave out nothing. When they ask you about witnesses, disclose anyone who is a witness to anything that happened. I know he did this stuff when no one was with you, but witnesses include people that you told about the events shortly after they happened. The fact that you told someone else adds to the credibility of your claims, and all of this is a credibility contest between you and Nolan."

"I understand," Sarah said.

"One more thing." Scott said, "Take a recorder and when the investigator meets with you to take your statement, tell him that you want to record the conversation. If the investigator is electronically recording, then the interview does not go forward unless you get to record, too. If he or she is not recording, chances are they still let you do it. Then we have the actual exchanges on record and they just have notes. If they are not recording and they don't let you record it, we'll use that fact as well."

"Can they fire me if I bring a lawsuit?"

"The law says no. They are prohibited from terminating or retaliating against you for reporting or bringing an action for harassment and discrimination. So they are not legally allowed to fire you for reporting it or pursuing it, but that doesn't mean they won't. It means that they have liability for that, too, if we can prove it happened. And it doesn't mean they won't treat you like an outsider or social pariah. Keep a journal of all words and actions that sound like retaliation by date and what occurred so that we have reliable evidence."

"I understand," Sarah said, nodding.

Scott asked, "Tell me about sexual harassment Nolan directed at you before the attack. Were there inappropriate comments about sex or your body? Anything like that?"

She was quiet for a moment and then said, "Yes. Like I said, several times he told me things like 'You look really hot today,' or 'Wow, you're looking good.' A couple of times he told me 'my husband is lucky to be climbing into bed with me.' He also had the habit of letting his eyes move down to my chest. I don't even think he cared if I saw he was doing it. It was all just those kind of actions and comments until last Tuesday, before the Seattle trip." She leaned back in her chair and took a deep breath.

"What happened Tuesday?" Scott asked.

"Tuesday, Nolan came into my office and told me that he wanted to make love to me. I was shocked and said that we were both married. He said we could really spice things up. He told me that I'd like it, too. It was pretty creepy."

"What was your response to that?"

"I told him that I didn't want to hear anything about sex, that it was not appropriate. He said 'I'll leave it for now, but I won't give up.' Then he added, 'I want you in my bed,' and then he walked out of my office."

"Did you talk to anyone about that conversation before the rape?"

Sarah shook her head. "I obviously should have, but I somehow thought I could deal with it at that point. Then came the trip to Seattle."

"To your knowledge, had he ever harassed anyone else in the workplace?"

"Not that I know of."

"Did he sleep with any other employees?"

"I don't know," Sarah replied.

"How is your relationship with your husband?" Scott asked.

"We are too busy, and don't get a lot of time together, but it's good."

"Still intimate?"

"Yes." She looked concerned. "Does this come out? I mean, do they get to ask me all about my sex life and my husband's as well?"

"No. We will be telling them nothing of your sex life. If they ask in your deposition, I will instruct you not to answer the question and we will fight it out in court if needed. We have a statute that says people bringing claims for sexual battery and harassment don't have to detail their sexual histories. This is an important protection, otherwise no one would ever want to come forward. This is all hard enough without some defense lawyer asking how frequently you've had sex and to describe your favorite position."

"Do they do that?"

"They often try and argue that it's relevant to whether what happened to you was voluntary. But like I said, you won't be answering any questions like that." Scott thought for a moment and then said, "Do you have any reason to believe that John has had any affairs. I have to ask whether the other side could locate evidence of anything like that. You know, hotel invoices, romantic meals, that kind of thing."

"Will they look for that as well?"

"They won't get it from us, but they will look around at social media and other outlets. Part of your injury claim is how the attack affects your relationship, so they will look around to see how strong the relationship was before this happened."

"Seems like there is no limit to what they will do to defend a case like this," Sarah said. After a moment, she added, "No, I am confident that John hasn't cheated on me. I know he thinks we haven't been as close as we once were, but I'm sure that John hasn't given up on us and hasn't been sleeping with others."

"Are there any videos on the web, Facebook posts, or anything public about your relationship with John, about Nolan, or about your work life?"

"No.

Scott smiled at her and nodded. He said, "Sarah, you come across credibly and we will take your case if you want us to represent you. You need to consider whether you want to move forward with an action against the company. It will be stressful to go through. Your deposition will be taken, and they will get to ask questions and try to attack your version of the facts. I will get to take Nolan's deposition, and I will go after him with everything we have. He needs to be held accountable for what he has done."

Sarah reflected a moment and then asked, "If a jury finds that he did this, is the company liable as well?"

"Yes, because this was business-related travel and he is your supervisor, and a company executive, the company will be on the hook if he is found liable."

"How do attorneys' fees work?"

"I will handle the case on a contingency fee basis. One third of any settlement up until sixty days before the trial date, then it goes to forty percent. You reimburse us for out-of-pocket costs like filing fees and court reporter charges for depositions we take as we incur them."

"And how long will this whole process take?"

"It will take a year or more to get to trial. During that time, both sides can send written questions that have to be answered under oath and requests to produce documents and take depositions to fully prepare the case." He paused and then said, "You mentioned earlier that Nolan said good things about your work or performance, is that right?"

"Yes, frequently."

"When was the last time?"

"The day before the trip to Seattle. He told me that my work made him look good and he planned to go to the Board and propose that I be promoted to Vice President of Finance. He said he didn't think he would get any resistance from any of the Board, because I had knowledge of the operations as well as the financials."

"Is it notated of memorialized anywhere?"

"Not to my knowledge."

"But, it was the day before the trip to Seattle?"

"Yes. In the same conversation in which he told me that he wanted me to go with him to his Seattle meeting."

Scott nodded. He reflected a moment and then said, "Sarah, I think you should consult with a psychologist or a counselor. These are life-altering events and the emotional part will usually far outlast the physical symptoms. I know that you are already battling depression, anxiety, fear, and damage to your self-confidence from this major trauma. You need someone to guide you through all of this emotionally, whether you elect to pursue a case or not."

Sarah thought a moment and then said, "I agree. I think Angie helped me realize that I was going to need some help getting through all this."

"You have any other questions of us?" Scott asked.

"I don't think so."

"If you have any questions feel free to call Donna or me. Spend the next few days thinking about whether you want to pursue an action and discuss it with your husband and then get back to us. I would be pleased to represent you, Sarah." They stood and shook hands and Scott said, "Whatever you decide to do, get a little counseling help and take good care of yourself."

Donna gave her a hug and said, "Call if you have questions or if you want to talk about anything. I'm so sorry this happened to you, Sarah."

Sarah smiled, and then she sat back down in her chair. They looked at her curiously and she said, "I want to do this. Let me sign your retainer agreement and let's get under way."

"Do you want to run it by John, first?"

"We talked about this. He said that if I liked and trusted you guys, and I was ready, then he was with me. So, let's do this."

* * *

When Sarah left Simmons and Winslow she drove to the mall to find anonymity among shoppers, while she obsessed about everything that had happened. She wasn't sure she had made the right decision, because she wasn't sure that she had the strength to go through litigation. She wasn't even sure that she could return to work. Her world seemed to be hanging by a thread.

She sat down on a bench near the center of the mall and called John. He was awaiting her call and answered on the first ring. "Hi, Sweetheart."

"Hi. I did it," she said. "I signed up with Scott Winslow."

"You liked him."

"I did. I like him and his wonderful paralegal. They were knowledgeable and pretty straight about what this would be like."

"Okay then, let's do this." He paused and then asked, "How do you feel?"

"Nervous. Scared about almost everything."

"I understand."

"Scott Winslow said I should talk to a counselor. Just like you and Angie told me."

"Are you going to do it?"

"I guess so. I'm not going to be able to pretend this didn't happen like I was hoping."

"Be better if you didn't," John said lovingly.

There was silence and then she asked, "How about you, John? How are you doing with this?"

"I've never been so angry in my life. And I'm sad. I would give anything not to have had this happen to you." Sarah heard him struggle to maintain composure. "I love you."

"I love you, too. And I get the anger thing. I've thought about killing him myself. It has become a pre-occupation of mine, thinking of different ways to get even."

"Damn good idea," he offered. "I'll start writing my ideas down as well. That is one alternative to actually snuffing the son of a bitch. I'm just not sure it will be enough."

She was quiet and then said, "Thanks for being with me through this. I know that it's hard."

He was quiet a moment and then said, "It's not hard to stand by you. It's just hard to see you suffer."

There was a few moments of silence, and then Sarah asked, "Do you have questions for me?"

"Like what?"

"Do you wonder if I provoked this or if I was somehow involved with him? The answers to these questions are no and never. I really want you to know that, especially since you and I have allowed some distance to grow between us. I have not cheated on you with him or with anyone."

"No, I don't think you did anything to bring this about. And just so you know, I've never cheated either."

"Can you take me out to dinner tonight?"

"You bet. I'll be home by 6:00 and we'll go wherever you would like. I love you, Sarah. Nothing will change that."

When she hung up, Sarah felt a little stronger. She called the District Attorney for King County, Washington and began the process of filing rape charges. The basics were taken down and a file opened. Forms would be in the mail for her to complete in detail. At least she had started that process. Next, she called the human resources department at work and spoke with the Director, Robert Berg, whom she knew well. There were many silences as she made her report of Nolan's comments and the rape. She could tell that he was taken aback by rape allegations against the CEO. He never strayed from script, asking her appropriate questions and then he said, "I'm traveling tomorrow, so can we meet Wednesday morning at 9:00?"

"Okay," Sarah replied. "I will see you in your office then."

Then Berg asked, "Are you okay, Sarah? Is there anything I can do personally?"

"No, I'm not okay at all. Thanks for being concerned, Bob. See you Wednesday."

When she hung up, Sarah called Laurie Spencer, the psychologist she met last year at a Chamber of Commerce business function. She remembered liking Spencer, after they spent fifteen minutes together talking about some of the challenges women face in the workplace.

After the second ring, Sarah got a recording. "You have reached the office of Laurie Spencer. I am in session or away from my desk. Please leave me a message and I will call you back as soon as possible."

Sarah hesitated, almost deciding to hang up. Then she said, "Hi Laurie. This is Sarah Willis. I don't know if you remember me from the Chamber function we met at last year. Anyway, I have a personal matter I would like to talk to you about. Please call me when you can."

Sarah hung up. She stood and walked toward the Starbucks a few stores away. Before she got there, her phone rang.

"Hello."

"Hi Sarah, this is Laurie Spencer."

"Wow. That was a quick response time."

"I remember you. I also remember that I enjoyed talking to you." She paused and then said, "How can I help you?"

"Laurie, do you have room in your practice? I'd like to make an appointment." Sarah took a moment to find the words, and then said, "I was raped and I need some help getting through this."

"I'm so sorry, Sarah. I will make room for you. Let me check something." There was silence for about thirty seconds and then Laurie said I have a cancellation for tomorrow at 10:00 a.m. Can you make it then?"

"I'll be there."

"All right. I will text you my info as soon as we hang up. You okay until tomorrow?"

"Yes, I think I'll be okay. I have support from a loving husband and a best friend, both of whom insist that I come get counseling."

"Okay. I'll see you in the morning. I want you to know that as hard as this is, you really can make it through."

"Thanks for fitting me in, Laurie." As she hung up, Sarah took a deep breath and felt better than she had since the attack. There were people around her who cared. For the first time, she felt like she really could survive this. Next, she dialed the Seattle Police Department, ready to report the attack while she still felt strong enough.

"Seattle Police Department," came the voice of a male operator.

"My name is Sarah Willis and I want to report a rape."

"Okay, please hold on for just one moment, and I'll put you through to the right person."

"All right," Sarah replied. Shook took a deep breath and got ready to tell the story one more time.

Chapter Four

Laurie Spencer emerged from her session room at moments after 10:00 a.m. Laurie had short, black hair and wore black-rimmed glasses. Her smile was warm, and her manner was relaxed and easy-going. "Hi, Sarah," she said, extending a hand. "Please, come on in." Laurie's session room was comprised of a couch and an armchair, both across a coffee table from Laurie's chair. There was also the obligatory back door, so that outgoing patients didn't have to come into contact with anyone in the waiting room. The room was neat and tidy, but with little to distract from the business at hand. Laurie had a small desk in the far corner of the room, which was free of files.

Sarah sat down in the chair.

"Would you like coffee or tea?" Laurie asked.

"Coffee, black, please," she replied."

Laurie poured her a cup from the pot on a side table and handed it to Sarah. She sat down and said, "I remember our meeting last year well. I thought that you were really great."

"Likewise," Sarah said. "I thought you had some great ideas." She added, "I remember that we made a connection."

Laurie said, "I remember that, too." She leaned forward in her chair and said, "I'm so sorry this happened, Sarah. Can you talk about it?"

Sarah nodded and then she burst into tears. Laurie stood and put her arms around Sarah and let her cry. After a few minutes, Sarah said, "I'm so sorry, Laurie. I really didn't want to do that."

Laurie nodded understandingly, and then gave her a smile. "I'm sure you didn't, but remember that you are here to deal with emotions, not to suppress them. This is the perfect place to be emotionally forthcoming. It's a good thing."

Sarah pushed the tears aside and began the story of all that had happened. She spoke of Nolan's prompts for sex, staring at her breasts, and his statement that he wanted her in his bed. Sarah then went on to describe how the trip to Seattle came about and the rape at the hotel. Sarah broke down as she described the helplessness of being over-powered and violated.

Laurie listened intently and then asked, "How have you been doing since the attack?"

Sarah was quiet a moment, and then she replied, "I've been someone else. Someone I don't recognize. Initially, I spent too much time in bed because it feels safe. Beyond that, I live in emotional turmoil. I am anxious and angry all the time." She put her head in her hand for a few moments and then said, "I also have sensations of helplessness. I'm afraid that he may get away with this and there is nothing I can do to stop him. I'm even afraid that it could happen again. This attack taught me that I'm not self-sufficient, and left me vulnerable and scared." She drew a breath and added, "I have always considered myself a strong and independent woman, able to deal with anything. Now I feel like everything I believed about myself was just a fantasy. I feel like a wounded animal. And I know that I have been really damaged, deep down. All these feelings swirl around in random order, and it all seems beyond my control." Laurie nodded, remaining quiet, and prompting Sarah to continue. "I have these awful dreams. A couple of nights ago, I woke up in the middle of the night in a sweat and screaming after dreaming someone had broken into the house and was coming after me.

Last night, I had a dream that I was being chased, and I knew the guy was going to catch me. Then, suddenly, this faceless man was in bed with me and forcing himself into me. It was happening all over again." She shook her head and added, "It's like some evil version of the groundhog day movie that has me reliving the most devastating experience of my life. I wake up in the middle of the night with my heart thumping like a freight train and I don't dare go back to sleep."

Laurie took her hand and said, "First, know that all of your feelings are entirely appropriate. All of this, depression, anxiety, anger, fear. It all comes with a violation like this. So it makes perfect sense that a healthy person would go through all of this." She paused and said, "You told me that you've got a pretty good support system, right?"

"Yeah, my best friend Angie has been incredible and my husband John has been understanding and supportive. I also met with a lawyer yesterday and really liked the guy. I plan to hold Nolan responsible for this."

Laurie smiled. "Wow. Awesome progress." She reflected a moment, and then said, "You know that going through the legal process will have you retelling the story and will open the door for the other side to attack you, right?"

"Yes, I know that," Sarah said. "The lawyer, Scott Winslow, told me that." She paused and then added, "Do you think that I should avoid legal action?"

"No, not necessarily. It can be a part of the healing process, however the case comes out, because you're shining a light on his conduct and you're standing up for yourself. I just want you to know that it won't be easy to do and the other side will likely say false things that will hurt." Laurie reflected a moment and then asked, "Do you feel guilt or shame?"

"Both. I feel like I was such an idiot to have let him into my room. It's like I'm responsible because I could have prevented it.

And somehow, I am ashamed of it all. Intellectually, I know he did this, but emotionally I am ashamed that I let this happen."

"And that is where they will attack in your lawsuit. They will suggest that guilt comes from being complicit, or leading him on in some way."

"I know, but I feel like I need to take this head on so that I don't remain afraid for the rest of my life. Another part of me just wants to hide. I just can't let that part control me."

Laurie smiled. "I think that you are a on the right track, Sarah. You are dealing with the emotional impact head on. Whatever you decide, I respect all you're doing to get past this attack and keep going."

Sarah was quiet a moment and then said, "I know that many rapes go unreported. Women just stay quiet, and live with the wounds. Then the guy who hurt them forever can forget all about it without a second thought, or just move to the next woman, feeling he can get away with it. I will not let that happen. I feel guilty enough that I let his leering at me and his comments go unreported. I should have owned it back then, rather than just hoping we could get past it all." She shook her head and said, "I knew that I needed to deal with it, but it's so hard, so I inanely hoped it would stop before I had to figure out what to do. It all seems so idiotic now." She sat back in her chair and asked, "Laurie, I know this is about me and not you, but have you ever been through anything like this?"

She smiled and replied, "This has to be about you and your needs, Sarah. I can tell you that I have worked with many women who have been harassed and others who were sexually attacked." Laurie took a breath, and then added, "We live in a society where there are now laws to protect us from harassment and attacks in the workplace, but it still goes on. It's about attitude and culture as well as laws, and there are so many power abusers that it continues to happen. You see it in the news all the time. All the powerful men who engage in harassment for years because they can get away with it. Recently, we've seen some of the celebs and politicians start to fall from grace, but it's a slow process. The 'Me Too' and Time's Up' movements are signs of a cultural shift."

Sarah said, "I'm going to human resources tomorrow to finish my formal complaint. If I'm up for it, I also plan to return to work."

"That could be really stressful."

"If he keeps me from my career, then the asshole wins, right?"

Laurie smiled. "You've got more fight left than you know."

"I won't let him take my career as well." She drew a breath and closed her eyes. When she opened them again, Sarah asked, "When can I see you again?"

"Friday at 9:00 a.m. okay?"

"I'll be here. Thanks."

"The other thing you should know is that the other side will likely subpoena my records during the course of the litigation so they can see if there are things in my notes that help them. I will make sure that Scott Winslow has a copy of my records, so that you guys can prepare."

"Thank you for everything," Sarah said. "I feel a little stronger with you on my side."

They stood, and as they walked towards the door, Laurie said, "I know this has been an awful experience, but you will make it through this. I'll see you Friday."

* * *

On Wednesday morning, Sarah met with Director of Human Resources Robert Berg. He listened while she described the attack and the rape by the company's CEO. Berg tried hard not to react, but he knew immediately that he had a corporate disaster on his hands. He was extremely respectful as he listened to the report of what occurred from Sarah. He asked her whether there were prior occasions of improper words or conduct by CEO Nolan.

She told him of Nolan's periodic comments and the conversation about getting her into his bed right before the Seattle trip.

When she finished, he said, "We will immediately commence an investigation and let you know our results as soon as possible. Do you want to go on leave until the investigation is complete?"

Sarah shook her head. "No, I don't want to go out on leave. I just want to be allowed to do my job, and to be protected from him. I don't want to deal with Nolan every day while this investigation is going on."

He nodded. "Okay. The first thing I want you to know that no one is entitled to retaliate against you for making your complaint and if they do, please come right back to me."

Sarah look directly at Berg and said, "Bob, we've worked with each other well and I know that this is difficult. Having to investigate the guy at the top won't be easy. I just hope they let you do it."

"We'll investigate, Sarah, don't worry."

* * *

Sarah returned to work to find countless emails and phone calls waiting for her. She started wading through it all. An hour later, Assistant Controller Melissa Carter appeared at her door. "Can I come in?"

Sarah nodded, "Sure, come on in."

Melissa sat down and said, "Okay, boss, spit it out. What happened?"

"How do you know anything happened?"

"Because I'm not an idiot. You not showing up for a presentation in Seattle would just never happen unless the earth flew off its axis. You not being here until now would never happen unless the whole world was on fire. And, if that's not enough, I can see it in your eyes."

"I'm not supposed to discuss it."

"What is that, the corporate investigation policy you're giving me? Screw that, I want to know if you're okay."

Sarah smiled. "Thanks for that, Melissa." She took a breath and said, "There's going to be an investigation. If I tell you, then you'll have to tell them that I did."

"So, I'll say you confided in me after I noticed you were upset. They can all get over it. I care about you."

Sarah nodded and said staring straight ahead, "Nolan came to my room in Seattle and raped me."

Melissa almost fell off her chair. "What? Oh my God." Shock filled her wide eyes. "Are you okay?"

"As okay as I can be under the circumstances. I am working to overcome depression, extreme anger and a feeling that I've been torn apart. The sense of violation is immense, Melissa. I feel like I've been really hurt to my soul."

"That son of a bitch," Melissa said, angrily.

"So, now that you got me to confide in you, you can't tell anyone else, okay? You have to keep this quiet. I don't want to be accused of sabotaging the investigation that I'm hoping will happen."

Melissa nodded her head. "How the hell does HR investigate Nolan?"

"Good question. I guess we'll find out." She paused, and then said. "Thanks for caring, Melissa. So, I guess we better get back to work. Were you able to get through the Dartmouth Plastics data?"

Melissa sat, transfixed. After a moment, she said, "You are so incredibly strong."

"No I'm really not. Let's talk business so I can focus on something that won't make me come apart."

* * *

Sarah worked quickly through the remainder of the day. At 6:00 p.m. Jim Nolan appeared in her doorway. He looked at her for a moment and then asked, "Have you had a chance to review those documents that I gave you in Seattle?"

He addressed her like nothing had happened and it was a gut punch. She was instantly angry. She drew a breath and kept her composure. After a moment, she replied, "No."

"Okay," he said with a friendly smile. "We'll discuss it tomorrow." He turned and walked away from her office. His pretense made her so angry should could scream. She wanted to annihilate him—to find some way to hurt him. She took a deep breath and pulled out the journal Scott Winslow had asked her to keep. She wrote down what had just occurred, and then she put the notebook away. Somehow, writing the event was therapeutic and she found her heart slowing to its normal pace. She put on her coat and headed for the elevator. It was time to go home and spend some time with John.

Chapter Five

Robert Berg called his boss, Vice President of Human Resources Ted Nelson, who was attending a series of meetings in New York.

Nelson saw the number and pushed a button. "Hi, Bob."

"Ted, we have a major issue."

"Okay, lay it on me. I've got about ten minutes before my next meeting."

"Sarah Willis met with me this morning to report some harassment over a number of months, followed by a rape while she was on the trip to Seattle."

"Jesus, that's awful. Does she know who the guy was?"

"Yes, and I hope you're sitting down."

"Too much build up. Just tell me."

"Jim Nolan."

"You've got to be kidding. Holy shit, Bob."

"Yeah."

Nelson thought a moment and then said, "How did she come across?"

"Ted, she's Sarah Willis, how do you think she came across? She came across as honest and injured."

"Did you talk to Nolan?"

"No, I wanted to check in with you first."

"Do it. It can't wait until I get back. Get his statement, you know how this goes."

"Am I supposed to tell Nolan that he's on leave while we investigate?"

There was a prolonged silence on the line, and then Nelson said, "That's the policy, so yes, that's what you need to tell him. Is he in the office?"

"He is."

"All right. Meet with him and get his side of it as soon as you can."

"I'm on it."

"Thanks, Bob. I suppose the good news is that if it happened in Seattle, there shouldn't be much knowledge of it around the office."

"That's some consolation, I suppose."

"This is not good," Nelson said. "Let's make sure we do everything right."

* * *

At 8:00 p.m., Bob Berg knocked on the door of the CEO's massive sanctuary. The desks in the outer office, like a wall that protected him from the unannounced, were empty. Berg walked between the desks and knocked on the door of the inner sanctum.

"It's open," came the response.

Berg opened the door and stepped inside. "Thanks for meeting with me, Mr. Nolan."

"Sure. Please, sit down Bob," Nolan said, pointing to one of four over-stuffed chairs and surrounded a ceiling-high fireplace. The environment was elaborate and intimidating. It spoke of wealth and power. "How can I help you, Bob?" Nolan asked smiling as he sat down at a right angle to Berg.

"Well, sir, we received a serious complaint today. Ms. Willis has filed a complaint alleging that you raped her in Seattle."

Nolan narrowed his eyes. "You're kidding?"

"No, sir, it's no joke."

"Why would she say something like that, Bob? Do you think she's angry with me for some reason?"

"So, it's not true, sir?"

"No, of course not."

"Do you mind if I take notes?"

"No, Bob, go right ahead."

Berg recorded the denials and then said, "Did you have any physical interaction with Ms. Willis on the trip to Seattle?"

Nolan leaned back in his chair and said, "This is embarrassing, Bob, but Sarah and I had an affair."

"So you had relations with her?"

"Yes, not that I think that should be anyone else's business."

"Well, sir, it becomes HR business when we get a complaint like this."

"Yes, so it does Bob." Nolan shook his head and then said, "I just can't believe she did this."

"Did anyone see you together in Seattle?"

"Not that I know of?"

"So what happened, Mr. Nolan?"

"We went to different meetings on Friday night and then we met in the bar. We had several drinks, one thing lead to another and we went first to my room, where we kissed, and then to hers, where we made love."

"All of this was with Ms. Willis' consent?"

"Right."

"Did she ever say that you were doing something she didn't like?"

"Never. In fact, she seemed to like it," he said, grinning as if sharing a secret with a buddy.

Berg felt a slight revulsion at this boast. He asked, "Did she ever ask you to stop doing anything you were doing?"

"No, never."

"Take me through all of it. Everything that happened and everything that was said from the time you met in the bar."

"Well, it was all friendly and overly flirtatious. We had drinks, we had fun relaxing and then we had sex. When it was over we agreed we would keep it to ourselves because it wasn't good for either of us given that we're both married. We also didn't want it to become office gossip."

"Anyone who can back up any of what you've told me?"

"We were in a public bar, but didn't know anyone there. Then we were alone in a couple of hotel rooms."

"What else can you tell me about what happened?"

"That's really it."

"Did you sleep in her room?"

"No, I returned to my room afterwards. Best for both of us as we're married."

Berg hesitated a moment and then asked, "She didn't present as scheduled the next morning, right?"

"Right."

"Any idea why?"

"No."

"Did she leave the hotel before morning?"

"I have no idea."

"But you know that she did not appear for her scheduled presentation on Thursday morning, right?

"Yes."

"Did you think that was unusual?"

"Yes, I did. I thought that she must not be feeling well, or something."

"Did you make an inquiry of her?"

"What?"

"Did you call her to see why she was a no-show?"

"No."

"Any particular reason?"

"I can't keep track of all the employees."

"Right, but this was an executive that you had been intimate with the night before, right?

"Yes."

"So when she didn't show up for her presentation, weren't you concerned?"

Nolan narrowed his eyes. The expression said that he had put up with enough annoyance. "I was concerned, but I was also busy. I thought we would catch up later."

Berg was thoughtful a moment and then said, "Mr. Nolan, we have a policy that says that when claims of harassment are made against an employee, they are to be suspended during the period of the investigation."

Nolan's eyes narrowed. "Sorry, Bob, I have way too much going on to sit on the bench. The Board has me busy every moment of the day, and the running of this company can't be sidelined because of a frivolous claim by someone who has had an attack of conscience after a voluntary affair."

"I understand, sir, but I'm just trying to do what the corporate policies say I must.

"I understand, Bob. Anything else? I have to get back to work."

"That's all I have for now, sir. I'll make an appointment if we need to talk further."

"That's fine. Have a good evening." Nolan said, dismissing Berg by turning his attention back to his computer.

Berg left the sanctum that belonged to Nolan feeling like this was going to be a son of bitch of an investigation. Nolan was right about the fact that the Board had him busy. The unspoken part was that the Board also strongly supported Nolan. Berg sensed that he was going to need the weight of Ted Nelson's authority even to have a shot at questioning the man further, without finding himself collateral damage. It was like bringing a challenge to the conduct of a corporate god.

Chapter Six

Donna walked out into the Simmons and Winslow lobby to greet Sarah. "Hi, Sarah, how are you doing?" Donna asked. Sarah gave her a look that said she was struggling. "Come with me to the conference room and we'll talk," Donna said.

As that sat down, Donna looked concerned and asked, "Are you okay?"

Sarah said, "I'm hanging in there. I feel like I've gone from golden child to someone simply being tolerated by top management. There's a whole new wall between me and them. I'm not sure if it's real or not, but I feel it."

"It has to be a tough functioning in that environment at this point," Donna responded.

"Make yourself comfortable and I'll let Scott know you're here."

"Okay."

Donna picked up the phone and said, "Scott, she's here." She hung up and said, "He'll be right in."

Scott walked into the room a few moments later with a concerned look, and a hand extended to Sarah. "Hi, Sarah, how are you?"

"Good days and bad," she offered. "Some days I can barely drag myself into work. Other days I convince myself that I can make it through."

"It's hard to go to work in that environment, knowing that some view you as persona non grata for coming forward. I respect your strength to keep up that fight." He paused and then asked, "What have you heard from the HR people about the investigation over the last three or four weeks?"

"Nothing. I checked yesterday and was told 'it's ongoing'—which is a way of saying nothing."

"Is Nolan still working? No suspension or interruption?"

"None. That's one of the things I wanted to talk to you about. He gave me an assignment to review some documents on the night of the attack. He has now asked me twice for my thoughts about the proposed project. He talks to me as if nothing has ever happened. It's like he's saying there was nothing to it—like he did nothing. I get so angry. I think that his repeated communication about this assignment is an attempt to just project business as usual. He wants to convey to the whole world that we are all doing just fine and he and I can deal with each other just like always."

"I suspect you're right," Scott said. "It's a little tricky because you can't refuse to respond to work given by the CEO. If you do, or if you don't do the work, he can use that to claim that you are insubordinate or that you have performance problems. But you don't want to get sucked into his 'everything is just fine game' either. The company is obviously not abiding by its policy of suspending him during the investigation, so let's be a little creative. Why don't you respond fully to his request for your evaluation, but respond to the HR Director and ask him to relay your thoughts. Tell him in the cover email that you have been emotionally devastated by what he did to you and you cannot deal with him directly, so please relay the requested information."

"I like that approach," Sarah replied. "I have assembled the information, so I will send the message and attachment to Bob Berg today."

"I know that working in that environment with him at the top of the food chain has to be difficult now."

"It is. Some days, I am ready to walk away." She shook her head and said, "I also know that Nolan has poisoned the well against me. No one ever says anything, but I see it in the way top executives look at me. I'm suddenly someone you don't go out of your way to talk to—and someone they have to watch because I might hurt the company. I've never felt like that before and it doesn't feel good."

Scott nodded. "I wish I could tell you that I think the work environment will get better, but it isn't likely." He gave her an understanding smile and said, "Let me give you an update from our end. We obtained the Right to Sue letter from the California Department of Fair Employment and Housing which is a procedural requirement before filing a harassment or discrimination lawsuit and we are now ready to file the lawsuit. Are you still prepared to proceed? It would mean that we file it next week and they will be served within a week or two thereafter."

"I'm ready," she said, without hesitation.

He handed her a document and said, "Here is a draft copy of the lawsuit for your review," laying a thirty page document on the conference table in front of Sarah. "Let's go over it together and make sure that all of the facts in it are correct. If we have any of the facts wrong, we want to correct them before we file."

Sarah looked at the document and said, "Thank you both for your support as well as your hard work. I'm really glad to have you guys on my team."

* * *

At noon, Sarah sent her analysis of the project Nolan assigned to HR Director Bob Berg, along with the cover email stating that she was responding to Mr. Nolan's request for a review of these documents. The email stated that, "I cannot deal directly with Mr. Nolan given what he did to me, and the devastating effect that his actions have had upon me. I will carry out any instruction provided, but I cannot deal with him directly at this time. I can provide a letter from my counselor substantiating these facts if desired."

About fifteen minutes after she transmitted the email, Sandy buzzed her. "Sarah, Bob Berg is on com-line 2."

"Hi, Bob."

"Hi, Sarah. Just wanted you know that I received your email and I will pass it on to Mr. Nolan."

"I hope you understand why I wanted to proceed this way," Sarah said.

"I understand completely. I don't think it should be a problem during the pendency of the investigation."

"Thanks, Bob. Any idea when the investigation will be complete."

"I don't have a precise date right now. I'll check on that and get back with you."

"Okay, thanks again, Bob."

* * *

At just after 6:00 p.m., James Nolan filled her doorway. His expression was stern. He waved a document in the air. He spoke angrily, "You sent a response to me through Human Resources rather than directly?"

"I did, and you know why," Sarah said, calmly.

"That is not acceptable. You have to be able to deal with your supervisor directly, otherwise you can't do your job. People who report to me, talk to me."

"It used to be that way, Jim, before you attacked me."

"Attacked you? What do you mean?" She immediately understood. This conversation was going to be the subject of documentation and deposition, so he would fill it with denials. Every conversation they had would be for the record.

She would take off the kid gloves. "You know exactly what I mean. You raped me."

"Of course not. Anyway, this is not working out. If you can't even communicate with your boss then we're going to have to let you go."

"You're firing me?"

"It's evident that you can't do your job, so there is really no choice."

Sarah said nothing more. She began gathering her belongings. When she looked back to where he had been standing, he was gone.

* * *

Sarah dialed Scott Winslow at 9:00 a.m. A female voice said, "Simmons and Winslow."

"May I speak to Scott Winslow, please? This is Sarah Willis."

"Hi, Ms. Willis. Hold on one moment."

A few seconds later, Scott said, "Good morning, Sarah."

"Hi Scott. That son of a bitch fired me last night."

"For what reason?" Scott asked.

"Like we talked about, I sent him the analysis that he wanted in writing through human resources rather than providing it in person because I didn't want more verbal interaction with him. Bob Berg told me he thought that would be fine. Then last night, Nolan told me that if I couldn't talk to him directly then I couldn't do the job."

"I suspect he was having difficulty being around you. You remind him that he is facing harassment and rape charges—and more to the point, that he's guilty." Scott paused and then added, "With your consent, we will revise the lawsuit to add claims for retaliation for raising complaints about the harassment and rape."

"Yeah," Sarah said, sounding suddenly tired. "Let's do it."

On her way home, her cell phone rang. She hit a button and then said, "Sarah Willis."

Melissa's voice said, "Sarah, it was just announced that you are no longer with the company. What happened?"

"Nolan fired me last night."

"What?"

"He said it was because I couldn't communicate directly with him anymore."

"No way!" Melissa said, clearly distressed.

"Are you at your desk?"

"No, I'm outside on my cell."

"The lawsuit will happen in the next couple of weeks, Melissa. I expect that the company lawyers will discourage you from interacting with me."

"Not happening. You're my friend and mentor and you don't deserve this."

"Thank you, Melissa. I just want you to know that I understand that you are caught between me and the company on this one."

"But, I'm not. I plan to call it as I see it, whenever anyone asks."

"Okay, but take care of yourself."

There was quiet for a time and then Melissa said, "I'm so sorry, Sarah. You should know that Marty's pissed off too."

Sarah replied, "Thank you, Melissa. You are very kind."

Chapter Seven

Ted Nelson walked into Jim Nolan's office and sat down.

Nolan observed his concerned expression and said, "What is it?"

"I talked to legal. We just got served with a lawsuit you should know about."

"What lawsuit?"

"A lawsuit by Sarah Willis that names you and the company. It includes claims for discrimination, sexual harassment and sexual battery based on rape and retaliatory firing."

Nolan reflected a moment and then said, "That bitch."

"What happened in Seattle, Jim?"

"I told you, we slept together."

"You want to add to or modify your statement in any way?"

"No. Why would I? That's what happened."

"No truth to her allegations?"

"No, I told you that." He paused and then said, "So, what do we do first?"

"We meet with the lawyers. I have us set up to meet with our General Counsel, Ed Perkins and the outside counsel we'll use at 6:00 tonight."

"Yeah," Nolan said. "See you then." His annoyance was clear.

* * *

At 6:00 p.m., the corporate General Counsel, Ed Perkins, HR Vice President Ted Nelson, HR Director Bob Berg and outside counsel Michael Graber waited for Nolan's arrival in the executive conference room. They spent time discussing the allegations of the lawsuit until Nolan walked into the room at 6:10 p.m.

"Sorry for the delay," Nolan said. "Now, where are we?"

Ed Perkins said, "Jim, this is Michael Graber. He and his firm will represent us in the litigation, so he'd like to ask a few preliminary questions."

"Yes, sure," Nolan replied.

Graber shook hands with Nolan and then said, "Mr. Nolan, let me get right to it. Did you sleep with Ms. Willis on the trip to Seattle?"

"Yes."

"Any time before or after that trip?"

"No. It was a one night thing."

"No force involved?"

Nolan looked irritated. "Of course not."

"Sorry, sir, but I have to ask those questions."

Nolan nodded. "What else?"

"Did you fire her?"

"Yes."

"Why?

"Because she couldn't do her job."

"Can you be specific?"

"She couldn't communicate with me about matters we needed to address." He paused and then added, "I also had been dissatisfied with her work over the past few months so I was contemplating merging the Vice President of Finance and Controller positions and replacing her with a real Vice President of Finance."

"Okay," Graber replied. "We can work with all of that." He paused and then said, "One more thing, Mr. Nolan. Does your wife know about the affair?"

"It was hardly an affair. It was a one-time fling."

"Okay, does she know?"

"No."

You should tell her. There's no way she doesn't find out about it, so it's best for your relationship if it comes from you."

Nolan did not respond. He asked, "So what do we do? How do we handle this now that we are in your forum, Mr. Graber?"

"Well, the first thing we do is kick it to arbitration. Get it away from a jury. Do we have an arbitration agreement signed by her?"

Nelson shook his head. "No. She was with us over four years. We implemented that practice after her start date."

"Can we get her into arbitration anyway?" Nolan asked.

"Nope. Arbitration is a matter of contract. The case only goes to arbitration if she signed an agreement to do so."

"So what is the plan?"

"We fight the claims with everything we can find. This is a credibility contest so we go after her credibility. Then we lock her into claims she can't support in deposition."

"Well, your firm has a few hundred lawyers, so I assume you've got the resources to get this done, right?" Nolan asked, pointedly.

"Yes, sir," Graber said. He added, "We'll also spend time preparing for your deposition. Scott Winslow is a good lawyer and he will work the case hard. Let's make this one a rough ride for him." He looked over at Nelson and Berg and said, "I need the investigation report as soon as possible."

Nelson nodded. "Jerry Orson is working on the investigation. Bob Berg and I are overseeing it."

Graber added, "I also want everything you can give me on her. Any prior complaints she has made, any complaints about her by anyone else, any performance issues, any behavior issues. Also, divorces, issues with marriage, social or legal problems, anything you can find that might be a source of stress or that might affect her credibility. Can you gents help with that?"

"Some of that is protected by privacy rights if it's in her file, isn't it?"

"Yeah, we can issue a subpoena for some of it."

"Okay," Nelson said. "We'll see what we can find."

"We'll get a look at social media, too," Graber said. "I can't tell you how many times people post facts on Facebook that are contrary to the allegations they are making."

Graber looked at Nolan. "Mr. Nolan, have there ever been any other sexual harassment or sexual battery claims against you?"

"No."

"Ever?"

"No."

"I mean this job and your prior positions?"

"No, none," Nolan said, sounding impatient.

"Okay, good," Graber said. He turned his attention to the General Counsel. "Ed, we should also talk to employees that she worked with and let them know that there is a dispute and we expect them to keep information confidential—not share any company information with her. Tell them to keep their heads down and work. We can't threaten employees who talk to her, but I want them to know that no good can come of trying to jump into the case on her side."

"One more thing. Any contact from the press should be referred to one central location so that the message is appropriate and consistent."

"Right," Ted Nelson said. "Bob and I will write a statement for Ed to approve and give it to the public relations people. Then all communications will be funneled through the PR department."

Nolan sat back in his chair. "Does that cover it for now?"

"I think so," Graber said. He looked around the room and asked, "Any questions?" No one spoke. "I guess we are ready to proceed then."

"Thanks, everyone," Nolan said. He stood and everyone knew it was time to leave.

* * *

Sarah walked into Laurie Spencer's office and sat down. Laurie walked in from a side door and extended her hand. After they shook hands, Laurie asked, "Well, how are you holding up?"

"Okay, I guess. It has been quite a week."

"How so?"

"I got fired, and the lawsuit is now in the courts."

"Tell me about getting fired—what happened?"

"I transmitted an analysis I did to HR and asked them to transmit it to Mr. Nolan because I didn't feel like I could deal with him directly after the injury he caused."

"Good for you, Sarah. I think that is awesome."

"He didn't think so. Nolan showed up at the door to my office the same evening and said 'it wasn't working out.' His people have to be able to deal with him so he was going to have to let me go."

Laurie nodded slowly. "How are you feeling about the termination?"

"Angry and betrayed. Also, a little scared that he's going to get away with saying that I voluntarily slept with him. I feel like I'm stuck in this truly awful place where he can get away with whatever he wants. How does a woman ever win a battle like this?"

Laurie nodded. "One of the hardest things to handle is knowing that the person who did this to you is going to lie through his teeth, and that he could get away with it. Like we've talked about, that is one of the big reasons so many women never come forward. You feel like a victim again and again. That's why," Laurie said, "I think seeking accountability is a two-edged sword. It can be both costly and therapeutic at the same time." She reflected a moment and then asked, "How is the case going so far?"

"Kind of early to know. My lawyer says that we are waiting for documents to be produced and questions to be answered under oath by the company and then he is setting the depositions of Nolan and the investigator."

"You have any support inside the company?" She asked.

"Yeah, my team is loyal, but they have no information about what happened in Seattle, so they can't help much." She was quiet a moment and then added, "I also don't want this to be a drag on their careers."

"How are you spending your time now?" Laurie asked.

"Obsessing over whether I can get through this and get my life back. I'm sitting outside because that son of a bitch…"

"You still having nightmares?"

Sarah nodded. "Yeah, four or five times a week. It's usually some faceless guy who is chasing me, and then suddenly inside me while I scream. Then I wake up, and I don't sleep anymore that night."

"Have you contemplated doing him harm?"

She shook her head reflectively, and then said, "In a thousand ways. Think Lorena Bobbitt; my favorite is to cut his dick off and throw it away—somewhere irretrievable. It's unoriginal, but a satisfying idea."

"Are you really planning to hurt him?"

"No. I know that you have to monitor such things to see if I am a danger."

"Have you thought of harming yourself?" Laurie asked.

Sarah closed her eyes a moment, visualizing, and then said, "Right after the rape, I had questions about whether I wanted to live. Not anymore. Now I want to find a way to make him pay. And I want to come out on the other side of all this."

"That sounds healthy to me," Laurie said. She paused and then asked, "How are things with John?"

Sarah smiled. "Amazing," she replied. "He is standing by me through everything. He has never expressed doubt about what happened. Through all this I've been realizing what an incredible guy he is."

"Sounds like he is," Laurie said, smiling. After a moment, she said, "I think it might be beneficial to you to attend a rape support group for a little while. I oversee one that meets once a week."

"It sounds depressing," Sarah said. "I'm not sure I want to hear all the stories of how men violated all those women."

Laurie nodded. "I know, but it has therapeutic value for many women. Something about knowing that you are not alone and that others have suffered violations and made it through."

"Let me think about that," Sarah said.

"Fair enough. Call me if you want to attend and I will get you in."

Sarah nodded. She thought for a moment and then asked, "Does anyone ever really get over an experience like this?"

"Not so much get over, as learn to live with," Laurie said.

Sarah nodded. "It is present all the time. The shame, the anger and the feeling of being damaged. I hope someday to let go of it."

* * *

Lee Henry was Scott's answer whenever he needed someone to go out into the electronic world, or the physical world, and come back with some evidence that would make a difference. He had uncovered critical evidence for Scott on several cases. Lee always found a way to get to information that seemed to be inaccessible to everyone else. Scott dialed the phone and waited. On the third ring, a familiar voice said, "Hi, Scott."

"Hi, Lee. Did you get the package I sent you on the Willis case?"

Lee replied, "I did, and I reviewed it last night."

"We're struggling a little bit. Sarah says it happened and I believe it's real. The proof part is going to be tough. This guy had no prior harassment allegations. His record with the company is clean, so I need some evidence of something."

"He was only with Ellison Company one year, right?"

"Right."

"And before that he worked for three years as the CFO, and then CEO, for Sunmont Builders."

"Yeah, it's heartening to know that you really do read the stuff I send you."

"I always like to impress the client by having some idea what they are talking about."

Scott laughed and said, "I've noticed that about you."

"Who's defending this case?" Lee asked"

"McMillan and Jensen. The partner on the case is Michael Graber."

"I vaguely remember him," Lee said. "Smart guy, but kind of an asshole?"

"Well, yeah, but that describes many of the defense attorneys I know."

"You might be a little jaded," Lee said, laughing.

"Only a bit," Scott replied. "And my cynicism grows daily." After a moment he added, "So what are your thoughts about Nolan?"

Lee said, "I am skeptical of his clean record. The guy seems practiced at this kind of thing. I mean he rapes a woman and then comfortably goes about his day to day as if he just had a fling. He pretends nothing ever happened when he talks directly to her. It's all a little cold blooded, so it's hard to believe that this is a first time. He may have been patient enough to wait a while, but I bet there's some other deviant shit back there somewhere.

"Will you see what you can find at his employment with Sunmont Builders?"

"I will. If he has been up to no good in the past, it might have come to light in the three years he spent at Sunmont. I'll dig into it."

"Perfect," Scott said. "Hopefully, you'll find something useful that I can get him to lie about under oath in deposition, and we will have him set up for trial."

"Sounds good," Lee said. "I really don't like arrogant assholes who think they are above accountability for whoever they decide to hurt."

"You and me both. Keep me posted on what you find, buddy."

"Shall do."

Scott hung up feeling that if there was anything to find, Lee was the guy to find it. Lee Henry went where others couldn't go. Lee's CIA background gave him abilities and connections that were mind-boggling. He found ways to look behind opaque curtains, at protected information. Barriers to most were not barriers to Lee, and somehow, he always seemed to find his way to circumvent any roadblock. If asked how he got to obscure or unavailable information, Lee would simply smile and say, "Isn't that why you pay me?"

Chapter Eight

For John Willis, it was hard to bear. Pain and fear had become a permanent fixture in his wife's eyes. She was doing her best to cope with the aftermath of terror, but it was taking its toll on every part of their lives. She had developed a startle reaction that she never had before. John could easily scare her by being unexpectedly nearby. She was often unable to sleep, and she sat up until all hours. It was heartbreaking to witness the fear deep within her. She could no longer comfortably close her eyes. There were the nightmares that caused her to wake up screaming—seeing someone coming at her and pinning her down. She feared sleep and what it would bring, and she didn't even want to try to go back to sleep after one of her nightmares. The pain reflected in her eyes was so much deeper than she shared.

John wondered whether he and Sarah would ever be able to make love, without the memories of the rape overcoming her. The Sarah who was bright-eyed and in love with living every day, had been cast into shadow. The sparkling eyes, ready for anything, had somehow been dulled by fear. There was an isolation borne of fear, which had never been present before.

The effects of what Nolan had done were visible a hundred times a day. John was growing angrier as the days passed, and he had no intention of letting Nolan's attack go unremedied. Sarah was dealing with the impossible already, so he couldn't show her the level of anger he carried. It would be something else she worried about. He had decided that she would see only unequivocal support from him.

John had been a star linebacker at Purdue and was expected to join the NFL until his right knee was irreparably injured in his senior year. He had been a monster on the grid-iron, but the consummate gentleman off the field. For many, that injury would have spelled disaster, but for John it meant only a change of focus. In the space of several years after college, he built a successful architectural career with commercial and residential work that was both uniquely beautiful, and practically efficient. He had gone from a small start-up, to a firm of five architects that was granted most of the projects it bid.

After college he attended a business function where he met the love of his life. The day he was introduced to Sarah was the day he first believed in love at first sight. She had eyes that lit up a room, and a smile that sped up the beat of his heart. He was all in on the first day, and he wanted to marry her by the third date. Their wedding day was the happiest day of his life and there had never been a day when he was out of love with her. They had both allowed busy careers to consume their energy, and they had foolishly allowed distance to build by not leaving enough time for each other, but he never wanted anyone but Sarah.

In her recent days of pain, Sarah was afraid of almost everything. That exquisite light in her eyes was still there, but it had been dulled by Nolan's attack. Sarah had loved her career, and now that had been taken as well. It was gone because she had complained about the actions of an assailant. John had silently decided that Nolan was going to suffer for every bit of the pain he caused. John would see to it, personally; it was his only consolation. He spent his free time devising plans to make Nolan pay, and it had become an obsession. Every time he saw the sorrow or fear in his wife's eyes, witnessed the nightmares or the myriad other ways in which the attack had affected the love of his life, he wanted to assure her that he would make it right, but he never spoke of the revenge he was planning.

It was after midnight. Lee Henry had dedicated the past three hours to searching through the confidential employment records of Sunmont Builders. He examined the personnel records of James Nolan, who had been its former CEO, and records of employee complaints that had been logged with human resources. He found his way into and searched through Nolan's emails. He found nothing related to any accusation of harassment, discrimination or battery against Nolan by anyone at Sunmont. Lee shook his head as he stared at the screen. Had this guy been well behaved for three years at Sunmont and another year at Ellison Company before suddenly raping a subordinate on a business trip? If he raped Sarah Willis, there just had to be something else in his past that could be uncovered.

Lee had devised several mechanisms for hiding his identity, were anyone to spot an intruder during his unauthorized record searches. There were a number of systems that could trace an electronic footprint left by an unauthorized visit, but with respect to most of his research, no one seemed to discover that they had been visited. Many companies didn't have the security sophistication to monitor his electronic footsteps, or simply never tried. He could often access records as needed, finding his way around most record systems as if he used them daily. For those with greater sophistication in their systems he had devised a number of curve balls that took them in the wrong direction in their electronic search to identify the visitor.

Lee had black hair, a wrap-around beard and penetrating blue eyes. He was six foot two and weighed about 210. He worked out regularly and was in great shape as he entered his forties. Lee was not just inconspicuous when he accessed electronic records, out in the world, he made an art of being entirely unnoticed while he watched his subjects go about their daily lives. He was in the center of every crowd and entirely inconspicuous. He could ask questions of a passersby and not be remembered. He saw everything, but almost no one saw him. Those who did see him could never provide a description. If he had to be in a specific location on a number of different days, he never looked the same twice. He altered his appearance with a variety of glasses, facial hair, wigs and contact lenses.

At 12:45 a.m., Lee shut down his computer. He looked out his home office window into darkness, thinking about his next move. He decided that it might just take a visit to Sunmont Builders to shake something loose. He thought about who should make that visit and concluded that it should be a visit from someone influential. Maybe someone associated with the FBI.

* * *

"Hi, Scott," Sarah said, as he came to greet her in the waiting room.

"Hi, Sarah. Please, come on back to the conference room. Today we'll rehearse for your deposition. I will play the role of the opposing attorney and ask lopsided and unfair questions."

"Sounds like too much fun," she replied. When we get done with this maybe we can pull out my fingernails one at a time."

Scott laughed. "It will be a tough couple of hours, but you'll learn how to answer critical questions in the best way possible. Many questions have several possible answers that are accurate. One of them might support your position, another might provide the other side with unintended ammunition to come after you. This rehearsal is about knowing the difference as you answer."

When they entered the conference room Sarah noted documents stacked in piles on the table. Each stack had a number beside it. "Grab some coffee and let's get comfortable," Scott said.

After Sarah sat down next to Scott with coffee in hand, she said, "This is all stuff that the company produced?"

"Yeah. Each stack is a response to one of the forty-five categories of documents that we requested. There's about four thousand pages."

She nodded, and then said, "Anything that's not bullshit?"

Scott smiled. "Yeah, a few things. Like policies governing discrimination, harassment and investigations. We also have your personnel file. It's full of documents concerning your good work, promotions and raises. It matches the version you gave me, so at least we know they didn't purge the good stuff from your file or add negatives that didn't exist before your termination. It paints a picture of an employee who was well regarded."

"Until it happened, I was," she said. "According to Nolan, I was going to be the next Vice President of Finance. I guess that went away when I wouldn't pretend nothing happened."

"There's nothing that supports any real reason for your termination. There's nothing critical of you. There's also nothing that says Nolan has been accused of anything before." "And you got the investigation report?" Sarah asked.

"We did. Interestingly, it was done by in-house HR. A guy named Jerry Orson. You know him?"

"I do. He's a relatively new guy who reports to Bob Berg, the HR Director."

"And?" Scott asked.

"I don't know him well. A relatively short-term guy with the company, and I don't know much about his background."

Scott smiled. "We will learn more about that at his deposition."

"What does the report say?"

"It consists of his statements about the verbal interviews of you and Nolan. Basically, he says that you say he raped you, and Nolan says you invited him to your room to have an affair. He concludes that it's a he-said, she-said thing, so there's not enough evidence to reach a conclusion. He doesn't say it, but the implication is, we don't know who to believe, so we will do nothing." Scott smiled.

"Why are you grinning?" Sarah asked.

"Because I see vulnerability that I will use in his deposition."

She shook her head. "In a way, this is an elaborate chess game for you, isn't it?"

"In the sense that I strategically determine how to use information, I guess so. But I know that we are dealing with lives and trying to get justice here, so I take every part of this seriously."

She thought a moment and then asked, "So my deposition is two weeks from today?"

"Right. Then Nolan, and then Orson, in that order."

She reflected a moment and then asked, "Can we win this if it's just a 'he said-she said'?

"We can, yeah. When two witnesses provide completely opposite versions of the facts, so one of them has to be lying, the jury gets to decide who they believe. To increase our odds, we want to enhance your credibility and attack his. So that's where the deposition testimony we get to take comes in, as well as the investigation we have Lee working on. If we can make it clear to a jury that he is not believable, then your odds of winning the credibility battle go way up."

Sarah nodded and reflected a moment. "My deposition will be hard, won't it?"

"It will. They are going to ask questions that suggest you had an affair and later decided to make false rape allegations to cover your indiscretions. They are going to argue that you are attempting to ruin Nolan's life to cover an affair that you don't want to admit you had."

"So, they cast Nolan as the victim." She shook her head and added, "No wonder many women just live with the violation."

Scott nodded. He said, "I want you to know that I admire you, and I think you are brave. When I raise issues that sound like they are good for the other side, it is only because we have to deal with them and not because I doubt you."

"Thank you, Scott." She nodded. "Okay, get to work, let's practice the cross-examination so that I can get used to the attack that's coming."

"Okay, but there's one more thing to talk about first. We are going to have a motion battle on a couple of points. They are going to make a motion to have you identify all intimate relationships for the year before the attack and since then."

She shrugged. "Well that's easy, it's only John."

"But they don't get to know that. The idea that someone who is raped should have to talk about their sex life apart from the rape is invasive and offensive."

"Wow," she said, smiling. "That gets you pretty fired up. I like that."

"I know," Scott said. "I get a little indignant about such things. The other part of the motion battle relates to our attempt to find out what meeting Nolan went to when he left you unprepared for the one you attended."

"I'd love to know that, but do we get to find out?"

"I don't know. I'm trying hard to relate it to the case, but they say it doesn't matter what meeting he went to as nothing happened at that meeting that is relevant to the case. They urge that it's company business that we have no need to know. I have to admit that I really don't know if there is anything helpful there. On the other hand, they are working pretty hard not to tell us what he was doing, which makes me think there might be something to find out."

"So what do we say in response to their argument that it's confidential business information?"

"We argue that it may lead to relevant information. For example, if he spent that time at a bar, we might get evidence of excessive consumption of alcohol that we'd be entitled to acquire. Relevant evidence may be out there, but we don't know what until we can look behind the curtain and learn what the meeting was all about."

"Can you sell that to the judge?"

"I'm not sure," Scott conceded, "but I'm going to try."

She smiled. "Thanks for explaining the strategy as we go. It helps me see how all the pieces fit."

"Let's get down to the prep for your deposition," Scott said. "Like we discussed last time, lawyers ask you leading questions that suggest the answer they want to hear. Questions that begin with words like, 'Isn't it true that...' Questions that suggest that they already know what happened. But it's a ruse; the defense lawyer didn't live any part of your life with you and he has no personal knowledge of what you lived through. He is just trying to make it easy for you to go along with what he wants to hear. So, if there is anything wrong with any part of the question, your response has to be, 'No, that is not right.' Be confident and tell it like it is. It doesn't matter if they don't like it. It doesn't matter if they rephrase the question, the answer is the same."

"Got it."

"The hard part is that you have to avoid letting them get under your skin. If you get pissed off, your answers won't be as thoughtful or as good. So, just remember the lawyer asking the questions has a job to do. However stupid or offensive the question, the answer is still delivered confidently, and respectfully. Make sense?"

"Yeah, I guess so."

"Well, let's try it. I'll be the defense lawyer with an agenda."

"Okay."

"Did you have sex with Mr. Nolan while you were both on the trip to Seattle?"

Sarah momentarily stared at Scott and then said, "No, we didn't have sex, I was raped."

"Did you kiss in his room?"

"No."

"Your lips and his didn't meet?"

She furrowed her brow. "He pinned me and kissed me, and then I got free and ran out of the room."

"And even after he did that, you let him into your room to rape you?"

Sarah sat back in her chair. She shook her head and said, "This sucks so much."

Scott nodded. "Yeah, I know, but I wouldn't be doing my job if I didn't alert you to what was coming. I don't want to scare you away, I just want you to be ready."

Sarah was quiet a moment and then asked, "Scott, do you think I'm doing the right thing here? I mean, is all this worth it?"

He smiled and said, "I think you are. I believe in the system and I believe in accountability. And if people in your position don't stand up, then people like Nolan do this again and again." He paused and said, "I also know how hard this is and I understand that some people just can't do it."

Sarah smiled and said, "I really want Nolan to answer for this. However bad this is going to be, I'm going to stay in it."

"And that's why," Scott said, "you are an inspiration to every other woman out there, however this case comes out."

Chapter Nine

Lee Henry wore a dark blue suit with a thin pin stripe, along with a new identity. For this meeting, he was Joseph P. Litton, a fifty-five years old, with thinning, grey hair and a beard. He carried a brief case and followed a young human resources representative, who introduced herself as Kim Denton, from the outer lobby down a long hallway, then down some stairs and into an office in the bowels of Sunmont Builders' corporate office in Pasadena. She had him take a seat in her small office and said, "So, Mr. Litton, I understand that you want to ask some of our employees questions about our former CEO."

"Right, nothing out of the ordinary. Your former CEO has been nominated for an important government post." He leaned towards her and spoke softly, as if sharing a secret, "I'm not allowed to say what post, but it's a good one." He smiled and added, "I've been hired as part of the vetting process. I just talked to neighbors, and now I have to talk to his former co-workers, just so we confirm that there is no reason he can't do the job. You understand, if all goes as expected, it's largely formality."

"I thought the FBI did that kind of door-knocking," Denton said, sounding perplexed.

"You're absolutely right. They often do. But they get busy chasing bad guys and they subcontract this kind of work to firms like ours. We can't hunt criminals, but we can help them interview friends and neighbors."

She nodded. "I get it," the young woman said, convinced it all made sense. "And we'd like to help Mr. Nolan get this appointment if we can."

Lee nodded. "I understand that you still employ about thirty-five employees that worked with Mr. Nolan, and twenty of those people dealt with him on a regular basis?"

"Right. When I heard this was happening, I made you a list." The woman handed him a typed sheet. "The seven at the top are the ones who dealt with Mr. Nolan all the time. They would know most about him."

"Come with me and we'll head to the conference room. From there, you can buzz anyone on the list and they will stop and answer your questions. It's only a couple of minutes of their time, right?"

"Correct. I'll be done and out of here in no time at all."

When they reached the small conference room that could seat three around a circular glass table, the woman said, "Oh, I need your business card."

"No problem," Lee said, reaching into his pocket. Then he rolled his eyes and said. "I left them in the car." The woman looked momentarily concerned. Lee said, "I will get one for you before I leave. If you prefer, I can go and get it now."

She hesitated and then said, "No, I guess before you leave will be okay."

"All right. This won't take too long and then I will bring it your way. Thanks again for your assistance. I think this is going to be a good thing for your former boss. I'm sure he'll be grateful if he gets the nod," Lee said, with a serious expression.

The woman seemed pleased as she said, "Great," and stepped out of the room. Lee checked the list and began calling in all of the women identified, one at a time. The first woman, Lilly Dawson, an obese, but pleasant looking woman in her early forties, took a seat and said "Hi, I'm Lilly."

"Hi Lilly. I'm Joe," he offered with a bright smile. "I'll just take a few minutes of your time." She nodded. "You worked with Mr. Nolan during his time here?"

"I did."

"How frequently did you see him?"

"Three or four times a week we would have a conversation and once in a while I would be in a big meeting when he spoke."

"What did you think of him?"

"I don't know, he seemed okay."

"Did he ever say or do anything that you didn't feel good about?"

She was quiet and Lee was anticipating. "Well, yes. His last year he said no bonuses after we had been told we would be getting them."

"That must have been disappointing," Lee replied.

"It was. We were counting on that money for Christmas."

Lee wasn't hunting Scrooge, so that didn't help much. He asked, "Anything else he either said or did that you thought was offensive?"

"Not that I recall."

"Or that anyone else told you offended them?"

"Like what?"

"Like anything inappropriate in the workplace."

She reflected and then said, "I can't recall anything."

Lee had similar conversations with eleven other women and three men over the next two hours. None gave him anything helpful on Nolan, but he was getting efficient at checking them off his list. He had three women and three men left to see, but the odds were looking bleak.

* * *

"Scott, I just took a call from Michael Graber while you were on the phone. He wants to have a meet and confer about his motion to compel identification of Sarah's sex partners and your motion to require them to answer the interrogatories about Nolan's meeting in Seattle."

"I'll give him a call."

Scott used the direct dial number he had for Graber. On the second ring he got, "Mike Graber."

"Hi Mike, Scott Winslow, returning your call."

"Right, so we have these motions coming up. I think you should pull yours off calendar."

"Why?" Scott asked. "Are you prepared to give me the information we are seeking?"

"No, I just don't think you are entitled to it."

"I believe that I am entitled to know where your guy was and what he was doing in the hours leading up to the rape. I also think that you should pull your motion off calendar. You don't get to invade Ms. Willis' privacy. Her sex life is none of your business."

"You'll remember that we believe this was an affair that she is trying to cover with these false allegations. We want to know how many times she has done this."

"That is absurd, Mike. As a matter of statute you don't get to explore her sex life."

"We'll have to let the judge decide it."

"I guess we will. See you next Thursday morning." There was a click and Scott was alone. "Pleasure chatting," he said into the dead phone.

* * *

Lee had only two more Sunmont employees to go. Either this idea was not working or there was just nothing to find. He wasn't sure which was true, but it wasn't good news either way.

Cherie Jackson, a woman of about thirty, walked into the room. He gestured to a chair and said, "Good afternoon, Ms. Jackson. My name is Joseph Litton. I'm here to ask about James Nolan, the company's former CEO. Did you know him?"

"I did."

"Can you think of any reason that he should not get an important job in government?"

She was silent. She looked down and away.

"Ms. Jackson?"

"I don't know what I'm getting into here."

"Well, you can tell me confidentially if you have any concerns about Mr. Nolan."

She was quiet again. After a time, she said, "I really shouldn't say anything."

"If you know anything, it's important you share it with me." She clammed up again and Lee thought he was about to hit a wall. He thought a moment and came up with an idea to pry some information from her. He said, "We have an idea that a woman may have had a complaint or concern about his behavior. Is that true?"

She looked up at him with wide, almost tearful, eyes, and began to nod slowly. He waited a moment and then asked, "Are you that woman?"

She hesitated a moment, and then replied, "No, but I know who you're talking about."

"Who is it?" Lee asked. She was quiet again and he added, "No one will know this information came from you if that is a concern."

"Margo Traynor. She used to work here." She looked to the side and shook her head. "He made her walk away from her career."

"Nolan?"

She nodded. "He was all over her."

"Did she report it to anyone?"

"I don't think so."

"Do you know why not?"

She shook her head in disbelief, and then said,. "I don't think you've ever been a woman who accuses a top executive of harassment. You start out as a disloyal whore, and it goes downhill from there."

Lee nodded. "So, where do I find Margo?"

"I don't know. I heard she moved to the Bay Area somewhere."

"Do you have any pictures of her?"

"No, but there might be a company picture somewhere."

"What does she look like?"

"Redhead. Pretty. Maybe twenty-six or twenty-seven when she left here, but that was about four years ago."

"Have you seen her on Facebook? Do you have any common friends who might know how to find her? Do you have any information that might help me locate her?"

"No, nothing else."

"Thank you for being honest, Ms. Jackson. You've been helpful." She nodded as she stood. "Will you allow me to call you if I think you can help me further?"

"Okay," she said with reluctance.

"What's your phone number?"

She gave him a number and then he thanked her once again. As she walked out, Lee gathered up his materials and got ready to leave the building. He was anxious to start tracking Margo Traynor. He wore a smile, because he had something to report to Scott Winslow that might just make a difference.

Lee walked over to Kim Denton's desk and said, "Thank you so much. You have been very helpful and extremely professional."

The young woman beamed and said, "Glad we could help. I hope Mr. Nolan gets the important job."

"You will likely hear the announcement on the news in the next month or so. Thanks again." He shook her hands and turned to go. After a moment he turned back to her and asked, "Does the company keep pictures of employees in their HR files?"

"Yes, do you need a picture of Mr. Nolan?"

He couldn't think of a good way to ask for a picture of Margo Traynor instead, so he said, "Well, yeah. Maybe something we can use for the announcement. More flattering than old footage the press usually digs up on a newcomer to a powerful position."

"Okay," she said nodding. He carefully watched her keystrokes as she pulled Nolan's picture from an employee gallery. She printed it and handed him the picture. Lee thought he looked like an egotistical asshole even then, but he had recent information to color that opinion. He smiled and the woman and said, "Thank you so much. I plan to write a letter to your supervisor about the great help you have been."

"Oh, no need," she said.

"Really, it will be my pleasure." He got her supervisor's name and walked from her work area. Before he reached the exit, he ducked into a small office and sat down at the computer. He went directly to the gallery of employee pictures and found a picture of Margo Traynor. He printed it quickly and exited the building, thinking it had been a pretty good day, and wishing he really could write a nice letter for Ms. Denton. It would be hard to send a letter from a guy who had no business being there and who didn't exist. Helping this phantom invader would not come out well for Ms. Denton, so it was just as well she would never hear from him again.

* * *

This time the dream wasn't some unidentified attacker, it was Nolan. The dream was painfully clear. She saw his face as he pushed her down on the bed. He smiled his best corporate success smile, as he forced himself into her. She could feel the pain and the terror all over again. She was saying, "Please, don't do this. Please, stop." And then she was screaming for help. She awoke as he thrust into her and sat up in bed, covered in sweat. The unforgiving cruelty of rape is that it never goes away.

John looked pained as he put his arms around her. "Was it the same nightmare?"

"This time I could see Nolan's face." She was shivering and breathing hard. "It was all so clear," she said, softly.

"That son of a bitch," John said as he held onto her while her pulse slowly returned to more normal levels. Something had to be done and it was up to him to do it. John held her for almost an hour and then they talked until day break. John fell back to sleep but Sarah didn't try.

John got ready for work and left for a meeting at 7:00 a.m. She knew that she didn't dare try to sleep again or it would all be back. Her attacker had changed her at some basic level. She was sad, anxious and vulnerable. The confidence that had defined her all her life had disappeared, along with her career, and now she had to convince people that she wasn't just a subordinate who fucked her boss and didn't want to admit it.

She called Angie. The answer came on the second ring. "Hi, Sarah, are you okay?"

"Not really. I keep having the dream. I'm afraid to try sleeping and I just needed to talk to you."

"Want to come over?"

"Yes," Sarah said, feeling grateful.

"Come over. I have some Danish, coffee and hugs."

"Angie, you are an amazing friend."

* * *

In no time at all, Lee located three Margo Traynors in northern California. One was eighty-two years old, so she was easily removed from the list of possibles. The next appeared to be around thirty and lived in Mountain View. The third was thirty-eight and lived in Fremont. She worked as a school teacher, so the age and change of occupation make her an unlikely candidate.

None of these women were active on social media, so Lee couldn't be sure if the Margo Traynor he wanted was any of the women he was considering. The Mountain View Margo was the best bet, however, so he decided to focus on her. The next step would be to find out where the right Margo lived and worked. He wasn't sure that she would have helpful information about Nolan engaging in harassment or sexual attacks in the past, and even if she did, she might not want to talk about it. She apparently left Sunmont rather than talk about it with HR, so he might have a challenge convincing her to talk to him.

Lee hit a button on his phone and waited.

"You again?" a male voice said.

"That is no way to talk to your best client. Come on now."

"Yes, sir, how can we help you," the voice said, sarcastically.

"Good words, but it would be much better if you meant them. I have an assignment for you."

"Of course you do."

"You are pretty feisty today."

"Just today? So, how can we be of assistance Mr. Henry?"

"I'm looking for a good-looking redhead, about thirty years old."

"Aren't we all?"

"Cute," Lee said. "This one is believed to be in the Bay area somewhere. Her name is Margo Traynor, and about four years ago she worked for Summont Builders."

"Got a photo?"

"Just so happens that I do. I just sent it your way. I need a current home and business address and phone."

"Have you tried Match.com?"

"Funny guy," Lee said.

After a short pause, the man said, "We just received the pic. We'll get on it and let you know what we find."

"How long?"

"Give us four or five hours."

"How about three?"

"We'll do it as quickly as we can."

"Good. I knew I could count on you guys for good work as well as bad humor."

Chapter Ten

Scott Winslow liked and respected Judge Elizabeth Burke. She was on her game. She read all of the briefs that lawyers submitted before a motion, and she reviewed the applicable law, so she was thoroughly prepared before oral argument occurred. She gave both sides a fair playing field and she didn't countenance any bullshit. Department 11, Judge Burke's kingdom, was a place well-prepared lawyers liked to be, and those who were faking it, were in for a hard day.

"Number 8 on the calendar, Willis v. Ellison Corporation and James Nolan."

Scott Winslow stepped up to the counsel table closest to the empty jury box and Michael Graber stepped up to the adjacent counsel table.

Judge Burke looked down from the bench. "Good morning, counsel."

"Good morning, your Honor. Scott Winslow on behalf of plaintiff, Sarah Willis."

"Michael Graber on behalf of defendants, your Honor."

"Good morning, counsel," Judge Burke replied. "We have two motions under consideration this morning. Let's start with the defense motion to compel disclosures pertaining to Ms. Willis' sex life. Mr. Graber, your motion, you have the floor."

"Thank you, your Honor. As the Court is aware, it's defendants' position that what occurred in this case is a consensual affair that Ms. Willis does not want to own. She got involved with her boss and doesn't want to explain it to her husband, so she manufactured a claim of sexual attack."

"Yes, I understand that is your position from your moving papers," Judge Burke said. "And?"

"And," Graber said, "We are simply trying to obtain and explore relevant evidence. If Ms. Willis did this sort of thing on other occasions, those facts are pertinent to her credibility and the credibility of the case she is attempting to make. We need to be able to assess those facts in preparation of our case."

Judge Burke turned to her attention to Scott Winslow. "Mr. Winslow, your position on that argument?"

"Mr. Graber's argument is the very reason that we have a code section in California that prohibits access to someone's sex life and sexual history absent a showing of good cause to the court. It is hard enough for a woman who has been harassed, attacked or raped to come forward knowing the scrutiny she will face without the harasser or attacker having the ability to explore every sexual relationship she has had. No woman would ever want to step forward if she would be subject to such attacks and invasion. What's more, a person's intimate life is a part of her right to privacy guaranteed by the Constitution of the United States and the California Constitution. You can foresee the countless abuses that would occur in deposition if the defense is suddenly entitled to intrude into the most intimate details of someone's life."

"Any response, Mr. Graber?"

"Yes, your Honor. The fact that this was really a consensual relationship that is being falsely called an attack by the plaintiff is the good cause for discovery of this information that the statute contemplates."

Judge Burke looked at Graber and said, "So what you're telling me is that whether or not the personal details of a claimant's sex life is protected hinges on the unproven defense that you are asserting?"

"Well, your Honor, it only requires the presence of good cause to access that information, which I believe we have presented."

The judge reflected a moment and then furrowed her brow. "I am not at all convinced, Mr. Graber. I believe that the statute protects disclosure of a claimant's sex life for good, public policy reasons. I do not think good cause is present that warrants disclosure of such information in this case. The motion is denied."

"Now, Mr. Winslow, let's turn to your motion. Please proceed."

"Thank you, your Honor. On the night of the attack, Mr. Nolan failed to attend a critical meeting that required his authority. He had Ms. Willis attend and she did not have the authority to act as the other side expected. Mr. Nolan said he had an emergency meeting to attend, but will not disclose what that was all about."

"Is that not the shoe on the other foot, Mr. Winslow? Isn't his privacy implicated in that context also?" Judge Burke asked, thoughtfully.

"No, your Honor. It was never advanced that this was anything, personal or private. To the contrary, defendants responded under oath that this was a business meeting."

"And if that is the case, how is this information relevant?" Judge Burke asked.

"Mr. Nolan returned from that meeting and raped Ms. Willis within the hour. We want to know if drugs or alcohol had been involved in his emergency meeting. There had to be some reason why he refused to attend a meeting in which he was a critical player to attend this other meeting he won't talk about and maybe it has something to do with something he imbibed or ingested."

"Mr. Graber, let me hear from you on this issue."

"Yes, your Honor. Mr. Winslow wants to fish through meetings that deal with proprietary information of the company, even while he argues out of the other side of his mouth that we shouldn't be entitled to look at Ms. Willis' background based on privacy."

"Your Honor," Scott Winslow replied, "This is apples and oranges. Ms. Willis' private sexual history is protected by statute. Defendant Nolan's failure to attend a critical meeting in favor of some other meeting shortly before he attacked Ms. Willis gives rise to questions about what happened while he was wherever he was."

The judge nodded. "Alright counsel, I am going to give this some additional thought. You will have my ruling on plaintiff's motion by email in the next day or two. The defense motion is denied. Have a good day, counsel."

"Thank you, your Honor," Scott Winslow said, feeling good about the fact that his motion had not been denied—at least not yet.

"Thank you, your Honor," Graber said, in a less appreciative voice as he gathered his notes and walked away from the counsel table.

The clerk said, "Number 9 on the calendar, Wilson v. Montoya," as Scott walked from the courtroom.

When he started back to the office, Scott's phone rang. He punched a button and said, "Scott Winslow."

"Hey, Scott, how are you?"

"Hi Lee. Doing pretty well. Judge Burke denied the defense motion to learn all about Sarah's sex life and took my motion to find out where Nolan went the night of the attack under advisement. You never know. She might go our way."

"That would be great," Lee said. "One way or another, we need to find out where he was that night. Even if it doesn't have anything to do with your client, I'm thinking that there is some reason they have to be so secretive about it all." He paused and then added, "I've also got some news. I have a possible witness on my radar."

"Really? Tell me about it."

"Margo Traynor was an employee of Sunmont Builders who left the company four or five years ago because of Nolan."

"Where did you get that?" Scott asked.

"I interviewed the Sunmont employees who worked with Nolan."

"How did you get them to talk to you?"

Lee was quiet and then said, "That is one of those things that you don't want to know."

"I withdraw the question," Scott said.

Lee added, "Of course, I don't have all the facts yet. I don't know if she left because he harassed her, or because he's just an asshole. Unless it's option number one, we will obviously hit a brick wall."

"So you'll make contact with her?"

"Yeah. I believe I have her located in the San Francisco Bay area. I'll try to call her, but if that doesn't work I will pay her a visit and try to convince her to help Ms. Willis."

"I know that you can be very persuasive," Scott replied.

"Naturally, it's all a matter of reason and charm," Lee said.

"Naturally," Scott replied. "So keep me posted."

"You got it. Let me know how your motion to identify the hole that Nolan disappeared into the night of the rape comes out."

"I will. Talk to you soon."

* * *

It was almost 9:00 p.m. when Jim Nolan punched numbers into the control panel and watched his gate swing open. He drove up the meandering driveway surrounded by expansive lawns, punched a button on the visor overhead and watched as one of the overhead doors of the four-car garage opened to let him slide the Jaguar inside.

He walked through the large, curved kitchen, and into the family room beyond, where Theresa sat with a glass of white wine and a book. She wore her robe, which suggested that she would soon be getting ready for bed. She looked up and said, "Hi, Jim. Jennifer left pork chops in the oven for you before she left for the day."

"Okay," he said, sitting down on the couch across from her. "How was your day?"

She looked a little surprised by the question. "It was fine. Today was the fundraiser luncheon at the club."

"What was this one for?" he asked, in a tone that suggested it didn't much matter.

"The children's fund in Zaire. Food and education."

"Oh, nice," he said.

"How was your day?" she asked, seeing as he asked first.

"Mostly good. Getting ready for the board meeting in San Diego next week."

"Mostly?" she asked.

He never shared his business with Theresa, but this was a little different. If she found out about the lawsuit some other way, the shit would fly, so tonight he would tell Theresa about it. It was the perfect opener. "Yeah, I have an employee lawsuit I'm defending, which is kind of a pain the ass."

"What kind of a lawsuit?" she asked, waiting to be shut down.

"A sexual harassment lawsuit."

"Against you?"

"Yeah."

"What does she allege you did?"

He walked over to the built-in bar on the other side of the room and poured himself a scotch. "She says that I harassed her. It's just impossible to prove a negative. I mean, how do you prove you didn't do something?"

Theresa nodded slowly. "What does she say you did?"

He was quiet for a moment and then said, "She says that I said I wanted to have sex and stared at her chest."

She put her glass of wine down and held his gaze. "Anything else?"

"Yes, she says I raped her." He added, "She also filed a criminal complaint, but it's all bullshit."

"Holy shit, Jim. You have to be kidding." They were momentarily frozen in place and wordless, then she asked, "So, your story is that you slept with this woman, right?"

He was quiet a moment and then said, "Yes, we spent one night together."

She shook her head and stood up. She looked disappointed as she said, "What happened to your promise that it would never happen again?"

"It didn't mean anything. It was just sex."

Theresa furrowed her brow. "Just sex? And when we sleep together, is that just sex, too?"

"No, of course not."

She hesitated a moment and then said, "Who is it? Do I know her?"

"Sarah Willis."

She shook her head. "I met her a few times. She doesn't strike me as a 'sleep your way to the top' kind of woman. And why would she say you raped her if it was an affair? There's something wrong with this, Jim."

"I don't know why she's saying that. We slept together one time on the Seattle trip, that's all."

"That's all?" She turned and started to walk from the room. She turned back to him and said, "You know, it's so sad. I'm not even surprised that you slept with someone else again. Just disappointed. I guess I wanted to believe your meaningless promises." She walked toward the bedroom and left him to sip his scotch alone.

It was 7:30 a.m. when Lee's phone rang. He looked at the incoming number and then answered with, "About time."

The male voice said, "Just trying to teach you some patience." Lee grinned, amused by this perpetual banter.

"Well, you've done that, but I hoped to get the information I need before I retire in twenty years."

"In that case, you're in luck. We have both a work address for Margo Traynor in Palo Alto and a home address in Mountain View."

"Are they good?"

"We are ninety-nine percent on the work address, but less sure about the home address. I'll text both of them to you."

"What's she doing?"

"She an assistant to a VP at Strilovent Technology."

"Which VP?"

"Let me see if we got that. Yeah, here it is. Corporate Planning. We also acquired an updated photo of her that I'll send your way."

"Great, thanks."

"We never let you down."

"Almost never," he replied. "Talk to you later."

Lee thought about how best to approach Traynor. In person was always best, but not the most economical way to get the job done. He decided to try to get her information by telephone. If that didn't work he would visit her in person to convince her to assist. If his information about her was correct, she had resigned from Sunmont rather than confront Nolan about his actions. Given her choice of flight over fight, she probably wouldn't be delighted to get involved in Sarah Willis' claims. He would have to find some way to approach her that didn't scare her away, and more to the point, that motivated her to put herself on the line.

* * *

Ted Nelson walked into Bob Berg's office and sat down on the couch that occupied the back wall. Berg sat at his desk and looked up from his monitor at Nelson. It was 6:30 p.m. and it was finally quiet. Support staff desks in the department were empty for the evening and the phones were quiet. Nelson sat back and asked, "So, how did it go?"

"It is miserable," Berg said.

"Because Nolan wouldn't allow himself to be suspended during the investigation?"

"For starters," Berg replied.

Nelson was quiet a moment and then said, "Who do you believe?"

Berg shook his head. "You don't want to have this conversation. It is possible that we are asked about our discussions concerning the investigation when trial rolls around."

"Yeah," Nelson said, "and I think you may have indirectly answered my question."

Berg said, "This is really uncomfortable. I mean we know Sarah and..." he let his words trail off. "There's no way I could have handled this one. That's why I had to hand it over to Orson."

"Is he strong enough to withstand challenge?" Nelson asked.

"Yeah, he's strong and he's good, just not as experienced as I might like. I mean, it would be good to have a ten year investigator on this, but like I said, I couldn't do this one."

Nelson replied, "Look, we now have a completed investigation, so that's what we rely on in making the decisions we need to make, which in this case is none, seeing as the investigation did not reach a definitive conclusion and Sarah is no longer here." He paused and added, "And if we are asked, we testify the same way. The investigation is what we relied on in this case like we do in every case; and that will be true."

"Yeah, I guess that's right," Berg said. He paused and then asked, "You're sure that Jerry Orson will hold up under cross-examination? I mean, he's going to have to defend the investigation."

"He'll do okay," Nelson replied. "I mean, he doesn't have years of experience, but he's gutsy and I think he has enough background to defend his conclusions. The lawyers will work with him to make sure he has it right."

Berg nodded and said, "This is such a tragedy, you know? I mean Sarah is good people."

"I know," Nelson said, "but you know that we don't deal the hand, it's our job just to play it out. We make sure to dot the 'i's and cross the 't's, right?"

Berg leaned back in his chair. Nelson was right, but none of this felt good.

* * *

Sarah's phone rang and she recognized the number immediately. She hit a button and said, "Hi, Melissa, how are you?"

"Been better," she replied. "How are you?"

"I'd have to say the same, I guess."

Melissa said, "I'm so sorry, Sarah. Truly."

"I know and I appreciate it."

Melissa said, "The corporate lawyer met with the department this morning and really pissed me off."

"You're probably not supposed to tell me about that," Sarah replied. "Don't get yourself into any trouble."

Melissa ignored the warning. "Get this. They assemble the whole department in the conference room, and the lawyer tells us that we are probably aware of the pending litigation involving you. He says that the company wants us to know that we don't have to get involved. He said that we don't have to talk to you or your representatives."

"I'm not surprised by that," Sarah said.

"That's not all. Then he tells us that it's better for all of us if we keep our heads down and steer clear of the whole issue." She was quiet a moment and then said, "I get angry all over again every time I think about it. The bastards impliedly threatened us if we get involved."

Sarah said, "Don't get on the wrong side of this, Melissa. You have a good career with the company and I don't want anyone to decide that you are not a team player like they seemed to have done with me."

"Screw them," she replied, angrily. "I am so mad at that son of a bitch Nolan. How dare he attack you and then behave like he's some kind of a victim?"

"Don't forget to take care of yourself, too. You have to survive this."

"I'll work here or I'll work somewhere else. What I won't do is abandon someone who has always treated me so well."

Sarah was deeply touched. "Thank you, Melissa."

"You hang in there. He needs to be held accountable, one way or another." She was quiet a moment and then she added, "I admire you, and I know it takes considerable strength to do what you're doing. Just know that you aren't alone. Not even here in the bowels of the beast."

Sarah chuckled. "Sounds like a great place to work," she said.

"The sad part," Melissa replied, "is that it used to be a great place to work, before the whole thing went off the rails. I miss working for you."

"Thank you, that really helps," Sarah said, suddenly feeling gratitude for those around her who were standing by her through all of this.

* * *

John Willis was struggling to compartmentalize; to be the loving and supportive husband in total control of his emotions when he was with Sarah, so that she had one less thing to worry about. When he was not with Sarah, his anger was right at the surface, and he was obsessed with how he would get to James Nolan. He drove to Ellison corporate headquarters and parked in the lot at about 7:00 p.m. and waited, eyes fixed on the building exit. Nolan emerged from the building shortly after 8:00 p.m and climbed into a black Jaguar XJ. John followed him as he left Woodland Hills and headed for the 101 Freeway. He drove north to West-lake Blvd. and turned right. They were now in Thousand Oaks. Nolan drove for about three miles and made a right and then a left turn past streets of magnificent golf course homes that were probably ten to twelve thousand square feet inside. One more turn and John could see Nolan slow his Jaguar to turn into the driveway of his estate.

From a couple of houses away, John watched as Nolan punched numbers into a mounted pad beside the driver's window and both halves of the massive, wrought iron gate began to swing open inwardly. As Nolan drove into the compound, John got out of his car and walked over to the gate, steering clear of the mounted camera. He glanced around, getting initial impressions of the estate. Inside the gate, he saw was a driveway that meandered around meticulously cropped grass to the front door of the estate, where Nolan had parked.

John looked around what looked like a fortress, surrounded by eight foot high block walls. It was a compound designed to protect the privacy of its wealthy owners. John smiled as he considered that, notwithstanding all this front loaded security, this estate was on a golf course. The front may look like a fortress, but no one built walls between their mansions and their golf course views. His way in would be on the golf course side of the house.

He checked his watch and decided it was time to go. His next trip back would be to explore access points. He would have to figure out how to disable video and alarm systems. As the architect for many elaborate residences over the years, he had contact with experts who knew those systems inside out. He would have to get closer to identify the specific systems that had to be shut down. He would return while Nolan was at work, when he could study and photograph the protective systems that surrounded the property. Once the systems were disabled, John fantasized about confronting him. Nolan would soon know what it felt like to be scared—really scared.

* * *

"Please, speak your piece," was the extent of Lee's latest voice-mail message, then came the beep.

"Hey, Lee, this is Scott Winslow. Give me a call back when you can..." Scott saw the notice of an incoming call from Lee. He stopped talking and hit a button. "Hi Lee."

"Scott, what's happening?"

"We got a ruling from Judge Burke. She denied both motions. The defense gets zero concerning Ms. Willis' sex life, and we don't get to know where Nolan went the night of the rape. In her ruling the judge says we can ask about what he had to drink or what he ingested, but not where he was before he came back to the hotel. From my perspective, that is not particularly helpful, because if he denies drinking, we have no way of checking the accuracy of what he says."

"Yeah, I get it. Let me think about other ways to look behind the curtain to see where he went. I'll get back to you. In the interim, I have an address for Margo Traynor and I'll talk to her to see if she will sign up to help. If she's hard to persuade, I'll head up to the Bay area in the next couple of days to see if I can convince her to do the right thing."

"Great. I hope she's amenable to being a witness for Sarah, although I have concerns about whether someone who didn't come forward with her own claims would want to be involved in someone else's."

"Yeah, I have those concerns as well," Lee replied.

Scott reflected a moment and then said, "If she won't talk voluntarily, I can compel her deposition near her residence with a subpoena. Then, she can decide whether she wants to perjure herself. One way or another, I plan to get her testimony. Let her know that if she'll sign a statement for us informally and agree to testify at trial, we can postpone her deposition for a while."

"I'll use that if I need it, but I'd like to be able to convince her to come voluntarily. She will be more open if we can get her to that point."

"Sounds good. Keep me posted."

"You got it," Lee said. "Talk to you later."

* * *

As Scott drove towards home, he hit preset one to check in with Lisa.

"Hello," a young, male voice said.

"Hi Joey, is mom there?"

"Hang on a minute. She's yelling at Katie right now."

"Okay, see if she can fit me in between the yelling."

"All right," Joey responded, in serious tones. Joey was now nine years old, going on ten, and popular with kids his age, but an independent spirit. He was his own man, already.

"Hi, Sweetheart," Lisa said.

"You done yelling at Katie, yet?"

"Is that what he said?" She chuckled. "I was talking to her about the fact that she is not old enough to wear make-up. She thought she would look good in eye-liner."

"She's eight for Pete's sake. Make-up?"

"Calm down, Dad. All the little girls want make-up and high heels. Dreams of being grown up, you know?"

"I'm going to be worried enough about her when she's old enough to date. I don't want to start now."

"You on your way to take your wife to dinner?"

"Yep. I should be there in about ten minutes."

"Good. I'm ready for a margarita, and maybe dinner, too," she said.

"Sounds great. You know, you are an inspiration to everyone around you. No wonder Katie wants to be able to dress like her mom."

"You are too sweet. Are you trying to seduce me?"

"Always. That sounds like the perfect after dinner plan."

* * *

John parked down the street from the Nolan estate and slowly walked over to the gate. It was 7:00 p.m., and if the past was an indicator, there was no reason to think that Nolan would be coming home for a couple of hours. His wife's Lexus was parked in front of the house but she was inside and out of view. He avoided the camera, as he looked at the keypad near the gate. He pulled out his phone and took a series of photos. He needed to know as much as possible about the entire security system, and how it was all tied together. He was going to make sure he was ready to handle the technology on the chosen day. After a few more pictures of the motion lights, he decided that it was time to head home to spend the evening with Sarah. The rest of this would have to wait.

As John walked along the street towards his car, he saw an orange Camaro with two passengers, both with eyes on him. As he moved past the Camaro, the driver lowered his window and asked, "Did you need something at that residence?"

"No sir, I'm just spreading the word of the Lord. I couldn't figure out how to get to that door though, so I think I'll have to choose another neighborhood."

"I see. You got any literature?" the man asked him.

"No, sir. I do it verbally." He thought a moment and then added, "He who trusts in his riches will fall, but the righteous will flourish like the green leaf." He smiled and said, "Important information from Proverbs. Particularly important for wealthy people." John hoped he didn't have to come up with anything else, because that was all he had handy. "Good day now," John added, walking away from the Camaro, and towards his car a block away. Once he got to the car, he took off quickly. He checked his rear view mirror, and was relieved that they didn't seem to be following. He had been caught and he hadn't even started to access the residence yet. He had sudden doubts about how effective he was going to be as a home invader. Lesson learned; situational awareness was a must.

* * *

They had a secluded table in soft lightning, and they toasted the evening with a clink of their wine glasses. Scott looked across the table at Lisa. "You are so gorgeous," he said, grinning. "Have I told you that lately?"

"That was the first time today, and thank you." She smiled and added, "Ready for some news? Well, apparently, your daughter got into trouble today."

"My daughter, huh? How so?"

"She apparently told several other children how they should be handling their relationships."

"Sounds like Katie. After all, she does know what's best for all of us."

"Well, this time she decided to tell two kids that they were rude and nasty. She told them that they needed to handle themselves with more respectability. That's actually the word she used."

Scott grinned. "Well, she's probably right."

"Don't tell her that, she already thinks that she's always right." Lisa shook her head. "Then she demanded that these two kids accompany her to meet with the teacher to discuss the matter. One of them told her to get out of town and the other just ignored her. Katie then took the matter to the teacher and demanded adult intervention to handle this unacceptable behavior. The teacher settled on talking to Katie about the fact that the dispute between two other kids was not her business to resolve. At that point, Katie shared that all students are affected by bad behavior at school, so she had a good reason to make things better."

"She is going to wind up as an international mediator or trade negotiator one day," Scott replied.

"Maybe, but that will be after many years of detention," Lisa replied. "For now, she needs to figure out the limitations on her own authority."

"Where does she get that from anyway?" Scott asked.

"Hmm, let me think," Lisa said grinning.

"You think that I climb into other peoples' affairs?"

"Only every day of your life. I mean people pay you to do that, right?"

"Yeah, but I have social boundaries."

"To Katie, that's a distinction without a difference. She's taking care of everybody else, just like her Daddy."

"That's kind of sweet," Scott said.

"Well, yeah, except for the part where she's getting in trouble for meddling," Lisa replied.

"Yeah, except for that." He paused. "Have I told you how beautiful you look today?"

"Yes, but that's only the second time today."

"I'll tell you again, as soon as I get you out of that dress."

She smiled. "Do you like the pearls?"

"I do," he said. "The pearls can stay. Everything else has to come off as soon as we get home."

She shook her head. "I like the way you think." She undid the top two buttons on her blouse.

Scott's eyes widened. "Better stop that or I won't be able to wait until we get home."

"It's good to know that some things never change," she said, smiling.

Chapter Eleven

The offices of McMillan and Jensen occupied the top six floors of the Western States Bank Building on Flower Street in Los Angeles. At 9:00 a.m., Scott Winslow and Sarah Willis were shown into a conference room with three massive chandeliers overhead and a marble conference table that could seat twenty. The court reporter and the videographer were already set up and in place. "Good morning, I'm Scott Winslow and this is the plaintiff, Sarah Willis."

"Hi, Mr. Winslow and Ms. Willis. I'm Charlie Gilbert, the videographer."

"And I'm Linda Farmer, the court reporter."

After greetings all around, Scott said, "Sarah, you sit next to the reporter in the seat of honor, and I will sit next to you." He picked up one of the microphones on the conference table and said, "We attach the microphones to our shirts so that we can be heard clearly on the videotape of the proceeding."

As she sat down, Sarah could see the camera directly across the table from her that would record her reactions and demeanor throughout the proceeding. When Scott told her about the video recording, she had been nervous about being on camera for hours at a time. He had told her to ignore the camera. She found it surprisingly easy to do.

After a few minutes, Graber walked into the room followed by Bob Berg. Berg looked at Sarah and said, "Good morning Sarah."

"Hi, Bob."

"How are you, Scott?" Graber asked.

"Good. You?"

"Also good." So much for the small talk. Graber asked, "Are we ready"

"Let's do it," Scott said.

The videographer stated the case name and number, the date and location. The court reporter then had Sarah raise her right hand and swear to tell the truth, the whole truth and nothing but the truth. Sarah confidently stated that she would do so.

"Good morning, Ms. Willis. I am Michael Graber, attorney for Ellison Company and Mr. Nolan. Are you ready to have your deposition taken?"

"Yes, I'm ready."

"Have you had any drugs or alcohol in the past twenty-four hours?"

"No."

"Is there anything that prevents you from testifying truthfully today?"

"No."

"Did you have an opportunity to speak to your counsel about the deposition process before be began today?"

Scott said, "Objection, attorney-client privilege. You are instructed not to answer."

"Come on, Scott, this is just part of the admonitions." Graber said.

"You don't get to know what we talked about. Objection and instruction stand."

"Fine," Graber said, sounding annoyed. "Did you have the opportunity to meet with your attorney at some point before today?"

"Yes."

"You understand that you are testifying under oath today, just as if you were testifying in a court of law?"

"I do."

"And you understand that if you give false testimony today, you can be prosecuted for perjury?"

"I object, that's a misstatement of the law," Scott replied. "Perjury requires intentional false testimony. Mistakes are false or inaccurate testimony, but they are not perjury."

Graber looked annoyed. "Okay. Do you understand that you can be prosecuted for perjury if you knowingly give false testimony?"

"Yes."

"If you don't understand any of my questions today, please tell me."

"Okay," Sarah replied.

"If you answer a question without telling me that you don't understand it, then I am going to assume that you understood it and I'm going to ask a judge to make that same assumption at trial. Understand?"

"I do."

"Your attorney may make objections for the record, but unless he instructs you not to answer I'm entitled to an answer to my question after he makes his objection for the record. Understand?

"I do, yes."

"Are you employed?"

"Not anymore."

"Who was your last employer?"

"Ellison Corporation."

"And your employer before that?"

"General Mechanics."

"For how long?"

"Three years?"

"Why did you leave?"

"A good opportunity at Ellison."

"So you left voluntarily? You weren't fired?"

"Objection. Compound and redundant. You can answer."

"Correct."

"Did you ever make any claims against that employer for harassment or discrimination?

"No."

"Any legal claims against that employer?"

I object. "Vague and ambiguous, overbroad and invasive of privacy, but you may answer," Scott said.

Sarah waited until Scott completed his objection and then said, "No."

"Before that?"

Scott said, "Before that what?"

Graber looked annoyed again, but clarified. "Before that where did you work?"

"Westpoint Engineering?"

"How long?"

"Two years."

"Why did you leave there?"

"Better opportunity."

"Entirely voluntary?"

"Yes."

"Did you ever make any claims against that employer for harassment or discrimination?

"No."

"Any legal claims?"

"Vague and ambiguous, overbroad and invasive of privacy, but you may answer," Scott said.

"No."

"Before Westpoint Engineering?"

Graber then took Sarah through her employment with her two prior employers. Then he took her back to her part-time jobs through high school, her college and graduate school days.

He asked about her areas of study in college and all subsequent training she had received in every discipline. He took her through professional organizations she had joined, seminars she attended and the initial training she received upon arrival at Ellison.

"How long did you work for Ellison Corporation?"

"Four years."

"Why did you leave Ellison?"

Sarah gave him a look that said you know why. "I was fired by James Nolan."

"Why?"

"I believe that it was because I complained after Mr. Nolan raped me."

"Why do you believe that? Did Mr. Nolan tell you that he was firing you because he raped you?"

Sarah choked back the desire to call Graber an asshole. "No, sir."

"Mr. Nolan gave you the reason for your termination, didn't he?"

"I object. Argumentative. You can answer," Scott said.

"He said it was because we couldn't communicate directly when I sent an analysis that I did for him through human resources."

"Did you do that?"

"Yes."

"So you couldn't communicate well with him directly, right?"

Sarah was quiet a moment and then said, "I did the work he asked and got it to him timely. And no, I didn't want to deal with him directly any more than I had to after he raped me."

"Mr. Nolan had other complaints about your performance too, didn't he?"

"Object, vague and ambiguous, calls for speculation. But you may answer," Scott interjected.

"No."

"He never voiced complaints about your performance?"

"No."

"Did he say anything about your performance?"

"Yes."

"What?"

"Before the attack in Seattle, he told me I was doing a great job and he was planning to promote me to Vice President of Finance," Sarah said.

Graber gave her a disbelieving look. "Anything else?"

"Anything else what?" Scott interjected. "Vague and ambiguous."

"Anything else he ever said about your performance?"

"Yes."

"What?"

"He periodically told me I was doing a great job, that he was really impressed, and on one occasion, that I was amazing."

"Did you document any of these occasions?"

"No."

"So, do you think he liked you?"

She was quiet, thinking hard about how to answer this without calling him a pig. "I think he knew I was doing a good job."

"And do you think he liked you on a personal level?"

"I don't know. I mean, how could you like someone and attack them?"

"Let's break for lunch," Graber said. "One hour okay?"

"Fine," Scott replied.

As Scott and Sarah rode down on the elevator and made their way to the soup and salad restaurant next door, Scott asked, "Are you hanging in there okay?"

"Yeah, I guess so." She was quiet a moment and then said, "This procedure is so intense, I don't know how you do this all the time."

"You're doing a good job," Scott said. "You come across as honest and direct."

As they sat down with their salads, Sarah said, "The worst is yet to come."

"It is, but you can handle it. Remember, don't let him get under your skin even if a question is insulting. We want your best answers, so don't let him get you off balance. There are times you will think he's being an asshole, and he may be, but he's doing a job. I will object when it's necessary to preserve my objections for the record, but I can only instruct you not to answer in limited circumstances, so take your time and give each question your best."

Sarah's stomach churned, and she ate only part of a small dinner salad, while Scott ate a turkey sandwich. An hour later, they returned to the conference room and waited fifteen minutes beyond the time agreed for the lunch hour before Graber returned. He entered the room and asked, "Everyone ready?"

"We're ready," Scott said. "Let's get it done."

The videographer announced the case name and number, the date, time and location and that we were now on videotape number two. Then he said, "Ready counsel."

Graber nodded. There was a moment of quiet and then he asked, "Did Mr. Nolan ever make sexual comments to you in the workplace?"

"Yes."

"What did he say?"

"He told me that I look hot a number of times?"

"When did he say that?"

"He said it on a number of different days over a period of seven or eight months."

"How many times?"

"Seven or eight."

"Were you offended by this?"

"I was," Sarah said.

"Why?" Graber asked. "Isn't it a compliment?"

"Object as argumentative. You may answer," Scott instructed.

Sarah's expression showed the emotion that came with all this. "I was a professional for this company: an executive. Not a contestant in a beauty contest and not anyone's girlfriend. I'm pretty sure he didn't make similar statements to male executives."

"So, if you were offended by this, I'm sure you would have reported it, right?"

"Object, vague and ambiguous, and argumentative," Scott interjected. "She can't tell you what someone would or would not have done, only what she did."

"Did you report this conduct to HR?"

"No."

"Not on any of these seven or eight occasions when you were deeply offended?"

"No."

"Did you report any of these occasions to anyone at the Company at the time they occurred?"

"No."

"Why not?"

"This may be hard to understand. I just wanted to do my job. To do a good job with my team and earn the promotion that was under discussion. I didn't want his improper behaviors to become the focus of who I was at the company. I hoped that he would stop this stuff."

Graber reflected a moment, and then elected to move on. "Any other comments he made that you found offensive?"

"Yes.

"On other occasions he told me that I looked really good."

"How many other occasions?"

"Approximately a dozen."

"Any other comments you found offensive?"

"Yes," Sarah said and stopped. Scott grinned. She was doing it right. Only answering the question that was asked.

"What are they?"

"A couple of times he told me that my husband lucky to be climbing into bed with me."

"What did you say?"

"The first time I was silent. Shocked. After that I told him that I thought that was inappropriate, and I asked him to stop."

"And what did he say?"

Anger showed in her expression. "He just grinned, like he was amused and proud of himself."

"Did you report these comments? To anyone?"

"No."

"Why not?"

"Because I hoped it would all stop and I could just be allowed to do my job."

"Anything else Mr. Nolan did that offended you?"

"Yes."

"What?"

"He would often let his eyes move down to my chest and stare."

"Did you complain to HR?"

"Ultimately, after the attack in Seattle, yes."

"How many times did this happen?"

"A lot."

"Ever complain to anyone between the time this conduct started and the time you went to Seattle?"

"No?"

"Why not?"

"Same reason I gave you before."

Graber sat back in his chair and asked, "Who are the witnesses that heard Mr. Nolan make any of the statements you've told me about?"

"I don't know of any witnesses."

"None? After all those occasions"

"Asked and answered, argumentative. Don't answer," Scott said.

"So no one can support your testimony that these statements were made?"

"I don't know. I can't identify anyone who heard the statements."

"That seems a little hard to believe."

Scott jumped in, "Argumentative. Save it for the jury."

"I don't think it's hard to believe," Sarah said. "He chose the times when he made these comments. He chose times no one else was around."

"Anything else that Mr. Nolan did that you found offensive?"

"Yes."

"What?" Graber asked, sounding annoyed that he had to pull it out of her.

"He came to my office and told me that he wanted to make love to me."

"What did you say?"

"I was shocked. I said we were both married to others."

"Did he respond?"

"Yes."

"What did he say?"

"He said we could really spice things up."

"Your response?"

"I told him I didn't want to hear comments like that."

"Did he say anything else?"

"No. Just smiled."

"You said you were offended?"

"Yes."

"But didn't report it at any time before Seattle?"

"Well, this was just a couple of days before Seattle, but no, I didn't."

"Why not?"

"The triumph of hope over experience. I just hoped he would stop and let me do my job."

"Now you've known the Senior HR team at Ellison since you began with the company, right?"

"Yes."

"How would you characterize your working relationship with HR Director Bob Berg?"

"Good."

"You got along well with Bob?"

"I did."

"And you think he does his job pretty well?"

"Yes."

"And you think that he cares about the company's employees?"

"I do, but I also think he has to protect the company."

"So why didn't you confide in Mr. Berg?"

"Asked and answered," Scott interjected. "She has told you repeatedly why she did not share this information. Just one time per question, counsel."

"I did," Sarah said. "After Seattle."

Graber gave a nod and said, "So let's talk about the Seattle trip. Why did you go on that trip?"

"I had a presentation to make, but I was asked to go a day early by Jim Nolan, to attend a meeting with him."

"And did you attend that meeting?"

"I did. He didn't."

"Do you know why not?"

"Object as calling for speculation. You may answer," Scott said.

"He said he had an emergency meeting to attend."

"Did you see him that night after the meeting?"

"Yes."

"How did that come about?"

"He called me when he came back from wherever he was and asked me to meet him in the lounge."

"What time was it when you met in the lounge?"

115

"Around 10:00 p.m."

"How long were you there?"

"Maybe half hour."

"Did you drink?"

"I had a drink."

"Just one?"

"Correct."

"Did Mr. Nolan drink?"

"Yes."

"How many did he have?"

"Three during that time, I don't know if he had been drinking before that."

"Did you leave the lounge together?"

"Yes."

"Why?"

"I told him I was tired and I wanted to go turn in. He asked me to stop by his room because he had a document he wanted to show me."

"Were you concerned about going to his room?"

"I thought I was picking up a document, so no."

"When you got there did you go in?"

"Yes."

"Did he give you the document?"

"Yes."

"Anything else happen?"

"Yes."

"What?"

"He pushed me against the wall and kissed me."

"Did you kiss back?"

"No. I did not."

"What did you do?"

"I pushed him away and ran out of his room."

"That night, did you see him after that?"

"Yes."

"How?"

"He came to my room and knocked on the door."

"And you let him in after he pinned you against the wall in his room?"

"Not at first. I told him I would see him in the morning."

"And did he leave at that point?"

"No."

"What happened?"

"He said he was really sorry for what he had done." Sarah was fighting back tears, and reliving it made her angry. "He said he felt bad and wanted to apologize. Just open the door long enough for him to say he was sorry."

"And you opened the door?"

"Yes, after resisting a couple of times. I shouldn't have trusted him."

"Move to strike everything after 'yes' as non-responsive," Graber said.

"What were you wearing?"

"My robe over my undergarments. I was getting ready for bed."

"Did he come in?"

"He pushed into the room as soon as I opened the door slightly."

"Did you kiss him?"

"No."

"Did you touch him?"

"To push him away after he pushed me onto the bed and started ripping my panties away."

"Did he rip them?"

"Yes."

"What were you doing this whole time?"

"I was yelling, and trying to push him away."

"Did you have sex that night?"

"What?" Sarah asked angrily. "Did we have sex? No, he raped me. He perpetrated the ultimate act of violence."

"Did he penetrate you?"

"Yes."

"And were you trying to resist the whole time or did you stop resisting?

"I never stopped resisting. I was overpowered."

"Did he ultimately withdraw from you?"

Sarah shook her head and answered, "When he was done."

"Then what did he do?"

Sarah began to cry and Scott said, "We are going to take a break now.

"I want an answer to my pending question first." Graber said.

"That's not happening," Scott replied and he left the conference room with Sarah following.

Once they were in an adjoining conference room, Scott said, "You okay?"

Sarah nodded. "I think so. This is just so hard to live through in such detail. Am I doing okay?"

"You are doing fantastic. You are a very credible witness. Just continue to tell it like it is." She nodded. Let's take a walk out to the lobby and relax a moment before we go back. Take a few deep breaths and know this will be over soon. Once Graber says he is done, we don't ever come back for any further deposition without a judge ordering it."

She nodded and said, "Thanks for all your support, Scott. I appreciate having you on my team."

They walked back into the conference room and sat down.

"Ready?" Graber asked.

"We're ready," Scott said.

The videographer stated the date and location, time and tape number for the audio record.

"How soon after he withdrew from you did Mr. Nolan leave the room?"

"Immediately."

"So what time was it then?"

"I'm not sure. Sometime after 11:00 p.m."

Graber nodded. "So at that point, who did you call to report this attack?"

"No one."

"Did you call the police at that point?"

"No."

"Why not?"

"I was emotionally devastated. I sat on the bathroom floor and cried until after 3:00 a.m."

"Did you call the police then?

"No."

"Anytime that night?"

"No."

"Why not?"

"I don't know."

"Did you call your husband anytime that night?"

"No"

"Why not?"

Sarah was tearing up. Scott knew that this was the most distressing and vulnerable part for Sarah because she felt guilty about not confiding in her John sooner. "You okay?" Scott asked. "Want to take a break?"

She shook her head and said, "I'm okay." She took a deep breath, pushed back tears and said, "I didn't tell him because I knew how much it would hurt him."

"So, what did you do after he left the room?"

"I took a long shower, repeatedly scrubbing and trying to get clean. Then I sat on the bathroom floor and sobbed."

"For how long?"

"Until about 3:00 a.m."

"What did you do after 3:00 a.m.?"

"Took a Lyft car to the airport, got a flight and went home."

"Did you file a report with the police the next day?"

"No."

"Why not?"

She was quiet for a time and then said, "Part of me wanted all this to go away. To pretend it never happened. I didn't want to relive the attack by describing it in detail."

"Did you tell your husband the day after the attack?"

"No, and I hope he can forgive me for not confiding sooner."

"Did you tell anyone?"

"No."

"Well, when did you first get around to telling anyone?"

"Objection, argumentative, but you may answer," Scott said.

"On Friday, the second day after attack."

"Who did you tell that day?"

"My best friend Angela and my husband?"

"Who first?"

"My best friend."

"Why her before your husband?"

"She had a way of getting it out of me."

"Did you file a complaint with the police that day?"

"No."

"Did you ever?"

"Yes. The day after that."

"So you waited almost a week before filing your complaint?"

Scott said, "I object, argumentative and asked and answered. Last time I checked, three days is not almost a week. Don't answer that question."

Graber looked agitated. "When did you first tell anyone at the company?"

"The same day. I called HR and set up an appointment with Robert Berg."

Graber sat back in his chair and took on a judgmental look. "Isn't it true that the reason you didn't talk to anyone about these events for three days was because they never really happened?"

"Argumentative," Scott interjected. "But you may answer."

"No, that's not true."

"Isn't it true that you were having an affair with Mr. Nolan?"

"No."

"You're under oath here Ms. Willis. Were you having an affair?"

Scott said, "Asked and answered, argumentative. Don't answer."

Graber was angry. "Counsel, you are obstructing my deposition. I'm going to go to court and get an order to reconvene this deposition and get sanctions against you."

"Anything you want to try. Just know that if you end this deposition, we won't be back. This is your shot. Use it or lose it."

"I want an answer to my question."

"You already have it. She said there was no affair. Now, do you have any other questions or are you concluding this deposition?"

Graber was fuming. "I don't intend to put up with you obstructing this deposition much longer."

"We're ready to leave anytime," Scott said. "But when we leave, we won't be back."

Graber shook his head and then asked, "When did you first see a counselor?"

"The same day I met with Mr. Berg."

"And that was Laurie Spencer?"

"Right."

"How did this particular counselor you've been seeing come to your attention?"

"She was someone I had been introduced to at a business event a year or so ago," Sarah responded.

"Had you ever seen her for any counseling, or for any professional reason, before the Seattle trip?"

"No."

"Had you ever seen any counselor before the Seattle trip?"

"No."

"How often have you seen her since the Seattle trip?"

"Twice a week since then?"

"Has she helped you?"

"Yes, she has."

"So you are better off than you were initially, right?"

"I would say that's true, yes. At that point I was barely hanging on."

"Were you suicidal?"

"I thought about it a couple of times in the first day or so, but I wasn't really going to do it."

"How is your emotional condition these days?"

She looked down at the conference table and remained quiet. After a time she said, "I feel like a part of me is missing."

"What do you mean?" Graber asked.

"I mean I've been a self-confident, optimistic person who loved her work for as long as I can remember. My confidence is shaken, I no longer feel safe and my career is gone. I'm pretty torn up."

"Do you have any other emotional symptoms today?"

"Yes."

"What are they?"

"Depression, anxiety, sleeplessness, nightmares and random crying spells. And that pervasive feeling that I am no longer safe. That I can't trust people." She was quiet a moment and then added, "I can't tell you how much I hate what has happened to me."

The questioning continued until 6:30 p.m., when Graber announced, "I just have to review my notes, but I think I may be done."

Sarah and Scott stepped outside into the hallway and took a short walk. "How did I do?"

"You did a good job, Sarah. In just a moment you can take a deep breath because you're almost off the hot seat."

"None too soon," she said, shaking her head.

They walked into the conference room and Graber said, "I have no further questions."

Scott noticed that as he said good-bye, Berg showed Sarah what looked like an empathetic expression. As they walked from the building Sarah said, "Thank you for everything, Scott. I'm so glad that you are on my side."

"My pleasure, Sarah. I'm sorry you have to go through all of that again, but we want to do everything we can to hold Nolan accountable."

She smiled and added, "Thanks for being so understanding. I judge me a lot harder than you do."

Chapter Twelve

Lee spent an hour searching through Sunmont Builders' employment files on line to assure that they had nothing he missed. As usual, security was lax and there was no difficulty getting in or perusing their confidential files, but he couldn't find anything helpful.

He decided that his next task was to find out where Nolan went the night of the rape. If the court wouldn't make Ellison tell Scott Winslow, he would find another way. Within twenty minutes, Lee had found his way into Nolan's Ellison Company email, and was searching for clues. He had been in for about two minutes when he could see alarms going off internally. Access was shutting down. He could no longer move between emails. And there was something else—someone was searching for the intruder. The programs were setting off alarms that were triggering a search for his IP address and identity. This was high end security that was not only defensively shutting down access, but proactively seeking out any invader. This was the fastest and most aggressive response he had ever seen. Lee quickly withdrew and shut down the programs, and then he shut down his computer and moved to his backup computer.

He waited for a few minutes and then climbed back into the program. This time the response was almost instantaneous. Access was shut down before he could see the first email. Lee shut down his second computer and walked over to the coffee pot. This guy's private email was fucking Fort Knox. He wondered why it was so tightly protected. More than ever, he wanted to know what secrets Nolan had in those emails that required the expense of incredibly sophisticated security. Very intriguing.

Lee called Margo Traynor at 6:30 p.m., figuring her workday would be over and she would be available.

"Hello."

"Hi, Ms. Traynor."

"Who is this?"

"This is Lee Henry. I'm an investigator in Los Angeles. I'm investigating a matter involving James Nolan, and I know you are familiar with him from your employment at Sunmont Builders."

She was quiet for a time and then said, "I don't have anything to say about Mr. Nolan."

Now, Lee knew he had the right person. "Ms. Traynor, this is really important."

"Yeah, so I understand."

"What do you mean?" Lee asked.

"I talked to my friend Cherie. She told me that Nolan was about to be given some big government position." She said it with distaste, and then she added, "I don't have anything to say about him."

"Anything you know could be helpful," Lee said.

"I have nothing to say," she replied. "Don't call me again." The line went dead. Lee considered what had just happened. It was good news because it was clear that what she would say about Nolan could be helpful. He decided to see her in person. Maybe face to face, he could get her to confide information that would help Sarah Willis.

* * *

"My wife and I are thinking about buying a home and becoming members," John Willis told the country club operations manager. "I thought I would get a look at the impressive facilities before I look at the price tag. I figure it will be less shocking if I know what I'm getting."

Carl Skinner laughed. "Sure, let me show you around starting with our restaurant." They walked into the adjacent building where the spectacular restaurant spanned a block in length. Its fourteen foot ceilings, magnificent chandeliers, high backed, leather chairs and walls of windows onto the golf course all screamed power and money.

"Wow," John said. "This is pretty impressive."

"And you haven't tried the food yet," Skinner said. "That's what gets most people. We have a phenomenal chef we stole from one of the best restaurants in Paris, and a staff that goes overboard to please."

"Wow, again," John replied, doing his best to sound impressed.

"I tell you what," Skinner said, "you and your wife come for dinner on us. I know that will sell the membership."

"Okay, sure," John said.

"They walked out onto a marvelous terrace that overlooked stone and marble fountains, and the manicured golf course."

Skinner's cell rang and he answered it, "Carl Skinner."

"Okay, I see. I'll be there in about five minutes." He hung up and said, "Sorry, I have an emergency. Feel free to hang out here and order a drink on me. Then take a walk around and see the clubhouse, the gym, the other two restaurants and the pools and tennis courts. Here's my card. Call me and tell me what night you and your wife would like to come for dinner."

"Thank you so much," John said. "Do you mind if I walk down to the course and take a look at the putting greens and the driving range?"

"Not at all. Enjoy."

He watched Skinner walk away and then looked out over the course to get his bearings. He made his way down to course level, and then pretended to stare at the extensive putting surface. He walked slowly toward the large homes that bordered the right side of the fairway. The homes had wrought iron gates, and low fencing that protected the views.

He counted the houses along the course, but could only view the first three. They were magnificent structures that seemed to spread out in all directions, around elevated decks that looked out onto the golf course. No walls, just a low wrought iron fence that accommodated the views and could get approval from the architectural committee. He smiled as he walked back up to the golf club restaurant. As soon as he got what he needed to disable alarms and cameras, he would be ready to go.

* * *

Lee left the courthouse after testifying in a case he had investigated. He enjoyed talking to juries. They listened well, and they cared. They wanted the information they needed to do a good job, and Lee played well to a jury. He was sincere and well-informed. He was hard to trip up on cross-examination because he was confident, well-prepared and could see where any line of questioning was going before it got there. He didn't go out on an unsupported limb. If he didn't know something, he owned it.

It was going to be another busy day. Lee had an appointment in San Jose in four hours, and then he planned to drive on to Mountain View to see Margo Traynor. He headed north on the 101 Freeway, toward San Jose, and decided to make a brief detour when he got to Thousand Oaks. He turned right on Westlake Boulevard and headed up to what was known as the 'north ranch' area, the area plush with meandering estates and private hedgerows. A place where power players had access to Los Angeles for their daylight dealings, but could escape the city at night. Lee wanted to see just how formidable the Nolan estate might be. If he couldn't get into Nolan's email externally, perhaps he would make a visit to his home computer and see what he could access. There might also be documents detailing his dealings during the trip to Seattle: where Nolan went and who he saw when he got there.

Lee drove past the expansive, gated residence. On the drive back the other way, he stopped and took pictures of the key pad and the camera that kept a watchful eye on the approaching driver. Undoubtedly, other cameras would be from the same provider, so ideally, he could learn how to shut them all down for his entrance. Many of the keypads were easily defeated because they targeted a would-be home invader, not a sophisticated electronics expert. Satisfied that he knew what he was up against, Lee took off and headed back toward the freeway. As he did, he saw an orange Camaro that he had noticed earlier in the trip. It seemed to be staying two cars behind him. He made a quick right and the Camaro followed. Lee slowed down and the Camaro did too. He turned a corner and increased his speed and the Camaro maintained its distance.

The driver of the Camaro had Lee's interest now. Lee drove to the mall and stopped not far from a primary entrance. The Camaro parked three rows away. Lee climbed out of his car without looking in the direction of the Camaro. He walked to the mall entrance, as two men climbed out of the Camaro and followed. Lee disappeared into a crowd near the mall doors, and then walked into the first store he came to, taking cover in an aisle containing racks of jeans. He could see the foot traffic outside, but could not be seen by passersby. Lee watched as the two men walked past the store, and looked around, trying to pick him out of the crowd. Lee left the store and walked back to the parking lot. He grabbed a tool from his car and made his way to the Camaro. He unlocked the door and pulled the registration from the glove box. Then he placed a small GPS device inside the rear wheel well, on the passenger side of the vehicle. Lee got into his car and drove to a parking spot that gave him a clear view of the mall entrance. He parked and dialed a number.

"I should have known we wouldn't go all day without a request. What do you need this time?"

"I need you to run a name. Thomas Walter Cummings of 2115 Las Villas Circle in Sherman Oaks."

"Is tomorrow sometime good?"

"Funny. You know me better than that," Lee said. "I'm following the guy now and I need to know what I've got here."

"Okay, give me ten minutes."

"You got it."

Five minutes later the two men came out, gesturing in animated conversation as they looked over at where his car had been. It appeared that they were arguing over whose fault it was that Lee had driven away unseen.

Lee watched as they climbed into the Camaro and drove away. He gave them a few minutes and then watched the GPS readout. He started following at a distance of two miles. He had only left the parking lot when his phone rang.

"Lee Henry," Lee responded.

"Okay, we have him. He is a private investigator. Looks like he does a lot of work in domestic cases. You know, take a picture of your spouse screwing somebody else, that kind of thing."

"Makes sense because he seems a little out of his element," Lee said. "Thanks, I owe you."

"I know, you tell me that all the time, but I never get what you owe me."

"You do. What you get is your exorbitant bills paid and then I call you again, even though I have to listen to your complaints. Later."

As Lee hung up, the GPS showed that the men had pulled off the road. He drove to where the car stopped and found that they were inside either a yogurt place or Starbucks.

He retrieved his GPS from the wheel well of the Camaro and then walked to the door of the yogurt place. The two men were the only two customers, sitting at a small table and eating yogurt. Lee walked over to their table as they looked up in a surprised stare. Lee sat down at their table and looked at them. He said nothing.

"Can we help you?"

"Hi, Mr. Cummings. Who's your associate?"

Cummings had a shocked expression on his face. "This is Mr. Jones. Can we help you?"

Cummings was a round man. A round head on a round body, much on the order of Frosty the Snowman. He wore a black shirt with sequined pockets. Mr. Jones was thin, had slicked back hair wore a polo shirt and jeans. Lee smiled. "Yes, Mr. Cummings, you can tell me why you are following me?"

"I think there must be some mistake," Cummings said. "We aren't following you."

Lee handed him his vehicle registration and said, "You may need this."

Cummings stared at him with a stunned expression. "Where did you get that?" he asked.

Lee stared at him a moment, and then said. "You know, if you're going to follow people, you need to be a little less obvious. I'd do away with the bright orange Camaro. You're driving something that looks like the sun, so it's hardly inconspicuous." Both men stayed silent. Lee said, "So now we come to the cooperation part of our program. Who hired you to follow me?"

"I don't know what you mean," Cummings said.

Lee sat back in his chair and said, "Let's cover some basics. You are a private investigator. You get hired for money. You were following me. Now, unless you have some weird personal interest in me, someone hired you to follow me. So, let me ask you again. Who was it that hired you?"

"I don't have anything to say," Cummings said.

"This is for your own good. You really need to tell me who hired you."

Both men's eyes grew big. "Wait a minute," Cummings said, "You can't threaten us."

Lee smiled. "I'll keep that in mind." He paused and then added, "All I need is a little information. Someone showed the poor taste to hire you to follow me. I need to know who that was." They were quiet. "You need me to convince you I'm not bluffing?" Lee asked. Neither man moved. Lee stood up and pulled out his phone. He took a picture of the two of them with their yogurt in front of them on the table.

"You don't have my permission to take my picture," the other guy said.

Lee smiled. "If only you'd said so earlier," he said, shrugging. He looked at Cummings and shook his head. "An orange car and a shirt that sparkles are not exactly insightful for someone in the business of not being noticed."

Lee walked from the yogurt shop and checked his watch. He needed to get back on the road to Mountain View, so he would have to converse further with Mr. Cummings later. He hit a couple of buttons on the phone and got an immediate answer. "What now?"

Lee said, "Patience, my friend, you need to slow down and enjoy life a little."

"And you're helping me do that how?"

"By making sure that you have business enough to assure your economic success. Then you can stop and smell the roses."

"Okay. So back to my original question, what now?"

"I just sent you a picture of Cummings and his associate. I need to know who the associate is, and whether he was hired by Cummings or someone else."

"Okay, I'm on it."

"Thanks, text me the results as soon as you can."

"I don't know how long it will take, because I don't know if we have background or database info on this guy. I'll let you know."

Lee was driving north through Salinas when his phone rang. He hit a button and said, "Hi, Scott, what's new?"

"Hi, Lee. I had a thought I wanted to kick around with you on the Willis case."

"Fire away."

"Well, you know that Sarah says she went back to her room alone and got ready for bed and then Nolan showed up and pounded on the door, needing to see her long enough to apologize. Nolan says that they walked to her room together, right?"

"Right," Lee said, and then added, "You're thinking video."

"Yeah, that's right. If the hotel has cameras that watch the hallways, we may be able to use the video to establish that Sarah and Nolan walked separately to her room to destroy Nolan's credibility."

"I like it," Lee said. "I'll get on it as soon as I visit Margo Traynor."

"Good luck. I think she may be a challenge."

"I'll give it my best shot," Lee said. "I know that she probably won't want to get involved, but it also appears that she is no friend of Nolan's. Maybe I can use that to our advantage."

Chapter Thirteen

"This is tape one of the deposition of James Nolan being taken on behalf of Plaintiff at the Law Offices of Simmons and Winslow, 1462 Lake Ave., Pasadena," the videographer announced. "May I have counsel introduce themselves for the record please?"

"Scott Winslow on behalf of the Plaintiff, Sarah Willis. Ms. Willis is also present."

"Michael Graber on behalf of Defendants and Robert Berg, Ellison's HR Director is also present."

"Ms. Reporter, will you please swear the witness?"

"Please raise your right hand Mr. Nolan. Do you swear to tell the truth, the whole truth and nothing but the truth?"

"I do."

Scott said, "Good morning, Mr. Nolan. You realize that you are testifying under oath today?"

"Yes."

"As a result, you are subject to the same penalties of perjury that apply to testimony in court, you understand that?"

"I do."

"Did you review any documents to prepare for your deposition today?"

"Yes."

"What did you review?"

"The company policies and the investigation report prepared by Mr. Orson."

"Anything else?"

"No."

Scott spent the morning taking Nolan through his employment history, dates of employment with each employer and positions held. He addressed the duties and responsibilities Nolan had at each employer, and his reason for leaving each. Then, he addressed Sarah Willis' positive employment history, including commendations, positive reviews and merit based increases reflected in her file. After all of this was completed, they broke for lunch at noon, returning at 1:00 p.m.

"Good afternoon, Mr. Nolan. You understand that you are still under oath?"

"Yes," Nolan said.

"This morning you told us that you reviewed policies to prepare for your deposition, correct?"

"Yes."

What policies did you review?"

"The Company harassment policies."

"Is raping someone while they are on a business trip with you something that violates the policy?"

"Objection, assumes facts not in evidence and argumentative. You are instructed not to answer," Graber said, visibly angry.

"You read the policy on harassment, Mr. Nolan. If an executive were to rape a co-employee while on a business trip, would that violate the policy?"

"Yes."

"And would staring at a female employee's breasts repeatedly violate the policies?"

"Objection, calls for speculation and a legal conclusion," Graber interjected.

"I'm not asking for a legal opinion, I asking for his under-standing, as the CEO of the company, of whether that conduct violates the policies. If he doesn't know, he can tell me that."

"Yes, I think it would."

"How about repeatedly telling a female employee she was hot, does that violate policies?"

"I don't know."

"Does telling a co-employee that you want to get her into your bed violate the harassment policies?"

"Yes, it would."

"Did you tell Ms. Willis that she was hot?"

"No."

"Ever?"

"No."

"Did you tell her you wanted to get her into bed?"

"When we were in Seattle we went to bed together."

"Move to strike as non-responsive. My question was whether you told her you wanted to get her into bed."

"In Seattle, maybe."

"How about before that?"

"No."

"Did you tell her that sleeping with you would spice up your sex lives?"

"No."

"Did you stare at her breasts at any time?"

"No."

"Did you ever make sexual comments of any kind to Ms. Willis?"

"No."

"To your understanding, would it violate Ellison Company policies to make sexual comments to an employee?"

"Yes."

"When you were in Seattle, did you say you wanted to get her into bed?"

"I don't recall how our lovemaking came about. Could have said something like that and she agreed."

"So, you said you wanted to get her in bed and she said, let's do it?"

"Not in those words."

"Well, tell me as closely as you can what you said."

"I may have invited her to go upstairs with me."

"To get some document you wanted her to look at?"

"Probably, yes."

"So, even in Seattle you weren't making sexual comments to her?"

"Right."

"Where were you when you asked her to stop by and get documents?"

"In the hotel sky-lounge."

"Was this after your separate meetings that night?"

"Yes."

"And what was her response, as closely as you recall?"

"She said something like, okay, let's go. So we went."

"Where did you go?"

"My room."

"Did you have sex there?"

"No."

"I kissed her and then we wound up in her room."

"How did you happen to go to another room?"

"I don't recall."

"Is there some reason you couldn't have stayed in your room to have sex?"

"No. No reason."

"Did you have a conversation about changing rooms?"

"Yes."

"What was said?"

"I don't recall precisely."

"What do you recall about what was said?"

"That we were going to her room."

"Whose idea was that?"

"Hers."

"She said let's go to my room?"

"Yes."

"Did she say why she wanted to do so?"

"No."

"Did you talk about why you were going to go to her room?"

"I don't recall."

"Did Ms. Willis leave your room before you did?"

"No."

"So, you left your room and walked to hers together?"

"That's right."

"Did you say anything about having sex in her room before you got there?"

"I did."

"What did you say?"

"That I wanted to make love to her."

"And what did she say?"

"That she agreed."

"She said, 'I agree?'"

"I don't remember the exact words. She said that was okay with her."

"How long after that conversation did you walk to her room?"

"Right away."

"How long were you in her room?"

"I don't know, half hour."

"And you had voluntary sex?"

"Yes, of course."

"Were you physically rough with her?"

"No, of course not. It was tender."

Scott paused and said, "Tender, is that what you said?"

"Yes."

"And did you rip her panties during the course of this tender love making?"

"I don't remember."

"But you might have?"

"I don't know counsel, I told you."

"Did you take her clothing off?"

"No."

"None of it?"

"No, she took her clothes off and I took mine off."

"Then what?"

"What do you think? Then we got in bed and made love."

"You use any protection?"

"No."

"Did you have any with you?"

"No."

"And neither of you discussed that?"

"No."

"You asked Ms. Willis to come to Seattle that day to attend a meeting with you, right?"

"Yes."

"You didn't attend that meeting, but you sent her, right?"

"Right."

"Why?"

"Something else important came up that I had to address."

"What was that?"

"Irrelevant, I instruct you not to answer," Garber told Nolan. He looked at Scott and added, "The Court already ruled that you don't get to know that confidential business information."

Scott continue to focus on Nolan. "But you did intend to go to the meeting you sent Ms. Willis to until that something else came up, right?"

"Yes."

"And when did that something else come up?"

"The same day as the meeting."

"Did you drink while at your meeting?"

"No."

"Did you take any form of drug?"

"No."

"Did Ms. Willis fly home in the middle of the night after you were in her room?"

"I don't know."

"You haven't learned that since then?"

"Yes, I heard that."

"She was to address a meeting you attended the next morning right?"

"Yes."

"And she was a no-show?"

"Yes."

"Were you ever aware of Ms. Willis not attending any event she was speaking at in the past?"

"No."

"So, were you surprised when she wasn't there?"

"Yes."

"You had no idea why she went home at that point?"

"That's right."

"So did you attempt to call her to find out why she didn't show?"

"No."

"Did it occur to you that she might be still in her room, maybe sick?"

"No."

"You had her cell phone number, right?"

"Yes."

"Why didn't you contact her?"

"I don't know. I was busy with other things."

"And then she didn't return to work, right?"

"Yes."

"Did you find out why?"

"No."

"Did you try?"

"No."

"Mr. Nolan, have you ever harassed or sexually attacked a woman at Ellison?"

"No."

"Have you ever harassed or sexually attacked a woman anywhere you worked before joining Ellison?

"Never."

"Have you ever inappropriately touched a woman anywhere you've worked?"

"Object as vague and ambiguous," Graber said.

"Well, let's make sure we are clear, have you ever grabbed, touched or fondled a female employee's breasts, buttocks or thighs?"

"No, absolutely not."

"Have you ever engaged in physical harassment of a female employee?"

"No."

"Any form of physical touching, other than a handshake?"

"No."

"Did you ever make sexual comments to any female employee?"

"No."

"Did you ever stare at the breasts of female employees?"

"No."

"Now, Ms. Willis returned to work after a few days, right?"

"Yes."

"And by the time she returned you were aware of her allegations against you, right?"

"Yes."

"And you fired her, right?"

"Yes."

"Why?"

"She couldn't communicate directly with me and I wasn't happy with her overall performance."

"She couldn't communicate directly with you refers to the fact that she sent her analysis of a project through human resources while her complaints were pending, right?"

"Yes."

"What was improper about that?"

"My executive employees have to be able to work with me. We have a lot to do and need to be able to effectively communicate."

"Ms. Willis only communicated with you indirectly on one occasion, right?"

"Yes."

"And that was approved by HR, wasn't it?"

"I didn't approve it, and she reported to me," Nolan said, dismissively.

"Did HR approve it?"

"I don't know."

"You've been informed that they did, right?"

Graber interjected. "You are not to divulge any of our communications, so you can answer as to information from any other source."

Nolan looked annoyed and then said, "In that case, I don't have such information."

"Did you have any understanding of how long a period Ms. Willis wanted to communicate indirectly?"

"I don't recall."

"Was any period of time discussed?"

"I'm not sure."

"Did you ask?"

"No."

"Why not?"

"It never occurred to me."

"How long had you been dissatisfied with Ms. Willis' performance?"

"Most of the time since my arrival at the company a year ago."

"So is that six months, nine months, how long?"

"Probably six or seven months."

"And what, in particular, were you not satisfied with?"

"The quality of her work."

"Can you be more specific?"

"No."

"Didn't you personally tell her she was doing a great job?"

"No."

"Did she get a bonus at the end of last year?"

"Yes."

"And was that bonus based on performance?"

"No."

"What was it based on?"

"The company's performance."

"Didn't some managers get bigger bonuses than others?"

"Yes."

"And didn't Ms. Willis get a bigger bonus than many other managers at her level?

"I don't know, maybe."

"Wouldn't that be based on performance, sir?"

"Not necessarily."

"Well what else would account for that?

"I'm not sure."

"Mr. Nolan, were you put out on administrative leave during the period of the investigation?"

"No."

"Did anyone talk to you about the fact that the policies call for you to be put out on leave while the allegations against you were being investigated?"

"Yes."

"But you weren't put on leave?"

"No."

"Whose decision was that?"

"Mine. I am far too busy to waste time."

Scott suppressed a smile at the arrogance. "Who talked to you about that policy?"

"Mr. Berg."

"And you told him that you weren't going out on leave?"

"Objection, assumes facts not in evidence," Graber said.

"Do you have the question in mind?"

"Yes, that's right. I told him I was far too busy, and that was not going to happen."

"Did you read that policy?"

"I don't know if I did at that point."

"Have you ever?"

"Yes."

"Is there an exception to the leave requirement for those who are busy?"

"No."

"Is there an exception to the leave requirement for your position?"

"Not that I am aware of."

Scott saw an opportunity and asked, "I noticed you checking your watch. Mr. Nolan. Do you need to take a break?"

"No. I need to get this over with and get back to work. This has killed a whole day."

"Mr. Nolan, did you tell Ms. Willis that you were going to combine her position with the Vice President of Finance position?"

"Yes."

"When did you tell her that?"

"Shortly before the Seattle trip."

"Was the Vice President of Finance position open at that time?"

"Yes."

"Did you tell her that you planned on promoting her to the Vice President of Finance Position?"

"No."

Scott asked, "Is there any document that you can point to that existed before the trip to Seattle which references inadequate or substandard performance by Ms. Willis?"

"I did not prepare such a document."

"And are you aware of any from any source?"

"No."

"Who did you tell that you had any dissatisfaction with Ms. Willis before the trip to Seattle?"

"I don't think I told anyone."

"So you didn't create any document reflecting any deficiency with Ms. Willis' performance, you didn't take any action based upon any deficiency and you never told anyone of any perceived deficiency in her performance, correct?"

"I object. Compound and asked and answered," Graber interjected.

There was quiet. "You can answer, sir," Scott said.

Nolan flashed an angry expression. "Yes, that's what I said."

It was 6:45 p.m. when the deposition was completed and Scott and Sarah left the conference room and walked to Scott's office. Sarah sat down in one of the visitor chairs in Scott's office and he sat on the edge of his desk. Her expression was hard to gauge.

"You okay?" he asked.

"I don't know. It's just so hard to hear someone so willing to lie like that."

Scott nodded. "It's a rude awakening for many when they hear what the kings of their industry will say to cover themselves. I see it a great deal, so I stopped being surprised a number of years ago. In truth, a number of highly placed people adopt an alternative reality to protect themselves from serious allegations."

"But it's about integrity," Sarah said.

"It is, I agree. And some people confronted with a tough scenario will tell the truth when it is not in their own best interests.

But a rapist is probably someone who's not going to score too high on an integrity scale either."

Sarah was quiet a moment and then asked, "So how do we win this if they are all prepared to lie?"

"That's the challenge, but credibility is everything. If we can support yours and attack his, it may help the jury choose the right answer. We also want as much of the evidence that supports your testimony as we can find, before we go to mediation. We want to make it hard for them to rely on their guy's credibility."

Sarah leaned back in her chair and said, "I know that we are going to mediation, but I don't know if this case can settle, with Nolan claiming an affair. In truth, I'm not even sure if I want it to settle."

"I understand. The approach I recommend is that if a reasonable settlement can be achieved, it is a worthwhile resolution. It allows you to move beyond all this and hold him accountability for what he did. But if there is no reasonable settlement offer, we let a jury make the decision."

"You have faith in juries?"

"I do. They are regular people who take the obligation to be attentive and follow the law seriously. It's a good system." He hesitated a moment and then asked, "How is John doing?"

"He's incredibly supportive about everything that has happened, but hard to read. He doesn't let me know how all of this is affecting him." She shook her head and asked, "You're married, right?"

"Yes."

"So if this happened to your wife, how would you be doing?"

Scott thought a moment and then said. "I don't honestly know. Part of me would want to go after this guy, so I admire the way John is doing the right thing. I really don't know what I would do."

Chapter Fourteen

Lee Henry drove from the airport to Strilovent Technologies in Menlo Park. Traffic was heavy, but he hoped to arrive somewhere around the lunch hour. His research showed that Strilovent was working on encrypting technology that would protect corporate messages from hackers seeking to sabotage or steal their work; the kind of technology that would make it harder for Lee to penetrate their records. Lee presented himself as an applicant for a position in the accounting department. He told the human resources representative overseeing applications for the position that he was going to be in the area and wanted to come by and fill out an application.

He reached the front gate of the facility to find extensive fencing and a guardhouse. A uniformed guard appeared as he pulled up to the gate and said, "Can I help you, sir?"

"Yes, my name is Michael Bailey, and I'm here to meet with human resources about possible employment."

"Who are you going to see?"

"Jordan Phillips," Lee said, having searched organizational profiles on line in case this question arose.

The guard nodded and stepped inside the guardhouse. He glanced at a monitor and then stepped back outside. He handed Lee a placard with a big number 16 on it, and said, "Proceed directly to building sixteen where human resources is located.

That's the only place this badge will allow you to visit. Drive inside the gate, take an immediate left and the third building on your right will have the number 16 on it. You'll find the human resources people you need to see right inside the door on the ground floor."

"Okay, thanks," Lee said and drove inside the gates. He made the left and saw building after building ahead. The place was enormous. Finding Margo Traynor in here would require him to get into Corporate Planning, wherever that was in this monolithic compound.

Lee drove ahead toward Building 16, and stopped as he approached someone walking near the building. He kept his placard out of view and asked, "Excuse me, sir, can you tell me which building Corporate Planning is in?"

"No idea, man."

"All right, thanks," Lee said. He saw a woman up ahead, and drove to where she was about to cross the street.

He put on his friendliest smile and said, "Can you tell me where to find Corporate Planning?"

She looked at him a moment and said, "Didn't they tell you at the front gate?"

He gave her an embarrassed smile. "They did, but I'm so wrapped up in my projects that my attention wavered."

She grinned. "You want building 11. You are going the right way. Pass buildings 16 and 12 on this road and then turn right and you are there. There is a giant eagle over the front entrance."

"Thank you so much," Lee said, and gave her a wave as he moved forward.

He decided to proceed directly to building 11, rather than stopping in building 16 to pretend to apply for a job. As building 11 came into view, he saw the giant eagle over the door. He parked in the visitor lot across the street and walked inside. There was a large waiting area that contained four different conversation areas comprised of chairs, couches and coffee tables.

Beyond the waiting room was a narrow hallway that led directly to a guard station. Lee decided that to approach the guard station was to motivate a call to the front gate to see why this guy without the right color pass was in the building. He decided he had no choice but to wait. He sat down and opened his IPad to check his email at 3:00 p.m. Nothing to do but wait and hope no one began to question his presence.

It was just after 4:00 when she came down the elevator and walked toward the lobby. She was a beautiful woman, looking just like the recent picture he had been given. As she approached he called out, "Hi, Ms. Traynor."

She looked at him a moment, assessing. Then she said, "Do I know you?"

"Sort of," Lee said. "My name is Lee Henry. I am an investigator and I called you on the phone to discuss James Nolan."

She tightened up immediately. "I have nothing more to say about him."

"This is not about finding him a job. This is about holding him accountable for his behaviors."

"I told you, I have nothing more to say," Traynor said. She turned and walked out the front door. He followed. By the time he exited the front door, she was fifteen feet away.

"Please, Ms. Traynor, give me just a couple of minutes." There was no response. She continued walking toward an adjacent building and never looked back. Lee thought about his next move as he walked to the car. She was going to be a challenge.

* * *

They sat in James Nolan's inner sanctum sipping coffee. "I don't know what he's up to, but the bastard needs watching," Tom Cummings said. "He caught us following him and approached us, demanding to know who hired us. The son of a bitch had pulled my car registration."

"So he sees you following him, and he winds up following and approaching you?" Nolan asked, incredulously.

"That's right," Jake Carlson, the man who was identified to Lee as Mr. Jones, responded.

Nolan silently assessed whether his team was up to the task of dealing with Lee Henry. "Jake, you understand that the story you just told me doesn't portray you guys in a particularly favorable light, right?"

"We've got our eyes on him now," Cummings said. "Next time we meet with him we will be in control of the situation."

"Jake?"

"That's right," Carlson echoed.

"Look, my tech people tell me that someone has been looking at records. I'm not sure who that is but my research tells me that Lee Henry is the guy who works closely with Scott Winslow. They also tell me that he's smart and ballsy, so don't underestimate him." Cummings and Carlson both nodded silently. "Maybe he's not the guy attempting to hack us, I don't know. I need you guys do what it takes to find out what he's up to so we don't have any surprises. If the answer is nothing, then we leave him alone and keep looking." He paused a moment and then said, "Jake, make arrangements with corporate security to get whatever time you need for this project. Tell Alan I blessed this deal so that corporate security isn't concerned about you taking time for some other project. I want you guys to report back to me as soon as you have something. I need to be sure that Lee Henry isn't getting where he shouldn't go. You with me?"

"Yes, sir," Cummings said.

"Okay, let yourselves out and update me before the end of the week."

"Shall do, Mr. Nolan," Jake Carlson responded. Carlson didn't enjoy looking like an idiot in front of Nolan. He had been paired with Cummings so that an experienced investigator could show him the ropes, but so far he wasn't impressed. It didn't feel like

Cummings had a clue. He just seemed to be waiting for something else to happen, which was not Jake's way of operating. He might have to take control of the situation himself if Cummings continued on his present path.

* * *

At 5:00 p.m., Lee sat on the steps outside a second floor condo on Wilson Court in Mountain View. From where he was sitting, passersby could not see him. Someone would have to be halfway up the stairs to the condo before he came into view. He made a couple of calls and wrote emails while he waited. It was just after 6:20 p.m. when Ms. Traynor appeared on the steps below him. She reacted with a jolt when she saw him sitting there. Her expression was some combination of fear and anger. "What do you want? I told you I have nothing to say. Please leave me alone."

Lee nodded and said. "I understand. Please give me two minutes to speak and then I will leave. You don't have to say anything, okay?" She was shaking her head. "Just two minutes he repeated, then I go away or you can call the police or whatever you want."

Her expression was skeptical, but she gave a brief nod.

"I am an investigator. I work with an attorney who represents a woman name Sarah Willis. She was raped by Nolan on a business trip. He raped her, and then he fired her for not being able to deal directly with him after the rape. Over the weeks and months before the rape, he engaged in a course of harassment that included telling her how hot she was, that he was going to get her into bed and often staring at her breasts. He now denies every bit of this and says that they had an affair."

She was looking at him attentively, with an inscrutable expression. As he took a breath, he had no idea if she would let him continue, so he said, "I can't put into words what this has done to her life. She was strong and independent, and a great manager, and she has been shaken to her core. Whether he can deny everything and get away with this is what is at stake. She is standing up to him, but it may not be enough." He shook his head and said, "I think that you can help her by coming forward about the way he treated you. Please, think about it. It is important to stop this from happening again."

She remained quiet for a time, but when she finally spoke, he could tell he had reached her by the emotion just below the surface. She was holding back. After a few moments, she said, "I will think about it."

"Thank you," Lee said, handing her a card. "I really hope you will. This kind of power abuser has to be stopped and that only happens if those who have seen it step forward." The look on her face said she got it. "Please, call me anytime." He paused a moment and then added, "I believe in this woman, and I believe that this guy needs to be stopped. If no one stops him, he continues ruining lives. I think you know something about how he does that." She nodded almost imperceptibly, as he walked past her and down the steps. At the bottom of the stairs he turned back to see that she was still watching him. "Thank you for your time, Ms. Traynor." He walked away, hoping that he had made the critical connection to a witness who could take Nolan down.

* * *

Every time John looked in Sarah's eyes, he saw the depth of the hurt. It was a constant reminder of the need to act; the need to hold Nolan accountable. He feared that she may not be believed, and that he may get away with what he had done. If the jury didn't believe her, it would be another soul crushing experience; one that would wound her even further. He had to act. Maybe, he could exact his revenge and walk out of the Nolan house unidentified. Probably not. Probably, he would go to jail. It didn't really matter so long as Nolan was made to pay for what he had done to Sarah.

For three days in a row John made early morning trips to the Nolan house. He parked down the street and stared at the residence, planning for the day he would enter and confront Nolan. He checked the list he carried in the glove box. He had the alarm system detail and the way to bypass the code, the camera system and shutdown mechanism, and the as-built drawings obtained from the county permit office. He reached under the seat and pulled out the gun, just to assure himself it was still ready for him. It was; loaded, safety on. He put the gun under the seat and the system notes and as-built drawings back in the glove box.

John sat in his car, a block away from Nolan's residence. He watched to see who came down the street. A FedEx truck came by, local traffic, and neighbors taking morning walks. He was alert to the times of the morning when most people were out. It was 7:45 a.m., and he had been parked and considering the options since 5:30. He took a walk closer to the house and studied the structure, the locations of its doors and windows and angles of visibility. After a time, it occurred to him that he may have been standing in one place too long, so he made his way back to the car. Everything had to be perfect. He couldn't afford to make a mistake. He figured that he should be ready within a couple of weeks. He started the car and headed toward his office, consumed with thoughts of making Nolan suffer. It felt good just knowing that he was going to do something to make this right.

* * *

Sarah took her customary chair in Laurie Spencer's office.

"You want some coffee, Sarah?"

"No thanks," Sarah said softly.

"How are you doing?" Laurie asked as she sat down across the coffee table from Sarah.

Sarah shook her head. "I guess it depends when you ask. Sometimes I think I can make it through this. There are days that I think I'm strong enough and I will be fine." She stopped talking.

"And other times?" Laurie asked.

"Other times, I get afraid something bad is going to happen, ot I think I'm not strong enough to fight back. When I feel like that, almost everything looks like a bad omen, and I just want to lock myself in my bedroom."

Laurie nodded and said, "I understand. You know all of this is still an open wound. You have to have safe places to be, and you need to put some distance between you and what happened."

"Will I ever be able to do that?" Sarah asked with some combination of sorrow and fear in her eyes.

"You will. You definitely will. You need support and time to heal." She paused a moment and asked, "The deposition of Nolan happened in your case, right?"

Sarah nodded. "Yeah."

"And how was that for you?"

She shook her head, and said, "He lied so easily. It made me feel like I didn't matter at all. He was so arrogant and self-important."

"Did good things come from it? How was your attorney?"

Sarah smiled at this. "Scott was great. He's a smart guy, and really tenacious." She hesitated and added, "Kind of like I used to be."

"What happens next in the case?"

"The next deposition is Jerry Orson, the guy who did the investigation. And then after that we go to mediation to see if the case can settle."

"Do you want the case to settle?" Laurie asked.

"Another split decision," Sarah said. "Part of me wants the case to go away, so that I don't have to relive any these events anymore. But, I guess that's based on a false assumption that if the case is gone I will be able to stop the replays in my head.

My other half wants to tell my story to a jury. I want to make them believe me."

"I can point out that if the case settles, it won't end your re-playing these painful events, but there will be fewer reminders. If it doesn't settle, by all means tell your story. Just know that whether they believe you or not, the facts are what they are. Even if Nolan succeeds in perpetuating a lie, it's still a lie."

"Yes, but it's a lie without accountability. That monster is cool and calm as he lies about what he did to me. I want to make him tell the truth."

Chapter Fifteen

Lee was still being trailed. There was no more orange Camaro, so they had apparently taken his advice and switched to the less obvious brown Ford Fusion that Lee saw several times a day. Presently, they were three cars behind and had been following him for the past half-hour. He made the effort to leave them behind only when there was some reason. Otherwise, they were welcome to follow him, and find nothing of interest.

Lee's phone rang. He saw the number and answered immediately. "What have you got?"

"We have an ID on the picture you transmitted. Your man with Thomas Walter Cummings is one Jake Carlson. He is a manager of operations in the security department at Ellison."

"Really?" Lee said. "So Jim Nolan has one of his own following me. Okay, one more thing. Run this CA license plate. F179246. Mr. Carlson and Mr. Cummings are its present occupants."

"Give me ten minutes."

Lee hung up thinking about how he might use Jake Carlson. He didn't seem to present much of a danger so long as he was teamed with Tom Cummings, but the possibilities were interesting. Nolan was nervous enough about what Lee and Scott Winslow were doing behind the scenes that he had people watching. Now it was just a matter of giving them something helpful to report to Nolan.

Lee made three trips around a regional mall's parking lot, with the Fusion in tow, when the phone rang again. They were aware he was screwing with them, but what could they do if the assignment was to stay with him?

"Hello."

"Wow, pretty unconventional response from you."

"Word economy. It's my new byword."

"Sure. We'll see how long that lasts."

"Funny. What have you got?"

"The car is a rental, so I hope they fill it up before they return it."

"Rented in what name?"

"Ellison Corporation."

"Perfect, thanks. Remind me to give you something special at Christmas," Lee said, hanging up.

Lee made a sudden left to leave the mall parking lot. He checked his mirror to see the Fusion, which had fallen about a quarter mile behind, accelerate to catch him before he hit the street. He waited patiently at the corner so they didn't get lost.

* * *

"How are you doing, Sarah?" Melissa asked.

"I'm hanging in there. Hoping to get the old me back soon. How about you?"

"Still angry. Yesterday we got a visit from the Executive Vice President for Administration. He wanted to tell us this litigation pertaining to the department was a real test, and we are all doing well. He said sometimes former employees bring frivolous lawsuits, and told us to steer clear of the entire matter. Then he thanked us for our loyalty to the company. Loyalty, that's what they are calling deserting you."

"I wish I could say I'm surprised," Sarah responded. "I'm suddenly on the other side of some big walls."

Melissa replied, "I've had enough of this stuff. I was ready to tell them what to do with this job, but then it occurred to me that maybe while I'm still here I could take advantage of the situation to be disloyal and help you."

"I don't want you to mess up your career, Melissa," Sarah said, earnestly. "It may be better for you to move on."

"That's what I mean. You're in the midst of a shit storm, and you still care about me. Management around here cares only about playing us to keep us on their side in the lawsuit. There is no compassion or concern, just a desire to win at all costs." She paused a moment and then said, "I really want to help you. Ask your lawyer if there is any way I can assist you."

"Okay," Sarah said, "I will ask Scott and one of us will call you back. Are you sure you want to get involved?"

"I'm sure, but call me back soon. I don't know how much longer I can put up with these guys."

* * *

Lee used the time to return phone calls as he drove nowhere in particular. He went through downtown Los Angeles, and then out to Westwood. He drove past the UCLA campus and then hopped on the 405 freeway north. He connected with the 101 north and then drove to Ventura, where he stopped for a hamburger. He then drove slowly back to Woodland Hills and took the Winnetka off-ramp. As he exited the freeway, he dialed a number.

On the second ring a voice said, "Detective Barton."

"Hi Don, this is Lee Henry."

"Hey, how the hell are you?"

"Doing good, buddy. We need to have a beer and catch up."

"I agree. When do you want to do it?"

"How about Thursday after work. Maybe 6:00?"

"That works. Where?"

"How about The Beer Buzz on Tampa."

"Yeah, I like that place."

"Good, I'll see you then. I also need a favor."

"Shoot."

"I have two guys following me in a Fusion. They've been on my tale all day and this is not the first day. I know they are privates hired to follow me around, but I want to have them shaken up a little. Can you guys pull them over and ask them to explain why they are following people. Mention harassment and possible restraining orders, that kind of thing."

"Where are they?"

"They are following me on Winnetka. We should pass the station in about two minutes."

"Well at least you're making it easy. What's the license number?"

Lee recited the license and then hung up. He slowed to allow the Fusion to get closer as they drove past the West Valley Station. A block later he saw the lights in his rear view mirror and grinned as a black and white stopped the Fusion. He made two left turns and headed back to the 101 Freeway and then proceeded north to Westlake Blvd in Thousand Oaks. He would take his new found freedom to get a better look at the Nolan residence while Cummings and Carlson were explaining their actions to L.A.P.D. cops. He smiled to himself, thinking that he would love to listen in on that conversation.

* * *

James Nolan stood by floor to ceiling wall of windows of his opulent office looking down at the busy downtown street below. It was 5:15 p.m., and he watched as cars emerged from parking structures to enter the fray that was the nightly drive home. He waited impatiently until the buzz he expected happened.

"Yes, Leslie," he said, without moving.

"Mr. Nolan, your conference call with the executive committee of the board is ready, and all of the members are now on the line."

"Thank you," he said, walking toward the telephone. He punched a button and said, "Good evening, everyone."

"Good evening, Jim. We are all here," Mark Dixon, the senior member and board vice president said. There was a moment of quiet and then he said, "Jim, we wanted to have this conversation before the board meeting happens. I think it's important that we all know where we stand on the Willis litigation before we meet next week." He hesitated and then added, "Obviously, this is going to remain strictly confidential and will be addressed only in private, with the exception of our general statements concerning the collective impact of all litigation the company faces that is included in the shareholder report."

Nolan had heard rumors of board discussion about the litigation, but no one had raised any issue with him directly. Typically, if the executive board had a concern about any particular issue, those concerns would be floated to Nolan informally, by an individual member over a drink. He wasn't happy to be confronted by the whole group, like it was some kind of an intervention. He sat down in his chair and said, "Okay, what do we want to discuss about the Willis litigation?"

"Jim," Dixon said, "We are concerned about this lawsuit. We understand your position on this case, but these kinds of allegations against the Company's CEO are a public relations nightmare."

"I obviously don't like these false allegations, either," Nolan said. "So what's the point?"

"The point is that the board wants to get this case settled and behind us."

"You have all been around business a long time," Nolan replied. "You know how litigation goes. We are going to have a mediation in the not too distant future, and maybe we can get it settled. If not, we'll have the court work it out."

There was silence and then Dixon said, "That's just it, Jim, we don't want this one worked out in court. Too much bad press for too long a period."

"So we buckle to a bullshit case?" Nolan replied, his anger emerging.

"Jim," this is Arthur Lindstrom. "There is more to it than that." Lindstrom was a brilliant leader who had built three successful companies, now sat on about a dozen boards and had been on this one for ten years. He spoke with authority, and the other board members listened to what he had to say. "These allegations are particularly harmful to the public's perception of both you and Ellison. The longer this drags on, the more likely our stock gets hit. And we would prefer not to have the publicity of a two week trial with articles about these allegations hitting the media eight times a day."

"I thought we were tough on litigation when we didn't think it had merit," Nolan responded.

Dixon said, "We are, Jim. But a number of us know and have worked with Sarah Willis. She is smart and credible, and we are concerned that she may be believed."

There was complete silence as this settled on the participants. "Are you saying that you believe her, rather than me?" Nolan asked.

"No, Jim. I'm not saying that," Dixon replied. "I'm saying that examining litigation risk is part of the job of this executive board, and we see risk here. We think it's better for the long term health of the company to be rid of a case like this if we can get it settled, rather than having it hang around all of our necks through a trial. The message you should take away from this is that we are trying to do what is in the best interests of the company."

"Yeah, that's right," Lindstrom responded. "You and Mark should meet with counsel and have a conversation about getting this case settled at the mediation. Then update the executive board."

"Are you valuing this case as a rape or a consensual relationship and false allegations against me?"

After a moment, Dixon responded, "We'll figure all that out with the lawyers, but for me the answer is neither. I would value this case as having inflammatory allegations that adversely affect the company just because those allegations exist."

"Fine," Nolan said. "We'll have that conversation, but you are giving this case far more attention than it deserves. The case is defensible."

There was a moment of silence and then Dixon said. "We understand your position, Jim." He hesitated and then said, "Do you want to have Leslie set up our meeting up with legal counsel between now and the Board meeting?"

"Yeah, Leslie will set it up."

"Anyone have anything else?" Dixon asked the group. They answered in the negative and Dixon said, "Okay, thanks all. We'll have one more conference call after we meet with legal counsel and before the board meeting next week."

They hung up and Nolan found himself angry, and oddly nervous. He didn't like the way this was going.

* * *

"Lee, call me back as soon as you can. I want to chat with you about some information I just received in connection with the Willis case. In the interim, I hope you're enjoying riding around town with those two paparazzi that have grown so attached to you." Scott chuckled as he hung up.

As Scott looked up, Donna stood in his office door. "You are pretty amused by Lee's new followers."

"I am. Mostly, because I know Lee will torture them for their efforts."

Donna shook her head and said, "Michael Graber just called. He wants to know if we want to agree on a mediator and a date for the mediation on the Willis case."

"Will you run with that, Donna? Suggest Linda Brewer as the mediator and we can set it up any time after the Orson deposition that works for everyone's calendar."

"Okay, I'm on it," Donna said, starting for the door. She stopped and turned back. "Can I attend the mediation?"

Scott smiled. "Yep. Love to have you there, so pick a date that works for both of us. Should be fascinating, don't you think?"

"I do. And I've become attached to Sarah."

"You and me both."

The intercom buzzed and Donna waved and left the room. "Scott" he announced.

"Scott, Lee is on line two."

"Okay, thanks."

Scott punched a button and said, "Hi Lee."

"You have me intrigued. What new information have you got in connection with Willis?"

"Sarah told me that she got a call from Melissa Carter, who reported to her at Ellison. Melissa is a big Sarah fan, and extremely upset about the rape and the way the company is treating Sarah. She's also pissed about implied threats from the company to employees who don't stay out of the case, so she wants to help. She says that if she can help we need to tell her soon because she's not sure how long she can continue to put up with the environment there."

"Wow," Lee said. "That has possibilities."

"I knew you'd think so. Anyway, give this some thought and between us let's see if there isn't some way to enlist her assistance while she's still inside."

"I've got a couple of thoughts already," Lee said. "Let me chew on that a bit and get back to you."

"You got it," Scott said. "How are the boys in the rearview mirror doing?"

"I had them pulled over by a cop friend, just to screw with them a little."

Scott laughed, and replied, "They must be a little ticked at you. Are they still following?"

"They still come and go. Nolan had a security manager from his own force join with a hired investigator and Ellison leased a car for the occasion. Makes me think that Nolan's nervous about what we're up to."

"Good. He should be nervous. With you and me coming after him in different ways, it should be a memorable experience for him."

"Hopefully so. I'll get back to you about how we might use that inside assistance," Lee said.

"Yeah. It's something we need to be careful with, because I don't want to get out of bounds here. I mean, no attorney-client communications or no trade secrets, and I don't want to get Melissa in a world of hurt either. When Sarah told me about this, she also said that she is concerned about a potential backfire for Melissa. Apparently, Melissa is pissed enough that she may be bolder than is in her own best interests."

"I get the need to avoid making her collateral damage."

"Take care of yourself out there, too. Maybe the contract on the Fusion will be up soon and those two guys will be following on foot."

Lee laughed. "It's hard to say what's next. I haven't ruled out horseback, or a team of Uber drivers. Talk to you soon."

As Lee hung up, he was already reflecting on doors that Melissa might be able to open for them to help the cause. Interesting indeed.

* * *

Scott was on his third cup of coffee and it was only 10:00 a.m. He decided that the moon must have been full last night, at least judging by the number of strange crises so far this morning. It had been all about handling emergencies and putting out fires on various cases since his arrival at 7:30 a.m. He hadn't yet had the opportunity to respond to ninety percent of the emails awaiting his attention.

The intercom buzzed one more time, and Nikki said, "Amy Curtis with the District Attorney's office on line one."

"Thanks," Scott said, and hit a button. "Hi, Amy, how are you?"

"Well, I'm okay, but I don't have good news for you."

"Today's the day for it," he replied. "Tell me."

"In connection with your client, Sarah Willis, we've determined that there is not enough evidence to pursue the rape case against James Nolan."

"You have to be kidding? In this culture of the "Me Too," and "Time's Up" movements, the D.A. won't pursue a rape case where the victim has a great reputation and is as credible as they come?"

"My boss says that it's too much a 'he said-she said,' kind of a case, with a credible executive who has a clean history on the other side." She paused a moment and then added, "We will also call Ms. Willis and tell her if you'd like."

"Yes, I think you should do that. She should hear this from you."

"Okay, that's fine. We're not closing the door on this," she added, "so if you come up with additional evidence, loop us in and we'll reconsider."

"You can count on it," Scott said. "This guy needs to be held accountable."

"I'm sorry, Scott. I understand that this is not what you or your client wanted to hear."

"You'll hear from us again," Scott said, "as I put additional evidence together."

"That would be fine with me. As a woman, I hate having to say no to this kind of a case."

"Thanks," Scott said. "We'll be in touch."

When they hung up, Scott dialed Sarah. Even though he wasn't letting the D.A. off the hook when it came to delivering the news of their decision to Sarah, he wanted to discuss it with her as well. This kind of a decision would reinforce that Nolan was getting away with this and could set her back emotionally. This was not a good day.

* * *

Lee called the Puget Sound Hotel and waited. He got a recording giving him several choices, none of them suitable to his purpose. He pushed zero and got a hollow ringing, followed by a distant sounding voice that said, "Puget Sound Hotel."

"Doug Turner, please."

"One moment while I see if Mr. Turner is available. May I say who's calling?"

"This is Lee Henry. I believe he's expecting my call."

"Yes, sir."

Tinny elevator music filled Lee's ear as he waited. After a few moments, a deep voice said, "Hello, Lee Henry."

"Hi, Doug. Did you get a call from Don Mills?"

"I did. He says you are a good guy."

"Don was your partner back in your L.A.P.D. days, right?"

Turner was effusive. "He was. My partner and almost my brother, so when he says that you've helped him out a couple of times, it matters." He paused and said, "So how can I help you, my friend?"

"I have a client who was raped by her boss in your hotel when they were on a business trip. There is nothing going on that targets the hotel, we are just seeking to prove our case against the arrogant asshole who perpetrated the rape."

"Wow, sorry to hear about it, man. So how do I help?"

"We have two different versions of what happened and we need to show that his is bullshit. She stopped by his room, which was 1474, because he wanted her to pick up documents. He pushes her against the wall and kisses her and she runs out of his room alone and goes back to her room, which is 1221. She gets ready for bed and then he shows up knocking and saying he wants to apologize. She resists, but after a while opens the door. That when he pushed his way into her room and raped her."

"Shit," Turner said.

"He says that they had an affair and that they walked together from his room, which was 1474, to her room on twelve."

"Got it. So you want help in showing that they went to her room separately."

"Right. Do you have video cameras covering the hallways?"

"Well, yes and no," Turner replied. "We have cameras at all entrances and exits on every floor. They don't yet cover all of the hallways entirely, but we will likely move in that direction." He took a moment and then said, "1221 and 1474 are both a good distance from the access points, so I know we won't have them at their room doors, but let me see if I can find footage of either of them walking the halls to the rooms. You got photos of both of them?"

"I'll get them to you today. I'll also text you the date and approximates times, to narrow the range."

"Perfect. Let me see what I can do for you, Lee."

"I appreciate it, Doug."

"No problem, man. If you get me the pictures today, I'll get back to you sometime in the next day of two and let you know what I find."

"Perfect," Lee said. As he hung up, Lee found himself wanting this one badly. He had to nail this guy.

Chapter Sixteen

At 9:30 a.m. the Scott and Sarah selected seats in the conference room of Simmons and Winslow. Michael Graber and Bob Berg were shown into the room. "Good morning," Garber said. "You know Mr. Berg, HR Director for Ellison."

"Hello, Mike. Good morning, Mr. Berg," Scott said.

"Good morning," Berg said, and then added, "Hi, Sarah." Sarah gave him a nod.

Graber and Berg took seats on the other side of the table, leaving the seat closest to the reporter vacant for the witness. A few minutes later, a thin, worried looking man was shown in by Donna. "This is Gerald Orson," Graber said, by way of introduction.

"Mr. Orson," Scott said, shaking a hand that was wet with perspiration.

The attorneys and the witness attached their microphones to their shirt lapels, and then the videographer stated the date and location of the deposition. He then turned the proceeding over to the court reporter.

"Please raise your right hand Mr. Orson. Do you swear or affirm that the testimony you are about to give will be the truth, the whole truth and nothing but the truth?"

"I do," Orson said, softly.

Orson's nervousness was evident from the line of sweat forming on his forehead as Scott began his questioning. "Mr. Orson, please state your full name for the record."

"Gerald Cameron Orson."

"Are you employed sir?"

"Yes."

"By whom?"

"Ellison Corporation."

"And your position?"

"Senior Human Resource Representative."

"How long has that been your position?"

"About three months," Orson said.

"You recognize that you are testifying under oath today, just as if you were testifying in a court of law?"

"Yes."

"Where did you work before Ellison?"

"Radiographs, Inc."

"What did you do for them?"

"I was a human resource representative."

"How long?

"About six months."

"Your duties were what?"

"Overseeing workers' compensation functions, benefits and employee discipline issues."

"What percentage of your time was spent on workers' compensation issues?"

"About fifty percent?"

"And what percentage did you spend on benefits issues?"

"I would estimate about thirty percent."

"And the remaining twenty percent was doing what duties?"

"Taking complaints and grievances from employees, writing memos about those complaints, and doing investigations."

"How many investigations did you do during your six months at Radiogaphs?"

"Three."

"How many workplace investigations had you done before you went to Radiographs?"

"One or two."

"Where?"

"At Lakeside Mortgage."

"How long were you there?"

After hesitation, Orson replied, "About five months."

"So you have done five or six workplace investigations in total?"

"Yes."

"And how many included allegations of a sexual attack or sexual battery?"

"One."

"How many included allegations of sexual harassment?"

He was quiet for a while and then said, "Two."

"What did the others involve?"

"Violations of company policy. One was about insubordination and another about failure to show up for work repeatedly."

"When you came to Ellison, what was the first investigation you were assigned?" Scott asked.

"The one involving Ms. Willis."

"Who gave you that assignment?"

"Robert Berg, the Human Resources Director."

"What instructions were you given?"

"To investigate Ms. Willis' claims."

"Which claims did you investigate?"

"The claim that she was raped by Mr. Nolan."

"Anything else?"

"Comments that she alleges he made to her."

"Anything else?"

Orson looked worried. Like he might be leaving something out. After a time he said, "I think that's it."

"Have you reviewed the lawsuit by Ms. Willis?"

"Yes."

"So you know it involves retaliation claims in connection with her termination?"

"Yes."

"Did you investigate the specifics surrounding her termination?"

"No."

"Why not?"

"No one asked me to do that," Orson said.

"What did you investigation consist of?"

"I reviewed written policies and interviewed witnesses."

"Which policies did you review?"

"The company policy on harassment and discrimination."

"Anything other documents?"

"No."

"Who were the witnesses you interviewed?"

"Mr. Nolan and Ms. Willis."

"Anyone else?"

"No. No one identified other witnesses."

"Did you get any training on conducting investigations at Ellison?"

"No."

"Anywhere?"

"At Radiographs I went to two or three seminars on investigations."

"How long was each?"

"One was a full day. The others a couple of hours."

"You interviewed Ms. Willis and Mr. Nolan only one time?"

"Correct."

Scott asked, "How long was your interview with Ms. Willis?"

"About half an hour."

"And with Mr. Nolan?"

"A little less. Maybe twenty minutes."

"You said you that you read the company policy on discrimination and harassment, correct?"

"Did you review the policy on conducting investigations?"

"Yes, a couple of times."

"So you know that when a harassment or discrimination claim is advanced, the written policy provides that the accused employee is to be suspended during the investigation, right?"

"Yes."

"Was Mr. Nolan suspended during the period of the investigation?"

"No."

"Why not?"

There was silence that Graber decided to fill. "Object as calling for speculation, lacking foundation."

More quiet. Scott said, "Do you have the question in mind, sir?"

"Yes, I think Mr. Nolan was too busy to be suspended."

"I see," Scott said. "And who told you that?"

"Mr. Berg."

"There is no exception to the policy for busy people, right, sir?"

"Right."

"Did Ms. Willis tell you that she had been raped by Mr. Nolan?"

"Yes."

"Did she tell you about other sexually inappropriate words and conduct by Mr. Nolan?"

"Yes."

"What?"

"That he made comments about her being hot and about wanting to sleep with her on several occasions."

"How many occasions did he tell her she looked good?"

"Several. I think about a dozen."

"And that is in your report, right?"

There was quiet while Orson reviewed the report. "Yes," he said, sounding greatly relieved.

"And what did Ms. Willis say she told him when he made such comments?"

Orson stared at the report a moment and then said, "That she didn't want to hear it or that it was inappropriate."

"How many times did Ms. Willis tell you he said something about sleeping with her?"

"I think two or three."

"And what did she report telling him when he made those comments?"

"That it was inappropriate."

"Any other actions of Mr. Nolan she told you about?"

"Yes, that he looked at her breasts during conversations."

"How frequently?"

"I don't know how often."

"Did you ask?"

"I didn't get a specific number of times," Orson said, sounding flustered.

"But she told you it happened frequently?"

"Yes."

"Did Ms. Willis tell you what she said to him when she observed him staring at her breasts?"

"I don't recall."

"And that's not in the report?"

"No."

"Your conclusion is that Ms. Willis states that the conduct happened, Mr. Nolan states that it did not, so no conclusive decision can be reached. Is that what you wrote in your report?"

"Yes."

"I don't find any credibility assessments in this report. Did you make any?"

"No."

"Have you been trained that in conducting a workplace investigation credibility assessments are important?"

There was prolonged silence and then Orson said, "I've heard of that, yes."

"You've heard of it? Have you been trained to make them?"

"I was told to make them when I can."

"By whom were you told that?"

"I don't recall."

"Have you also been told that such assessments are an important part of the investigator's job?"

"I was instructed about that, yes."

"Why did you make no such findings in this case?"

"I didn't have sufficient information."

"What information did you need that you didn't have?"

"I don't know. Something that told me I should or shouldn't believe one of them."

"Did you find Ms. Willis to be credible?"

"Yes, but I also found Mr. Nolan credible."

"Was there anything that detracted from Ms. Willis' credibility?"

After another prolonged silence and nervous glances at Bob Berg, he said, "Only one thing?"

"What was that?"

"She didn't report the alleged rape immediately."

"Anything else?"

"No."

"Did you learn that Ms. Willis took a flight out of Seattle at after 4:00 a.m.?"

"Yes. Was that undisputed?"

"Yes."

"Did she fail to attend a program that she was presenting at the next morning?"

"Yes."

"Was that also undisputed?"

"Yes."

"Had she ever failed to attend any event at which she was presenting before?"

"I don't know."

"Did you endeavor to find out?"

"No."

"Did Mr. Nolan fail to contact her to see why she wasn't at the morning meeting she was to speak at?"

"I don't know."

"You never asked?"

"No,"

"Mr. Orson, as an investigator concerning claims of harassment and discrimination, you're aware that it is not at all unusual for a woman not to complain about harassment, discrimination and sexual battery for protracted periods, aren't you?"

Graber interjected, "Vague and ambiguous as to what constitutes a protracted period."

"You can answer," Scott said.

"Yes, I'm aware."

"In this case, Ms. Willis left Seattle at 3:00 a.m. and complained to human resources within a couple of days thereafter, right?"

"That would be correct, yes."

"You are aware of cases in which women go for weeks or months without reporting attacks, aren't you?" There was silence as Orson took a deep breath and looked to Berg. "Mr. Berg cannot help you answer the question, sir."

"Yes, I'm aware such things occur."

"As a matter of fact, we've seen a great deal of it in connection with politicians and Hollywood people of late, right?"

"Yes."

"Mr. Orson, I see from the report that Mr. Nolan stated that Ms. Willis' performance was unsatisfactory and as a result he was contemplating combining her position with the CFO position and eliminating her."

"That's correct."

"Did you ask Ms. Willis about her performance?"

"Yes. She said she had been repeatedly informed that her performance was excellent and that she had bonuses and commendations from many including Mr. Nolan."

"Was she right about any of that?"

"I don't know."

"Did you check her human resources file?"

"No."

"Why not?"

"I didn't think it mattered to the charges that I had been called upon to investigate."

"It might have mattered to the credibility of Ms. Willis and Mr. Nolan though, right?"

"Object as calling for speculation," Graber interjected.

Orson was quiet for a time, and then replied, "Maybe, I don't know."

"When you interviewed Mr. Nolan, did he take you through the sequence of events that occurred in Seattle?"

"Yes."

"Did he have a meeting on the night of the attack in Seattle?"

"Objection, assumes facts not in evidence as to an attack," Graber said. "I'm not letting him answer a question that assumes an attack occurred. If you want to use that reference, ask about the alleged attack."

"On the only night Ms. Willis was in Seattle for these events, did Mr. Nolan attend a different meeting than Ms. Willis?"

"Yes."

"Did you find out where his meeting was?"

"No."

"Why not?"

"I didn't need to know that."

"How do you know?"

"Objection, argumentative," Graber interjected.

"Do you know if he was drinking or taking drugs at this gathering?"

"No."

"Wouldn't that be important to know?"

"It could be."

"And you never asked?"

"No."

"How many drinks did Mr. Nolan have at any time on the night of the event?"

"I don't know."

"Did you ask?"

"No."

"Why not?"

"Object as argumentative," Graber said.

Orson looked momentarily relieved, and then Scott said, "You can answer, sir."

He looked at Graber, who nodded agreement. "I don't know. It wasn't an issue that anyone raised."

"Including you, as the investigator?"

"Yes."

"Did you ask Ms. Willis who she told about Mr. Nolan's behavior before it was reported to human resources?"

"No."

"Why not?"

"I didn't see any reason to do so."

"Mr. Orson, we talked about the fact that credibility is important to whose version of the story you believe, right?"

"Yes."

"As an investigator, isn't it important to know if Ms. Willis made any contemporaneous statements about her claims to anyone else?"

There was a moment of quiet while he wrestled with how to answer, then Orson said, "It could be."

"And if it could be important, you need to know those facts, right?" Scott was suppressing a smile, knowing that there was no way out of this.

Orson had a helpless look on his face. "I guess so."

"But you never found out, correct?"

"Asked and answered, I object," Graber said.

"You can answer, sir," Scott said.

"No, I didn't."

"Did you make an audio recording of the conversation?"

"No."

Scott handed him ten pages of handwritten documents. "Are these are of your notes in connection with this matter?"

"Yes."

"We will attach them to your deposition as Exhibit 1," Scott said, handing a copy to the court reporter and another to Graber.

At 5:25 p.m., the deposition concluded. Scott gathered his documents and thanked the court reporter and the videographer. He and Sarah walked back to his office and sat down.

Sarah smiled widely and said, "Thank you, Scott. That was just amazing. However this all comes out, I appreciate the way you fight for me."

He smiled and said, "My pleasure, Sarah."

She grinned and said, "You know, you really shook that guy. He was a deer in headlights several different times."

Scott nodded. "He has some vulnerabilities and I think his bosses know it. Maybe that motivates the defense team to try and reasonably resolve the case."

"Whatever happens," Sarah said, "I'm pretty sure he won't be looking forward to seeing you again at trial."

Chapter Seventeen

Lee's phone rang around 7:00 a.m. He looked at the number and grabbed it. "Lee Henry," he said and waited.

"Hi, Mr. Henry. I hope it's not too early to call."

"No, Ms. Traynor, no problem," Lee responded cordially and then waited for the substance of her message.

"I wanted you to know that I didn't forget about our conversation. I'm more than a little conflicted about this." She was quiet a moment and then said, "I can't tell you how much part of me wants to walk away from this. I know you must think that I'm a coward, but I've known a number of women who have accused powerful men, and it doesn't ever seem to go well. The man remains powerful, and the woman is branded as a troublemaker, or a whore, and her career is suddenly stalled."

"I know that it can be very difficult," Lee replied.

"My best friend complained her boss about a co-worker grabbing her breasts and wanting sex. She was all of a sudden looked upon as a corporate traitor. Three months later, she was the subject of a layoff that everyone knew was a way to get her out." She took a moment and then added, "That's why I decided not to file formal complaints against Nolan."

"I know that what you say is true," Lee said, "so I do understand your hesitation. What I can tell you though is another undeniable fact. If no one comes forward, it never stops. The power abuser who does this stuff is confident he can get away with it, and there will be more victims."

"I get it, I really do. It's just so hard. Just thinking about it turns my stomach." She reflected a moment and then asked, "This woman you want to help was raped by Nolan on a business trip?"

"Yes, there was a business pretense to get her to his hotel room, and then he came after her. He forced her against the wall and kissed her. She ran out of his room and back to hers. Then he came to her room telling her that he just wanted to apologize for forcing himself on her. She opened the door to let him apologized and then he over-powered her."

She was quiet a moment and then said, "I believe he could do that. I will never forget what he did to me."

Lee wondered if this was the right time to ask what Nolan had done to her, but decided to get her agreement to help, first. "Will you assist Sarah?" he asked.

"I don't know," she said. "I just don't know if I can."

Lee was trying hard to get her to commit. "Will you talk to Scott Winslow, the attorney who represents her and who I am working for on this case? He's a good guy and he can give you more information and answer any questions that you have. Can I have him give you a call?"

"Yes," she said, "I'll talk with him."

"When is the best time for him to call you?"

"Any evening after 6:00 would be okay. I'm usually home by then."

"I want you to know that we appreciate this."

"I haven't agreed to get involved, yet," she said. "I'm just agreeing to talk to the lawyer."

"I understand," Lee said, "and thanks for doing that."

* * *

John was confident that he had it figured out; the cameras and the circuitry that linked them, as well as the external and internal alarm systems. He looked at the plans open across his desk, and then nodded his satisfaction to the empty office. He was ready. John rolled up the plans and put them in a backpack. His questions about how to circumvent an alarm system had raised suspicion with one of his colleagues, but it didn't matter. Once he was inside, he would let the chips fall as they may. The only important thing is that he would have Nolan alone inside the house, and the opportunity to hold Nolan accountable.

John would get one more weekend with Sarah before it happened. They would take a long walk, go out to dinner and to a movie and spend time to be treasured for years to come—just in case their future together was cut short. On Monday morning, he would make a final trip to the Nolan residence to make sure he had all of the circuitry right, and to figure out the best access point from the golf course to the back of the Nolan residence. Early Wednesday morning, before Nolan left to work would be the best time to make it happen. From time spent following Nolan, he knew that Mrs. Nolan left early Wednesday mornings. That would give him a window of about a half-hour when Nolan was alone, before he left the house for work.

* * *

"You can be yourselves here," Laurie Spencer told the ten women seated around the table. "You can cry, you can laugh and you can just be you. You can share, knowing you have support from everyone in this group. The only judgment you will experience is against those who hurt you." Sarah sat two seats away from Laurie, looking around the room at the other wounded women, and wondering if this was a good thing. "Who will start us of today?" Laurie asked.

"I had a bad week," a blond woman of about forty said softly.
"What happened, Linda?"

The woman nervously drew a deep breath and said, "On Monday evening, I picked up a couple of things I needed from the grocery store a block away from my apartment. There was a man walking behind me. I tried to stay calm, but I felt a rising panic. Then I looked back and as he passed under a light post I saw his face. It looked like him in the shadows; the man who raped me two months ago." She shook her head. "I was terrified. I dropped my groceries in the street and ran back to my apartment."

"Did he follow you?"

"I never saw him again. I just locked myself in my apartment and didn't leave for two days. I was just so scared that..." She let her words trail off and hugged herself as if warding off the cold weather.

"I understand, Linda. That had to be very scary," Laurie replied, empathetically.

"The worst part is that at some level I knew that he wasn't really the guy, but I'm scared of most men I don't know at this point. I'm also worried that if I don't make some progress I'm going to lose my job. I can't keep calling in sick for too long, just because I'm scared to go outside. It's starting to wear on my work teammates, even though they are doing their best to be supportive."

"Anyone else have any thoughts to share?"

A woman of about thirty, with dark eyes and olive skin shook her head and said, "Getting past this stuff is one step forward, five steps back, but little by little, we make progress. For me, it has been a year now, and I am slowly getting stronger. You will too, Linda. Thanks for having the courageous to speak about it. My bet is that when you get home tonight you will feel that this has been a good day, and you will be glad that you shared."

The woman seated next to Sarah nodded. Laurie said, "Jan, share what you are thinking."

A woman who was about forty-five, with brown hair and a kind face said, "The healing process is slow and painful, but it's real. It has been nine months for me, and I feel like I'm starting to get some of the old me back. I'm recognizing how injured I have been. Don't get me wrong, it's not all gone and it probably never will be, but I can tell that I am stronger, and the panic attacks I used to get daily, are now just occasional."

Two other women spoke and Sarah shared their pain and the feeling that they were damaged as they spoke with heavy hearts and tear-filled eyes. The meeting was amazing, but emotionally exhausting.

"Anyone else?" Laurie asked.

Sarah nodded and slightly raised her hand. "Thank you all for this afternoon. It has been really helpful to know that things get better, and to know that I am not alone." She paused and took a deep breath, then she said, "I was raped in a hotel room by a coworker. He had forced a kiss on me and then theoretically came to apologize for his behavior. I made the mistake of opening the door and he came into my room and raped me. I am not only scared and feeling vulnerable like I have never felt, I feel like it's partly my fault for letting him in. I should have known better, but I really believed he want to say he was sorry."

Sarah saw looks of recognition around the table. The woman seated next to her left touched her hand and said, "I get it. My name is Carla. I went out with a guy I met on line. I had a drink with him and the next thing I know I'm naked from the waist down in his car and this guy is on top of me." She ran a hand through her hair. "I couldn't move, so I couldn't even fight back. When it was all over, I blamed myself for not better screening who I went out with and for taking a drink from someone I didn't know." She shook her head and said, "There is lots of opportunity to blame yourself when you get attacked, and that is one final injury that your attacker delivers. I mean, I know women who have blamed themselves because they were in the wrong place at the wrong time. You know, the 'if only I hadn't gone' to wherever it happened." She shook her head and added, "When someone is shot, we don't say they shouldn't have been where the bullet was going, we realize that the attacker is responsible. This is no different."

Sarah nodded slowly and said, "Makes sense. Sometimes takes a while for the emotions to catch up with what makes sense intellectually."

"Amen to that," Laurie said. "Logic and emotion are often a long way apart, and sometimes competing, but they are both very real. Anyone else?" Seeing no more hands she said, "Thank you all for coming. It has been another really good day."

The group said brief goodbyes and headed out of the building. Sarah walked out with Laurie and after the group members moved toward their cars, she said, "Laurie, thanks for encouraging me to attend today. Somehow sharing and knowing that I'm not alone in enduring this makes me feel stronger."

Laurie smiled. "I'm so glad you came."

"What do I owe you for today?"

"Nothing," Laurie said. "There's no charge for being a part of this group. Will you come back?"

"I will. I think it really helps you see that progress can be made. I feel like after seeing some of these strong women make progress, maybe I can too. I'm encouraged, and maybe I won't always be stuck where I am today."

"Good message to take away from this meeting. Nice work."

"Thank you, Laurie. You have been so great."

Laurie gave her a hug and said, "Well done, Sarah. You are on the right road."

* * *

Sarah took a walk through the local park. She watched kids play on swings, oblivious to any problems the world presented, she watched pigeons battle over a piece of bread and she watched the sun move in and out of clouds over the afternoon sky. There was something wonderful about watching the world from an anonymous portal, and being out in the afternoon air. She sat down on a park bench and pulled out her phone, calling a number she had on speed dial.

"Hi Sarah," a recognizable voice answered. "You doing okay?"

"Yeah, I'm doing okay. How about you?"

"I'm okay, I guess. I miss my old boss and the way this place used to be, but I think those days are long gone. It's amazing how your perspective about a company can change so drastically in short order."

Sarah thought a moment and then said, "Melissa, I don't want this to poison the well for you. I mean, there's more to the company than Nolan."

"The company poisoned the well for me in the way they have handled all of this. The whole 'keep your head down and stay out of the affray' message gets me riled up."

"I understand. Are you still interested in helping this side of the battle?"

"Very much," Melissa responded, without hesitation. "What can I do?"

"Is anyone occupying my office these days?" Sarah asked.

"No, not yet."

"Scott's investigator, Lee Henry, would like to access my computer."

"Sure, that can be arranged."

"The company would not approve, Melissa. So he would have to come into the office under some pretense. As a client meeting you, perhaps."

"That's fine," Melissa said.

"Melissa, there is reason for you to say no to this request. I don't know exactly what Lee wants to access, but it is likely that the company will be able to determine when someone used my computer and what they accessed. So there could be questions that come back to you. In other words, feel free to decline and it is not a problem."

"If anyone comes back to me, I just had a visitor who wanted to use a vacant office for a minute. That's all I know."

"You sure about this?"

"I'm sure. Tell Mr. Henry to call me to make an appointment as whoever he is going to be."

"Okay, I will pass on the word. Thanks again, Melissa." As she hung up, Sarah had second thoughts about making that request. It was troubling that she didn't know why Lee Henry wanted this access. The last thing she needed to do was screw a friend who was trying desperately to help.

* * *

Scott and Donna sat in Scott's office conducting one of their frequent impromptu meetings to discuss pending cases. "I just emailed you additions to the Martin Brief," Scott said. "Can you get it finalized so we can get it out of here by tomorrow?"

"Yep."

"Next, where we are on the Hernandez interrogatory responses?"

"In rough for you to look at by the end of the day," Donna said.

"Great. We also need initial discovery on the Farris age discrimination case and we need the revisions to the Complaint on Porter."

"I started initial interrogatories on Farris, but I haven't had a chance to prepare the Request to Produce Documents for your review. I'll calendar completion of that for the end of the week. On Parker, I'll get your revisions to the Complaint completed today."

"Sounds fine," Scott replied.

There was a buzz and then Nikki, the receptionist, said, "Scott, Michael Graber is on line one."

"Okay, thanks Nikki."

Scott punched a button and said, "Scott Winslow."

"Hi Scott, Mike Graber. I just wanted to talk a little bit about the mediation in connection with the Willis matter."

"Okay," Scott said, "Good timing, I'm working on our Mediation Brief today."

"Well, I just wanted to make sure that we were on the same page here. From our perspective, this is a defensible case. It's all he said, she said, and our guy is extremely credible. Well respected company leader and no history of harassing anyone, so he is going to be believed."

"Interesting assessment. From my perspective, Ms. Willis is extremely credible and will likely be believed at trial. Not only that, she was also a great performer, fired in retaliation for raising her claims. Her performance was exceptional, and is well-documented. Your guy's statement that he was unsatisfied with her performance is undermined by the company's own documentation."

"So, we agree to disagree," Graber said. "My concern is your level of expectation for settling this case. Obviously, we don't see the case the same way, so we probably don't value it the same."

"Probably not," Scott said. "Which is pretty much the story of every case." He paused and then asked, "Is your message that you don't want to go through with the mediation because we are likely to value it differently? I mean, if you think this case is not of significant value, then I don't want to waste my time either."

"We want to go to the mediation in good faith to see if we can get somewhere, but we obviously do disagree about the likely result. Get me a reasonable settlement demand the week before the mediation, so that I can run it past my people. We want to know where you are coming from before we get there."

"We can do that. Ms. Willis and I are coming to the mediation to see if we can negotiate a reasonable resolution, but we are not holding a fire sale here. We are happy to take it to trial if we can't reach agreement. So, if you think we are not going anywhere, call me when you get the demand, and we can decide whether to cancel the mediation."

Graber replied. "We will probably go forward to see if we can make any progress even if we think the demand is excessive. I just want to make sure that both sides give it their best shot. This is the best chance to resolve the case and if you are over the top with your demand, my client will likely dig in and spend the money getting ready for trial. We will be prepared to go to trial as well, because we think our guy has a great reputation as an executive and a credible guy who has nothing by way of harassment in his background, but we will come to the mediation prepared to work on a resolution."

Scott rolled his eyes and Donna smiled. Scott said, "Great. I'll look forward to seeing you at the mediation in three weeks, and you'll have our settlement demand a week before that."

There was a moment of quiet and then Graber asked, "Are you working with Lee Henry on this case?"

"Confidential information, Mike. Why do you ask?"

"I heard that there was some kind of a run-in between Mr. Henry and a security representative of Ellison."

"Really? What kind of a run-in?"

"I don't know, but the Ellison security representative interpreted it as a threat, so I thought I would give you a heads-up."

"Well, thanks for the information." Scott smiled. "Lee is a really professional guy, so if he were working on this case, I can't imagine him threatening anyone, even if the Ellison guy was doing his best to provoke a response. Lee is always cool and collected."

"Okay, just thought I'd let you know."

"Thanks. Talk to you soon, Mike."

* * *

"Ms. Traynor, this is Scott Winslow. Have you got a few minutes to talk?"

"Yes. Hi, Mr. Winslow. I told Mr. Henry I would talk to you, although I'm still not sure I want to be involved." She was quiet a minute and then added, "Mr. Henry is a pretty persistent guy."

"He is that," Scott replied. "Will you meet with Sarah Willis and me? I really think you should meet her and hear her story before you make a decision."

"Well, I don't know how I can. You know that I'm in Mountain View, right?"

"I do know that. We will come to you and meet at a hotel conference room nearby. We can meet after your workday or on the weekend. We'll do whatever works for you."

She was quiet a moment and then she said, "Okay, how about Saturday afternoon?"

"Perfect," Scott said. "How about 1:00 p.m.?"

"Okay, that will work," Traynor replied.

Scott said, "We will call you back in the next half-hour with a location close to your house."

"That will be fine," she said. "You have to know, Mr. Winslow, I am reluctant to get involved in this because it never ends well. The woman who complains gets trashed and the pervert lives to harass another day."

"Please, call me Scott. I want you to know that I really understand the price a woman pays for coming forward. Especially if she stands alone. But I've represented many women who decided to fight, and I know that their fight can make a big difference. If a guy who abuses his power never gets challenged, then he's more convinced than ever that he can do whatever he wants to women with impunity." He paused and then added, "I hope to convince you that the fight is worthwhile on Saturday. I look forward to meeting you then."

"Yeah, you sound like a nice guy. Doesn't mean I'll do it, but I will meet with you and Ms. Willis Saturday."

"See you then, Ms. Traynor."

* * *

Melissa Carter picked up the phone on the first buzz. "Melissa Carter."

"Your three o'clock appointment, Melissa."

"Okay, send him up. Thanks," As she put down the phone, Melissa was more than a little nervous. She was now a part of a plot that her employer would not approve. She tried to focus on the email she was in the middle of composing, but she was too distracted by what was about to happen. She looked up from her desk to see a tall, white-haired man with a moustache and wire-rimmed glasses standing in her doorway. He wore a grey suit and a friendly smile.

"Good afternoon, Ms. Carter. I'm Jack Landon." He extended a hand, which she shook. "Thanks for making time to see me." At that moment his phone rang. "Hello," he said. A moment later he said, "I see. Wait a minute." He looked at Melissa and said, "I'm so sorry, it seems that we have a mini-crisis to address. Do you have a place where I can take this call for a few minutes?"

Melissa smiled and said, "Yes, of course." She led the way down the hall and pointed to the larger office that had been Sarah's. "You can use this office. Feel free to close the door for privacy."

Lee stopped at the door and looked at her. He spoke quietly, asking, "Are you sure about this?"

She smiled and said, "Yep. I would do most anything for Sarah."

"I've heard that she thinks highly of you as well," Lee said with a smile. "But you don't know anything about what I'm doing here—I'm just a potential client, right?"

"I'm just giving you access to a place where you can have privacy for your call. That's all I know."

Lee grinned. He already liked this lady. She was smart as well as attractive. Maybe, he would get another chance to talk to her sometime. Of course, he was dressed up as a non-existent character and next time he saw her she wouldn't recognize him, but one thing at a time. "Thank you, Ms. Carter. This call shouldn't take too long."

"No problem. I'll be in my office when you are done."

He gave her a nod and then walked into Sarah's former office and closed the door. The computer had already been turned on as he requested, so he was able to jump right into the system. As he suspected, the networked computers of the department were not only linked, they worked on the assumption that executives inside the network had the right to access company data, so there was considerably less security. Within a few minutes he was able to access James Nolan's email.

Twenty minutes later he left Sarah's office and walked to Melissa Carter's. He knocked briefly and she looked up and waved him inside. "Thank you, Ms. Carter, you've been very helpful."

"Call me Melissa," she said, smiling. She was happy to be aiding Sarah, whatever it was that this guy was doing to make that work.

He handed her a file. "Here is a proposal that I put together for Ellison, should anyone inquire about the nature of our meeting today." She nodded. He paused a moment and then said, "I really hope that I get to see you again sometime soon."

"You, meaning Jack Landon?" she asked, grinning.

"No," he said smiling.

* * *

Lee Henry dialed Scott Winslow as soon as he made it to the car. "Simmons and Winslow," Nikki's voice said.

"Scott Winslow, please."

"Hi, Mr. Henry. Just one moment."

After a brief pause, Scott said, "Hi, Lee. How did it go?"

"Good. Really good. I know what Nolan was doing in Seattle the night of the attack."

"What have you got?"

"You won't believe it. I found out who he met in Seattle on the night of the rape. Based upon that information, I did some research that told me exactly what the meeting was about. Now I just have to convince a guy in Seattle that it's in his best interests to give us information he won't want to share. Scott, I think we've really got something here."

Chapter Eighteen

The Hilton Hotel in Mountain View featured a post-modern lobby with smatterings of bright color on walls, and wall-to-wall carpet that encircled white columns. The conference room Scott Winslow reserved was big enough for ten, because although there were a number of great seating areas in the hotel, none of the others available were sufficiently private.

Scott and Sarah met Margo Traynor in the lobby of the hotel at 1:00 p.m. They smiled and she walked toward them. She was an attractive woman in her early thirties, who wore blue jeans, a tan blouse, and a look of concern. Scott extended a smile and a hand, which she shook. "Good afternoon, Ms. Traynor. It is a pleasure to meet you. This is Sarah Willis."

Sarah shook her hand and said, "May I call you Margo?"

Traynor nodded. "Sure," she replied, sounding tentative. She said, "I should tell you up front that I'm not at all sure that I am going to be able to help you. I would like to be able to assist, but I'm not at all sure that I can. As a matter of fact, I almost decided not to come today."

"Okay," Scott said, giving her an understanding smile. "We will talk it through and see where we come out. We have a conference room booked right over here," Scott said, gesturing across the lobby and down a hallway. They walked into the conference room and grabbed coffee. They sat down with Sarah at the end of the conference table and Scott and Margo on each side of her as pre-planned. Scott wanted Sarah to be the focus of this meeting.

"We really appreciate you meeting with us, Margo," Scott said. "We want to be open with you and we want you to know what we are dealing with here. James Nolan had a habit of making inappropriate statements to Sarah. He told her how hot she was, he regularly stared at her breasts and then he started talking about having sex with her and getting her into bed. She did her best to cope with this and then he asked her to go on a business trip to Seattle. He wanted her to attend a meeting with him. Then, at the last minute, he didn't go to the meeting, but sent her alone because there was another meeting he had to attend. They got back to the hotel and he wanted to meet her in the bar. He had three drinks, and when she said that she wanted to go back to her room and get some sleep, he asked that she stop by his room to pick up documents he wanted her to review." He stopped, and then said, "I'll let Sarah tell you what happened from there."

Traynor had a look on her face that said she really didn't want to hear this. Sarah said, "Margo, whatever happens, thank you for coming. This means a lot to me." She drew a breath and then said, "I walked into his room and he handed me the documents. Then, as I turned to leave, he forced me up against the wall and kissed me. I pushed him away and ran out the door. I ran back to my room in shock, and started to get ready for bed, shaken by what had happened.

Sarah stopped long enough to take a deep breath. The emotional impact of this retelling was evident in her expression. "Then there was a knock at my door. I asked who it was and he said he was so sorry for what he had done. I said, you can apologize in the morning. He kept asking that I please open the door and let him apologize face-to-face. He said that he wanted to make things right, and I was foolish enough to believe him."

She bowed her head and said, "I opened that door, God help me, and he pushed in and closed it. I stood there in my robe, just frozen. Then he pushed me down on the bed, tore open the robe and ripped off my underwear. I have never known what it's like to be overpowered like that. It was so awful. I fought back as hard as I could, but he forced himself into me." Sarah was breathing harder and there was a tear in her eye. "I just couldn't stop him." She wiped a tear away, determined to make it through this and then said, "I took a shower, but I couldn't get clean. I sat on the bathroom floor crying until about 3:00 in the morning and then I packed and took a plane home. I couldn't even show up for a presentation that I was supposed to give in the morning. I didn't call anyone. I just didn't show." Margo reached out and took Sarah's hand, as Sarah continued, "I went home and crawled under the covers. For the first couple of days I didn't tell anyone, and then I realized that I was really hurt. That I had been damaged and that I couldn't make it alone."

When Sarah stopped talking, Margo was fighting tears of her own. She shook her head and said, "That son of a bitch."

"After I filed a complaint with the company, Nolan fired me." She stopped and drew a deep breath. Then she said, "So now, I'm caught in this he said/she said purgatory, where he says that we had this consensual affair, and that I'm making up the rape charges to hide the affair." She shook her head. "I want to hold this guy accountable. I want him to admit what he did and if he won't, I want a jury to tell him that they know he did this to me. He has ruined my career and damaged me in ways that I can't even describe." She shook her head, and then added, "I'm not even me, anymore. I have to make him answer for this."

Margo was quiet for a long while, trying to regain her composure, and then she wiped a tear from her eye, and then she nodded slowly and said, "If I agree to help, how will it go?"

Scott said, "You tell us what happened to you and I will create a declaration telling your story for you to sign under oath. If anything is inaccurate when you get it, you call us and we will fix it. Then I will have to take your deposition in this area before trial because you are too far away for a subpoena to compel your attendance in a Los Angeles courtroom." Scott hesitated and then added, I would love it if you came to trial so the jury can hear how well you come across and see your face as you let them know what he did to you, but that will be up to you."

Margo nodded slowly. "Okay, I will help." She took a deep breath and then said, "Let me start by telling you what he did to me. I was an executive assistant at Sunmont and I was assigned to work with Nolan on a couple of different projects over an eight month period. The first time I was alone in a conference room with him he said, 'You look great in that suit.' I said 'thanks,' and then he said 'I bet you look even better without it.' I was shocked, so I stayed quiet. He then said, 'Why don't you show me those gorgeous tits.' I had never been spoken to like that before, especially by an executive of the company where I work. I didn't know what to do, so I just left the room. I was embarrassed and I didn't say anything to anyone."

"Did anything else happen?" Scott asked.

"Yeah. About a week later he came into my office and closed the door. He stood there grinning and said, 'You and I are going to have some great sex. Just wanted to give you a heads-up. I know how to make you cum long and hard.' Then he left. I know I should have reported it, but I was so embarrassed and just went back to work and never told anyone." She shook her head and said, "I was such an idiot to do nothing. So about three weeks go by and then we are in a meeting. I was wearing a skirt and I was seated at the conference table when he came into the room. He sat down next to me and addressed the five people present. Then he asked one of them to update on a couple of items. While that guy is talking, he puts his hand on my knee under the table. I try to move away and he gripped it tighter. Finally he let go. The meeting went on another twenty minutes and then he dismissed the group, but said he had a question for me and asked me to stay. The others walked out of the room and he put his hand back on my knee and said, 'We need to get to know each other better.' Then he moved his hand between my legs and all the way up to my crotch. I threw my chair backwards and stood up. He held his hands up in the air like okay, and then he walked out. I was really shaken up, so I called HR and talked to a representative about what happened. The HR rep told me that I could file a complaint if I wanted to, but if I did it might affect my position on the team. I was shocked and angry and I didn't know what to do." She took a breath. "So I made a bad decision. I decided to confront Nolan. I made an appointment and then went into his office. I told him that the things that he did to me were not okay and that I only wanted to be left alone to do my job. He just stared at me. Then he said, 'you really are beautiful, you know.' He stood up and walked around his desk. He sat on the corner of the desk and said, 'One way or another, you are going to fuck me.' He was smiling. Then he said, 'I want you to know how this is going to work. If you complain to anyone, your job is gone.' I stood up and walked out of his office. I went to my office and cleared out my belongings. I quit, effective that day. I was so angry, and I wanted to fight him, but I knew that I couldn't win that fight. He was too important, and I just didn't matter. Whatever he said, is what the company did."

Scott asked, "Did you give them any reason for your decision to quit?"

She shook her head. "No. It all seemed so pointless. I just said I'm quitting and walked out."

Scott thought a moment and then asked, "You talked to your co-worker, Cherie Jackson, about what happened, right?"

"Cherie has been my friend since I started at Sunmont, so when I left I told her that I had been harassed by Nolan." Margo was quiet a moment, and then she looked at Sarah and said, "I don't know how much help I can be because there is no written record of any of this, unless HR recorded my call, which I doubt."

Sarah smiled at her and replied. "I'm sorry for what you went through, Margo. You know, I've been feeling like you felt. No one is going to believe me and he will just get away with this." She put her hand on Margo's and then said, "I could really use a friend here. Even without a written record, you can help if you will testify."

Margo nodded. "I will help. Maybe if I had done something sooner, what happened to you..." She let the words trail off.

"No way, Margo," Sarah said. "We have to stop blaming ourselves for the misconduct of men. That's where we start to draw a line."

Margo said. "I'm so sorry for what he did to you, Sarah." She drew a breath and nodded slowly, and then added, "Count me in. I'll sign the declaration, let you take my deposition and I'll come to trial to testify. I'm in for all of it."

"You're sure?" Sarah asked. "I can't pretend that this won't be stressful."

"I'm uneasy about it." Margo reflected and then added, "Not uneasy, scared." She was quiet a moment, and then she took Sarah's hand and said, "But it's time for me to take a stand for you, and for me."

* * *

Donna walked into Scott Winslow's office and heard him signing off on a call. She sat down in one of the visitor chairs and after he put the phone down said, "Linda Brewer confirmed her availability to serve as mediator in the Willis. So we have ten days to complete the brief and send out our settlement demand to the other side if we are going to get both done a week before the mediation."

"That works," Scott said. The first draft of the brief is done, although I've since pulled about three additional pages of deposition testimony that I want to incorporate in various portions of the brief."

"I know," Donna replied. "The briefs always get longer as you think about the possibilities."

"Yep. And we're going to have to scale this one back a little. The first draft was thirty pages and that's without the latest additions and without exhibits."

Donna smiled and said, "I could just eliminate every third word."

"You could, but it would be embarrassing if no one noticed."

Donna laughed and asked, "Did you talk to Sarah about what our initial settlement demand should be?"

"I did. We are going with a demand of two million dollars and we will negotiate down to one million to resolve the case."

"You think that Ellison Corporation will pay that?"

"Nope. Not based on my conversation with Mike Graber. He still thinks it's a 'he said/she said' case and that his guy is credible, so they're likely to offer a hundred thousand or less." He shrugged. "But, by now he has received our notice of taking Margo Traynor's deposition, so he can start having conversations with Nolan about whether he had any issues with her. Nolan will deny anything happened, and he'll also remember that she didn't file a complaint. I'm sure that they will find her deposition very interesting, because then he'll have to start denying what two women say under oath."

Donna nodded and said, "Sarah is a great person and I'd really like to see her do well. I feel in my gut that she's telling the truth, and as a woman, I want to nail dirt bags like Nolan."

"Yep. You and me both." Scott paused and then added, "And hopefully a jury will feel the same way if we have to go to trial."

* * *

The Ellison Board of Directors were seated in the Windsor Complex at the Hotel Del Coronado in San Diego. The annual retreat was part planning meeting, partly devoted to addressing pending problems and partly dedicated to good times in beautiful surroundings. The Hotel was magnificent. Windows on the ocean, magnificent suites, chandeliers and planned sports and activities. The Windsor Complex was a large conference room with lengthy boardroom tables in a U-shape, underneath a beautiful chandelier in the shape of an inverted dome. At the open end of the U were floor-to-ceiling windows that looked directly out at the ocean, only fifty feet away. The wide, leather chairs were occupied by the Board members as they moved through an agenda of critical topics.

"Next item for discussion is the Willis litigation," Senior Vice President Mark Dixon said. He stood in the center of the room, between the tables and looked at Nolan, who was seated at the top of the U-shaped table and said. "I know that you want to push back hard on these claims, Jim. I really get that. It's just not in the best interests of the Company. We are dealing with the fallout from bad headlines, and it will only get worse. This is also a distraction from things that we need to get done. So I think we need to get this one resolved." He paused and said, "Tell Mike Graber to come in here and let's get his report."

A young man seated at the table closest to the door opened it and gave a signal. Graber walked into the room. "Mr. Graber," Dixon said, "Can you give us an update on the latest in the Willis litigation? Start with your take on the Orson deposition."

Graber nodded and donned a serious expression. "Good afternoon ladies and gentlemen. Well, Mr. Orson did a reasonably good job of getting his position across."

He hesitated, and Dixon said, "I hear some hesitation. What's the downside?"

"Well, there is vulnerability. Scott Winslow did a pretty good job of setting up things that the investigator could have done and didn't do. I'm sure he plans to attack legal adequacy of the investigation as part of his case."

"What do you think we should do with this case," Mr. Graber.

"Settle it reasonably, if you can."

Dixon smiled and said, "And what is the potential range of the jury verdict in this case?"

"I guess that's the big question," Graber said. "It could be defensed, but if it isn't, the verdict range is likely mid six figure range. Maybe it gets to seven figures."

There was quiet while this settled on the room. "Mr. Graber, give the Board your assessment of the good and the bad in the case."

"In a nutshell, the good news is that Mr. Nolan is credible and testifies that the relationship was consensual. That, along with the fact there are no prior occurrences, help us make our argument that this is just a woman who is unhappy with the fact that her performance was under scrutiny and maybe didn't want to tell her husband about a relationship."

Dixon nodded. "Now tell us the bad news."

"Ms. Willis is also very credible, and likeable." He paused and then said, "If the jury likes her, they could hit us pretty hard."

"What do you think our odds of resolution are? Do they want to settle?"

Graber frowned. "I know Scott Winslow and he will be prepared to go to trial. He will not recommend settlement unless he believes that the amount is reasonable. I think his view of what is reasonable will be in the high six figures."

Dixon looked around the room and asked, "Any questions?" No one spoke. Dixon nodded and said, "Thanks, Mr. Graber. We appreciate you making yourself available to meet with us. Now, go enjoy this facility."

"Thank you, everyone," Graber said and walked out of the room.

"Okay," Dixon said. "Let me open this for debate by saying that I think this case is dangerous. I don't like the press it gets us and I want to see it resolved. I submit that we should be prepared to go to at least five hundred thousand dollars to get it settled at the upcoming mediation."

"That's crazy!" Nolan said. "You heard the lawyer. Willis was unhappy with criticism of her work and wanted to cover an affair. This is a bogus claim."

Don Myer, a new member of the Board spoke next. "Sounds like a lot to me. I mean, we have a defense that sounds strong. We have a decent chance of winning outright, and, if not, having a verdict smaller than that proposed settlement number."

Julie Brock, who was president of her own company, and seated on about three boards, said, "Let me enter the affray, here. How many of you have read the deposition testimony of Ms. Willis?"

Dixon said, "I have reviewed parts of it. I can't say I've read it all."

"Well, I have," Brock said, "and I have to tell you that this woman sounds very credible and very professional. I think that we may well have jurors who believe what she says. As a woman, I can be harsh on other women in business, but I know someone who comes across well when I hear it." She paused and said, "Jim, I'm not saying that you aren't telling the truth. What I am saying is that she comes across well, and credibly. Some of the jurors who hear what she has to say may accept her version of what occurred as accurate."

There was quiet in the room. After a moment, Arthur Lindstrom, one of the heavy weight voices on the Board said, "I agree with what Mark and Julie have conveyed. This is a dangerous case and we should get it resolved."

"Okay," Dixon said, "I move that the Board authorize up to five hundred thousand dollars to resolve the case at the mediation. All those in favor?" Hands went up around the room until almost ninety percent sat with hands raised. Dixon looked around the room and said, "The ayes have it. Motion carried."

* * *

On Monday morning at 7:30 a.m., John Willis parked his car a block from the Nolan estate and walked toward the front gate of the residence. There were a few neighborhood cars taking off from driveways and heading toward the main streets that lead to schools, businesses and wherever else people felt the need to chase early in the morning. As he walked along the street, he feigned a telephone conversation to present himself as a guy who belonged—just one more resident planning for the day's activities as he took a morning walk.

John made his way to the Nolan driveway and looked around, surveying the premises and remembering the location of access points he could see from this angle, as well as the camera locations. He satisfied himself that he had it right and walked back to the car. He drove to the country club and parked, and then he walked down on the course to get a final look at access to the adjacent estates from the golf course. He nodded to himself, satisfied he knew access points, camera locations and the alarm system. He would shut them all down before he made his entrance onto Nolan's estate. He was confident that he knew the route and the obstacles.

* * *

While Lee waited on hold, he thought about how this conversation should go.

There was a rustling and then a nice voice said, "Melissa Carter."

"Hi, Melissa. This is Lee Henry."

There was a moment of quiet and then she said, "How are you?"

"I'm doing okay, how about you?"

"I'm okay, too."

"First, I wanted to thank you for what you did."

Melissa replied, "No need. I was doing the right thing."

"Yes, I think you were."

"You know, I have so much respect for her," Melissa said, avoiding using Sarah's name just in case someone was listening or recording her call. "And I don't like how she has been treated around here since it happened. She was nothing but devoted to this Company." She took a breath and added, "Sorry about going on about this, but that's what happens when I talk about it."

"I understand," Lee said, "She seems to be a pretty remarkable woman. I'm glad you're so passionate about supporting a friend." He paused a moment and said, "Would you have coffee with me?"

"I think I would like that. How will I know you?"

"I'll be the one walking directly toward you and smiling." He paused and said, "Or I could come as Jack Landon, so you'd know me."

"Nope. I want to meeting the real you. When?"

"Does tomorrow at 3:00 p.m. work for you?"

Melissa thought a moment and then replied, "Let's make it 3:30 in case my 2:00 meeting runs long. Where?"

"Do you know The Coffee Canyon, a couple of blocks from your office on Wilshire Blvd?"

"Yep. I will see you there."

* * *

Since having the Fusion stopped by the police, Lee hadn't seen Jake Carlson or Tom Cummings again; until right now. He thought that they had finally gotten the message and given up, but apparently not. They were three cars behind him, as he drove north on Ventura Blvd. Lee turned right and a block later turned right again. Then he made a third right and drove back to Ventura Blvd. The three hundred sixty degree turn let them know that he was aware they were following. He slowed and made them slow as well, and then he took off and disappeared into traffic as they struggled to follow.

He dialed a number as he drove. On the second ring, the phone was answered, "Hello?"

"Hi. Mr. Cummings. Just thought I would check in and see where you and Mr. Carlson would like to go today. I have a little time before my next appointment, so I can be flexible." There was silence. "Hey, I have an idea," Lee said, "maybe we should all go in the same car so that you guys don't get lost." After a moment, Lee heard the click as Cummings hung up.

* * *

After Cummings hung up, he looked over at Carlson, who was shaking his head. "That guy is an asshole," Cummings said.

Carlson grinned. "Yeah, maybe, but he's pretty good at what he does."

"So, now you admire this dickhead?"

"Yeah, I think he's all right. I mean, we are chasing him all over creation and he knows it. So he reacts in a way that tells us we're not fooling anyone."

Cummings said, "I just want to smack that son of bitch."

"Calm down, Tom. Not good for the blood pressure."

Chapter Nineteen

Lee Henry walked into The Coffee Canyon at 3:30 p.m., exactly. When wearing no disguise, Lee's cropped wrap-around, black hair and penetrating, blue eyes, and inquisitive smile added up to memorable good looks, particularly for someone so practiced at going unnoticed.

As Lee entered the coffee shop, he saw Melissa Carter sitting alone at one of the elevated tables and gazing out the window. His first thought was that she was captivating. She wore a business suit in shades of gray over a blue blouse. She projected an image of elegance and confidence.

He walked towards her and she looked up at him and smiled. She extended a hand across the table and he shook it as he sat down. "Hi, Lee." She smiled and said, "So, this is what you really look like."

"This is me," he said. "I hope you're not disappointed."

She smiled and said, "Nope. No disappointment here. And you?"

"No way. But I had the advantage–I saw the real you before, so I knew how beautiful you are."

"Wow. Thank you. You certainly know how to boost an ego."

They walked to the counter and ordered coffee, and then sat down together. Melissa looked at him a moment and then said,

"So, did I really help? I mean, did Jack Landon find what he needed?"

"You did and he did. Thank you for that."

"It was my pleasure," she said. "I only hope whatever you found will be helpful to Sarah."

"I think it just might," he said.

"I'm sorry our conversations all begin like a meeting of the Sarah Willis fan club, but I can't tell you how much she has meant to me in getting my career going. She hired me from about fifty applicants, and she has been my mentor ever since. I learned a lot just watching her move through corporate circles so brilliantly."

He nodded and said, "And from what I see, she is a woman of courage and integrity," he said. "Both are qualities I truly admire." He was quiet a moment and then asked, "So how's it going now? I mean for you; are you doing all right with Ellison?"

"Not really. I mean I enjoy the work, but I'm angry with them for the way they abandoned Sarah and treat her like she has done something to betray the company. Management is projecting a company versus Sarah mentality that I really hate. I'm not sure how long I can stay in that environment."

Lee nodded, and replied, "I get it. I think I would feel the same way."

She smiled and said, "So, what about you? Do you spend all of your time being other people, or just when the urge to be an actor strikes?"

He grinned. "I guess I must have that frustrated actor gene in me somewhere, but it's more the case that it lets me move around without being recognized. If you aren't the same person the second time you meet someone, you can watch them without them watching you."

"So, I know that you are a private investigator. Were you a cop in the past?"

"I spent about twelve years with the CIA."

"Wow, so you learned to be invisible with the best of them."

"Something like that." He reflected and said, "But, it's not always good to be invisible."

"No?"

"Nope. Like right now. I want to be very visible to you."

She smiled and said, "So, Lee Henry, are you going to ask me out?"

"I am, indeed. How about Friday night?"

"Friday is good."

"Dinner at around 7:00?"

She nodded. "Okay."

"Shall I pick you up or would you prefer to meet me there?"

"Come and pick me up," she said. She wrote her address on a napkin and handed it to him. Handing him the napkin, she said, "This is how they used to do it. A little more romantic than staring at a cell phone and texting."

He put his hand on hers and said, "Thanks for interrupting your day to meet me. I'm already looking forward to Friday."

"Yeah, me too," she said, momentarily holding onto his hand.

* * *

Sarah walked down an abandoned street late at night. There were houses all around her, but all of their lights were turned off and the residents were either out or asleep. There were no cars on the narrow residential street, but she could hear footsteps behind her. She looked behind her and saw nothing, but the footsteps grew closer and louder. She began to run as the footsteps drew even closer. Now, someone was right behind her. She ran into an alley that led to garages behind the houses. It was suddenly darker. She turned to see a shadowy image materialize behind her. Sarah awoke with a wail and sat up in bed, shaking, and her heart racing.

She took deep breaths and tried to return her pulse to normal levels. She looked around to the comfort of her bedroom to assure herself that everything was going to be okay. Then she discovered that John was not in bed next to her. "John, are you here?" she called out in the dark room. No answer. Glancing at the clock, she saw it was 3:00 a.m. She climbed out of bed and slipped on a robe, then made her way down stairs. She reached the bottom of the stairs and made her way into the living room, where John stood staring out the window, fully dressed.

"John? What are you doing up in the middle of the night?"

He was startled and turned to look at her. "Just couldn't sleep," he said. "I thought I would go into the office early today." She had a distressed look on her face. "Did you have another dream?" he asked, walking over to her. She just nodded. John put his arms around her and said, "I'm so sorry, sweetheart."

There was sadness, but there was also anger in his voice. She nodded and held him tight. "Come back to bed with me," she said whispered. He kissed her softly at first, and then passionately, as all of their fear and anger that they harbored gave way to an urgent need for closeness. She threw off her robe and he took the nightgown from her shoulders, and let it fall to the floor. She unbuttoned his shirt and then tore at his belt and took his pants fell. They pressed against each other and never made it back to bed. She laid back on the couch and he put his arms around her and held her tight as he entered her. They clung tightly to one another and there was nothing in the world but the two of them, getting ever closer together, kissing deeply, moving together and making sounds of love, softly at first and then louder as they reached climax. Sarah was lost in ecstasy, with no remnants of the attack or the attendant nightmare. They held each other tightly, not wanting to let go of the moment and then gradually drifted off to sleep. After a time, John asked, "Are you okay?"

Sarah nodded and said, "There were a couple of tough moments at first, but after that I was able to let go and it was just you and me; no intruder."

It was 5:15 a.m. when John awoke, still wrapped in Sarah's arms. He carefully extracted himself and retrieved a blanket. He placed it over Sarah, and kissed her cheek, softly. He stood and looked at the face he loved a moment longer, before running up the stairs to dress. Twenty minutes later, he was ready to go. John sat at the kitchen table and composed a note to the love of his life, and left it on the kitchen table. If things went bad, he would not be a free man the next time she saw him. At that point, it would be too late to try to explain.

The cold air struck him as he stepped outside, and made his way to the car in the early morning darkness. He looked back at the house and blew Sarah a kiss, knowing that what he was about to do might come between them. He drove quickly towards the Nolan residence, thinking of the wonderful lovemaking he and Sarah had just shared. There was almost no traffic, but John drove below speed limits to avoid attracting the attention of law enforcement. He exited the freeway and drove northbound on Westlake Blvd, only a few early morning travelers sharing the road. John parked on the street, not far from the golf club. He opened his laptop and called up the program he needed. He pulled up the image of the Nolan house and entered a code, then he checked his watch. He needed to allow sufficient time to reach his destination, but not so much that he was trapped on the golf course, waiting for a program timer to complete its countdown. He keyed in a time that gave him twelve minutes to reach his destination. Satisfied, that he could comfortably arrive at the Nolan house in the next twelve minutes, John reached under the seat and grabbed the waiting gun. He climbed out of the car and locked it, and slid the gun under his belt. He moved quickly, back towards the club's vast, empty parking lot. He walked around the building to the golf course viewing patio, where food and drinks were served during daylight and evening hours. The tables were empty and the umbrella over each was folded closed. John made his way down to the first tee in the darkness. The only light across the fairways came from intermittent lampposts that provided small areas of illumination in an ocean of night. The lampposts were stationed about two hundred feet apart, intermittently on the left and right sides of the fairways.

As John moved to the right side of the first fairway, he realized that everything looked different in darkness. He couldn't yet make out the Nolan estate, but he searched for a landmark he had noted–the big Cypress tree that he remembered was adjacent to the second estate's wrought iron fencing along the golf course.

To reach his destination, John would have to get past three of the lampposts that bordered the right side of the course. He began to walk across the uneven, grassy fairway surface. He kept an eye on the houses off to his right, to assure that no lights went on and that no motion lights or alarms were triggered. The lampposts were to be avoided, as they could make him suddenly visible to the residents abutting the course. As he approached the first of the lampposts, he moved away from the houses and toward the darkness in the center of the fairway. He moved faster, so as to spend as little time as possible, as a distant shadow cast in the light of the lamppost. He was breathing harder and could feel, and almost hear, his racing heart. He moved beyond the light cast by the first lamppost, and then back toward the right side of the fairway, where distant streetlights from the front side of the homes helped him discern the shapes and locations of the houses. As he passed the third house, a light came on in a window that looked out onto the golf course. John laid down on the wet grass and remained still. After a time, when it was clear that no one was emerging from the house, John got to his feet and moved quickly in a crouching position. The next house remained in darkness as he passed it by. He slowly turned three hundred sixty degrees to assure himself that there was no one watching. He saw nothing but the darkness and intermittent light ahead.

John moved to the center of the fairway as he passed by the second lamppost, then returned to the right side of the fairway. He continued on, moving as quickly as his crouched position would allow. He moved to the center of the fairway again, passing the third of the lampposts. The houses to his right remained in darkness. Up ahead, in total darkness was the second big Cypress tree, which he had identified as adjacent to the Nolan house. He pushed a button on his watch, so that he could see the time. He had three and a half minutes left. With the target in sight, he moved faster. John reached the house with two minutes to spare, and then he laid down on his stomach near the wrought iron fence that bordered the Nolan estate, to assure he wouldn't be seen. He found himself soaked from some combination of midnight golf course watering, and early morning dew. He checked his watch again. In less than two minutes, it would all be shut down; the cameras, the alarms and the external lighting, but he would not be able to tell whether it had worked until he approached the first of the motion light. If his movement did nothing to light up the house, it had worked as planned. If it didn't work, or if there was other lighting that was independent of the house's sophisticated system, he would light up like a stage actor and there would be nothing he could do about it.

He checked his watch one final time and saw that he was one minute beyond the time set to trigger the shutdown. He climbed onto his feet and over the wrought iron fence. There was no sound and no lights went on. He kept low and moved quickly toward a rear window that the plans had identified as a guest room. For what seemed like a mile, he felt totally exposed and vulnerable, but there were no immediate effects: no flashing lights, no sirens and no one emerging from the estate. When he reached the window, he knelt down and looked around. There was no movement other than his own. He was in darkness and all was according to plan.

* * *

Sarah heard the click of the door as John stepped out into the early morning darkness. She reached out to find that he was no longer next to her. She sat up and called out to him, and then realized that the door she heard closing was John leaving. She felt warm all over from their love-making, and she wanted to let him know that she felt better than at any moment since the attack. With a smile, she walked into the kitchen and started to make coffee. As her Keurig spit coffee into her cup, she caught sight of the note on the kitchen table. She sat down and started to read the note. As she read, she began to feel panicked.

> "*My Dearest, Sarah. I love you more than I can ever say. You have filled my heart with light since the day I first got lost in those eyes. I cannot live with what that man has done to you. The sorrow and depression in those wonderful eyes, the relentless nightmares and the fear of strangers. Every day I am reminded of how badly he hurt you and I have felt so helpless. You have been courageous and now it is my turn. I am going to hold him accountable for what he has done. He will soon know the meaning of fear. You cannot call the police, my love, or they will be after me. Please, destroy this note and tell no one. It is my turn to show some courage. My love for you will always be, John.*"

Sarah stared at the note, reading it again. John was going to get himself arrested, or worse, on her account. She could not let this happen, but what could she do? John was right–she couldn't call the police to tell them that her husband was about to take vengeance on her attacker. Who could she call? She picked up the phone and dialed Scott Winslow's cell phone number.

"Scott Winslow."

"Scott, it's Sarah. I'm sorry to call you so early, but I need help."

"What's happening, Sarah?"

"John, took off a short time ago and left me a note. He is planning to hold Nolan accountable for what he's done to me. His note says don't call the police or he will wind up in jail." She was having trouble getting air and took a deep breath. Then she said, "Scott, he's going to get himself arrested or shot. What do I do?"

"I'm on my way. I'll see if I can get Lee involved. I'll call you back as soon as I can."

As they hung up, Sarah stared at the note. She could lose the man who had helped her survive all of this. "John, what the hell are you doing?" she cried out to the empty room. She closed her eyes and said a prayer that John would be okay, and that he would be alive and not in prison at the end of the day.

* * *

Lee hit the button on his phone as he sipped his morning coffee. "Lee Henry."

"Lee, it's Scott Winslow. I have an emergency."

"What's up, buddy?"

"John Willis is on his way to Nolan's for some kind of vigilante justice. He is planning to get even for what Nolan did to Sarah. I don't know if he's going to shoot him or torture him, but whatever it is, it won't be good."

"I'm on the way. I'm at my place in Simi Valley, so at this time of then morning I can get there in about fifteen minutes or so."

"I'll see you there–on the premises somewhere. I'm struggling with whether to call the police at this point."

"Let's try to keep John's ass out of jail," Lee said. "I'll approach from the golf course, while you approach from the front."

"Fine, but if things go bad, or if they are already bad when we get there, I'm going get the cops involved."

"I agree," Lee replied, "we don't want anyone dead even more than we don't want John in jail."

* * *

Another moment of truth was on the horizon. There would be the screech of alarms, or there would be silence. John was nervously looking around, his heart racing. He reached into his jacket pocket and pulled out a fist-sized rock. He stood and looked in the window. The room was dark and there was no sign of movement in the house. He struck the window right below the horizontal beam and there was the sound of shattering glass. He waited a moment, but there were no other sounds. He reached through the broken glass and unlatched the window, then he slid it open and climbed inside. John made his way across the room to the door. He opened it slowly and found himself looking down a darkened hallway. He pulled the gun from his waistband as he moved from the room and walked down the hallway with his back to the wall. He passed three other closed doors, which he remembered from the as-built plans were other guest bedrooms and bathrooms, and then came upon a stairway.

He waited a few moments to see if there was any reaction from the floor above. It remained quiet. John slowly made his way up the stairs until he reached the landing. He looked around the corner and found himself looking down another hallway. This time there was a light on at the far end of the hall. He moved slowly past two other closed doors, and as he approached the light, could see that the room was a kitchen, as he expected. He moved cautiously, with gun leading the way. He stopped momentarily at the kitchen door, where he could see James Nolan, dressed in a suit. He sat at the table drinking coffee, and looking at documents.

John stepped into the kitchen, as a wide-eyed Nolan looked up at him. There was dread in the eyes, as he recognized what was happening. Seeing him at close range, John's anger overcame his fear.

"You son of a bitch," John said, pointing the gun at his head. "You know who I am?" Nolan nodded, saying nothing. "I should just shoot you right now."

"Wait," Nolan said. "Please, put the gun down and we will work things out."

"Things, huh?" He shook his head and said, "You mean things like you raping my wife?"

"Just be careful with that gun. Please, I'll do whatever you want."

John stared at him coldly, and then said, "The first thing you're going to do is admit that you did it."

Nolan was quiet a moment. As John silently raised the gun to his head, Nolan said, "All right. I admit it. I'm sorry. I'm really sorry. Just don't shoot me."

John walked closer to him and smiled. "You are human trash. I want you to know that I'm going to hurt you, and I might kill you. You just won't know when it's coming."

"Please, I know we can find a way to work this out. What do you want? What can I do?" Nolan said, raising his hands protectively.

John was quiet for a time and then he smiled and said, "Now you get to find out how it feels to be really scared. And you aren't going to know whether you will be shot in ten seconds or ten minutes. All you can do is wait for the bullet." John sat down at the table and stared at Nolan, pointing the gun at his heart. "You have no idea how much I hate you, you rapist, son of a bitch."

"I like Sarah," Nolan said. "She's talented and smart."

With that, John stood and leaned over the table. Nolan froze. John swung at Nolan, who tried to move out of the way. The punch struck his left cheek and ear. He was momentarily stunned, and almost fell from his chair. As Nolan gathered himself, his ear was ringing loudly. His right cheek was beet red, and burning.

"How could you hurt her?" John yelled, emotion cracking his words.

"I know that she's a great lady" Nolan said, pleadingly.

John hit him again, this time striking him in the nose. Blood poured from Nolan's nose. He raised a hand and touched the wound, and then said, "Please, no more."

"Do you even know what you did to her?" John screamed. "You perverted mother fucker. You read your newspaper and enjoy the world every day, while she lives the damage you did. It is never over for her." John saw a butcher block housing several knives on the kitchen counter. He walked over to the butcher block and selected a large wide-bladed knife. He walked over next to Nolan, who was leaning as far away from John as he could without falling out of the chair. John raised the gun to Nolan's head, and then he said, "Put your hand on the table."

"Please, don't do this to me," Nolan said, pleading for mercy.

"You are the coward that I thought you would be," John said, pushing the gun against Nolan's head. "This is the last time I'm going to tell you. Put your hand on the table."

"No, please," Nolan said. "I'm sorry, I'm really sorry." Nolan began to cry.

John said, "Put the hand down or I slice the arm."

Nolan began to move his arm toward the table, sobbing as he slowly moved it forward. There was a sound of glass and then footsteps. John looked up to see the shadow of a man running towards him. He pointed the gun in that direction, and Lee became visible and stopped at the doorway, with arms raised.

"John, you can't do this," he said, imploringly. "Sarah doesn't want you to go to jail, she needs you." As Lee spoke, the front doorbell began to ring, and then there was a pounding.

John hesitated, and then yelled, "You know what this demented bastard has done to her?" John's eyes filled as he spoke.

"I do know, John. I really do. But not this way. This is just the way you lose your life with Sarah."

John hesitated, standing motionless. There was a sad expression on his face as he said, almost pleadingly, "I can't let him get away with this, don't you understand?"

Lee nodded. "I do understand. I really do, John. But not like this."

Lee walked slowly to where John stood and reached out. "Let me have me the gun, okay John?"

John hesitated, a soul deep pain in his eyes. He wanted desperately to make Lee understand why he had to do this. "This man hurt her so much," John said quietly. There were tears in his eyes now.

"I know he did, John, and he will answer, but this can't be the way it happens, my friend." Lee slowly reached out and took the gun from John's hand. There was no more resistance. Lee took the knife from John and placed it back in the empty slot in the butcher's block. He leaned on the counter and drew a breath.

"You're going to jail, you bastard," Nolan screamed. "I will see you behind bars for years. I'm going to get you for this." He stood and walked rapidly towards John.

Lee said, "No more, you asshole." He grabbed Nolan by the shoulder and spun him around. He hit Nolan in the stomach and Nolan doubled over, and then fell to the ground.

"Let's go, John. We'll use the front door and find Scott on the way out." They ran toward the front door and opened it.

"Everyone okay?" Scott asked.

"Yeah, no permanent damage," Lee replied. "How did you get into the compound?" Lee asked.

"I couldn't get the gate open, so I came over the wall."

"No shit, I didn't know lawyers could scale walls. Not bad." He grinned and then added, "Let's get out of here. Nolan's going to get to his feet and get the police here shortly."

"Get to his feet? What happened to him?"

"He got a little too hard to take, so I helped him find the floor."

Scott looked at John and said, "This is going to be a real mess."

John nodded. "I just couldn't let him get away with it. He had to feel what it's like to be really scared."

Scott said, "Let's go," and they ran around the side of the house and back onto the golf course. As they reached where John and Lee had parked, Lee looked at John and said, "You and I are going to get arrested, my friend."

Scott said, "When it happens, acknowledge that you understand your rights and say nothing else. The only words you utter the whole time in custody are, 'I want to talk to my attorney.' Your attorney will be Barry Corbin, an excellent criminal lawyer and a friend of mine. He will make arrangements to have you surrender for the arrest, so that you don't get cop cars outside your house and taken away in handcuffs. Then, he will get both of you out in no time. Got it?"

John nodded. "I've got it."

"I plan to do the same," Lee said.

John replied, "I'm sorry you guys. I got everyone in deep shit."

"Tell me you aren't going to try anything like this again."

"I won't," John said, shaking his head. "No more."

Scott nodded and said, "Don't forget what I said. Tell them nothing more than I want to talk to my lawyer." Scott shook his head and said, "And call Sarah on the way home and let her know that you're okay, and Nolan is too. She's worried out of her mind."

"I will," John said, and climbed into his car.

Lee and Scott jumped into Lee's car and Lee took off, heading towards where Scott had parked in front of Nolan's house.

"This is going to be a real clusterfuck," Scott said.

"True, but at least we prevented John from torturing the son of a bitch."

"Yeah, there is that," Scott said, "although half of me can't decide if that's the good news or the bad news."

As they reached Scott's car, they could hear the sounds of fast approaching sirens.

"Lee, thanks for being there and jumping into this with me," Scott said.

"Anytime my friend. I didn't have anything this exciting planned for this morning."

Scott smiled, and then climbed into his car. They took off as the sirens grew louder and police cars began to appear in their rear view mirrors.

On the drive home, John punched a button in the car and his home number appeared on the panel in front of him. As he waited for Sarah to answer, he thought about what the criminal charges he would soon face. If Scott and Lee had not stopped him, it would have been much worse. Still, this low-life who hurt Sarah found out what it was like to be really scared for a while, so maybe it was worth it. Or maybe not. Maybe, it was a horrible mistake that didn't make anything better.

Chapter Twenty

When he walked in the door, Sarah threw her arms around John and held him tight. "I was so scared," she said. Then she pulled back and looked at him. "You have a gun on you. Were you planning on killing him?" she asked, alarmed.

"No." He paused and then added, "I just wanted to hurt him, and to let him know real fear." He drew a breath and looked into her eyes. "Seeing what he has done to you made me so angry, Sarah. I had to find a way to make him answer for it." He shook his head, and then added, "I wanted him to know what it was like to be really hurt, and to think he might die."

"You broke into his house?" Sarah asked. "What happened in there?"

As he began to share the details, the phone rang. He picked it up and said, "Hello." Then he was silent for a prolonged period. After a time, he said, "I understand. I'll be there."

He put down the phone and Sarah regarded him quizzically. "What was that?"

"That was Barry Corbin, the criminal lawyer Scott contacted for me. I have to be at the Valley Division of LAPD at 2:00, to be formally arrested and finger-printed. Corbin arranged for me to turn myself in so that I don't get picked-up while the neighbors watch. He'll be back with us to talk about the arrangements for a bond so that I can be out of there in a couple of hours, pending arraignment on felony charges in the next day or two. He's says it's likely that I will be charged with burglary, breaking and entering, assault and maybe battery or attempted murder."

"Holy shit, John, if you are convicted of those things you can get years in prison." He nodded and she asked, "Does he think these charges will stick?"

"He hasn't said yet."

"Burglary? You weren't there to steal anything."

"No, but he says that doesn't necessarily mean you came to steal. It means breaking in with the intent to commit a felony."

"You're going to tell them that you never intended to kill him, right?"

"Right, but I was carrying a gun that I pointed at Nolan, so I don't know whether they will believe me."

"What are we going to do, John?" she asked, with fear in those stunning eyes.

"I don't know. I guess we're going to fight hard and hope the sentence isn't too long." He shook his head sadly, realizing that his actions were only going to add to her anxiety.

* * *

John and Sarah sat in the lobby of the police station with Barry Corbin for twenty minutes, and then John was escorted back to a processing area by a uniformed officer, where he was finger-printed. As each finger was rolled with precision over an ink-pad, John felt like a criminal for the first time in his life. In fact, he reminded himself, he was a criminal. He had done a lot of what he was being accused of, and now it was a question of how many of the charges would stick, what kind of a deal could be made somewhere along the way, and whether he would spend months, or years, in prison.

An hour later, John and Sarah walked with Corbin to the front door of the police station. "You can go back to your life, John. Just make sure you are at the courthouse Friday morning to plead not guilty at your arraignment. I'm confident you will get released on your own recognizance, or with minimal bail, pending trial."

"How about Lee Henry?" Sarah asked. "Will he be okay?"

"Yeah," John added, "That guy jumped into the middle of it to stop me. He doesn't deserve to be charged with anything."

Corbin nodded and said, "He's being charged with battery and trespass, but his circumstances are pretty compelling. I don't think a jury is going to want to do much to someone who is there as a rescuer trying to prevent bad things from happening, and I hope that the prosecution will recognize that as well. That means the trespass doesn't amount to much, but he did punch Nolan in the gut."

"And Scott?" John asked. Is he in the clear?"

"Scott hasn't been charged with anything yet," Corbin replied. "That doesn't mean it won't happen, but I doubt it. I don't think a prosecutor will make much of him being at the front door trying to prevent an attack, although it's not a given. I know that Nolan wants everyone prosecuted."

John nodded. "I owe Lee and Scott a great deal. As far as I'm concerned, these guys are heroes. If they hadn't shown up, I don't know where it would have gone from there."

Barry Corbin said, "I understand, but we'll have to figure out what to do with that before trial. We certainly can't entertain the possibility of you testifying on your own behalf if you are going to say that if they hadn't shown up, you might have killed Nolan."

John shook his head. "I wasn't going to kill him, but I did want to scare him, and I wanted him to know what kind of pain he caused Sarah."

Corbin nodded and said, "I understand. I know you've been through a great deal and a jury might sympathize, but a jury won't be instructed that there was any legal justification for breaking into his house or hurting him."

"I get it," John said.

"Anyway, the case won't be set for trial for a number of months, so there will be an opportunity to consider what kind of a deal can be made."

"Thanks, Barry. You've been great."

Sarah and John shook hands with Corbin, and then they walked across the parking lot. John silently considered the additional stress of all this on Sarah. It had all seemed so right while he was preparing his plan to hold Nolan accountable, but now, nothing was clear. Sarah took his hand as they walked to the car together. When they arrived at the car, he opened the passenger door for her and said, "I wasn't too smart, was I?"

She smiled at him and said, "No, but it was very chivalrous, my love." She kissed him softly, and then added, "You still sweep me off my feet, even without Don Quixote type attempts to right wrongs. Now we have to figure out how to keep you out of jail after that grand, insane gesture."

* * *

On Friday morning, Lee walked into Department 22 and met Barry Corbin and John Willis at defense counsel table. A young man in a grey suit sat at the prosecution's table. He looked over and gave Lee a smile and a subtle nod. Lee knew Tyler Cornell from times he had testified for the prosecution. He returned the nod, and then sat down next to Corbin as Judge Alex Markham took the bench.

"Good morning, ladies and gentlemen," Judge Markham called out to the half full courtroom. He had a round face, black hair cut short and glasses that were precariously perched half way up on his nose. "We have twenty-one arraignments set for this morning, so I'd like to keep this moving along. Mr. Corbin, I understand that you have requested priority for two matters that you are handling this morning, because you are engaged in trial in Department 44, is that correct?"

"Yes, Your Honor. I have a preliminary hearing set to begin at 9:00 this morning, in Department 40."

"Very well, then. The Court calls docket number B1946219, The People v. John Willis"

"Barry Corbin, for Mr. Willis, Your Honor. Mr. Willis is also present."

"Tyler Cornell for the People, Your Honor."

Judge Markham studied his computer screen a moment and then said, "A very unusual set of circumstances. First, how does Mr. Willis plead?"

Corbin Stood up. "Not guilty, Your Honor."

"This is set for Preliminary Hearing on May 23 at 8:30 a.m. I am inclined to release Mr. Willis on his own recognizance. Any objection?"

Cornell stood and said, "Yes, your Honor, we think that serious crimes are charged and that significant bail is warranted, if Mr. Willis is going to be released."

Judge Markham furrowed his brow at Cornell and said, "I don't see the reasoning. Mr. Willis runs an architectural firm, and is a well-established member of the community. He has no priors and this incident was a highly personal matter, if it happened. There is no information that I have that suggests that he is a flight risk or a danger to anyone in the community. Do you have any contrary information?"

"No, your Honor, but these are serious allegations. Attempted murder, assault, breaking and entering…"

"I know the charges. Anything else, Mr. Cornell?"

"No, your Honor."

"Mr. Willis is released OR. You are to return to this Court for your preliminary hearing on May 23, 2019 at 8:30 a.m. If you are not here, a warrant will issue for your arrest and additional charges may result. Understand, sir?"

"Yes, thank you, your Honor."

"Have a good day, sir."

The Judge pushed his glasses further up on his nose and said, "All right, Mr. Corbin, let's call your other matter. Case number B1946219, The People v. Lee Henry." He leaned back in his chair and looked at Lee. "Good day, Mr. Henry. I've seen you in my witness box, but never in this role before."

Lee nodded, "True, your Honor. This is not a role I ever envisioned for myself either."

"How does Mr. Henry plead?"

"Not guilty, your Honor," Corbin said.

"After reading the file, I have questions about why this case exists, Mr. Cornell. Talk to your boss about whether pursuing this makes sense."

"He did enter the victim's home and strike the victim, Your Honor."

The judge stared at him silently, looking thoroughly unconvinced. After a moment, he said, "You're not going to tell me bail is needed here, are you?"

"No, Your Honor, we know Mr. Henry is not a threat to others or to flee the jurisdiction."

"You are also released on your own recognizance, Mr. Henry. See you at your preliminary hearing on May 29," He furrowed his brow, and then looked at Cornell and said, "if there is to be one. Good day, everyone. Next case is Docket Number B1932391, People v. Johnson."

Lee and John walked out of the courtroom with Barry Corbin. In the hallway, Corbin looked at Lee and said, "I like the way Judge Markham looks at this. He knows you and he views your role as a rescue attempt, so there may be some pressure on the District Attorney's office not to pursue the charges where you're concerned."

"Yeah, maybe," Lee said. "And likely there will be some pressure from the Nolan camp to keep it on calendar."

"That could be," Corbin replied. "I have to run guys, I've got that other matter about to start."

"Thanks, Barry," Lee said.

"Yeah, thank you," John said.

"As Lee and John walked out of the building together," John said, "Do you think I did damage to Sarah's civil case against Nolan?"

"I don't know. Seems to me that what he did to her isn't affected by your attempt at holding him accountable, but you should run that by Scott."

After a few quiet moments, John said, "Lee, I am really sorry that I got you into this mess. I hope you get off the hook or get a misdemeanor deal without any trial."

"I hope so, too," Lee replied. "And even if the case against me doesn't go forward, I'll still be there to testify for you."

"Thanks again for making this come out better than it would have if you hadn't shown up when you did."

Lee nodded. "My pleasure. Take care of yourself and that beautiful lady of yours. I really don't blame you for wanting to do something about Nolan. I'd want to fight for her, too."

* * *

Lee pulled up in front of a building containing three, two story townhomes. A white, picket fence surrounded the front yard of all three units. Lee walked to the white gate in the center of the fence and stepped into the front yard. There were three pathways, each leading to the front door of a residence. Melissa emerged from the unit on the left, and he could see her warm smile, even before she reached the gate where he waited.

"Good evening," Lee said, giving a slight bow.

"Hi, Lee," she said, as he held the gate open. She wore black slacks and a blue and white top, partially covered by a blue sweater. "Good to see you."

"Likewise," Lee said. "I have been looking forward to this evening."

She nodded and replied, "Yeah, me too."

They walked to the car and he opened the passenger door for her. He walked around the car and hopped in the driver's side, fastened his seatbelt and looked up to see that she was looking at him with anticipating eyes.

He looked at her and said, "What?"

"I talked to Sarah. She told me that you jumped into John's planned revenge on Nolan, to save him from disaster."

"It was pretty wild," he said, shaking his head.

"You can't stop there," Melissa said. "I want to hear all about what happened."

Lee started the car and pulled away from the curb. He looked over at Melissa and smiled. "You're pretty animated about this."

"I am, now tell me what happened."

"Well, Sarah told you that John left her a note, telling her not to call the police, right?"

"Yes, that's right. So she called Scott Winslow instead. She joked that it was pretty weird to call your employment lawyer when you probably need a SWAT team."

Lee laughed. "Yeah, that's right. Then Scott called me, and we both raced for Nolan's place. I got there first and followed John's path, accessing the house from the golf course. I found the window he had broken and went inside to find him making Nolan sweat bullets. Part of me wanted to just stop and watch him torture Nolan, after what he did to Sarah, but I had try to keep John from getting himself in too deep."

"You hit Nolan, right?"

"Yeah, he was being a pain in the ass, so he needed a little help to mellow out."

Melissa shook her head and said, "That could have really been bad. Do you think John would have killed him?"

"I don't think so, but he would have inflicted some suffering. He was about to stab him in the back of the hand with a kitchen knife, when I arrived."

"Sounds like you got there at the right moment." Melissa smiled, and added, "Sarah says that he's grateful to you for preventing what might have happened."

"John's a good guy," Lee said. "And I can't say I blame him for wanting to go after the guy who attacked his wife."

"You would do that?" she asked, smiling.

"Maybe devise something a little less obvious, but I would definitely go after the guy in some creative way."

"Right, some kind of a spook thing–like Jack Landon and a bunch of friends who look like FBI agents raiding his home?" she offered, smiling.

"Not that I'll admit," he said, grinning. "It seems like you know me pretty well for a first date."

"I've never gone out with a smart, successful guy, who may go to jail shortly," Melissa said thoughtfully. "It makes for interesting beginnings."

"I'm glad you're taking it so well," Lee said. "Some women might not appreciate the irony—or the uncertainty."

"It's exciting," Melissa said. She gave him a thoughtful look and said, "Maybe, you're the bad boy my mother warned me about." He laughed. She considered a moment and then said, "You came to the rescue of the woman I most respect. I want you to know how much I admire you for jumping in to help."

"Thanks," Lee said. He was quiet a moment and then said, "I know a small family restaurant in Glendale that has atmosphere and great food. Does that sound okay?"

"You bet," she said. "It sounds great."

Fifteen minutes later, they pulled into the parking lot of Chez Luv and walked into the restaurant.

The restaurant was a couple of adjoined storefronts on a retail street. They walked in and Lee said, "Two, please," to the young hostess with a short skirt and blue hair.

"Okay, we have a booth for you if you'll follow me." She led the way carrying menus and gestured to a booth with two candles on the table and soft, overhead lighting. "Is this okay?" the hostess asked.

"Yeah, it looks great," Lee said.

They say down and looked across the table at one another. "What are you thinking?" Lee asked.

"I'm thinking that this is really nice."

A young man appeared at their table, presenting a big smile. He was thin, with thick black hair and wore the restaurant's signature, green vest. "Good evening. My name is Derrick, and I'll be serving you tonight. Can I start you out with drinks?"

"Do you have a house Pinot Noir?" Melissa asked.

"We have a great Peacock Pinot from the central coast that I recommend."

"Sounds great," Melissa replied.

"Make it two," Lee said.

"All right. Our specials tonight are blackened salmon on a bed of rice and chicken piccata, served with asparagus. I'll be right back with the wine and give you a couple more minutes to figure out what you want."

"Thanks," Lee replied.

He smiled and replied. "I agree, this is really nice. I know we are just getting to know each other, but one good sign is that I feel comfortable talking to you."

She nodded. "Definitely mutual." She was quiet a moment and then asked, "So, do you date a lot of women?"

"Not really. My business doesn't offer the opportunity to meet people that I might care to spend time with, you know? I mean, half the time I'm somebody else, the way you met me the first time. The rest of the time, I'm moving around the state, or the internet, in search of evidence."

Derrick appeared balancing two glasses of wine and a basket of bread on a silver tray. He set the drinks in front of them, and then placed the bread on the table. "Are you ready to order?" he asked.

"I'll try the salmon," Melissa said. "Sounds great."

"You won't be disappointed. It's a favorite. And you, sir?"

"I'll try the halibut," Lee answered.

"Okay, thank you folks. I'll get your order in right away." The young man smiled, and then moved away from the table.

"Were you ever married?" she asked Lee.

"No, not so far."

"Ever close?" He gave her a sideways glance that made her add, "If it's too personal, you can tell me that."

"I don't mind sharing. I'm just making a mental note of these relevant questions so that I can send them back your way, shortly." He drew a breath and then said, "There was a college relationship that everyone assumed was going in that direction."

"What happened to it?"

"She was really unhappy with my decision to go work for the CIA. You know, all the time and travel it would require. She demonstrated her unhappiness by hopping into bed with someone else. I heard rumors from friends, and then I confronted her. After dodging the question for a while, she admitted that she was involved with someone else. I broke it off with her and we both moved on to what was next. For me, that was a trip to Langley, Virginia for training. I don't know what that was for her." He smiled and said, "Tell me about you. Someone as pretty as you must be asked out a lot. Has there been someone special?"

Melissa's expression became more serious as she searched for the right words. "I haven't been dating much." She grew quiet.

The waiter appeared and placed their dinners on the table. "Is there anything else I can get you?" Melissa shook her head and Lee said, "No, it all looks great, thanks." With that, the waiter gave a slight nod, and then walked away from the table.

Lee picked up where he left off, saying, "I don't want to intrude if it's something you're not ready to discuss."

She smiled and said, "I haven't talked about it much, but I can tell you. I was married for almost four years. It ended really badly a couple of years ago." She drew a breath and said, "Turns out he had something of an addictive personality. He lost his job and then he started drinking too much. He stopped trying to find a new path, and then, he started gambling with the money I brought home. Ultimately, I told him either he got help, or I was getting out. He got angry and slapped me, and then he spent a week apologizing. He said he would get help, but he only went to one meeting, and then went back to his old habits. A few weeks later he got angry and punched me in the stomach. When I caught my breath, I picked up a vase and broke it over his head. Then, I packed my bags and I moved out. He called me every day for two months, telling me he was going to kill himself if I didn't come home. That kind of stuff."

"How did you handle that?" Lee asked.

"I told him that he should get help to save his life, but whatever he did, we were over. I heard through friends that he started getting help about a year ago, but that's the last I heard." She took a breath and added, "I really hope he makes it."

"Did you have any kids?" he asked.

"No, and I'm glad we didn't. One day I want to have kids though. How about you?"

"No and yes." He grinned. "I haven't so far, but some day."

She grinned and asked, "Do you envision a whole bunch of mini covert operatives running around?"

"That's a scary thought. I'll settle for kids playing in the yard, and getting into trouble for not cleaning their rooms."

She smiled. "I don't know, I like the image of two foot people in beards and trench coats."

They finished the meal in laughter and then Lee gave the server a credit card. When the card was retrieved, they walked out into the well-lit, Glendale downtown, where some people walked briskly, while others strolled. Some of the businesses were still open and the shop windows alight. "Shall we walk a little?" Lee asked.

"Yes, let's do."

They began walking down Glendale Boulevard, and as they reached the corner, Lee saw them out of the corner of his eye. The brown Fusion was a block away, lights out, silhouettes of its two occupants in the front seat. Jake Carlson and Tom Cummings were watching them together.

"Shit," Lee said, softly.

"What is it?" Melissa asked with concern.

"There are two investigators who work for Nolan. They've been following me off and on for a couple of weeks, and they are watching us now. That means it will get back to Nolan that you are out with a guy they link to Scott Winslow and Sarah."

She let it settle for a moment and then said, "I don't care."

"They may approach you at work. They may question your loyalty."

"That's fine. I'll leave that much sooner. Sarah's my personal hero and she tells me great things about Scott Winslow." She smiled and then added, "I'm coming to like you quite a bit, too."

"That is definitely mutual," he said. "Come on, there's a great little coffee shop straight ahead. We can see them, but they won't see us." He took her hand and they walked towards the coffee shop. As they walked, Lee considered that at some point they might learn that someone named Jack Landon was given access to Sarah's office by Melissa, and that Landon accessed the corporate intranet. Now that they also know that he was seeing Melissa, might they also suspect that Jack Landon, who they won't be able to find, might be him? She was going to have to be very convincing when it came to knowing nothing about Landon and his activities, so he couldn't let her know what he did during that visit. Suddenly, there was a need to protect her from what he was doing.

Melissa must have seen concern on his face, because she stopped before they reached the coffee shop. He stopped and looked at her, curiously, wondering why she had stopped. She asked, "Is everything okay?"

"I don't want these guys to make your life difficult because you're seeing me."

"It's okay," she said, smiling. "As a matter of fact, as long as they are busily watching, let's make it interesting." She pulled him towards her and kissed him passionately. For a few moments, Lee was unconcerned with the fact that they were being watched, what they might think or, for that matter, everything else going on in the world. It was a really good kiss.

Chapter Twenty-One

The day of the mediation was overcast and cool, with grey clouds looming over the tops of the skyscrapers that populated downtown Los Angeles. Sarah and Scott met in the thirty-seventh floor reception room of Linda Brewer's office, and then an assistant led them to a conference room that seated eight. There were floor to ceiling windows that looked onto downtown traffic, so that as the day of mediation progressed, they could observe first hand just how bad the freeway snarls had become.

"You feel okay?" Scott asked Sarah, as they waited for Linda Brewer's arrival.

"Yeah, I guess so. A little anxious because this is another stranger to talk to about things all so personal, you know?"

"I get it," Scott said.

There was a knock on the door and then it opened. "Hi Scott," a tall woman with short brown hair and glasses said, "Good to see you again." They shook hands.

"Hi, Linda. This is Sarah Willis."

Brewer extended a hand that Sarah shook. "I'm really glad to meet you."

"Good to meet you, too," Sarah replied.

"How are you holding up?" Brewer asked, looking at Sarah with concern.

She shook her head and said, "I've been struggling. First the attack, followed by being treated like a pariah when I reported it. Then, I was fired by an employer who thought I was wonderful until I reported the rape."

They sat down, with Brewer placing herself closest to the door. "I like to sit here because I will be back and forth between this room and the conference room where the defense are set up." She looked at Sarah and said, "Tell me how you are doing these days, emotionally?"

"I still have nightmares about being attacked a few times a week. They are usually about being chased and overpowered by faceless men, who suddenly appear. I am really angry about how he violated me, and how he is lying about it now. I'm depressed, and my anxiety levels are pretty high." She took a breath and then said, "You know, Ms. Brewer, I have always been a strong and confident woman. I could hold my own with the tough guys and the assholes. He took that away from me. I have second thoughts like never before and my own future direction is so unclear." She started to tear up, but then pushed it back. "And I will not cry," she declared. "I also have fear that I never had before. Fear of strangers, unlit streets and large men. I guess that's because I couldn't stop it the first time, it could happen again."

"My role is as a neutral here. Meaning I have to stay unbiased to have the ability to persuade in both rooms." She shook her head. "But I understand what you've been through, and I'll do my best to get a good resolution of the case for you."

"Thank you," Sarah replied.

Brewer looked at Scott and asked, "You have a trial date set in this case, right?"

Scott nodded. "Yes, trial is set for six weeks from Monday."

"Okay," Brewer said, "so both sides know there is a lot of work and expense ahead." She leaned forward in her chair and looked at Sarah. "Before we move on with the mediation, I would like to cover a few basic ground rules. As I'm sure Scott has explained, I have no power to order anyone to do anything. My job is to try to facilitate a settlement between the parties, so that everyone avoids the costs associated with a trial; both economic and emotional. Throughout the day, I will be discussing the legal and factual questions with both sides and seeing what I can do to help the parties achieve a resolution. You should know that I will often be bringing you the position of the other side on critical issues. I want you to know that does not mean I agree with their position, but simply that I am presenting the positions they have taken for your consideration. Any questions so far?"

"No, I understand," Sarah said.

"Do you want to get the case settled?" Linda asked.

"Maybe. I mean, if there is a reasonable settlement, we will get it done, but part of me wants to tell a jury what happened, because I want Nolan to be held accountable."

Linda Brewer turned her attention to Scott and asked, "I see from your mediation brief that you conveyed a settlement demand to the other side about a week ago. Did you get any kind of a response?"

"They didn't send me a check," Scott said, with a grin. "No other response either."

"Well, it probably won't surprise you to hear that they think your demand is too high."

"No, it doesn't surprise me, given that is the response I get in every case."

She was quiet a moment, and then Linda asked, "So, is it true that your husband went after Nolan, at his home?"

Scott said, "There are criminal charges pending, so we won't say much about that. They did have an impromptu meeting, however."

Linda looked at Sarah and said, "I can see where it would be very hard for him to standby and do nothing, knowing what someone had done to his wife."

Sarah nodded. "John is a good husband and a good man."

"How frequently are you going to counseling now?" Linda asked.

"Twice a week," Sarah replied.

"And it continues to help you?"

"Yes, it really does."

Linda looked from Scott to Sarah and back again. "Well, you know their position. In a nutshell, the whole 'he said/she said' thing, with no evidence that he had engaged in this kind of conduct before."

"There are a few holes in that argument," Scott replied.

"Tell me the holes. I need holes to work with in that other room."

"Sarah is a four year employee with a great record, suddenly fired when she complains about harassment and rape. Sarah told three people of the rape within a week after it occurred, so there is a contemporaneous record that all three of those people will support. Then there is the "never done anything like that before" argument. He has and we will have testimony to that effect shortly. The deposition of Margo Traynor is on the calendar in a week, but they don't know what she will say, and I don't want to let that cat out of the bag yet."

"What will she say?"

"That he harassed her at a former employer, both verbally and physically, including reaching under her skirt and running his hand all the way up to her crotch."

"Really?" Brewer asked, with wide eyes. "Did she report his conduct?"

"She told an HR rep, who told her that if she files a complaint, it may cost her spot on the team. After that, she left her job because of him."

"You have a statement from her?" Brewer asked.

"Yes, I do," Scott said, with a grin.

"All right. Let me go and talk to them and see if we can get this started. I'll wrestle with the crew in there and bring you back an opening offer sooner or later."

"Who's here for them?"

"Nolan, two board members, Michael Graber and the HR Vice President."

Scott shrugged. "Seems like we have their attention, anyway."

"I think you definitely have their undivided attention." Linda stood and walked to the door, then turned and added, "You know where the kitchen is if you want coffee or snacks."

When she walked out, Scott asked, "What do you think of her?"

"I like her. I think she wants to help," Sarah said. "That can't hurt, right?"

"I think she believes you," Scott said. "She'll do her best with these guys, and we'll see if we get anywhere."

Scott and Sarah grabbed coffee and then spent time going through documents. It was an hour before Linda Brewer returned, shaking her head.

"Where are we?" Scott asked.

"It was a slow start, but I have an initial offer of $50,000, which isn't a bad starting point."

"Well it wouldn't be if we were interested in working towards twenty percent of our demand, but we're not. I gave Mike Graber a heads up that although we have some room for negotiation, the demand reflects what we think the case is worth." Linda nodded. "Give us just a moment to talk, will you Linda?"

"Sure. I'm in the office next door when you're ready to talk."

As she closed the door, Scott said, "We have to get these guys moving to six figures before we do much. I suggest we tell her that we will move to $1,950,000, but no more until they are over $100,000."

Sarah nodded and replied, "I think that sounds good. I'll follow your lead."

* * *

Lee Henry walked onto the Alaska Airlines flight with blond hair and a moustache. He carried an expensive brief case, and today he was Robert Stimson, a wealthy investor. In a couple of hours, he would arrive in Seattle, where he would meet with Greg Munson. Munson was a financial advisor with McKinley Bass and Rieger, whose name Lee obtained when Melissa allowed him access to Sarah's former office. It had been a very productive twenty minutes. The Ellison Company Intranet had allowed access to James Nolan's email, where he found the connection he needed. On the night of the rape, Nolan had scheduled a meeting with Greg Munson.

Lee called Greg Munson and made an appointment seeking investment advice for Robert Stimson. He told Munson that he was in the process of selling his business and would have several million dollars that he needed to put to work for his retirement. Greg Munson had happily rearranged his schedule to see Robert Stimson promptly. Lee would meet with Munson first, and then he would visit Security Director Doug Turner at the Puget Sound Hotel.

As the flight took off from Los Angeles International Airport, Lee opened his briefcase and pulled out notes he had prepared. As he began to review the notes in anticipation of his meeting with Greg Munson, he looked out the window to watch the plane ascend through dense grey and white clouds, and into direct sunlight. It was a good thing that his latest alter ego, Robert Stimson, was making this trip, because Lee Henry was not allowed to leave the State of California without consent, while he was on OR release pending trial. If Jake Carlson and Tom Cummings had been talented enough to follow him to LAX and see him board a plane, they would have information that he was in violation of the terms of his release, and could get revenge for his antics. His thoughts strayed to his date with Melissa and then to

240

the kiss she had initiated for the benefit of that twosome tailing them. She was a good kisser. He found himself smiling as his thoughts moved to their second kiss; the one he had initiated at the end of the date. He could still taste her lips, and he could still see those eyes drawing him in. With a wide smile, he forced his attention back to the documents on the laptop in front of him.

* * *

At 4:00 p.m., Linda Brewer made her sixth trip into the conference room where Scott Winslow and Sarah Willis waited. After seven hours of back and forth, with periodic legal arguments advanced by both sides and offers and counter-offers exchanged, Scott and Sarah had come down to $1,675,000 and the multitude in the other conference room representing Ellison Company had come up to $250,000.

Brewer sat down with Scott and Sarah and laid her notes on the table. "Well," she said, "they have offered $300,000, and they are beginning to make noises that they are nearing the end." She shrugged and then said, "They are not at the end yet, and it's possible that they would go to $400,000, maybe even a little higher if something in that neighborhood would get the case settled."

Scott smiled and said, "I won't recommend that to Ms. Willis. It looks like we are not going to get the case resolved today, but I appreciate your efforts in trying to make it happen."

Brewer donned a thoughtful expression, and after a moment said, "How about a mediator's proposal in the range of $700,000? I don't think they will go along with it, but I'll push it hard if you guys would do it."

Scott shook his head and said, "We won't do it either, so not much point in making that proposal."

"I don't want to give up," Brewer said. "Give me a response to the $300,000 offer and let me take it to them."

"Okay, our response to that is $1,625,000."

Linda Brewer shook her head. "I should tell you that the last couple of times in that other room, Nolan has been talking about your client's husband breaking into his house to attack him. He's angry and he wants to push the prosecution, and he plans to file a lawsuit against John. If we could reach agreement," Linda said, "maybe we can make all of this go away."

Sarah felt the anger rise. She took a deep breath and said, "John's actions may have been misguided, but he was responding to a dreadful attack by Nolan. He stood up for me. If they think that they can make us lay down by threatening John, they are sadly mistaken. Please let them know that for me."

Linda Brewer smiled and said, "I will let them know."

* * *

Lee's plane landed at just after 4:00 p.m. He summoned a Lyft ride to downtown Seattle as the plane stopped at the gate, and when the front door opened, grabbed his carry-on luggage and made his way through the airport. The ride from Sea-Tac Airport to downtown Seattle was only thirteen miles, but at this time of day he'd be lucky to get there in forty minutes. Still, he was going to be on time for his 5:30 p.m. meeting with Greg Munson.

The Lyft driver, as it turned out, was a mother of three who loved her job because she could work during the few hours that she wasn't consumed by family issues. She also drove like Danica Patrick. There was a constant need to pass the next car ahead, and she wasn't influenced by whether there was sufficient room to do so. Lee told her that he needed to get downtown as fast as possible, and she got him there by 5:15 p.m., ten minutes faster than he thought possible. He gave her a good tip, and felt like he should kiss the ground to give thanks for a safe arrival, before heading into the building.

Lee took the elevator to the fifth floor. As he exited the elevator, to his left was an enormous reception area with a now empty reception desk, with the name McKinley Bass and Rieger in large red letters on the wall behind the desk. It occurred to Lee that red was the wrong color to use to display your name if finances were your business. He stood at the desk for less than a minute, before a man appeared from an interior hallway and announced, "Good afternoon, I'm Greg Munson. You must be Mr. Stimson."

"Correct," Lee said, with a smile.

Munson extended a hand, which Lee shook. Munson was a husky man, with the neck of a defensive lineman. He had a closely cropped, brown beard, showing no signs of gray, and short, brown hair. He wore an expensive suit. "Come back to my office," Munson said. "I've prepared a few opportunities to show you that I think you will like."

"Great," Lee said. "You lead the way."

They walked down a hallway surrounded on both sides with offices and conference rooms. Windowless, internal offices on the right and floor to ceiling window offices on the left. Where your office was parked in the suite apparently said a great deal about your stature within the firm. They turned right down another hallway and walked all the way to the end, and then into the corner office that featured floor to ceiling walls of window on two sides, a large desk and a conference table that sat eight. Apparently, Mr. Munson had done well and was rewarded accordingly.

On the conference table were portfolios that waited. Munson said, "Let's sit at the conference table where we can spread out. Would you like coffee, or maybe something stronger?"

"No, I'm fine, thanks," Lee said, smiling.

Munson said, "Nice digs, right?"

"Very nice," Lee said, smiling.

"Comes with being the senior guy in the Firm now."

"What about the named partners?" Lee asked, feigning curiosity.

"All gone now. Ted Bass was last to go and that was five years ago." Lee nodded as they both sat down. "My thought was to start you with the opportunity to get in on the ground floor of a major acquisition," Munson said, lifting one of the portfolios. "I think you'll be impressed with this opportunity Robert. May I call you Robert?"

"Sure," Lee said, smiling, "but before you go too much further, let me give you a little more information about why I am here."

Munson sat back in his chair and nodded. "Okay, that might be helpful to assist me in knowing your preferences."

"This is an important meeting for you, Mr. Munson," Lee said. He let the words settle as Munson's face took on a look of confusion. "I am not here as a potential investor. I am a private investigator with connections to the government. I've was assigned to investigate a transaction of yours, and I found things that are bad for you." Munson appeared to be stunned and remained quiet, so Lee continued. "You've worked with James Nolan for a number of years now. You shared with him that General Data Corporation was going to be the white knight that acquired troubled Lattimer Chemical Company. With your guidance, Nolan picked up five thousand shares of Lattimer before word was out that the deal was going to happen. Then information of the pending acquisition hit the media."

"You need to leave and call my lawyer," Munson said.

"Sure," Lee said, "I just want you to have a little more information before I go." He leaned forward and continued, "When you learned that General Data completed its due diligence and the deal wasn't going to go through, you met with Nolan right here in your office and told him that the deal was going to crash. He sold his five thousand shares the next day at a substantial gain, while the stock value was still inflated by the expected acquisition that you and Nolan knew was not going to happen. Two days later, word leaked out and Lattimer lost half its value." Lee leaned forward and added, "Naturally, we have dates and documentation of all that I just told you."

After a few moments of silence, Munson said, "Leave and go talk to my lawyer."

Lee shrugged. "I'm happy to, but that will negate your opportunity to minimize the impact on you." Lee shook his head and then added, "You understand this is a violation of Section 10(b)(5) of the Securities Exchange Act, otherwise known as insider trading, and the penalties are rather harsh for using insider information to profit, right?" Munson remained silent, looking some combination of angry and distressed. Lee said, "Now, I don't know what other clients you helped benefit from that inside information, but we can find out. You may not be aware, but people you illegally notified of such opportunities are known as 'tippees' under the Act. So far, the only one I identified was Nolan. If you cooperate with me concerning your assistance to Nolan, I won't look at what happened with respect to your other clients." He folded his hands and added, "In my experience, any financial advisor who engages in this practice does it for more than one client because there is a lot of money to be made, and what the hell, once you're in, you're in, right? So there's almost always many clients who benefitted from the same information. Think about it carefully."

This one hit a nerve, as Lee could see the depth of concern on Munson's face. "What do you want from me?" Munson asked.

"I want you to sign an affidavit. It acknowledges that you advised Nolan that this acquisition was about to happen, and states the date that occurred. The declaration also states that you advised Mr. Nolan that the acquisition wasn't going through the night you met with him, and that you both knew that the failure of the deal would become public within the next few days. You sign the affidavit, and I won't ask about what information you gave other clients about the pending acquisition that allowed them to profit by trading on inside information."

At that point, Lee got the question he wanted to hear. "How do I know you won't look further?"

Spoken like a guilty man who needs to cover his ass, Lee thought. He said, "You don't know me, but I give you my word. I will not ask anything else about anyone other than James Nolan."

"Whoever you're working with is really after Nolan?" Munson asked.

"I can't comment on that. Do we have a deal?" Munson was quiet, thinking hard. Lee gave him time to stew and then added, "It doesn't matter to me one way or the other. If we don't reach agreement today, all of this will come out within the next twenty-four hours, but there will be a lot more discussion about your conversations with Nolan and all the others you spoke with about the planned acquisition and its subsequent failure."

Munson said. "Let me see what you want me to sign."

Lee opened his briefcase and pulled out a folder. "Take your time and review this affidavit," he told Munson. "If it meets with your approval, sign it."

Munson stared at the document silently for a while, and then he looked up at Lee and said, "I can't do this." He paused for a moment, and then asked, "Can you assure me that no one will come seeking information about other clients?"

"No," Lee said, "but I can assure you that I won't and that I won't have any discussion about any of your other clients with anyone else."

"I don't know," Munson said, sweat forming on his brow.

Lee nodded and then said, "Fine." He reached for the document and said, "But remember when the shit hits the fan, you did have a chance."

"Wait," Munson said. He grew quiet again, while Lee waited silently. "I'll think about it, okay?"

Lee smiled and said, "I wouldn't think about it too long. Once the information is transmitted to regulatory agencies, we'll have nothing left to talk about. I'll be fine with that, how about you? I'll be in touch only one more time." He walked from the office, while Munson sat in stunned silence.

* * *

Sarah punched in a number and waited. After the third ring, a woman's voice said, "Mr. Cushman's office."

"Good afternoon, this is Sarah Willis calling for Art Cushman."

"Hang on one moment please."

There was a brief delay and then a voice said, "Hi Sarah, how are you doing?"

"I'm hanging in there. How about you, Art?"

"Really busy, otherwise okay."

"And Louise? Are she and the kids okay?"

"Louise is great. The kids are teenagers, which pretty much says it all."

"So sorry," Sarah said. "The good news is that it is a curable. It's all a matter of time."

"Praise heaven," Art replied. "I'll try to keep that in mind when I feel like strangling one or both of them."

There was a brief pause and then Sarah said, "You've been chasing me to join Richert Industries for about a year, and I'm ready to do it."

The pause was a long one. "I really don't have anything right now, Sarah."

"I see. You know, Art, you and I have always been straight with each other. Let's not screw that up now. What's really up?"

"The official answer is the one I just gave you. The real one is that I approached my boss about hiring you. I got unequivocal direction to stay clear of the dispute between you and Jim Nolan. They seem to think that hiring you will plant us in the middle of the dispute and could cost us some contracts."

"I understand," Sarah said. "Thanks for giving it to me straight, Art. I appreciate it."

"I'm pissed about it. You would be damned good for this company."

"Thanks again. Glad I still have some friendships that Nolan can't damage."

"No way," Art said. "I hate what they did to you."

"If you hear of any opportunities at my level, let me know, will you?"

"You can count on it."

* * *

Lee went down one floor and found the men's room. Before going in, he made sure that there were no cameras covering the hallway in front of the restroom. Satisfying himself that there were no electronic eyes monitoring him, he stepped into the restroom as Robert Stimson and three minutes later, emerged as Lee Henry.

Lee made his way to the elevator bank, hit a button and waited for a ride down to the street. The door to the middle elevator opened and Greg Munson was looking out at him. Neither gave any sign of recognition to the other. Lee stepped into the elevator and said, "Good afternoon." Munson just nodded, apparently deep in thought. They rode in silence to the ground floor and when the doors opened, Munson raced towards the building exit at top speed. Maybe he was off to alert key clients that there may be some problems in connection with money they made recently, or maybe he was going home to pack his bags and head for a new life in Grand Cayman. When the elevator doors opened, Munson took off at a good clip. Lee walked at a leisurely pace outside to the street, and summoned a Lyft to take him to the Puget Sound Hotel. For this next meeting, he could be himself.

Chapter Twenty-Two

The morning was been crazy busy, and the afternoon was even worse. Melissa had no time for lunch and spent the whole day putting out fires. As she grabbed another cup of coffee, she thought about her experience working with Sarah, and how she knew how long Sarah had been at work by the quantity of coffee that had been consumed. Melissa took a sip of her coffee and allowed herself a minute to think about tomorrow night's date with Lee Henry. Later today, he would be back from some mysterious trip that he couldn't tell her about, and she could hardly wait to talk to him. She recognized that she was sitting in her office all alone and grinning; a sure sign that she was getting in deep. An intercom buzz brought her back from her reverie.

She hit a button and said, "Melissa Carter."

"Melissa, this is Bob Bennett. Ted Nelson and I would like to meet with you."

"Okay. When do you want to set it up?" she asked, hitting a few keyboard strokes to pull up her calendar.

"Now," Bennett replied. "It's a good time because we are together now."

"Where?"

"Ted's office."

"Anything I need to bring or be aware of for the meeting?"

"No, we'll talk when you get here."

"All right. See you in a few minutes," Melissa replied. As she hung up she had a foreboding about this sudden meeting. Why would the Human Resources Director and the Human Resources Vice President need to have an emergency meeting with her? She grabbed a notepad and her iPhone and made her way to the elevator. She rode up four floors and nodded to Liz, the floor receptionist, as she got off the elevator and made her way down the corridor of offices. She appeared at the open door of Ted Nelson's large office to find Nelson, Bennett and General Counsel Ed Perkins sitting on the couches that faced each other over a coffee table. Bob Bennett stood and said, "Come on in Melissa. Have a chair." He gestured to the chair at the end of the coffee table, perpendicular to both couches.

She nodded and sat down. She looked at each of the three men and then said, "Is there some information you need about a pending project? How can I be of assistance?"

"What is your relationship with Lee Henry?" Nelson asked.

"What?" Melissa asked, furrowing her brow. "Why would you need to know that?"

"You know we are in litigation with Sarah Willis, who is represented by Scott Winslow, correct?"

"Yes."

"Mr. Henry does work for Mr. Winslow. I assume that you are aware of that fact, as well?" Nelson asked.

"So, I've heard," Melissa said, her annoyance beginning to show. She couldn't believe this interrogation was actually happening.

"We need to be sure that no sensitive information about this company is shared with Mr. Henry. You understand, Ms. Carter?" Ed Perkins interjected, speaking for the first time.

Melissa sat silently staring at him in disbelief. After a time she said, "Are you accusing me of something?"

There was more silence while the three men studied her, and then Bob Bennett said, "No, but we want you to be aware of the importance of what we're saying. Nothing you learned here can be conveyed to Lee Henry."

"I understand," Melissa said, suppressing her anger. "Is there anything else?"

"No, Ms. Carter, there's nothing else," Nelson said. "Just know the situation is sensitive and Ellison information cannot be shared."

"I am aware," Melissa replied. She stood to go and then said, "You know, I don't think I've ever given any of you any reason to believe I'd give out confidential information." She walked to the door, and then turned back and added, "Come to think if it, Sarah Willis never did either." She walked from the room knowing that last line would blow up her relationship with the company. She would now officially be persona non grata. These bastards want to see if she's loyal to the company, after the disloyalty they showed Sarah? The hypocrisy was amazing. She made her way back to her office fuming, and wondering if she could continue to work for Ellison. It occurred to her that whatever Lee Henry, alias Jack Landon, did in Sarah's office might also be identified at some point. Then they would learn that Melissa let him in there and the puzzle would be complete. Maybe she needed an immediate exit strategy.

* * *

Lee greeted Doug Turner with a handshake and said, "Thanks for meeting with me, Doug."

"Sure thing," Turner said, grinning. "Don Mills told me you are quite a character, and there isn't much you won't take a shot at." Turner was a solidly built black man in his mid-fifties with no facial hair and a big smile.

"Well, you were his LAPD partner, so you know Don was open to most anything. He and I had some great CIA adventures together. Most of them still classified or I'd tell you what kind of shit we were up to."

"I'd love to have a beer and talk about all the things we can't talk about," he replied. He shook his head and said, "So, I've been through the camera footage covering the 12th and 14th floors for the critical night. The bad news is that both rooms are midway down the corridors and the cameras don't reach either. I can't identify your client or Nolan on the videos because neither was close to the elevators or the emergency exits at the critical time." He shrugged. "So that didn't go anywhere, but I did pull the employee schedules and talked to my security employees, the bell team, room service and food service employees who were on duty during the critical hours."

"Great," Lee said. "You've taken this further than I would have expected. Thanks, so much."

"Yeah, and I have good news. I got one hit. We have a young man who was working room service that night who has some information. His name is Jason Chambers and he will be here to meet with you in," Turner hesitated and looked at his watch, then concluded, "forty minutes."

"Doug, I owe you my friend. Really great work."

"I heard the kid's story and I think you'll find him helpful."

"Mills was right about you," Lee said. "Let's see, how did he describe you? Yeah, a brilliant guy who's less of a pain in the ass than me."

Turner chuckled. "That sounds a lot like Don. No doubt about it."

The two men laughed and joked as they awaited the arrival of Jason Chambers, an employee who just might provide some great evidence.

* * *

"Scott, Mike Graber is on line 3."

"Okay, thanks." Scott punched a button and said into the speaker, "Hi Mike, what's happening?"

"I kept working at trying to move settlement forward after our negotiations stalled during the mediation, and I have good news to report. My client just had a meeting and gave me the authority to settle the case for $500,000, naturally with full release and confidentiality provisions. It's a good deal and you should run with it."

"Thanks, Mike. I will pass it on to Ms. Willis and get back to you."

"Will you recommend it to her?"

"No."

"You're kidding! This is a great deal and it won't last."

"Like I said, I'll pass it on."

"Okay. Just so you know, I have full authority to do the deal from the board of directors, so the agreement can be put together and the settlement paid within a couple of weeks."

"I'll let Ms. Willis know."

"But you still won't recommend it?"

"Right. Thanks, Mike." Scott dialed Sarah Willis to let her know. He wasn't going to recommend the deal, but at least they had Ellison's full attention.

* * *

Sarah reached out to her many contacts and applied for a number of jobs that she was well-qualified for, but had no luck. Somehow, her attempts to find a new position were going nowhere, even though she had been offered no less than five different jobs in the year before she was fired by Nolan. She had been known as an industry dynamo. She was the talented go-getter everybody wanted, right up until the day she was fired. Now, no one wanted her. She was an industry pariah, and she suspected that Nolan had to be behind it.

She drove to the grocery store to pick up a few household items. It was almost 5:30 p.m. and the store was busy, with shoppers freed from their daily grinds and thinking about dinner.

She parked a few rows from the store and another car pulled in right next to her. It was so close that she couldn't open the driver's door. The driver of the other car stared directly at her with an angry expression. After a moment, he signaled that she should lower her window. She did nothing, frozen in fear. The driver again gestured to open the window with a hand circular motion. She clutched at her phone, punching 911 and hit the 'speaker' button, and then the 'send' button. Then she opened the window just slightly. "Yes?"

"Ms. Willis, I have a message for you."

"A message from whom?" she asked.

"The message is that you need to take the money being offered and settle your case. You don't know what you're about to come up against and you don't want to find out. Settle your case."

"Who are you? Are you threatening me?" Sarah asked.

The man stared at her and then started his engine. Before driving away, he said, "This is not a joke. Settle your case. There will not be another warning."

Sarah was shaking as the man sped away. She had to get information about his car. She noted that it was a white Chevy Malibu or Impala. She looked for the license number, but there was no plate. She tried to follow the man, but he disappeared too quickly. She tried to calm herself, taking deep breaths, as she heard the 911 operator's voice and picked up the phone.

* * *

When Lee landed in Los Angeles and turned on his cell phone, there was a message from Scott Winslow. "Lee, give me a call as soon as you can. More weird stuff to kick around."

Lee hit a button and waited. "Simmons and Winslow," the familiar reception's voice announced.

"Hi Nikki, is Scott available?"

"Yep. He told me to interrupt his meeting to talk to you. Hold on one moment, Lee."

"Hi, Lee, how was the trip?"

"We got what we wanted in one meeting, and we are a maybe in the other."

"Really? Tell me more."

"Yeah, I think that Greg Munson is going to sleep badly for a while. I'm not sure if he'll tell Nolan about our meeting, but my guess is that he'll just try to lie low and pretend our meeting didn't happen, while he frets over whether to sign the affidavit. We have him on the ropes, so if I give him one more push, we may get it done."

"I agree. If he tells Nolan about your visit, it is going to be a very uncomfortable conversation, so maybe he stays quiet. Tell me about the hotel meeting."

Lee said, "The Security Director at Puget Sound Hotel didn't have camera footage that helps, but he found a service employee who witnessed Nolan standing at Sarah's hotel room door alone, and then knocking on the door. We can undercut Nolan's story that they walked to her room together. He'll sign a declaration and he'll come down to testify for trial."

"Incredible," Scott replied. "You are amazing."

"Ah, shucks," Lee replied, laughing. Then he said, "So, I got your message. What's the latest weird occurrence?" Lee asked.

"A guy pulled up next to Sarah as she stopped in a grocery store parking lot in Woodland Hills. He was so close to her driver's door that she was pinned in the car. He signaled her to roll down the window, and then told her she needs to take what's being offered and end the lawsuit. He told her that there would not be another warning. Then, the guy sped off and left her."

"What did he look like?"

"Husky dude. Round face and blond hair that could have been a wig."

Lee immediately thought of Thomas Cummings. "What kind of car?"

"She said it was a late model, white Malibu or Impala, with no license plates."

Lee reflected that if it was Cummings, at least he was smart enough not to use the same Ford Fusion that he and Jake Carlson had been following him around in for weeks.

"This guy was alone?"

"Right."

"All right. Let me look into it. I think this could be Tom Cummings, the investigator who was part of the team chasing me around."

Scott was quiet a moment and then replied, "It seems kind of stupid to be the one making threats if you can be readily identified."

"I agree, but you have to know this guy. He wants to be tough, but he's not the sharpest tool in the shed."

"Thanks for checking it out."

"Sure. Did she report it to the PD?"

"Yeah, right away."

"Good. I'll keep you posted if I learn anything."

"Thanks, Lee."

* * *

"So how are you holding up?" Laurie Spencer asked Sarah as soon as they were seated in their usual positions in Laurie's office.

"I've been better," Sarah said, "although not lately. I have a husband charged with several crimes for going after Nolan and a stranger who pulled up next to me in a parking lot and threatened me if we didn't take a settlement offer. If that's not enough, my attempts to get back to work are going nowhere, because none of the firms that wanted to hire me until I was attacked want to get at odds with Nolan and Ellison Corporation."

"I'm sorry," Laurie replied. "Tell me about your emotional symptoms."

"I'm doing okay, all things considered. Horrific dreams are fading slowly. At least there are less of them, and I feel like I'm getting stronger little by little."

"Okay, but your anxiety level has to be pretty high with all that you just told me."

"It is." She reflected a moment and then said, "I can't get mad at John for a misguided attempted to take care of me, but now I'm worried how all that plays out in court." Sarah paused and then added, "I also really want to get back to work, so it would help if the people who used to want to hire me didn't treat me like I had the plague." She shook her head, "And being threatened was all I needed to top it off."

Laurie said, "Believe it or not, I find cause for optimism in what you just said."

"Really?" Sarah replied. "Help me find it, will you?"

"Yes. Having a full awareness of the sources of your anxiety is helpful to understanding why you have the physical and emotional symptoms that manifest."

"You sound like a text book, but I get it," Sarah replied, smiling.

"Glad to see that your sense of humor is still there, and that you're keeping your spirits up. Both are really significant and tell us that you are making progress."

"I feel like I am. I'm also not taking any unnecessary chances."

"Well, that sounds good," Lauric said. "Mcaning what?"

"I'm careful where I go, and what time of day I go there. I also carry both pepper spray and a stun-gun."

"Really?" Laurie asked.

"Yep. Any guy who gets too close to me will get a million volts and be laying on the ground before he realizes that wasn't a good idea."

"Sounds like you may have some nervous friends," Laurie said, grinning.

"Damned straight," Sarah replied, laughing.

Laurie was quiet a moment and then said, "I know that you are going through a lot right now, but I think you are getting stronger each time I see you, Sarah."

Chapter Twenty-Three

Scott and Sarah walked into the Hilton Hotel conference room in Mountain View, meeting Margo Traynor at the same location as their first meeting. This time, there was a court reporter and a videographer setting up and Mike Graber was in the lobby on his phone.

Scott said, "Good morning, Ms. Traynor. It's nice to see you." She wore a black skirt, white top and a light blue jacket. She looked professional and ready for what lay ahead.

"Good morning," she said, shaking his hand.

"Thank you for this," Sarah said, taking Margo's hand. "I know this isn't easy and I appreciate it."

"I want to do this," Margo said.

"You get the seat of honor today," Scott said, gesturing to the chair that was the focus of the camera. "Just ignore the camera and look at the questioner. I will be asking questions first, and then the attorney for Ellison and Mr. Nolan will get the opportunity to ask you questions."

"Got it," she said. "Let's do this."

Mike Graber walked into the room and said, "You're Ms. Traynor?"

"Yes."

"Hello, I'm Michael Graber. I represent the defendants in this case."

"Hello," she said, shaking his hand.

"Are we ready?" Scott asked the room. Everyone nodded. Scott said, "Take it away," to the videographer. "This is tape one of the deposition of Margo Traynor, noticed by the plaintiff, Sarah Willis." He recited the name of the hotel, the address, and the date and time. Then he said, "We are ready to swear the witness."

After Margo was sworn, Scott too her through each of the incidents of harassment she had relayed to him. She described each confidently and in detail, ending with her quitting her position when the company after she spoke to human resources and was told that a formal complaint might end her position on the team. When his opportunity to question came around, Graber focused on the absence of any written complaint or investigation that supported her allegations.

When it was all over, Scott walked from the room with Margo Traynor and said, "Thank you, Margo. However this comes out, both Sarah and I appreciate how hard it is to relive all of this."

She shook Scott's hand and nodded. "I just hope I did all right."

"You did a great job, Margo. You were very credible."

She was quiet a moment, and then said, "I figured out that I needed to do this for me, as well as for Sarah." She smiled and said, "Call me to let me know when the trial is happening and I'll be there."

* * *

Lee punched in a number and waited.

"You again?" came the response.

"There's always more to do."

"How can we help?"

"I got your message that Thomas Cummings is not of record as owning a white Chevy Malibu or Impala. See if you can identify relatives of Thomas Cummings and his family members within a hundred mile radius of his address. I need to know who they are and which of them owns a late model, white Chevy Malibu or Impala. I have a hunch that we are going to make a connection between the car and his family."

"You got it. Give me a couple of hours."

"You guys are amazing, you know that?"

"Of course."

Lee pulled up in front of Thailand West, a restaurant featuring great Thai food and an eastern ambience defined by overhead lantern lighting and red brick interior walls, with tables seemingly randomly placed to defy any discernable pattern. He walked inside and spoke to the hostess. He was directed to the left side of the restaurant, through an alcove and to another room of tables, where he spotted Melissa. She smiled widely, stood up and waved to get his attention. She wore a brown coat over a tan blouse and blue jeans. She was still beautiful.

He walked over to her and they embraced. Then they kissed, before they sat down. They ordered a glass of pinot noir from the waiting server. She smiled at him and said, "How was your trip?"

"Quite productive," he said. "Definitely worthwhile."

"Glad to hear that." She paused and said, "I missed you." She looked a little nervous and then said, "I hope it's not too early in our relationship to say that."

"It's not, and I missed you, too. I've been looking forward to tonight."

She looked a little worried as she said, "I was called into HR, and with two HR executives and the company lawyer present, they raised questions about why I was spending time with you."

"Really? I guess I'm even more unpopular with them than I knew. What did they say?"

"That you were associated with Scott Winslow and he represented Sarah Willis, so they wanted to make sure I knew that I had to honor my confidentiality obligations."

"Guilt by association, right?"

"Right, and I'm a little worried that they will piece together the fact that you were there as Jack Landon and come after you."

He shrugged and said, "They're already after me for breaking into Nolan's house with John Willis, so what's one more charge." He smiled and said, "Are you okay there? I mean, I don't want them coming after you because of me."

"I am disappointed and angry at them. It's not a feel good kind of place for me these days, so I've been talking to couple of the headhunters that are always chasing us. If I make the right connection, I will be out of there."

Lee's phone rang and he said, "Excuse me, this should be quick." Melissa nodded. "Speak to me." There was a few moments of silence and then Lee said, "I thought so. Great work and very helpful."

He hung up the phone and then asked Melissa, "Did you hear about the threat to Sarah?"

"Yes, I talked to Sarah yesterday and she told me about it."

"I think I know who did it," Lee said.

"Really? Are you going to turn him in?"

"I'm going to pay him a visit and chat a little first."

The server emerged with a big smile and said, "Are you ready to hear about tonight's specials?"

Lee looked at Melissa and smiled broadly. Then he took her hands in his as they semi-listened to the recital of the specials, immersed in thoughts of being in each other's company.

* * *

"The Executive Committee of the Board are now on the line, Mr. Dixon," a voice said into the speaker on Ellison Vice President, Mark Dixon's desk. He hit a button and said, "Good morning, everyone. Thanks for being available so quickly. I wanted us all assembled to address the Willis litigation. As you know, we authorized going up to $500,000 to settle the case at the mediation. Our counsel is on this part of the call. Mr. Graber?"

"Yes, sir. I'm here."

"And what is the current status of discussions?" Dixon asked.

"Their last demand was $1,625,000. They have not responded to our $500,000 settlement offer."

"I think they did," Dixon said. "They responded with the deposition of Ms. Traynor that you told us about. You all received an email from Mr. Graber outlining her testimony in that deposition. The upshot is, they now have a witness who says that Jim engaged in some serious harassment and sexual misconduct directed towards her." He drew a breath and said, "Jim, you're on this call because you're our CEO. This call is to decide what, if anything else, we need to do in light of this new testimony."

Arthur Lindstrom said, "Mr. Graber, if there is a plaintiff verdict in this case, tell us what you now believe is the likely range of that verdict."

Mike Graber hated that question. They wanted him to forecast how twelve unknown strangers would value a case that would be hard for anyone to value. "I have to give you some pretty wide parameters," Graber said, "because the possibilities are quite broad. I'd say somewhere between $250,000 and something into the seven figure range."

"Okay, Mr Graber, thanks for your participation. You can sign off now."

"Okay. Good-bye everyone," Graber replied. There was a click as he hung up.

Jim Nolan was then first to speak. "Let me remind you that you're talking about throwing more money at a case that should be a defense verdict." He was trying hard to sound analytical, rather than defensive, given that his conduct was implicated in all of this.

Arthur Lindstrom said, "Jim, you're our CEO and we always value what you say, but you have a horse in this race. We have to consider that as well."

"Of course I have a horse in this race, I'm being falsely accused."

There was a protracted silence while that statement was digested, and then board member Lloyd Meachem said, "I think we need to stand behind Jim. If he says it didn't happen, that should be our corporate position. I vote we don't increase the offer and we take our chances."

Silent until now, Bob Anderson said, "I agree. Let's give the lawyer flexibility to go up ten percent from where we are, but if that doesn't work, let's try the case."

Michelle Barnes said, "I have to disagree. I understand the desire to be loyal to Jim, but this is a business decision at this point, and knowing the verdict potential, I suggest that we go close to a million to get the case settled."

"Let's stand with Jim," Lloyd Meachem interjected, "I move that we go no more that 10% above the $500,000 offer to settle."

Bob Anderson said, "I second."

"Pamela, are you on the line to get the voice vote?" Mark Dixon asked.

"Yeah, I'm here," Pamela Martin replied.

"So the vote is, how many want to go up by no more than ten percent from our $500,000 offer?"

"Right," Martin said. "I'll call the voice vote."

When Martin collected all of the "ayes" and "nays," the motion carried six to five.

"Okay," Dixon said, with concern. "Our recommendation to the full Board tomorrow is that we go up no higher than $550,000. Thank you for your participation everyone."

* * *

At 8:30 a.m., Nikki buzzed Scott's office. "I have Mike Graber on line 1."

"Okay, thanks Nikki," Scott said, and hit the button.

"Hi Mike."

"Scott, how are you?"

"I'm good. What's up?"

"You never got back to me about our settlement offer."

"We wanted you to hear from Traynor to see if that helped your perception of the case before responding. Now we are prepared to get to our bottom line. I have authority to settle for one million dollars if we do it now."

"Too bad," Graber said. "I have authority to go to $550,000, and that's it."

"I'll pass it on, but I don't see us accepting it. I will call you back by the end of the day tomorrow to let you know one way or the other."

"Okay, thanks," Graber said. Scott heard the click and wondered why Traynor's testimony hadn't made a bigger impression. It meant that the case was not likely to settle and it was time to put it in the hands of a jury.

* * *

Lee drove to 2115 Las Villas Circle in Sherman Oaks, the residence of one Thomas Walter Cummings. The orange Camaro was parked in the driveway, as inconspicuous as ever. Lee shook his head and walked towards the front door. He knocked and waited. After a few moments, the front door opened and Cummings stood there, a shocked expression on his face.

"What do you want?" he asked, angrily.

Lee shook his head. "That's sounds down right unfriendly. And I'm here to do you a favor."

Cummings squinted and repeated, "What do you want?"

"I wanted to give you a heads-up."

Cummings was sneering at him. "A heads-up about what?"

"About what deep shit you are in."

"Get the fuck off my porch."

"Not just yet. Not until we have a serious conversation." Cummings flashed angry eyes, his muscles tightening. Lee, unimpressed, continued, "You threatened Sarah Willis if she didn't dismiss her lawsuit. As you and I both know, that is criminal assault. And, of course, you can be sued civilly for your threats of harm to Ms. Willis. I think juries in both cases will think that your conduct was despicable. Should be jail time in one case and a big verdict in the other."

"I don't know what you're talking about."

Lee nodded slowly. "Well, maybe I can jog your memory a little. You have a sister in-law named Stephanie Johnson. Nice lady. Turns out she owns a white Chevy Malibu, just like the one you were driving when you threatened Sarah Willis."

"I didn't..."

Lee held up a hand and interrupted him to say, "Don't bother denying it. I met with Ms. Johnson, and she confirmed that you borrowed her car for the occasion." Lee laughed, "She also mentioned that you removed her license plates, but apparently you forgot to put them back on the car. You left them on her backseat." He shook his head. "I bet I would find a blond wig in your house if I looked right now."

Cummings said, "No, you wouldn't."

"Well, I'm glad that you at least managed to dump the wig." He shook his head. "Did I mention that I don't think you are cut out for this kind of work?"

Cummings face was bright red. He took a sudden swing at Lee, but his fist hit nothing, when Lee stepped aside. Cummings' inertia brought him toward Lee, who punched him in the gut, and watched him fall to the ground. Lee pulled up a porch chair and sat next to Cummings, who laid on his side, groaning. "Well, you didn't do great work with this little gambit, but at least you took my advice and didn't use that orange neon sign of yours," he said, gesturing towards the Camaro in the driveway. "Now, I have assembled all of the information that I just shared with you and it is packaged up ready to go to the D.A. If you don't want that to happen, you can do a small favor for me." Cummings was on his side, still holding his stomach. He groaned. "Are you listening, Mr. Cummings? Please nod if you hear me." Cummings nodded. "Great. So, what's it going to be Tom? Would you prefer to assist me with a small favor or address all of these troublesome issues with the local prosecution team?"

Cummings drew several deep breaths, and then he nodded again. "What do you want?" he asked in a hoarse whisper.

"Here's the thing, Mr. Cummings. Sometimes good deals are made by negotiating through lawyers, while other times back channels can accomplish things that no one wants to say on record. So your job is to become one of those back channels."

Cummings slowly climbed to his feet and sat down on the porch chair next to the one Lee occupied. "How?" Cummings asked.

"I understand that there is a quarterly industry event that happens tomorrow evening. I don't know if Mr. Nolan typically attends such events, but you are going to tell him that he should definitely attend this one."

Cummings looked at Lee, still working on normalizing his breathing, and said, "Why?"

"Because, Ms. Willis will be there to seek out her contacts so that she can find work. You should advise Mr. Nolan of the negotiating importance of back channel communications. I think he will understand that concept. Tell him that he should personally approach Ms. Willis with a proposal. He should suggest that he will advise the District Attorney that he doesn't want to pursue any case against John Willis, and that he won't testify if that case is brought. In exchange, he suggests that Ms. Willis accepts the pending settlement offer. Both cases are over, and you get to be a hero."

Cummings was listening hard. He was quiet for a time, and then asked, "What's the catch?"

Lee responded with his most sincere nod. "The only catch is that you never say that you got any information from me. If you do, I deny it and the packet I mentioned goes in the mail. If you do this right, I never send that package, and no one finds out that you were the guy who threatened Ms. Willis."

"Yeah?" Cummings wheezed. He was red in the face and still breathing hard.

"Yeah."

"Okay, but I can't guarantee that Mr. Nolan will heed my advice."

"You need to be your most persuasive self, Tom. Give it everything you can, because if it doesn't work, the package gets mailed, and the D.A. has one more important case to work." Lee said, "Have a great day," and then turned and walked towards his car. When he looked at the house as he pulled away, Cummings was still sitting on the porch. Lee smiled as he watched Cummings trying to figure out how he was going to persuade Nolan to show up and make the offer.

Chapter Twenty-Four

Scott and Sarah were seated in a conference room at Scott's office, a cup of coffee in front of each. "Are you sure that I should have a recording device?" Sarah asked, sounding concerned. "He may never approach me, assuming he even shows up at the event."

Scott shrugged. "He may not, in which case we are no worse off. On the other hand, if he does, maybe we can use it to get John off the hook." Scott said. He smiled and added, "Either way, Lee identified the guy who threatened you, and made sure that we can take him off the threat list."

"He did, didn't he?" She nodded.

"He's pretty remarkable," Scott said.

"I'm hearing that from Melissa, too," Sarah said beaming. "It's pretty clear that those two have a thing for each other."

"Yep," Scott replied. He grinned and added, "Seems that Lee is pretty taken with your friend." After a moment, Scott said, "You ready to practice your testimony for trial?"

"I guess so. I'm pretty nervous about it and I'm going to try not to be too emotional."

"My advice is to be who you are. Listen carefully to each question and respond only to the question asked. And remember, on cross-examination, don't let him get under your skin, even if he asks offensive questions. If he can get you upset, your testimony won't be as good as it should be if you remain calm." He reflected a moment, and then added, "One more thing. If you get upset or cry, it's okay. Be who you are. You have nothing to try to hide and the jury is composed of real people who will see that your reactions are genuine."

She nodded and then asked, "You have a lot of faith in the legal system, don't you?"

He nodded. "I really do. Juries take the job and the solemnity of the proceedings seriously, and they try to get it right."

"All right. I'm ready," Sarah offered.

"First, we will go through direct examination. Consider it you and I talking. I'll ask you questions that you answer in your own words. In that way, we will tell the story of everything as it happened. Then, we'll practice cross-examination and I'll ask you yes or no questions that try to box you in, and give you little chance to explain anything."

"I can hardly wait."

"Just like your deposition. You handled it great there. This time the questions will be less broad and more focused on the issues: what happened, how it happened and the effects that it all had on you." He smiled and added, "You can hold your own, and I've already seen that."

"Thanks for your confidence, Scott." She paused and added, "However this comes out, thank you for everything. You and your team have helped me through all this and I'm not sure where I would have been without you."

"Our pleasure. Okay, here we go. State your full name for the record please."

"Sarah Willis."

"Are you married, Ms. Willis?"

"I am. Happily married to my husband, John."

"How long?"

"We've been married for eleven years. Our twelfth anniversary in next month."

"Where were you last employed?"

"Ellison Corporation,"

"And when did you work for Ellison?"

She leaned back in her chair and was quiet a moment, and then she said, "I'm already nervous. This is already stressful and this is just practice on my team."

"Yep. Wait until I do the mock cross-examination. That will really make your day."

She shook her head. "Just shoot me now."

"No way," Scott said, "you're not getting out of this the easy way," and they both began to laugh.

* * *

Lee pulled up in front of Melissa's place and walked slowly towards the front door, tired after a couple of long days and nights of work. He knocked once and she answered. She smiled widely as she held the door open. Then she gave him a kiss and said, "Come on in." Just like that, he felt revived, exhaustion suddenly gone.

They walked into the kitchen and she said, "Want a beer?"

"Sounds great," he said, sitting down on a bar stool at the kitchen island. She pulled two beers from the refrigerator and handed one to him. He took a drink and then asked, "How are you?"

"I'm good," she replied. She sat down next to him, and then added, "Especially now."

"Yeah, me to," he said. He put his arm around her and gave her a kiss.

There was a moment of silence while they focused only on the kiss, and then she said, "So, tell me the news. Did you pay that visit to the guy who threatened Sarah?"

"I did." He smiled. "And we have him."

"Have him?"

"Yep. I was able to convince him that he is in legal jeopardy, so he is going to do us a favor in an attempt to keep us from revealing his identity."

"What kind of a favor?" He just smiled, so she added, "Okay, something I shouldn't know?"

He nodded. "Not quite yet, but soon." He gave her another kiss, and then said, "I think that is becoming addictive. It's almost an involuntary response."

She replied, "I think so, too."

He touched her hair and said, "You know, I could get lost in those amazing eyes of yours." She smiled and took his hand. He asked, "So, where would you like to go tonight?"

She looked at him thoughtfully, and then said, "I thought maybe we should stay home tonight. Relax and shed our worries and concerns." He nodded, and then she added, "And our clothing."

His smile grew wide and he said, "Now that sounds excellent." He kissed her softly, and then passionately. Their clothes started to peel away as they made their way to the bedroom. When they arrived, they were both naked, leaving a trail of clothing from the kitchen and down the hallway. Melissa laid down on the bed and he kissed her lips, her neck, her breasts and then slowly moved downward between her legs. He kissed her again and again. He began to move his tongue, and she began to moan. She laid back and closed her eyes, overcome by the depth of her reaction. The sensation built quickly and she gasped as she came. He moved on top of her and entered her as they kissed deeply, and moved slowly. The entire world suddenly disappeared and there was only them, and only the moment. There was only touch, feeling and ultimate pleasure. They reversed positions and she climbed on top, now moving more quickly. Their breathing grew louder, and they held each other tight as the moment of climax came. Wrapped in each other's arms, the world disappeared as they fell into that mystical, peaceful sleep that follows lovemaking.

* * *

Sarah looked around the big auditorium. She wanted to run for the door. There were accounting and finance people everywhere, and many familiar faces. The program had been an hour of panel presentation containing ten minutes worth of information. It was boring, but during the presentations she hadn't had to talk to anyone. Many in this room knew of her situation and of the litigation. A number of them had once upon a time approached her about leaving Ellison to work with them. Now, none of them had a position for her. She was treated with vague smiles and distance. She was someone not to get too close to, because whatever she had, just might be contagious. Being her friend might be cause for retaliation against anyone deemed to be too close. Tonight, everyone spoke to her cordially, and then promptly moved on to speak with others.

She held a glass of champagne and looked around the room. A grey haired man walked over to her and said, "Hi, Sarah."

She smiled and said, "Hi, Jack." Jack Porter was a Vice President at Pivotal Engineering and a nice guy. "How have you been?"

"I'm good. You?" he asked, watching her expression.

She shrugged and said, "I've had better times."

He was quiet a moment and then said, "Sarah, you are a terrific and talented person. Your issues with Ellison don't change that."

"Thank you," Sarah said. "I've always thought highly of you, too, Jack."

"Don't give up, Sarah. You will find the right spot," he said, giving her a warm smile. "I better go find my wife," he said. "I think she's ready to get out of here."

"Good to see you, Jack."

"You, too."

With those final words, he disappeared into the crowd. She looked around to see John caught up in a crowd, and then she saw a familiar face approaching and felt relief. Melissa almost ran up to her and threw her arms around Sarah, making it clear that she was quite comfortable consorting with those on the outcast list. "Hi, Sarah. Sorry that I'm so late in getting here, but I had one more emergency at the end of the day."

"Glad you made it," Sarah said. "I feel like an injured deer, in a forest of wolves."

"Wow, well, that's not so good."

"No, it's really not." Sarah grinned. "Everyone is superficially friendly, like strangers offering a greeting in the supermarket. Then, they move on to talk to people who aren't blacklisted."

"I get it, the chicken-shit bastards."

"So how are you and Lee doing?" She saw the glow on Melissa's face, and added, "Well, that is good news."

"I think I've really found someone incredible," Melissa said. "He's an amazing guy."

Sarah glanced to her left to see James Nolan standing there. She looked back to Melissa and continued talking as he made his way toward them.

Without any greeting, he said, "Can I talk to you privately?" Melissa looked alarmed. "Just for a minute," he said.

Sarah was quiet a moment, and then said, "I can't imagine what we have to talk about."

Nolan said, "Just one moment. I think it's information you will want."

There was an extended silence while Sarah regarded him. Then she said, "Okay, Melissa, can you give us a moment?"

"I'll be right over here if you need me," she replied, gesturing to a nearby table. There would be no doubt that her boss would know whose team she supported.

Melissa moved a few feet away, and then Sarah looked at Nolan and said, "What is it?"

"I wanted to let you know that I think we should resolve our little problem in a way that serves both of us. You accept our last offer to settle your case, and I will advise the D.A. that I do not want to pursue any charges against John for his attack on me at my house."

Hearing him describe the rape as "our little problem," instantaneously made her blood boil. She wanted to slap him across the face. Instead, she took a deep breath and said, "I'll think about it." Then she walked away to rejoin Melissa and didn't look back.

As they walked from the auditorium and into the parking lot together, Melissa asked, "What in the world was that about?"

Sarah replied, "He proposed that we accept his last offer and in exchange he will tell the D.A. that he doesn't want to proceed with the criminal action against John."

Melissa looked shocked. "Is that legal?"

"I don't know, but I know that your boyfriend made it happen."

Melissa smiled, liking the reference to Lee as her boyfriend. "How?" she asked.

"I'm not sure, but Scott knew it might happen, and had me ready to record the conversation in case it did."

"You recorded it?" Melissa asked, her eyes wide.

"I did," Sarah replied. "I have it all on tape."

Melissa wore a questioning look. "What's going to happen with the recording?"

"No clue. I'll give it to Scott and he can tell me what should be done with it."

Melissa shook her head. "You know," she said, "in a lot of ways Scott and Lee are a team in the same way that you and I are a team. They just kind of belong together."

Sarah nodded. "I think that's right. Even though you and I don't see each other every day at work anymore, let's make sure we stay close friends, forever."

"You can count on it," Melissa said.

* * *

At 11:30 a.m., Scott arrived back at his office after arguing a motion on an age discrimination case. He grabbed the awaiting stack of phone messages from Nikki, but before checking his email or returning any of those calls, he called Lee.

On the second ring, the familiar voice said, "Hi, Scott."

"He did it," Scott said.

"I thought he might," Lee replied. "Not that Cummings wielded much influence with Nolan. I think it's just that Nolan liked the idea. If he could get Sarah to take the deal and end the case in exchange for letting go of any desire to prosecute John, it's a pretty clean deal for him."

"That's right. I suspect that this case is getting Ellison and its management much more attention than they'd like."

"Right," Lee said. "So what do we do with the tape now that we have it?"

"I have to be careful with this," Scott said, thoughtfully. "It's unethical for a lawyer to do something like using a threat of criminal action to obtain an advantage in a civil case. On the other hand, there are often deals made, called civil compromises, which allow resolution of a civil case with a criminal case."

Lee laughed. "I'm glad that one is your quagmire, and not mine, good buddy."

"Yeah, I bet you are."

"So, do you know how you want to handle it?"

"Yes. I'm having it transcribed. That's where you come in."

"How?"

"I want to have you drop off copies of the transcript of the conversation between Nolan and Sarah to a couple of key members of Ellison's board of directors, at their respective homes."

"You want copies to land in their mailboxes, without explanation?"

"Exactly," Scott responded. "Then they can think about the implications of these statements by Nolan and how it would look if they became public. I think it will stimulate conversation about Nolan, and about how hard they want to push on the criminal case against John Willis."

"I like it," Lee said. He reflected a moment, and then added, "You know, for a by the book kind of guy, once in a while you can be as devious as me."

"Thanks. I'll take that as a compliment."

"Oh, it is," Lee said. "I place a high value on getting things done when people don't know that you're doing them."

Scott laughed and said, "The transcript will be done in an hour or so. I'll email it to you shortly."

"Great," Lee replied. "I'll identify key board members and get them a copy at home, so they can have that first drink at the end of the day with some good reading material."

"Perfect," Scott said. After a moment, he added, "By the way, I keep hearing that you and Melissa are a pretty good thing these days."

Lee replied, "She is really special, man. I think I have a crush, an addiction or something. Heaven knows, I may even be in love with this woman. I find myself grinning like an idiot every time I think about her. I'm doing it now, for Pete's sake."

"Yep. Pretty serious. I think that's a love symptom. I'd get that treated right away or it could be permanent."

"I think it may already be too late," Lee said, "because I have no desire to get treatment."

* * *

Lee parked his car curbside about two blocks from his intended destination. It seemed that that Tom Cummings and Jake Carlson had finally given up tailing him as he ventured around the city. Carlson probably went back to his real job at Ellison and he was pretty sure that Tom Cummings never wanted to see him again.

The sun was shining in the cloudless, blue sky. It was a beautiful southern California afternoon, now approaching 5:00 p.m., and the sun still hovering far above the horizon. Lee grabbed an envelope and locked the car. He walked past large estates with expansive lawns and elaborate landscape and hardscape. He made a left at the second corner and was greeted by a dark haired woman he estimated to be in her late forties, walking a standard poodle.

"Beautiful afternoon," the woman said.

"It sure is," Lee said. "Nice day for a walk."

The woman gave him a flirtatious smile and said, "Do you live around here?"

"No, I'm just visiting," he responded. "I'm on my way back to Iowa first thing in the morning."

She smiled and replied, "Too bad I won't see you on future walks."

"Right, too bad," he said. "Maybe next trip." She gave him a wide smile and he said, "Have a great afternoon." He walked on without looking back. He made the next right, and then saw the address he was after. The two-story estate was a tasteful gray and white with symmetrical bay windows, and large dormers. He walked to the curbside mailbox and delivered the unstamped envelope to Ellison Vice President, Mark Dixon. Then he turned and walked back to his car. Next stop was the home of Arthur Lindstrom, in Encino, where he would drop off the second identical envelope. He smiled, thinking it would be great to see the expressions on their faces as they read the transcript of the conversation between Nolan, and Sarah Willis, without explanation. It should make for some stimulating Board conversation.

* * *

At 5:00 p.m., Melissa entered the circular foyer of Diversified Development on the thirty-ninth floor of the Bascom Building. The reception area was expansive and opulent, with three massive chandeliers over travertine tile. Two conversation areas, each consisting of two large sofas facing each other over marble coffee tables, were situated so that occupants could view the city below through floor to ceiling walls of window.

There was a reception desk that guarded the door to the inner sanctum. The blonde woman seated at the desk looked up from her screen and smiled. "You must be Melissa Carter," she said, extending a hand. "I'm Tory Mills. You will be meeting with Vincent Harper, our Executive Vice President. Please have a seat for a moment and I'll let him know that you're here."

"Okay, thanks," Melissa said, walking toward the astonishing view from this ivory tower. The day was clear, and as she looked west, she could look between the other monolithic structures of downtown, to see traces of the distant ocean.

After a few minutes, a slender man in his early fifties stepped into the lobby and walked towards her. He had salt and pepper hair and a warm smile. "Good afternoon, Melissa. I'm Vince Harper." They shook hands, and then he said, "please, come on into my office."

She followed him through the inner sanctum doorway, and down a hall to the office at the far corner. The office consisted of two walls of windows from floor to ceiling, a large desk holding three computer monitors and a conference table that seated eight. He gestured to her to take a seat in one of the two visitor chairs beside his desk. Rather than walking around the desk to his chair, he sat in the other visitor chair and turned it to face hers.

Harper leaned forward and said, "So, Melissa, I reviewed your resume and it is impressive, but I'm not sure of the fit. You know that we are looking for a VP of Finance to oversee all financials for the parent company and thirteen subsidiaries," he paused and corrected, "soon to be fourteen, subsidiaries. Tell me why you are the best person for this job."

"I've got the academic credentials and I've been in senior finance and accounting roles in three major corporations. I've also been trained by the very best."

His eyes widened and he asked, "Who would that be?"

"That would be Sarah Willis, at Ellison."

He nodded slowly, but said nothing for a time. Then he asked, "You would have reported to her throughout your time at Ellison, right?"

"Until recent events that I'm sure you've heard about."

He nodded, and replied. "Yes, I've heard about it."

"Sarah is the best I have ever seen. She was also highly regarded at Ellison until what happened." She paused and then added, "I was responsible for half of the subsidiaries while I reported to her."

"I understand." He paused a moment and then said, "But, Ellison didn't elevate you with her departure, right?"

"Yes, that's correct."

"Forgive me for being direct, but I can't help wondering why," Harper responded. "I mean, they have someone with expertise, trained by the best as you say, yet they are looking outside the company to fill that critical position."

Melissa gave him a sideways grin and replied, "I hope you don't mind if I am also direct. There is something of an "us versus her" culture war at Ellison. I think highly of Sarah and I consider her a friend, as well as a mentor. Ellison doesn't like the fact that I am close to her, and supportive of her." She shrugged. "I am not okay with sacrificing a great employee because she came forward to complain about harassment, and an attack on her. I think integrity, as well as the law, requires more."

He leaned back in his chair and reflected. After a moment, he said, "I like you, Melissa, and I like that we can both be direct and candid. You have an impressive resume, but I don't think you have enough experience for this position. A few years from now, but not yet." She listened carefully, without visible reaction, as he continued. "What if I were to offer you a Director level position that reported to the position you came here about? I consider it to be on the same level as the position you hold now."

She thought a moment and then said, "Depends on the terms."

"Fair enough," he said. He picked up a small file from his desk, took out two sheets of paper, and handed them to her. "Here's what we can do," he said.

She read over the terms sheet. The starting salary was fifteen thousand dollars higher than her current annual salary, and there was profit sharing, and 401K benefits.

She reflected on the oppressive atmosphere she faced as an outsider at Ellison, and then said, "I'm interested."

He smiled. "I think you'd be a good fit and the job is yours if you want it. We'll allow you two weeks for notice to Ellison, and then we'll make sure that you are more than busy."

"Okay," she said. "I would like to work with you." They stood and shook hands. She hesitated and then, before turning to leave the office, added, "I'm on board whatever you choose to do, but Sarah Willis would be the right person for your top job. Just something for you to consider."

He gave her a look that said he didn't want to step into that mess and then replied, "You certainly are supportive of her." He grinned and added, "Thanks for the suggestion, but you are joining us regardless of who we choose for the VP of Finance role, correct?"

"Yes, that's right," she said, feeling deflated that he had seemed to have no interest in considering Sarah. How could she blame him? No one wanted to walk into the Willis and Ellison dispute. They all steered clear. "I look forward to working with you, Mr. Harper."

He smiled. "It's Vince."

"Okay, Vince. See you in two weeks."

"Great, I'll have HR email the necessary forms to get you signed in around here, so that we don't waste time on your first day."

"Perfect," she said, and walked from the office down the hall, taking in what would soon be her new surroundings. She wasn't going to miss working at Ellison these days, that's for sure.

* * *

"Scott, Michael Graber on line 3."

"Thanks, Nikki" Scott said, punching a button.

"Hi, Mike. What can I do for you?"

"I thought you were a straight shooter, Winslow. Now I guess I know better."

"What does that mean?" Scott asked, sounding as innocent and uninformed as he could.

"You had your client record mine without his knowledge. It is unlawful to record someone without their consent in this state."

"What are you talking about?"

"You're going to tell me that you don't know anything about your client recording this conversation?"

"I'm not telling you anything at the moment, I'm just listening to you complain."

After a moment, Graber said, "Your client recorded my client's suggestion that they resolve this case, along with the criminal action against her husband. Your client taped the conversation without his consent."

"How do you know that?"

"Come on, Scott. A transcript of the conversation just happened to turn up in the mailboxes of two Ellison board members. At their homes, no less!" He sounded angry.

Scott waited a moment and then said, "This hasn't been released publicly, right? I mean, the media doesn't have it, right?"

Graber quieted his tone and replied, "Not that I know of so far."

"Well, that part is good, right?"

"That's not the point. Your client had no right to make an unconsented recording."

"Yeah, I did hear you say that." Scott responded evenly.

"This may be unlawful, and it's certainly unethical to try to influence a civil action using a criminal action."

Scott was quiet for a time, suppressing a smile. After a moment, he said, "Well, isn't that exactly what your client was doing? I mean, Mr. Nolan suggested a resolution of the civil action on certain terms and he end the criminal action. Based upon what you have told me, my client only listened to his suggestions, isn't that right?"

"You son of a bitch," Graber said, in angry tones. "I know you choreographed this."

"You seem awfully upset, Mike. Seems like the only ones who know about this, at least so far, are your own clients."

"Are you threatening to release it?"

"I'm not threatening anything. You called me, remember? I'm just listening to you telling me what happened. Maybe we should both give it some thought. Perhaps some kind of an answer will suggest itself." There was a click as Graber hung up. Scott smiled. That had gone rather well.

The intercom buzzed again, "Scott, I have Amy Curtis with the D.A.'s office on line 1."

"Okay. Thanks, Nikki."

He hit a button and said, "Scott Winslow."

"Hi, Scott. This is Amy Curtis."

"Hello, Amy. I didn't think we'd ever hear from you again. What's the news?"

"The news is that we are seriously considering going forward with the case against James Nolan for rape. We reviewed the Margo Traynor deposition transcript that you forwarded and concluded that it may give us enough for a good shot at a conviction."

"Good, I'm glad you are seriously considering filing," Scott said. Then he added, "but you can't file it yet."

"Why not?"

"Because we go to trial a week from Monday. If you file your case, then Nolan will assert his Fifth Amendment rights, and the judge will probably continue until the criminal case concludes." He paused and then added, "Not good. We are ready and want to go to trial."

"I don't know," she said. "I don't know if we can do that."

"You've taken this long to decide you want to go forward. You can wait another three or four weeks before making a final decision, right?"

"I'll have to check with Russell Hanks."

"Fine. Please have him call me if he has any questions about this. We spent a lot of hours preparing the case and we don't want to get kicked down the road for six months or a year."

"I'll let him know and call you back," Curtis said.

"Thanks," Scott told her. "You can also tell him we will share our evidence with him." Scott already decided that if the decision was other than to delay the filing, he would contact the D.A. himself. They had waited a long time for the prosecutor to decide to go forward. They prosecutor could wait thirty more days while the civil case went to trial.

"Okay, I will tell him. Talk to you soon."

"Thanks, Amy."

As Scott hung up, he shook his head. Their timing was remarkable.

Chapter Twenty-Five

Melissa opened the front door and saw Lee standing there smirking.

"What?" she asked.

"This," he said, and took her in his arms for a passionate kiss. By the time he pulled back, she was smiling, too.

"Nice," she said. "Keep that in mind for all future greetings."

"I have been thinking about you rather obsessively," he confessed. "I've been day dreaming about your face, your kiss, and all of you."

"Come on in before we wind up naked on the front porch," she replied.

He walked in and kissed her again in the entryway. He raised a foot and pushed the front door closed, without interrupting the kiss. When they pulled apart, she slowly opened her eyes and said, "My, you do that well."

"I can't seem to get enough," he replied.

"Come on in," she said, taking him by the hand. They walked into the dining room where wine and cheese waited. "We are celebrating," she said, smiling.

"Yeah? What is the news?"

"I got a new job today."

"Where?" he asked, excitedly.

"Diversified Development. I'll be doing financial reporting for the parent company and fourteen subsidiaries."

"Sounds wonderful," he said. "Here's to a great new position," he offered. "I know that Ellison has been a source of major stress these days, so that has to feel great."

"It feels so good knowing that I don't have to work with the people who betrayed Sarah anymore. I am so ready. I'm giving my notice tomorrow," she added, pouring them each a glass of pinot noir.

He touched her hand and said, "Tell me more about the job."

"It is Director of Finance. I actually applied for the Vice President of Finance position, but didn't get it, which isn't surprising, because it's so senior and requires more experience than I have. It would be the ideal position for Sarah, so I tossed her name out there"

"How did that go?"

"Not well. They clearly weren't going there. He wanted me to assure him that I would come no matter who they hired for the senior position. Anyway, it will be everything I do at Ellison, and a little more, and it pays better."

"We'll, here's to your exciting new position," Lee said, raising his glass.

"Thank you," she replied, and they clinked glasses.

After a moment, she put down her glass and put her open hands on his cheeks. "Do you want to make love before or after dinner?" she asked grinning.

He looked thoughtful for a moment and then said, "How about both?"

She nodded and said, "Good answer." She took him by the hand and they walked to the bedroom. At the doorway, she put her arms around his neck and said, "I want you to know that I love being with you. I really hope you plan to stay in my life."

"That's exactly what I'm planning," he said, and then he closed the bedroom door with the same foot that had handled the front door.

* * *

"Scott, Amy Curtis, line 2."

"Thanks, Nikki."

Scott hit a button and said, "Hi, Amy. Thanks for getting back to me quickly."

"No problem," Curtis replied. "I talked to Russell Hanks about our conversation and he says that we will hold off on making a final decision about whether we proceed for thirty days. He said to tell you that he understands that you had to wait a long time for us to consider whether we had enough to file against Nolan, so we owe you a little cooperation."

"Tell Russell that I appreciate it."

"I will," she said. After a moment, she added, "He said you better not lose the case, though, because if Nolan prevails when the burden of proof is a preponderance of the evidence, then we are going to have to rethink whether we have a shot at satisfying the beyond a reasonable doubt standard that we have to overcome."

"Yep, I understand. We'll give it everything we've got."

"I know you will," she said. "Good luck."

"Thanks," Scott replied. "I'm sure that the press will keep you posted on how it's going."

"I expect so," Curtis responded.

"Talk to you later."

* * *

"You told Sarah Willis that if she would accept our last offer to settle her case, then you would tell the D.A. that you didn't want the criminal action against John Willis to go forward?"

"I did," Nolan said to the Executive Board members. "I saw it as an easy way to end all this for everyone."

"She recorded your conversation, right?"

"Yes, it seems so."

"So, she had to know that something was coming," Dixon said. "It's either that or she carries recording capability at all times just in case something interesting happens."

"Seems that way, yes." Nolan said.

"Where did she get this insight? How could she know that you were going to make this proposal?"

"We were set up," Nolan replied.

"Obviously, but how?"

"Our own investigator, Thomas Cummings, told me to approach her with this offer."

Arthur Lindstrom replied, "This is more than an idea that didn't work; Cummings had to be in on it. How else could Sarah Willis be ready to record the conversation?"

"You're right, Arthur," Dixon said, "So, what should we do about it?"

Nolan, angrily replied, "I'll talk to that little son of a bitch, Cummings. I find out why he sold us out."

"As to what we do about the tape and transcript," Dixon said, "I guess nothing for now. They haven't released it, so they just want us to know it's out there."

"That's my feeling, too," Lindstrom replied. "Maybe it will get released if Jim testifies against John Willis, but probably not until then."

"I'll find out what I can from Cummings," Nolan said. Then we can decide what to do about it. Maybe we just let them release it. Why do we have to care?"

"It's bad press, Jim," Dixon said. "You offering to walk from supporting a criminal action if they take what you're offering in the lawsuit? The talking heads will be all over it." He was quiet a moment, and then said, "Okay, no action for now, other than grilling Cummings," Dixon concluded. "Let's update in a couple of days."

Tom Cummings sat in the waiting area adjacent to the CEO's office. He knew why he was here; there could be no other reason.

"Mr. Nolan will see you now, Mr. Cummings," the mid-thirties brunette seated behind the desk offered. "Follow me."

"She entered a door and he followed her down a hallway. She opened another door and he found himself in a luxurious office that featured exquisite furnishings and breathtaking city views. There was a conference room table that seated eight in one quadrant of the room. A fireplace and two armchairs occupied a second quadrant. The remainder was dedicated to a large desk by the windows, with two elegant visitor chairs.

Nolan stood and gestured to one of the visitor chairs. "Sit, Mr. Cummings."

"Yes, sir," Cummings replied, and walked across the immense room to the seat designated. He sat and said nothing, conscious of the fact that he was already sweating.

"We have a problem, Mr. Cummings." Cummings said nothing. "It seems that you gave me some bad information." Still no reply. "You told me to approach Ms. Willis with a suggestion that we walk from supporting a criminal action against her husband if she would accept our last offer." Nolan leaned forward in his chair, studying Cummings' reactions. "You remember giving me that advice, right?"

"Yes, sir."

"Turns out that not only was that bad advice, Ms. Willis recorded our conversation, so she clearly knew what was coming." He furrowed his brow and asked, "How did that happen, Mr. Cummings?"

Cummings felt the sweat on his forehead. "I don't know, sir."

"That is not a satisfactory answer. Try again." He paused and said, "The way I see it, you had a conversation with Scott

Winslow or his investigator, Lee Henry, to set this up. Why don't you tell me about that?"

Cummings did not know what to say. He wanted to confess to Nolan, but he couldn't. Lee Henry had him by the balls, and if he said a word, he would get charged for his threats to Sarah Willis. There was just nowhere to go with this. "I don't know how that happened," Cummings repeated. "I thought that this would be a way to end the whole thing—to help you."

"And why did you think that?"

"I don't know."

Nolan snarled, "You don't know? What kind of bullshit is that?"

Cummings reassessed the situation and there was no doubt what he had to do. His first priority was to avoid criminal charges. "I don't know," Cummings repeated. "I don't have any additional information."

"Goodbye, Mr. Cummings. You are disloyal and you have made an enemy of this Company. Not only will you never again work for us, I will do everything I can to assure that you are never hired by anyone." He shook his head. "Now, get out of my office."

Cummings stood up slowly. He was shaking and felt sick to his stomach. He moved slowly towards the door, trying desperately to find some satisfactory answer he could give to Nolan. Nothing came to mind. Maybe this guy could hurt his business opportunities, but he could stay out of jail and still return to his bread and butter, following disloyal spouses and filming their affairs.

* * *

Lee dialed the phone and waited. "McKinley Bass and Krieger," a soft, female voice answered.

"Greg Munson, please," Lee said.

"Can I tell him who is calling?"

"Yes," Lee said, "Tell him it's Robert Stimson, a potential client of his."

"Just a minute, please." There was a couple of minutes of elevator music, and then a voice said, "Greg Munson."

"Hi, Greg."

The response was distinctly cold. "What do you want?"

"We need to meet one more time," Lee replied. "I have some important and very private information for you."

Munson was quiet for a time and then said, "Okay."

"The day after tomorrow at noon?"

"All right," Munson said, tentatively.

"See you then," Lee said.

Chapter Twenty-Six

Judge Elizabeth Burke had a regal appearance on the bench, which lent an appropriate air of dignity to the proceeding, and kept jurors attentive. She also had a common sense and an insightful approach to every issue presented.

Scott Winslow and Michael Graber stood at their respective counsel tables arguing a pre-trial motion to the court before the newly-selected jury was seated to begin the trial. "I've read the briefs from both sides in connection with the defense motion to exclude the testimony of witness Margo Traynor. Mr. Graber, in a nutshell it is your position that Ms. Traynor's testimony concerning prior harassment by Mr. Nolan should not be admitted because this is a rape case and because she never reported the incident to her employer. Is that correct?"

"That's right, your Honor. Both of those issues are critical, and to allow her testimony creates prejudice against the defendants. A bell that cannot be unrung."

She furrowed her brow and nodded. She asked, "Mr. Winslow, do you want to be heard?"

"Yes, your Honor. Let me address both points briefly. As to the first, there are indeed rape allegations here. There are also harassment allegations that pre-date the rape. Additionally, Mr. Nolan testified in his deposition that he had never harassed, improperly touched or made inappropriate sexual comments to any employee in the workplace. Accordingly, Ms. Traynor's testimony directly impeaches Mr. Nolan's deposition testimony. As to the statement that Ms. Traynor did not report Mr. Nolan's conduct to her employer, first, the evidence will show that she did, but even if she had not, I would remind the Court that many women who are harassed do not report. They are intimidated, they feel trapped, and don't know what to do. Not reporting the conduct is a question of credibility, not admissibility. Finally, your honor, this evidence is only prejudicial in the sense that bad facts hurt a party's case. This is not a case of probative value being outweighed by the prejudice of evidence of dubious relevance."

"Mr. Graber, your response?"

"Yes, your Honor. We now live in a world where many come forward with claims of harassment, and we have to be careful not to give weight to the unproven. That is the source of the prejudice. In this case, Ms. Traynor's allegations were never tested because she never filed a report."

"Your Honor, if I may," Scott interjected. "It is inaccurate to state that these allegations were not reported. To the contrary, she told the HR department and they failed to act. They ultimately told her they could file a formal report, but if they did, her status as a 'team member' might be called into question."

"All right. Counsel, I have fully considered the motion, and the motion is denied. Mr. Graber, you can question Ms. Traynor as to her allegations, and you can argue her credibility, but these are questions of fact and do not present a basis to exclude the evidence."

"Thank you, your Honor," Scott said.

"Thank you, your Honor," was echoed by Graber.

* * *

The courtroom was a big rectangle, cut in half by a waist-high, gated wall that separated the press and the spectators from the participants. The gate opened to a walkway that allowed access to the witness stand and the counsel tables that faced the judge. The bench was elevated and the jury box was to the judge's left as she looked into the courtroom, allowing her, as well as the jurors, to get a good look at the demeanor and appearance of each witness. On the judge's right side was a cubicle similar to the witness stand occupied by the court clerk. In front of the judge, the court reporter was positioned so that she could hear and see witnesses as they testified, and counsel as they asked questions. On the judge's far right was another desk, where the Sheriff's officer who served as bailiff kept an eye on the courtroom proceedings. There was a lectern near the separation wall, just a few feet from the jury box, where both counsel could station themselves to make their statements to the jury, and to question witnesses.

When they returned to the courtroom, Sarah Willis sat next to Scott at the counsel table closest to the jury. She wore a gray suit, and was doing her best not to appear nervous. The bailiff seated the carefully-selected jury in the box, and returned to his seat. The seven men and five women in the jury box, who had taken a day and a half to select, awaited what came next, attentively. Judge Burke looked at the jury and calmly stated, "Ladies and gentlemen, we are now ready for opening statements from counsel. Opening statements are not evidence. Rather, they are statements by counsel of what they believe the evidence will show."

Judge Burke turned her attention to the counsel tables and said, "Mr. Winslow, are you ready?"

"Yes, thank you, your Honor," Scott said, as he stood and walked to the lectern.

He turned to the jury and said, "Good morning, ladies and gentlemen. As you know, I am Scott Winslow, and I represent the plaintiff, Sarah Willis in connection with this matter. This case is about harassment, and rape, by Ellison's CEO, James

Nolan. It is a case about abuse of power." He let that statement settle on the courtroom. "The evidence will show you that Sarah Willis was a talented and devoted employee with four successful years of service at Ellison Company. You will see that she had good evaluations, and was well-respected. That matters, because shortly after complaining about rape and harassment by James Nolan, Ellison's CEO, fired her.

The evidence will show you that the defendant made sexual comments to Ms. Willis. Many times he made comments to her like "You look really hot today," and "Wow, you're looking good." He told her that her husband was lucky to be climbing into bed with her. He also made it a regular practice to let his eyes slide down to her chest. Then, he told her that he wanted to make love to her. He told her that they could really spice things up.

The evidence will show that those last statements happened right before he asked Ms. Willis to go to Seattle to attend a business meeting. She went to Seattle to find that Nolan would not attend the meeting, leaving her to cover it alone, even though it was outside of her area of responsibility. When she returned to the hotel, the defendant called her and said he was back from an emergency meeting he had been called upon to attend, and that he needed to talk to her in the hotel lounge. She met him in the lounge, where he had three drinks, while she sipped from a single glass of wine. She told him that she was tired, and wanted to go back to her room and get some sleep. He asked her to stop by his room on the way, to pick up documents he wanted her to review. Ms. Willis will testify that when they arrived at his room, he handed her the documents he wanted her to review. As she started to leave, he pinned her against the wall, and forced a kiss on her. She broke away and ran out of the room. She went to her room, distressed by what had happened. She began to get undressed for bed, putting a hotel robe over her undergarments. Then, the defendant was pounding on her hotel room door. She asked what he wanted and he said to apologize. At first, she told him he could apologize tomorrow. He repeatedly pleaded for just a single moment to apologize in person. When she opened the door, he pushed inside and closed the door. Then, he threw her on the bed, and he raped her. You will hear her testify that she fought hard, but was unable to fight him off. When it was over, he then left her devastated and bleeding. She will tell you how she showered, but couldn't seem to get clean, and how she then sat on the bathroom floor sobbing. At about 3:00 a.m., she got dressed and made her way to the airport to fly home. You will learn that she had been scheduled as a speaker the following morning and never attended. She went home and went to bed. At first, Sarah felt torn apart and was hopeless, and she stayed in bed. The rape was Wednesday night, and she returned home the early morning hours of Thursday morning, in desperation and feeling lost. On Friday morning, she confided in a close friend, who convinced her to tell her husband, to the report the rape to the police and to the human resources department at Ellison."

Scott could see that the jurors' eyes were locked on his, listening carefully to every word. He continued, "Sarah has been profoundly affected in every aspect of her life. She has suffered from depression, anxiety, attack dreams multiple times each week, sleeplessness and a lack of confidence. Sarah has always been a self-assured woman, charged with responsibility and happy to fulfil it. Now, she faces a lack of confidence for the first time. She is afraid. She is afraid because the defendant overpowered her. He stole her sense of safety, and the fear is always there: It happened once, and she now lives in fear that it could happen again.

The defendants are going to tell you this was a one night affair, but when you listen to the testimony from Ms. Willis and all of the other witnesses, you will know that is just an attempt not to accept responsibility for the deplorable act that James Nolan perpetrated. You are the judge of the credibility of witnesses. You decide who to believe and whose testimony doesn't hold up under scrutiny. The case also presents questions of retaliatory termination for complaining about the rape and harassment by the defendant." He gestured disapprovingly toward Nolan, and then continued, "The defendant fired Ms. Willis after she complained about his behavior. The defendant will tell you that he fired Ms. Willis for two reasons. Both of which are clearly false. One false reason was that his subordinates needed to be able to communicate with him directly and her submitting an analysis through the human resources department was unacceptable. In fact, the human resources department had approved her sending the analysis to Nolan through them. The second false reason for the termination was alleged poor performance. The evidence will show that Ms. Willis had an outstanding performance record and that Mr. Nolan talked about promoting her shortly before the attack.

In this case we are seeking damages for the devastating consequence of the harassment and rape, the emotional consequences that don't go away. You will hear from Doctor Laurie Spencer, who will talk to you about the emotional injury that Ms. Willis suffered because of the actions of the defendant. Doctor Spencer will tell you about Ms. Willis' condition after the attack and through today. We are also seeking recovery of her lost wages and benefits.

One final word about the burden of proof we are required to meet in this case. This is not a criminal case and the burden of proof is not beyond a reasonable doubt. It is a preponderance of the evidence. Meaning that a simple majority of the evidence is enough to satisfy the burden of proof. Thank you for your careful attention ladies and gentlemen and I look forward to speaking with you again after all of the evidence has been presented for your consideration." Scott walked back to his seat and John caught his eye from the gallery and gave him a nod. He sat down and Sarah squeezed his arm. She whispered, "Thank you, Scott."

"Mr. Graber," Judge Burke said, "your opening statement."

"Thank you, your Honor." He walked to the podium and then looked at the jurors.

"Good morning," he said, and then added, "My colleague, Mr. Winslow, is a good speaker, but like the judge told you, opening statements are not evidence. In this case, the facts will show you that Ms. Willis and Mr. Nolan had a brief affair and then she panicked. For whatever reason: guilt, not wanting her husband to learn what she had done, or not being able to accept the truth, she made up this story about a rape." He took a breath and then continued. "Now, it's true that Mr. Nolan flirted with Ms. Willis. That happened. And she flirted back. It carried on for some time, until they found themselves on a business trip in the same hotel in Seattle. They had a couple of drinks together and they made love. Affairs sometimes happen in the business world. People work together and they get close. That was all there was to it, until Ms. Willis falsely accused Mr. Nolan of rape. Mr. Nolan will testify that he is embarrassed about all of this. Embarrassed that he had an affair with a co-worker and embarrassed that it led to this hideous, and ill-founded, accusation. Imagine, if you will, how dealing with such allegations affects the reputation of a hard-working and successful business man with a large company to run. Ms. Willis was terminated by Mr. Nolan, not for filing these claims, even though they are false, but because of his concerns about her performance and for failing to be able to work with him. Now, we know that harassment happens in the workplace. Rape happens as well. And we know that such an experience is a great hardship. But consider that when such allegations are made falsely, they have a devastating effect on the accused." He paused a moment and then continued, "Harassment and rape are completely intolerable, but none of it happened here. This was a consensual relationship that turned bad only because Ms. Willis could not live with the decision that she had made to become involved with her boss. This is a time for accountability, to be sure. It's a time to be truthful and account for the decisions and mistakes that one makes, including having an affair with your boss. The facts will show you that Mr. Nolan and Ms. Willis became involved, and that she refuses to own that truth. Maybe it is because she is married and didn't want to admit that she strayed. Whatever the reason, she fabricated these claims and she needs to be held accountable. For that reason, we are going to ask you to help her face those facts by returning a verdict for the defense in this case. Thank you ladies and gentlemen."

Scott was watching the jurors as Graber spoke. The jury also seemed to be following him closely, but there wasn't much body language revealing their thoughts.

Graber sat down and Judge Burke said, "Mr. Winslow, call your first witness."

"Yes, your Honor. We call Ms. Sarah Willis to the stand."

Sarah stood and walked to the witness stand. She took a seat and the clerk asked, "Do you swear to tell the truth, the whole truth and nothing but the truth, so help you God?"

"I do," Sarah said.

Scott stood and said, "Good morning, Ms. Willis."

"Good morning," she responded.

"Tell us a little about your background. Do you have a post high school degree?"

"I have a Bachelor's in Finance and an MBA."

"Tell us about your employment history." Sarah took Scott and the jurors through the three companies she had worked for before Ellison, and the positions and promotions obtained at each.

"Ever fired from any position before Ellison?"

Graber looked like he was about to object, but remained silent. "Never," Sarah replied.

"Who did you report to at Ellison?"

"The CEO, James Nolan."

"How long was he your supervisor?"

"Since he started with the company. About a year."

"Did you made a trip to Seattle, shortly before you were terminated?"

"Yes"

"Let's talk about the time between Mr. Nolan's arrival as your supervisor and the Seattle trip. During that period, did he do or say anything that you found to be offensive or inappropriate?"

Graber stood. "Object, your Honor, overbroad and vague and ambiguous."

"Overruled," Judge Burke ordered.

"Do you have the question in mind?" Scott asked.

"Yes, I do. And the answer is yes."

"What words or actions were those?"

"Mr. Nolan repeatedly told me that I was hot. He told me that I looked really good. On a couple of different occasions he told me how lucky my husband was to be climbing into bed with me every night, which I found really creepy. Then, shortly before the Seattle trip, he told me that he wanted to have sex with me. That we could spice things up."

"Anything else that he said or did that you found offensive or inappropriate?"

"Yes."

"What?"

"He had this habit of letting his eyes fall to my chest and he would stare at my breasts. He did that on many occasions."

"Let's talk about your response to these events. What, if anything, did you say to him when he would stare at your breasts?"

"At first, I let it pass. When he kept doing it, I said that my eyes are up here. He just laughed. Then on a couple of other occasions I told him that he was making me uncomfortable."

"What did he say in response?"

She shook her head. "He just laughed at that, too."

"What was your responsive to his comments that you look good or hot?"

"The first time I said nothing. The second I told him that made me uncomfortable."

"And what did he say?"

"Nothing. At that point he was looking at my breasts and said nothing."

"How frequently did he tell you that you were hot or looked good."

"Many times; well over a dozen."

"What was your response to his statements that your husband was lucky to be climbing into bed with you?"

"I told him that I did not want to talk about sex or my sex life. I told him that I just wanted to do my job."

"When he told you that he wanted to have sex with you, how did you respond?"

"I was angry. I said that it was inappropriate and that I only wanted to talk about work."

"And how did he react?"

"He grinned, apparently amused, and then he said he wanted me in his bed and walked out of my office."

"How did the trip to Seattle come about?"

"Mr. Nolan told me that he wanted me to go. That he had another meeting to attend and I needed to cover the one he originally scheduled."

"Your response?"

"I was a little confused. This meeting was about a corporate acquisition that Ellison was making and it was not finance related. In other words, it was out of my area."

"How did he explain that?"

"He didn't. I raised that issue, but he just said he couldn't make the meeting so I needed to cover it."

"I had to be up in Seattle for a presentation that I was making the following day, so it just meant going a day early. The only hesitation was that these guys would have questions and concerns outside of my area of expertise, and they did."

"So you went to this meeting?"

"Yes."

"And then what did you do?"

"I returned to the hotel around 9:30. I was exhausted, so I went up to my room. Then I got a call from Mr. Nolan telling me he had to talk to me and to meet him in the bar."

"Did you do that?"

"Yes."

"What happened in the bar?"

"He had three drinks while thanking me for covering the meeting he couldn't attend."

"Did you have anything to drink?"

"I sipped on one glass of wine that I never finished, and then I said I was going to bed."

"And did you leave at that point?"

"No."

"Why not?"

"Mr. Nolan told me that on my way up to my room I needed to stop by his and pick up some documents that he needed me to review and give him an opinion after I digested them."

"And you agreed?"

"At first, I suggested that I just look at them in the morning because I was tired."

"He said it will only take a minute to pick them up and take them with you, so I reluctantly agreed."

"Then what happened?"

"When we got in the room, he handed me a folder and as I turned to leave, he pushed me against the wall and kissed me."

"What did you do?"

"I pushed him away and ran out of his room."

"Did you go to your room?"

"I did, I went to the room and put on one of those hotel robes while I washed my face and got ready for bed."

"Did you hear from Mr. Nolan again that night?"

"Yes."

"What happened?"

"I was getting ready for bed and there was this knock at the door. I asked who it was and he said Jim Nolan. I asked what he wanted and he said that he just wanted to apologize. He said that he shouldn't have tried to kiss me and that he felt really bad about it. He said he wanted just a moment to apologize, face-to-face."

"How did you reply?"

"I told him that we could talk about it tomorrow, because I was really tired. He said, please, just one minute. I told him again that we could discuss it in the morning. He said he felt really bad and just needed a few seconds."

"How did you respond to that?" Scott asked.

"I didn't do anything and then he knocked again. I said tomorrow we could talk and then he pleaded again for just one minute." Sarah began to fight back tears as she said, "God help me, I opened the door to let him talk."

Scott waited a moment and then asked, "Are you okay to continue?"

"Yes, thank you," she replied softly.

"What happened when you opened the door?"

She looked directly at Nolan and said, "He stepped into the room and pushed the door closed. He stared at me in my robe. I asked him to get out, but he didn't move. Then he pushed me backwards onto the bed and threw himself on top of me." She was quiet a moment and tears appeared in her eyes that rolled down her cheeks. She pushed one tear away and let out a breath. Then, she said, "I fought as hard as I could, but he was too strong and I couldn't make him stop."

"So what happened next?"

"He forced himself inside of me." Her expression was first angry, and then turned sad.

Scott took a moment as he watched the jury carefully watching Sarah, then he asked, "I'm sorry to have to ask something so distasteful, but did he finish?"

She just nodded, solemnly.

"I'm sorry, Sarah, I have to ask you to answer with words so that the court reporter can get your answer,"

"Yes," she said.

"And then?"

"And then he stood and straightened his clothing and ran out of the room."

"What did you do next?" Scott asked.

She was fighting tears as she said, "I felt totally violated, and totally lost. Time went by and I was sobbing. At some point, I went into the shower and scrubbed and scrubbed, but I didn't feel like I could get clean." She fought emotion, releasing a deep breath, and then added, "Finally, I climbed out of the shower and sat down on the floor of the bathroom. I sat there crying until around 3:00 in the morning. At that point, I threw everything I had together in my suitcase and left. I got a ride to the airport and went home, where I climbed into bed for the next two days."

"Did you tell your husband what happened?"

"Not at first. I couldn't bring myself to tell him what this man did to me. So, I told him I didn't feel well."

"You said you stayed in bed for a couple of days?"

"Yes."

"And then what?"

'Then a close friend of mine, Angie, called and I began sobbing on the phone. I told her everything."

"What did she say?"

"She was horrified and supportive and everything a best friend should be. She also told me that I had to tell John, and that I had to report it to the police and to the company."

"And how did you respond?"

Sarah was quiet. She shook her head and said, "At first, I didn't know if I was strong enough to do all that. I just wanted the horror of it all to go away." She cupped her hands over her mouth a moment, and then added, "And then I realized that I had to do it. I had to stand up and tell my story and I had to make him accountable for what he did. So, I told John, and then I reported the rape and the previous harassment to the police and to the company."

"To whom did you report the rape and harassment at the company?"

"Bob Berg, the Human Resources Director."

"How did he respond?"

"He said that they would investigate."

"Did you talk to him further?"

"I did."

"What was said?"

"I told him that I was given an assignment by Mr. Nolan, but I couldn't deal with him directly because of the attack."

"What did Mr. Berg say?"

"Bob said I could turn in the assignment to him, and he would deliver it to Mr. Nolan."

"Did you do that?"

"I did."

Scott nodded and asked, "And did you get a response from anyone?"

"Yes, from Mr. Nolan."

"What did he say?"

"He told me that if I couldn't deal directly with him, I couldn't do my job, so he was firing me."

"What was your reaction?"

"Total shock. I told him that it was because of the attack."

"Then what happened?"

"I'll never forget the look on his face as he smugly told me that no one was going to believe me."

Scott let that answer settle on the room for a moment, and then asked, "How did the rape affect you emotionally?"

Sarah was quiet a moment and then said, "It has changed my whole world." Tears began again, and she said, "I'm so sorry," looking over at the jury.

Scott nodded slowly, and then said, "Tell us what you mean by that."

"I couldn't sleep for the longest time and when I did, I started having nightmares about being attacked, being chased and being over-powered. I woke up covered in sweat and sometimes screaming. I also suffered from depression and anxiety and periodic panic attacks. Every day I'm either focused on the violation, or it's in the corner of my mind. I can't seem to get free of it, no matter what I do." She looked over at the jury and said, "I was raised to be strong and independent and I really believed that I was both of those things. But now I know it was an illusion. My self-confidence and my belief that I can do anything are just gone." She pushed a tear back and added, "And I hate it so much."

"Have you sought treatment?"

"Yes. I have been seeing psychologist, Laurie Spencer."

"How often?"

"Twice a week for the first few months, and now I see Dr. Spencer once every week."

"Has she helped you?" Scott asked.

Sarah nodded. "She really has. I think I am better than I was."

"Have you been seeking re-employment?"

"Yes, since about three months ago. As soon as I felt I could."

"And did you find another job?"

"Not yet. The same people who used to encourage me to leave Ellison and join them are distant, and staying away."

"Sarah, you know that the defense in this case claims there was no rape. That you had an affair with Jim Nolan that you just don't want to admit. What do you say to that?"

"I say that they are lying. I was never involved with Mr. Nolan and just wanted to do my job." She shook her head and added, "You know, that is why women don't want to come forward when they are attacked. They get victimized all over again. First physically, and then their reputation is put on trial. It is not right." She leaned forward in the jury box and said, "I want Jim Nolan to be held accountable for what he did."

Graber stood and said, "I object, your Honor. Non-responsive. I move to strike everything beginning with why women don't come forward."

"Objection sustained and motion granted. The jury will disregard the statements about why women don't come forward."

Scott smiled inwardly, because that important point had been made, and everyone in the room knew it was true. He said, "Let me have you take a look at Exhibit 12." Sarah turned to Exhibit 12 in the book in front of her and said, "I have it."

"What is that document?"

"My W-2 for last year."

"Does it accurately depict your earnings?"

"It does."

"Look now at Exhibit 13. What is that document?"

"This is the statement of the value of my 401K at the beginning and the end of last year."

"Let me show you Exhibit 14, contained in this baggy. What is Exhibit 14?"

Sarah stared at the exhibit with a sad expression. After a time, she said, "My torn underwear from the night of the rape."

Scott was quiet a moment and then said, "One more thing. You told us that you left the hotel at around 3:00 in the morning on the night of the attack, correct?"

"I object to the word attack," Graber interjected, standing."

"Well," Judge Burke responded, "that's certainly the way she characterized it, so I'll overrule the objection."

"Do I have that correct?" Scott asked.

"Yes."

"And you were scheduled to do a presentation the next morning?"

"I was, but I just couldn't go."

"Did Mr. Nolan ever call you or leave you a message asking why you were a no-show that morning?"

"No."

"Did he ever suggest that he didn't know why you weren't there?"

"Never."

"Thank you, Ms. Willis, that's all I have for now," Scott said.

Judge Burke looked towards the defense table and asked, "Mr. Graber, cross-examination?"

"Yes your Honor," Graber responded, standing and walking to the lectern. "Ms. Willis, you were in a management position at Ellison, correct?"

"Yes, correct."

"You supervised other employees?"

"I did."

"And you were required to know the human resource policies that governed all employees, right?"

"Yes."

"You consider yourself to be someone that tried hard to comply with company policies that pertain to your employment?"

"Yes."

"And you knew that the policies require a supervisor to act immediately to report any harassment, right?"

"Yes."

"But you didn't report the fact that Mr. Nolan was supposedly looking at your breasts?"

"Objection, your Honor, argumentative as to the word supposedly."

"Overruled, this is cross-examination."

Graber asked, "On the occasions that you believed Mr. Nolan was looking at your breasts, did you never report that conduct before the trip to Seattle, correct?"

"No."

"Who witnessed him staring at your breasts?"

"I don't know."

"You can't identify anyone?"

"No."

"Comments he made to you about you being hot or wanting to sleep with you, you never reported those at any time before the trip to Seattle, either?"

"Yes, that's right."

"Who heard those comments?"

"I don't know of anyone."

"So, you never reported any of these things and no one heard them?"

"Argumentative and asked and answered, Your Honor," Scott interjected.

"Sustained," Judge Burke ruled.

"In Seattle, you went with Mr. Nolan to his room, right?"

"Yes, to pick up documents he requested I review."

"And you kissed in his room?"

"Wrong. He pushed me against the wall and forced a kiss on me while I struggled."

"So, you were highly offended by his conduct?"

"Yes."

"So much so, that you ran out of the room and back to your room, right?"

"Yes, that's right."

"Then, you took your clothes off and let Mr. Nolan back into your room, right?"

"Object, your Honor, misstates former testimony. She was not without clothing covering her," Scott said.

"Sustained."

"You put on a robe?"

"Yes."

"With only undergarments beneath your robe?"

"Yes."

"And then you let this man who kissed you against your will and whom you were so offended by into your room, is that it?"

"Yes, unfortunately, I gave him a chance to apologize after several attempts. It was the biggest mistake of my life."

"After your trip to Seattle, you testified that you returned home and went to bed."

"Yes."

"As far as your husband was concerned, and everyone else for that matter, you pretended to be sick, right?"

"I wasn't pretending. I was seriously damaged by what happened in Seattle."

"But you didn't tell your husband the truth?"

"Not immediately, no."

"You had a good relationship with your husband?"

"Yes. Did and still do."

"But you still kept these important things from him?"

"For a couple of days."

"You had a good relationship with Bob Berg in Human Resources as well?"

"It was a working relationship, but we got along fine," Sarah replied.

"Yet you didn't report all these offensive occurrences to him either, right?"

"Like I said, not until a couple of days after the Seattle trip."

"You've been seeking reemployment, right?"

"Yes," Sarah responded.

"And as soon as you find a job, you are ready to get back to work?"

"I really want to, yes."

Graber reflected a moment and then asked, "You're not trying to blame Mr. Nolan for the fact that you haven't found a job yet, right."

It was Sarah's turn to think for a moment, and then she replied, "I cannot prove that he has stopped me from finding a position."

"You are not aware of him saying anything negative to any prospective employer about you, right?"

"Right. I just know that a number of these companies were chasing me to get me to work for them for a couple of years before my termination, and then all of a sudden, the same people don't want to talk. In fairness, it could just be that some are aware of the dispute and don't want involvement."

Graber turned to the judge and said, "I move to strike everything after the word 'right' from the answer as non-responsive, your Honor."

"Granted," Judge Burke said, "the jury is to disregard the answer given after the word 'right.'"

Graber was thoughtful a moment and then said. "I am still a little confused about how a manager, knowing that she's required to report all occurrences of harassment doesn't report any of them."

Scott stood and interjected, "I object, argumentative. That's not even a question."

Judge Burked nodded. "Sustained."

"Of course, none of these things would have been reported if you were flirting and involved in a voluntary relationship with Mr. Nolan, right?"

"Objection, your Honor, argumentative, and an incomplete and inappropriate hypothetical question." Scott said, again.

"I agree, sustained. Mr. Graber, you can ask her if she was involved in a voluntary relationship if you choose."

"Thank you, your Honor. I have nothing further," Graber replied.

"Redirect, Mr. Winslow?" Judge Burke asked.

"Yes, your Honor," Scott replied.

Scott stood and said, "Let's ask the direct question that counsel was indirectly alluding to with his questions. Did you ever have any affair with Mr. Nolan?"

"No, I did not," Sarah said, firmly.

"Did you flirt with him?"

"I did not."

"Did you have any relationship with him other than your working relationship?"

"No, sir."

"Did you ever want to?"

"Never," Sarah replied.

"That's all I have, your Honor."

"Mr. Graber?" the Judge said, turning her attention in his direction.

"No, nothing further with this witness, your Honor."

"Okay," Judge Burke said, "you may step down Ms. Willis."

As Sarah walked back to the counsel table to sit next to Scott, Judge Burke said, "Call your next witness, Mr. Winslow."

"Yes, your Honor. We call James Nolan to the stand under California Evidence Code Section 776."

Judge Burke looked towards that jury and said, "Ladies and gentlemen, a witness being called under this Code Section can be treated as a hostile witness because he or she is associated with the opposing party."

Nolan walked to the witness stand and was sworn in. Scott walked to the lectern and looked at him a moment before asking, "Mr. Nolan, you are the CEO of Ellison Company?"

"Yes, sir."

"And you were also Ms. Willis' immediate supervisor for about a year before the trip to Seattle took place?"

"Yes."

"As the corporate CEO, you have to be familiar with corporate human resource policies, right?"

"Yes."

"You know that the company had a so-called "zero-tolerance policy" where sexual harassment is concerned, correct?"

"Yes."

"Why don't you tell the jury what a zero tolerance policy is, sir?"

"It is a policy that says that we don't tolerate any form of sexual harassment."

"That includes, sexual comments and sexual advances, right?

"Yes."

"And it also includes any inappropriate or offensive touching?"

"Yes."

"You are also aware that engaging in inappropriate touching and making sexual comments are both prohibited by law, correct?

"Yes."

"So, did you ever make any sexually oriented comments to Ms. Willis?"

"Probably, we were flirting and got involved." Scott hesitated a moment as this was entirely unexpected. He had to suppress a smile as he glanced at Graber, who knew the significance of what his client just said, and looked concerned. This was Nolan trying to better his testimony by taking the position that those who are involved make sexual comments. A decent position to take, unless your deposition had been previously taken and you didn't testify the same way.

"I see. So, exactly what comments of a sexual nature did you make?"

"I don't remember, but people who are romantically involved say intimate things to one another."

"You remember any of the intimate things you said?"

313

"No."

"How many times did you say intimate things to Ms. Willis?"

"I have no idea. I didn't count them."

"Your Honor," Scott said, looking toward Judge Burke, "I propose to read from page 111, line 22 to page 112 line 6, of Mr. Nolan's deposition."

Judge Burke flipped to the pages in the deposition in front of her. "Counsel," she said to Graber, "any objection."

"Yes, your Honor. It lacks foundation as to his knowledge of the policies."

"Overruled," Judge Burke said. "You may proceed, Mr. Winslow."

"Thank you, your Honor."

"Commencing on page 111, line 22 and continuing through page 112 line 6. Question: Did you ever make sexual comments of any kind to Ms. Willis?"

Answer: "No."

Question: "To your understanding, would it be violative of Ellison Company policies to make sexual comments to an employee?"

Answer: "Yes."

Scott closed the transcript and looked up at Nolan. "That was your testimony under oath, correct sir?"

"Yes, but..."

"It was a yes or no question, sir."

Nolan looked angry and the jury could see it. His arrogance could only be contained for so long, so Scott wanted to keep pushing."

"Mr Nolan, did you tell Ms. Willis that sleeping with you would spice up your sex lives?"

"No."

"Did you stare at her breasts at any time?"

"No."

"Did you tell her that her husband was lucky to be climbing into bed with her at night?"

"No."

"Did you tell her that she looked hot?"

"No."

"You asked her to stop by your room to get a document, didn't you?"

"Maybe, that's how it started."

"And when you got to your room, did you give her a document?"

"Yes."

"And then, did you force her up against the wall and kiss her?"

"No, I kissed her and she was willing."

"Did she tell you that?"

"No, when you move to kiss someone and they participate you know they are willing."

"Was she still willing when she ran out of your room?"

"She didn't run out of my room."

"Did you both stay in your room?"

"No."

"What did you do?"

"We both went to her room."

"Why?"

Nolan got the message about what happened when he strayed from his deposition testimony and he wasn't going to do it again. "I don't know."

"Is it your testimony that you both walked to her room together?"

"Yes."

"You didn't go from your room to hers separately then?"

"Right."

"So there was no time that evening when you were knocking on her door and asking to be let in."

"That's right."

"Did you, when you were in Ms. Willis' room, force her onto the bed and rape her?"

"No, sir. Of course not. We had consensual sex."

"I believe that you described it as tender, is that right?"

Nolan looked uncomfortable, but he wasn't risking changing his testimony. "That's correct."

"So, tender, that you ripped her panties and caused her serious bleeding, right?"

"Objection, your Honor, argumentative."

"Sustained," Judge Burke responded.

Scott nodded and asked, "Her panties were torn off her, weren't they?"

"No."

"Any idea how they got torn?"

"Calls for speculation, I object, your Honor," Graber interjected.

"Overruled."

"Do you have the question in mind, sir?" Scott asked.

"I don't know if or how that happened. We were pretty enthusiastic though."

"I see, you were enthusiastic." Scott said.

"Objection, argumentative."

"Sustained," Judge Burke ruled.

"Mr. Nolan, you left Ms. Willis' room after a short period, right."

"I'm not sure how long I was there"

"Was it more than a half hour?"

"I don't know."

"Why did you leave?"

"We needed to get some rest for the following morning."

"You both had presentations to make, right?"

"Right."

"Did you make yours?"

"Yes."

"Did Ms. Willis show up for hers?"

"No."

"You must have been concerned about her absence after being with her the night before, right?"

"No, I don't think so."

"Weren't you worried about the fact that she wasn't there? That she was sick?"

"No, I was really busy."

"Mr. Nolan, at some point you were told there was an investigation into Ms. Willis' complaint that you sexually harassed and raped her, right?"

"Yes."

"A human resources representative told you that Company policy that you be suspended during the investigation, right?"

He was quiet for a moment, and then said, "Yes."

"Who told you that?"

"Human Resources Director, Bob Berg."

"And he was right about that, wasn't he? I mean, it was Ellison Company policy that when sexual harassment complaints are made against any employee, they are to be suspended during the period of the investigation?"

Scott could see Nolan thinking about a way to evade answering. Scott reached for an exhibit and Nolan said, "Yes, that's right."

"And what was your answer, sir, when Mr. Berg told you that the policy called for your suspension?"

"I told him that I was too busy to be suspended."

"And as a result, you weren't suspended, correct?"

"Correct. The demands on a CEO running a big company are unrelenting," Nolan offered.

Scott nodded and then asked, "Sir, within two weeks after the investigation commenced, you fired Ms. Willis, right?"

"Yes."

"Why?"

"I need those at the top to be able to communicate directly with me on important issues and she couldn't."

"Any other reasons?"

"I had concerns about her performance."

"Really? For how long?"

"About six months."

"Is there any document that you can point to that existed before the trip to Seattle which references inadequate or substandard performance by Ms. Willis?"

"No."

"Who did you tell that you had any dissatisfaction with Ms. Willis' performance before the trip to Seattle?"

"I don't think I told anyone."

"Now let's address this issue of communication. Do you know that Ms. Willis told HR that she was concerned about communicating with you directly because you raped her?"

"I don't know."

"Are you aware that Bob Berg told Ms. Willis she could submit her work through HR during the period of the investigation?"

"I don't know if I was aware of that at the time?"

"But you did at some point find out that was the case, didn't you?"

"Yes."

"So you fired her for doing what HR said was acceptable?"

"Like I said, my people at the top have to be able to communicate with me directly. It's critical."

"Or did you fire her because she complained about you harassing and raping her?"

"Object, your Honor. Argumentative, as the witness already answered," Graber interjected.

"Overruled," Judge Burke replied.

"No, sir. I fired her for the reasons I gave you."

Scott said, "One more thing, sir. Did you ever make sexual comments to any woman at Ellison or anywhere else you worked?"

"No."

"Did you ever sexually or inappropriately touch or grope any woman at Ellison or anywhere else you worked?"

"No."

"Did you ever tell an employee at any place you worked that you wanted sex?"

"No."

"Did you ever reach up under a female employee's skirt at any place you worked?"

No."

"Did you ever tell any female employee that she was going to have sex with you and if she were to complain, her job would be gone?"

"No."

"That's all I have, your Honor," Scott said.

Judge Burke nodded and then said, "Mr. Graber, direct examination?"

"Yes, your Honor."

"Good afternoon, Mr. Nolan," Graber began.

"Good afternoon."

"Let's address the key issues, sir. Did you rape Ms. Willis?"

"Absolutely not."

"Did you have sex with her?"

"Yes, it was something that shouldn't have happened, but we had consensual sex."

"How long was the relationship?" Graber asked.

"Just one night, when we traveled to Seattle for business."

"You said it was something that shouldn't have happened. What did you mean by that?"

"Well, two things actually. First, we're both married, and secondly, sexual relationships with subordinates are ill-advised, even though consensual."

"So, Mr. Nolan, the jury has to grapple with the fact that Ms. Willis is accusing you of something that you have stated you did not do. Why would she do that?"

Scott considered objecting and decided to let this play out. "Maybe she felt guilty about our sleeping together," he said. "I really can't be sure."

"When you became aware of the claims that had been made by Ms. Willis, what was your reaction?"

"I just couldn't believe it. I assumed that she must just have regrets about her decision and be looking for cover."

"Move to strike, your Honor. Self-serving speculation," Scott said, jumping to his feet.

"Sustained, the rest of the answer is stricken after the witness said, "I just couldn't believe it.""

"And when you fired Ms. Willis, did it have anything to do with claims that she made?"

"No. Her false claims were not a factor."

Scott looked over at the jurors. Some were inscrutable, but a couple looked skeptical.

"So why did you terminate her employment?"

"We have many deadlines on projects that are critical to the company and its shareholders. If someone cannot communicate to get things done, then we have a big problem."

Graber spent another twenty minutes going over the organizational structure and the important role that Ms. Willis' position played in securing financial reporting from each of the subsidiaries. He then took a different tact, asking, "Mr. Nolan, you've told us that you are aware of the corporate policies governing harassment. You've also been involved in making sure that those policies stay current and protective?"

"Objection, leading," Scott interjected.

"Sustained," Judge Burke replied, nodding.

"What, if any, role have you played with respect to the corporate policies of the organization concerning harassment?"

"I have repeatedly encouraged our HR executives to stay current on the law, and to assure that all legal protections become part of our policies. I have also asked them to enlarge training from every two years to every year."

"I have nothing further," Graber said.

"Anything more, Mr. Winslow?" Judge Burke asked.

"Yes, your Honor." Scott stood up and thought for a moment. He never liked to ask any question he didn't know the answer to in advance, but this one was geared at making a point for the jury and there was no great down side. "Mr. Nolan, please confirm for me that it was only nine days between the time you learned of Ms. Willis' rape and harassment complaints and the day you fired her."

"I believe so."

"To whom in human resources did you instruct that you wanted to increase training from every other year to every year?"

"That would be Mr. Berg."

"And when did you give him that instruction?"

"I can't exactly recall."

"Approximate for me, sir."

Nolan looked like he was thinking hard, and then said, "I guess five or six months ago."

Scott nodded and then asked, "So that was after this case was filed, correct?"

"Yes, correct."

"Nothing further, your Honor," Scott said.

"Mr. Graber?" Judge Burke asked.

"Nothing further, your Honor," Graber replied.

Judge Burke said, "You may step down, Mr. Nolan." She looked at the jury panel and said, "Ladies and gentlemen, let me remind you of the admonition that I gave you at the outset, and which I will likely give you every time we part company. You are not to discuss this case with anyone, including family members and other members of the jury, until the case is given to you for deliberations. You are not to do any research or exploration about any matter brought to your attention in this courtroom and you are not to do research on this case or any party involved in this case. No reading articles in the paper or on line and no googling any topic addressed here. We will reconvene tomorrow morning at 9:00 a.m."

Chapter Twenty-Seven

Lee entered the lobby of McKinley Bass and Rieger in downtown Seattle at 11:45 a.m., appearing as Robert Stimson. He checked in with the receptionist, who made a brief call on the intercom and reported, "Mr. Munson will be right out."

"Thank you," Lee said, smiling at the young woman.

"My pleasure," she said, returning the smile.

Lee carried a briefcase and looked out the windows to the city below. Within moments, Munson appeared and said, "Follow me." He did not smile and he did not attempt to shake hands. He led Lee to a small, internal conference room. It was windowless and offered only the table and four chairs. It was obviously designed for practicality and not to impress any potential client.

"What do you want to say, Mr. Stimson, or whoever you really are."

"I wanted to let you know that I have completed assembling the information that I told you about earlier."

"Meaning?"

"Meaning that I made some startling discoveries when I compared your client list with those who benefited from the sale of stock the week before the acquisition failed."

"How did you get access to my client list? That is confidential and proprietary information you are not allowed to access."

Lee looked at him without expression. After a moment, he asked, "Do you want to know what discoveries I made?"

The man looked at him, assessing, and then simply nodded his head.

"There are no less than sixteen of your clients who collectively made or saved hundreds of thousands of dollars by dumping stock in that very narrow window. A remarkable coincidence that they suddenly sold at precisely the correct moment, don't you think?" Lee asked. "Take a brief look so that you can satisfy yourself about what I have learned," Lee said, pushing a thick folder towards Munson. "Each of the tabs, one through sixteen pertain to the trades of individual clients that you counseled." As Munson began to review the folder, Lee added, "For each of your clients on this list, you will find the number of shares and dates of the purchase and sale of the stock. I also identified the amount of money that each client made or saved." He paused and then added, "It seems that you did very well at making money for each of these clients. The only down side of each of these transactions are insider trading violations."

Greg Munson considered a moment and then said, "If you were planning to give these to federal agencies, I think you would have already done so."

Lee smiled, sardonically, and replied, "That's a very risky calculation, Mr. Munson. You should know that I am quite prepared to turn all of this over to the authorities. I hope you have another line of work in mind, because they will pull your license. And with the number of violations and the amount of money involved here, you will probably have to defer seeking other work until you are paroled."

"I don't like to be threatened, Mr. Stimson."

"No one does, but you and I know both know how this goes if all of this gets investigated," Lee said. He shrugged. "Simply a statement of fact."

Munson was quiet as he turned his attention back to the documents. His angry expression gave way to apparent tension and anxiety. He moved back and forth through the pages for an extended period, and then he put the file down and looked at Lee. "What do you want from me?" he said in angry tones, laced with desperation.

Lee spoke calmly, saying, "I want to make a deal that serves your interests as well as mine."

"Specifically?"

"Like I told you before, I am interested in only one of your clients. I want you to sign the affidavit containing the deals concerning the very questionable stock trades made on behalf of Mr. Nolan. If I get that signed declaration from you today, I will have no interest in your other transactions and no need to share them with the applicable authorities. As far as I am concerned, those never happened."

"You son of a bitch," Munson said, raising his voice. "You are trying to extort me."

Lee shook his head. He closed his files and put them back in his briefcase. "I won't waste your time or mine any further," he said as he stood and walked towards the door. "Good day, Mr. Munson," he said cordially.

"Wait a moment," Munson said. "Just wait a moment."

Lee turned and looked at the man. "My time is valuable, Mr. Munson." he said, evenly.

"Sit down and I'll look at what you want me to sign."

"You've already seen it," Lee said. "Like I said, I don't have any more time to waste." He shrugged and said, "Let's just put it all out there and let the chips fall where they may. I'm okay with that if you are."

Munson looked weary. "Please, sit down," he said, giving up the fight. "I'll sign it."

As he signed, Lee said, "I will talk only about the single client of yours we discussed. When you get inquiries in the near future, tell the truth about what you know about Nolan, and you will get no push back from me, and I will give out nothing on these other clients."

"I understand. Anything else?"

"No, that's it. Thanks for your time, Greg. I just wanted you to know that I will honor the deal, provided that you are true to the affidavit you gave me regarding Mr. Nolan's activities."

"I get it."

Lee picked up the signed affidavit and said, "Have a good day, Mr. Munson." He walked to the door. He was confident that Munson understood that he had no wiggle room. However unhappily, he would tow the line.

Chapter Twenty-Eight

At two minutes before 9:00 a.m., Judge Burke took her seat on the bench and said, "The record will show that all members of the jury are present as are counsel for the parties and the plaintiff and defendant are present. Mr. Winslow, you may call your next witness."

"Your Honor, Plaintiff calls Ms. Margo Traynor to the stand."

All eyes were fastened on Margo as she walked from a seat at the rear of the courtroom to the witness box. She wore a conservative business suit, and her red hair was cut a little shorter than the last time Scott had seen her. She sat down and was sworn in by the clerk, as the jury watched her carefully, readying to assess her as a witness."

"Good morning, Ms. Traynor," Scott said.

"Good morning," she responded with a nervous smile.

"Are you employed?"

"I am."

"By whom?"

"Strilovent Industries in Menlo Park."

"And how long have you worked for them?

"About three years."

"What is your position?

"I am an executive assistant in Corporate Planning."

"Where did you work prior to Stilovent Industries?"

"I worked for Sunmont Builders."

"What did you do there?"

"I was an executive assistant."

"In that position, did you have occasion to work in the same physical location as Mr. Nolan?"

"I did."

"For how long"

"About eight months."

"What was his position at the time?"

"He was Sunmont's CEO."

"During this eight month period, did Mr. Nolan ever say or do anything that you found inappropriate or offensive?"

"Yes, I do."

Scott nodded and asked. "When was the last time you worked with Mr. Nolan, relative to your departure date?"

"I was working with him at the time I quit."

"Why did you quit?"

"Because of Mr. Nolan's behaviors. His offensive conduct."

"Were the behaviors you are speaking of words or actions?"

"Both," Margo said, shaking her head.

"What was the first event that you found offensive?"

"The first time I was alone in a conference room with him he said, 'you look great in that suit.' I said 'thanks,' and then he said 'I bet you look even better without it.' I was shocked and I stayed quiet. He then said, 'Why don't you show me those gorgeous tits."

"How did you react?"

"I was shocked. I had never been spoken to like that by an executive of the company where I work. I didn't know what to do, so I just left the room. It was all very embarrassing."

"Did anything else happen?" Scott asked.

"Yeah. About a week later he came into my office and closed the door. He stood there grinning and said, you and I are going to have some great sex. Just wanted to give you a heads-up. I know how to make you cum long and hard.

"Did you report that?"

"No. I didn't want to cause any investigation, I just wanted to get past it, and do my job."

"Did any other occurrences that you regarded as offensive or inappropriate occur?"

She nodded with a pained expression on her face. "About three weeks later we are in a meeting. I was wearing a skirt and I was seated at the conference table when Mr. Nolan came into the room. He sat down next to me and addressed the five people present. Then he asked one of them to update us on a couple of items. While that guy was talking, he put his hand on my knee under the table. I tried to move away, and he gripped it tighter. Finally, he let go and the meeting went on another twenty minutes. He dismissed the group but said he had a question for me, and asked me to stay. The others walked out of the room and he put his hand back on my knee and said, 'We need to get to know each other better.' Then he moved his hand between my legs and all the way up to my crotch. I threw my chair backwards, and stood up. Then he just grinned and walked out.He"

"Did you report this occurrence?"

"Yes. I called HR and talked to a representative. He told me that I could file a complaint if I wanted to, but if I did it might affect my position on the team. I was shocked and angry and I didn't know what to do."

"What did you do?"

"I decided to go see Mr. Nolan. I made an appointment and then went into his office. I told him that the things that he did to me were not okay and that I only wanted to be left alone to do my job. He just stared at me. Then he said, 'you really are beautiful, you know.' He stood up and walked around his desk. He sat on the corner of the desk and said, 'One way or another, you are going to fuck me.' Then he said, 'If you complain to anyone, your job is gone."

"What did you do?"

"I quit my job. I left Sunmont and never returned." She shook her head. "He was the guy at the top, and HR made it clear they didn't want to help, so there was just nowhere to turn."

"Thank you, Ms. Traynor. I have no further questions," Scott said.

Judge Burke asked, "Cross-examination, Mr. Graber?"

"Yes, your Honor," Graber said, rising from his chair.

"Ms. Traynor, you found this experience you've described difficult?"

"Yes."

"But you never filed any claim or lawsuit of any kind, correct?"

"Correct."

Graber folded his arms and said, "And there is absolutely no written record of any such complaint anywhere, is there Ms. Traynor?"

"I would not know that, sir," Margo replied.

"There is nothing that backs up anything you've said, right?"

"I object, your Honor. It's not the witness' job to conduct investigations."

"Overruled. The witness can answer to the extent of her knowledge."

"I don't know."

"Have you met with Ms. Willis?"

"I met with Ms. Willis and Mr. Winslow."

"And you like Ms. Willis?"

"I don't know her well, but she seems nice."

"Have you been offered anything to testify today?"

"No."

"Are your expenses being paid?"

"No."

"So, you are here at your own expense to testify?"

"Correct."

"All this is your way of getting some revenge against Mr. Nolan for some incident that isn't even documented?"

"Objection, argumentative," Scott interjected.

"Overruled," Judge Burke replied.

"You may answer," Graber said.

"Not revenge, just accountability."

"You could have had your complaint investigated, but chose not to do so, right?"

"Well, I was dissuaded."

"HR told you that you could file a formal complaint?"

"Yes."

"And you never did?"

"Right."

"So your matter was never investigated?"

"That's correct."

"So Mr. Nolan never had a chance to respond to any allegations, right?"

"He did when I confronted him, personally. After HR told me that I could lose my position on the team, it was clear there was nowhere to go."

"And these events that you are telling us about go back more than three years, is that right?"

"Yes, sir."

"You've been harboring anger toward Mr. Nolan for a long time and looking for some way to get even for your perception of what occurred?"

Margo was quiet a moment and then said, "I was angry and confused. I was anxious, depressed and helpless. When a woman is subjected to horribly invasive conduct, it affects her life in every way, sir. Mr. Nolan cost me my job, and caused me a great deal of distress. So yes, I want him to be held accountable. I want him to know what he did to me, and what he did to Ms. Willis, is not okay."

Graber didn't want that to hang in the air too long. He asked, "You don't personally know what did or did not happen to Ms. Willis, right?"

"That's right."

"You only know what she told you and what you want to believe because of your own history, right?"

"I only know what she shared, that's right."

"And you never heard Mr. Nolan's side of this dispute from any source except whatever Ms. Willis chose to reveal to you, right?"

"Right."

"I have no further questions, your Honor."

* * *

Lee waited at the airport. The flight was supposed to have arrived forty minutes ago, but the latest update said it wouldn't arrive for another fifteen minutes. They would be cutting it close and Scott might have to do some courtroom stalling until they got there. Lee knew that judges were routinely unhappy when a lawyer wasn't ready with the next witness as soon as the last one stepped down, but until the plane landed, this witness just wasn't going to be there. He had tried to talk Jason Chambers into coming earlier, but it wouldn't work. Chambers had a family funeral to attend in the morning, so the late morning flight was the only answer. Scott would have to find some esoteric point to argue to buy them a few extra minutes. Or maybe he could tell a few lawyer jokes to entertain the jury. That thought made Lee chuckle to himself.

It was 2:45 p.m. when the plane landed. Lee met Chambers in the loading and unloading zone in front of the Alaska Airlines terminal and, as soon as Chambers climbed into the car, he raced as quickly as traffic would allow. The freeway wasn't moving, so Lee raced over a myriad of meandering side streets, finding every back door he could find until he pulled up in front of the courthouse.

Lee looked at Chambers and said, "Walk quickly to Department 11 and take a seat outside the courtroom. Scott is going to need you anytime now. I'll be there as soon as I can park."

Chambers nodded, and then he climbed out of the car and moved quickly towards the enormous glass doors that fronted the downtown courthouse. Lee parked and made his way from the parking structure to the courthouse. He reached Department 11 just in time to see the member of the Sheriff's team assigned as bailiff step into the hallway and call for Jason Chambers. Lee gave Chambers a nod and then followed inside. He took a seat in the rear of the courtroom as Chambers walked to the witness stand. Scott looked back and gave Lee a quick smile, noting that the witness sitting next to him was in the courtroom.

* * *

As Margo Traynor was excused from the stand, Judge Burke said, "Mr. Winslow, please call your next witness."

"Yes, your Honor. Plaintiff calls Jason Chambers to the stand.

The judge nodded and said, "Mr. Bailiff, will you please check for the witness in the hallway?"

The uniformed Sheriff's Deputy said, "Yes, your Honor, and walked toward the opaque wooden doors to the hallway outside. Scott was relieved to see him return followed by the witness, a young man of about twenty, with blond hair and a well-trimmed, light colored beard.

The young man took the witness stand and was sworn in by the clerk.

"Good afternoon, Mr. Chambers," Scott said.

The young man forced a nervous smile and said, "Hi."

"Are you employed, sir?"

"Yes."

"By whom?"

"The Puget Sound Hotel in Seattle."

How long have you worked there?"

"A little over a year?"

"And your job?"

"I work for food service. Primarily delivering room service orders to guests throughout the hotel."

"Were you working on April 8, of this year?"

"Yes. I worked 3:00 p.m. to midnight, which was my typical shift."

"Let me ask you to take a look at the two men seated at the defense counsel table. Have you seen either of the men before?"

"Yes, sir. I have seen the gentlemen on the right."

"Your Honor, please let the record reflect that the witness referred to Mr. Nolan."

"It will so reflect," Judge Burke said.

"When did you have occasion to see Mr. Nolan before?"

"I was working at the Puget Sound Hotel. I was delivering some food to someone on the twelfth floor at about 10:30 or 11:00 p.m. and he was pounding on a door in the hallway."

"How long did you see him doing this?"

"From the time I stepped out of the elevator, until I walked to where he was, I'd say two minutes."

"Did you speak with him?"

"I was about to ask him if he was locked out of this room and needed help, but he seemed to be speaking to someone in the room. As I approached where he was, the door was opened and he went inside."

"Could you hear what he was saying?"

"No, I could see his mouth moving, but couldn't hear what he was saying. It seemed clear that he wanted someone to let him in."

"What did you do next?"

"I continued on and made my delivery."

"That's all I have, your Honor."

"Mr. Graber, cross-examination."

"Yes, your Honor."

"So, you only saw that person in the hallway for a minute or two, right?"

"And you were looking at his profile, rather than straight on, right?"

"True."

"And this person never spoke to you."

"That's right."

"How do you know it was that particular date?"

"I couldn't remember the specific date he was there, so we looked it up."

"You don't know whose door it was that he knocked on, right?

"Right."

"How do you happen to remember it was the twelfth floor?"

"Because that was the time when I was delivering a special request for a truly bizarre dish of pigs feet. It's really pretty gross, but the same guy orders it every time he comes to the hotel and he always stays in the Parker Suite on the twelfth floor."

"So you assumed that he was on the twelfth floor that night, too?"

"Yep."

"Has he ever stayed in any other room in the hotel?"

"Not that I know of."

"Do you also visit the fourteenth floor for deliveries?"

"I do."

"So if the guy with the pigs feet order was staying on the fourteenth floor this trip, then that was where you saw the man knocking on a door?"

"That would make sense, but my manager checked what floor that fellow stayed on and it was confirmed that is was the Parker Suite on the twelfth floor."

"Why did you or your manager confirm the floor where he stayed?"

"We were asked to do so."

"By whom?"

"The investigator who works with Mr. Winslow."

"I have no further questions," Graber said.

"Redirect, Mr. Winslow?"

"No, your Honor."

"You may step down, Mr. Chambers," Judge Burke said. She turned her attention to the jury and said, "Okay, ladies and gentlemen, that will conclude proceedings for today. We need you here by 8:45 tomorrow morning so we can get started by 9:00. Remember my daily admonition. You may not discuss this case with each other or with anyone. Don't investigate anything or anyone involved in the case and don't subject yourself to any news about the case. See you all in the morning."

* * *

Scott gathered up his trial notebook and portions of the three banker boxes of documents. He assembled one box of materials and pulled it behind him on a dolly as he and Sarah walked from the courtroom together. They remained silent as they walked down the corridor, and during the elevator ride down, just in case jurors were lingering nearby.

Once they stepped outside and started moving toward the parking structure, Sarah said, "I have something that I want to say to you, Scott."

He looked at her and said, "Sure."

"I am very grateful for all you have done here. I mean, however all this comes out, you and your team have given everything possible." She teared up a little and then added, "I can't express how much all of it means to me, but I feel like I am being heard. Like you, Lee, and the judge, and the jury are all listening to what happened to me and you all care. Thank you, Scott."

Scott smiled at her and said, "You deserve nothing less. I can never be sure how a jury will interpret the evidence, but we are holding our own in there."

Sarah said, "The way the jury interprets the evidence won't change a thing. I will always be grateful to you." She gave him a hug, and then said, "Thank you, you have already done great things for me." With that, she moved two aisles away to where her car was parked. She looked back and he gave her a wave. He couldn't help but feel great. What he just experienced was the very best part of the job.

Chapter Twenty-Nine

At nine the next morning, Sarah sat next to Scott once again.

Judge Burke announced, "The record will reflect that the jury members, counsel, Ms. Willis. Mr. Nolan is not here today, but you are not to draw inferences from his absence. Mr. Winslow, please call your next witness."

"We call Doctor Laurie Spencer to the stand."

Laurie Spencer wore blue slacks, a white top and a blue jacket. She moved quickly to the witness stand and was sworn in by the court clerk.

"Mr. Winslow," Judge Burke said, "You may proceed."

"Thank you, your Honor. Good morning, Doctor Spencer."

"What is your profession?"

"I am a psychologist and counselor."

"Have you testified as a witness in the past?"

"I have."

"How many times?"

"Well, including my time as an evaluator for social services and criminal court evaluations, probably about fifty to fifty-five times."

"What is your practice these days?"

"I see private clients. I also do evaluations for government agencies and the courts."

"What percentage of your practice is seeing and counseling private clients?"

"About sixty percent."

"Have you provided psychological counseling to Sarah Willis?"

"I have," Laurie said, an involuntary smile emerging.

"How did she come to your attention?"

"She called me. She remembered me from a prior business meeting we both attended. She told me about what she had experienced and that she needed assistance."

"And did you meet with her?"

"Yes, I met with her the following day."

"Describe the treatment you provided to Ms. Willis," Scott asked.

"After initial psychological testing, I provided counseling to her."

"How often have you counseled her?"

"At first, it was twice a week. Then, later, we cut it back to once a week."

"What was your diagnosis?"

"Severe depression and anxiety secondary to a traumatic event, and specifically, rape."

"Was she also given medication?"

"Yes, she was given anxiety medications by a psychiatrist that I work with and who saw her once a month."

"Can you describe her condition as of the time you first saw her?"

"She was emotionally in danger. Her whole life had been turned upside down and she was barely hanging on. She was depressed, anxious, self-confidence had been taken away and I was very worried about her."

"What history did she give you?"

"She told me that she had been raped by her boss on a business trip."

"Did she describe what had happened—I mean, how it had all happened?"

"Yes."

"What did she tell you?"

"May I consult my notes, because I want to make sure I get it completely correct?"

"Yes, feel free to do so."

"After a meeting in Seattle, they met and he asked her to stop by his room to pick up documents. While they were there, he pinned her against a wall and kissed her. She ran out and back to her room. Then a while later he was pounding on her door and wanted to apologize. She attempted to put him off until the morning, but after he persisted a while, she opened the door. He came in and pushed her down on the bed and forcibly raped her."

Scott glanced at the jury as she spoke. All seemed to be totally consumed as she spoke. Scott asked, "Did she tell you of other comments and actions she thought were inappropriate before the rape?"

"She did."

"What did she tell you?"

"She told me about numerous times that he told her she looked good or looked hot. She told me that he frequently let his eyes fall to her chest, that her husband was lucky to be climbing into bed with her and that he said he wanted to have sex."

"When you hear a patient describe harassment and a rape, do you do your own credibility assessment?"

"I do."

"And what was your assessment of Ms. Willis' credibility as she told you about the rape?"

"She was telling the truth—unquestionably."

"What led you to that conclusion?"

"The affect as she talked, the emotion that flowed, and the parts that she could barely get out. It was an emotional upheaval just to tell me what had happened."

Scott let that settle on the courtroom. He glanced at the jury and saw they were attentive to her testimony. "Was there a time when you believed Ms. Willis was a suicide risk?"

"I grappled with that at first. She was so devastated, I felt I needed to watch her closely. We talked about whether she might do something to herself for the first four or five visits, but I concluded she was not going to attempt to take her own life. Being able to talk about it in a protected environment was critical to her slow progress."

"Do you think that she would continue to benefit from counseling?"

"Yes."

"How long should counseling continue?"

"I think another six months to a year, on a slowly reduced basis, would be appropriate to help her recover."

"Will she ever get entirely past this event?"

Laurie shook her head. "No. It is an emotional scar that doesn't go away, but it becomes more distant, and a survivor acquires tools to help accept what has happened and move forward, functionally."

"Is Ms. Willis able to work at this point?"

"Yes, I think it will help her to get back to a busy environment that she loves."

"Did you formulate any other opinions about Ms. Willis?"

She smiled and said, "On a personal level, I think she is a brave, compassionate woman and I like her."

"Thank you," Scott said, "I have no further questions."

"Mr. Graber, cross-examination?"

"Yes, your Honor. Good morning Ms. Spencer—it is doctor Spencer?"

"It is doctor, as I have a Ph.D. in psychology."

"But you are not a medical doctor, correct?"

"Correct."

"You told us that you like Ms. Willis, right?"

"Yes."

"And you want to help her?"

Scott stood and interjected, "Vague and ambiguous. Help her how, medically?"

"Please clarify, Mr. Graber," Judge Burke responded.

"Well, do you want to see her do well in this trial?"

"I am here as a witness. I don't know what do well means in that context, but I do want to optimize her emotional recovery."

"You told us that you took a history from Ms. Willis?"

"Yes."

"So, that means you got her version of the facts, right?"

"Correct."

"But you never spoke to Mr. Nolan and got his side of the story, correct?"

"That is correct."

"And you don't have any personal knowledge of what happened between Ms. Willis and Mr. Nolan, correct."

"Yes, that is correct."

Graber took a moment and reflected, and then he asked, "You never did report to any agency that Ms. Willis was a danger to herself or others, correct?"

"No."

"And you are aware that the law requires you to do that if you believed that she was suicidal?"

"Yes, sir."

"Ms. Willis told you that she shares the blame for what she said happened, right?"

"She only blames herself for letting him into the room."

"She's a married woman, right?"

"Yes."

"But she didn't immediately tell her husband about the alleged rape, right?"

"Yes, I think it was a couple of days before she told him."

"One reason a woman might not tell her husband about such an event would be if she had a voluntary sexual relationship and didn't want her husband to know?"

"Are you asking me about this case or whether that is a general possibility?"

"Well, first, generally."

"Yes, that could be a possible situation."

"It could be the situation here, if Ms. Willis wasn't being honest, right?"

"No."

"Why not?"

"Because here, I have seen Ms. Willis first hand and been able to evaluate the truth of what she says and the toll these events have taken."

"But, the only version of the factual history that you have to rely on is the one that she provided."

Laurie shook her head. "Yes, I told you that."

"And Ms. Willis considers herself partially blameworthy, right"

"Well, she feels like she should not have let him in to her room."

"And she admitted that she feels partially blameworthy because of her role?"

"Well, she says that she wishes she had never let him in, but I don't consider that blameworthy. He was purportedly there to apologize. You know, sir…"

Graber cut her off, "There's no question pending."

Scott stood and said, "Your Honor, she is an expert witness and should be permitted to give her full answer to the question."

"Overruled, you can address any additional issue on redirect, Mr. Winslow."

"You would have to agree that Ms. Willis has made great progress in her recovery, right?"

"Yes, I think she is doing well."

"And she is able to return to the type of career that she held with Ellison?"

"Yes."

"How long has she been emotionally capable of working?"

"I'd say the past couple of months."

"Thank you, I have no further questions."

"Mr. Winslow, redirect?" Judge Burke offered.

"Yes, your Honor." Scott walked to the lectern and paused a moment. "Doctor Spencer, Mr. Graber asked you about whether Ms. Willis felt blameworthy for opening the door, do you recall that?"

"I do."

"Is guilt an unusual reaction in someone who has been attacked or raped?"

"Not at all."

"Please explain."

"Women who are raped go through tremendous emotional turmoil. Part of that is obsessing over what they might have done to avoid being raped. Sometimes it is not wearing a blouse that showed some cleavage. Sometimes it's not leaving fast enough when a situation occurred. Sometimes it's just being in the wrong place at the wrong time. The most important thing to remember, however, is that we are talking about victims who have been through horrendous experiences and are trying everything they can just to cope and go on with life."

"You told us that the injuries suffered by Ms. Willis will improve, but that this kind of event never goes away. What did you mean by that?"

"I mean that a woman who is raped will live with that trauma for the rest of her life. There is never a single day it is forgotten. Not ever."

"Thank you, Doctor Spencer," Scott said. "Nothing further, your Honor."

"Mr. Graber?"

"No, your Honor, nothing further."

"You may step down, Doctor Spencer," Judge Burke said.

"Any further witnesses, Mr. Winslow?"

"No, your Honor. Plaintiff rests."

"Mr. Graber, you are up when we resume at 1:30 this afternoon."

"Yes, your Honor."

* * *

At precisely 1:30 p.m., Judge Burke called the court to order and then said, "Mr. Graber, your first witness, please."

"We would like to recall Mr. Nolan to the stand."

He sat down and looked first at the jury, and then toward Graber, who asked, "Mr. Nolan, you understand that you are still under oath this afternoon?"

"Yes, I do."

"Mr. Nolan, how do you feel towards Ms. Willis?"

"Objection, your Honor, relevance." Scott interposed.

Judge Burke hesitated and said, "I'll let him answer and we'll see where this goes."

"I have no anger towards her. She has her own demons to cope with."

"Objection, your Honor, improper opinion and irrelevant. I move to strike."

"Sustained and motion granted. The jury will disregard Mr. Nolan's comment."

"Mr. Nolan, did you make sexual comments to Margo Traynor?"

"No."

"Did you improperly touch her?"

"No. I never knew why she suddenly left her employment with Sunmont Builders and I haven't heard of her since."

"Did you ever harass her in any way?"

"Never."

"Did anyone at Sunmont ever suggest that you had?"

"No."

"Did you ever attack Ms. Willis?"

"No, of course not."

"But you did sleep with her?"

"Yes, we had a one night encounter."

"Nothing further, your Honor."

Judge Burke said, "Mr. Winslow?"

"Yes, your Honor." Scott stayed behind the counsel table and asked, "Mr. Nolan, you worked with Ms. Traynor on a couple of different projects over eight months, right?"

"That sounds correct," he replied.

"She was a good employee, right?"

"I guess she was okay. I don't recall anything that stands out either way. She was simply one of many employees I worked with."

"And you told her that she was going to fuck you?"

"No."

"And you grabbed her crotch?"

"No."

Scott shook his head, knowing he was being rather dramatic.

"I never harassed these women," Nolan volunteered.

Scott furrowed his brow and asked, "Mr. Nolan, how many other women have you not harassed in a similar fashion throughout your career?"

"Objection, your Honor, argumentative," Graber said, angrily leaping to his feet.

"Sustained," Judge Burke said.

Scott said, "I have nothing further of this witness, your Honor." It was delivered with distaste.

"Anything further, Mr. Graber?"

"No, your Honor."

"You may step down, Mr. Nolan. Please call your next witness, Mr. Graber."

"The defense calls Gerald Orson."

Orson took the stand and was sworn in by the clerk. He looked even more nervous than he had in his deposition. Before the first question there was a thin band of perspiration on his forehead.

"Good afternoon, Mr. Orson."

"Good afternoon."

"Are you employed, sir?"

"Yes, I am a Human Resources representative with Ellison."

"Were you called upon to investigate Mr. Willis' claims of harassment and rape?"

"I was."

"Who asked you to conduct the investigation?"

"Human Resources Director Robert Berg."

"Had you done investigations concerning harassment in the past?"

"Yes, for two prior employers as well."

"As part of your investigation into Ms. Willis' claims, did you interview her?"

"I did."

"And did you limit what she could say in any fashion? In other words, was she allowed to tell you all of her concerns?"

"Yes, sir."

"Did you interview Mr. Nolan as well?"

"I did."

"And did he answer your questions?"

"Yes, he did."

"What did you conclude in conducting this investigation?"

"That there just wasn't enough evidence to establish Ms. Willis' claims."

"Did you give a recommendation as to what, if anything, should occur based upon your investigation?"

"I did."

"What was that recommendation?"

"That because there was not sufficient evidence to establish the claims, no action should be taken."

"And to whom did you make these recommendations?"

"To Mr. Berg, the HR Director."

"Did you give him your findings in a written report?"

"Yes sir, I did."

"I have no further questions, your Honor."

"Mr. Winslow, cross examination"

"Yes, your Honor."

Scott stood and looked directly at Orson. The momentary silence seemed to make him sweat more. Scott asked, "You had only ever done two investigations involving sexual harassment in your entire career before this one, right?"

There was a moment while Orson considered and then he said, "Yes."

"And you were a three month employee at the time of the investigation of this matter, right?"

"Yes, sir."

"You were aware that, in addition to rape and sexual harassment, Ms. Willis alleged that she was terminated unlawfully and in retaliation for her complaints, correct?"

He looked increasingly uncomfortable as he said, "Yes."

"But you never investigated any of those allegations, did you?"

"Well, I investigated the rape and harassment allegations."

"Did you investigate her allegations that she was terminated in retaliation for her complaints, sir?" Scott asked, reaching for a copy of Orson's deposition transcript.

Orson watched Scott for a moment and knew that impeachment would be coming, so he said, "No, I did not investigate those allegations."

"Why not?"

"No one asked me to."

"Was Mr. Nolan suspended during the investigation?"

"No, sir."

"Doesn't Ellison policy call for suspension of employees while they are being investigated for any form of harassment?"

"Yes."

"So, why was Mr. Nolan not suspended?"

"He's the CEO, sir, and very busy."

"There is no exception to the policy for busy people, right sir?"

"Right."

"And there is no exception to that policy for CEOs, right?"

"No, not that I have seen."

"Did Ms. Willis tell you that Mr. Nolan raped her?"

"Yes."

"Did she tell you about other sexually inappropriate words and conduct by Mr. Nolan?"

"Yes."

"What?"

"That he made comments about her being hot and about wanting to sleep with her on several occasions?"

"How many occasions did he tell her she looked hot?"

"Several. I don't have an exact number."

"And what did Ms. Willis say she told him when he made such comments?"

Orson stared at the report silently, and then said, "She said she told him it was inappropriate."

"How many times did Ms. Willis tell you Nolan said something about sleeping with her?"

"I think two or three."

"And what did she report telling him when he made those comments?"

"That it was inappropriate."

"Anything else she told you about?" Scott asked.

"Yes, that he looked at her breasts during conversations."

"How frequently?"

"I didn't get a specific number of times," Orson said.

"But she told you it happened frequently?"

After a lengthy hesitation, Orson said, "Yes, that's what she said."

"Ms. Willis told you about the rape in Seattle, correct?"

"Yes."

"She told you that after it happened, she cried on the bathroom floor until around 3:00 in the morning?"

"Yes."

Scott nodded. "Did she tell you that she then took a cab to the airport and flew home?"

"Yes."

"Anything inaccurate in her description of what happened from the time of the attack until she got home?"

"Not that I know of."

"Ms. Willis failed to attend a presentation she was scheduled to give on Thursday morning?"

"True."

Scott took a step closer to the witness and then asked, "Ms. Willis never failed to attend anything that she was set to attend, did she?"

"Object as calling for speculation," Graber interjected.

"Overruled," Judge Burke responded.

Orson was quiet for a moment, and then said, "I don't know."

"Did you attempt to find out?"

"No, I didn't believe I needed to."

"Did you think about whether that would be helpful?"

"I don't know."

Scott nodded and asked, "Had you formed any opinion of Ms. Willis' credibility before the investigation?"

"No, I didn't know her well."

"Had any other person told you anything about Ms. Willis' credibility before the investigation?"

"No."

"Your conclusion is that Ms. Willis states that the conduct happened, Mr. Nolan states that it did not, so no conclusive decision can be reached. Is that what you wrote in your report?"

"Yes."

"I don't find any credibility assessments in this report. Did you make any?"

"No."

"Have you been trained that witness credibility assessments are important?"

"Yes, I was told to make them when I can."

"By whom were you told that?"

"I don't recall."

"Have you also been told that such assessments are an important part of the investigator's job?"

"Yes."

"Mr. Orson, you are aware that in some instances, women go for many weeks, months or even years before reporting harassment or rape, right?"

"Yes, I am aware of that."

"You are also aware that there are lots of reasons for delays in reporting?"

"Yes."

"And you're aware that Ms. Willis only delay reporting the rape for a couple of days, right?"

"Yes."

"In conducting your investigation, sir, did you ask Ms. Willis whether she had reported her allegations to anyone else shortly after the rape?"

"No."

"Why not?"

Orson was having difficulty finding words. "I can't recall."

"Have you been trained that in conducting an investigation it is important to find out whether contemporaneous sharing of the allegations occurred?"

"Yes."

"By that I mean, have you been trained that allegations are more credible if the facts were shared with others shortly after they occurred?"

"Yes, I think so."

"You think so?" Scott repeated as a question. There was silence.

"At the conclusion of your investigation, sir, were you aware that another woman said that she was also harassed, verbally and physically, by Mr. Nolan at a prior employer?"

"No."

"As an investigator, could that fact be important to your assessment and conclusions?"

"Yes."

"And by the conclusion of your investigation, had you learned whether any hotel employee saw Mr. Nolan standing alone in the hallway of the twelfth floor, banging on a door of Ms. Willis' hotel room?"

"No, sir."

"Would it be important to your conclusions to know the details surrounding that information?"

"Yes sir."

"I have no further questions, your Honor."

"Redirect, Mr. Graber?"

"Yes, your Honor," Graber replied, standing and smiling at the witness. "Mr. Orson, was everything that you did in performing this evaluation consistent with the training you had been given?"

"Yes, sir."

"And did you have any predisposition about how this investigation should come out at any time before you reached your conclusions?"

"No, sir."

"Do you feel that your findings were fair and complete?"

"Yes, sir."

"I have no further questions, your Honor."

"Mr. Winslow?" Judge Burke asked.

"No, I have nothing further for this witness."

"You may step down, sir."

"Next, Mr. Graber."

"Your Honor, may counsel approach the bench?"

"Yes, come on up."

When both counsel stood near the clerk and away from the jury, Graber quietly said, "I was just advised that my expert witness, who is my only remaining witness, had a family emergency and is requesting to be on first thing tomorrow morning. Given that it is about 3:30, your Honor, I'd like to request that we reconvene to complete testimony in the morning."

She looked at Scott, who said, "I guess a family emergency is a good reason."

Judge Burke looked annoyed, but nodded. After counsel returned to their respective tables, she turned to the jury and said, "We have a slight delay with the next witness. Sorry, ladies and gentlemen, I generally like to take testimony until at least 5:00 each day, but today we need to break early. She admonished the jury as she did at the conclusion of each session, and sent them on their way.

* * *

The restaurant was noisy and animated, with video games in all corners, a train that was suspended just below the ceiling and kids everywhere. It was not the best place for conversation, but kids, including Katy and Joey, loved it.

"I want my birthday party here," Joe announced.

"Okay," Lisa said, "but your birthday is still two months away."

"Yeah, I know, but I thought you might need to tell them we want to come here. Maybe with eight kids."

"Eight nine year olds? You think they can handle that many?"

"Very funny," Joey replied.

Scott smiled and asked, "How about you, Katy, you want your seventh birthday here?"

"Nope. It's way too noisy here. I want my party at home with just my friends and scary movies." She turned her attention back to her macaroni and cheese.

Lisa looked at Scott and said, "So, you are nearing the end of the trial?"

"Yeah, last witness tomorrow morning and then closing arguments. I'm so glad I have these family moments to get me out of my head for a while."

"It's still going okay?"

"I think so." He shrugged. "The evidence is going in okay, but you can never quite figure out what a jury is thinking. But by mid-afternoon tomorrow, the judge will instruct them and they will start deliberations."

"How is Sarah holding up?"

Scott smiled. "Stressed, but I think she is doing okay. You know, I wouldn't mind keeping her and John as friends when this is all over."

Lisa nodded. "I only met her briefly in your office, but she seems really great."

"From your lips to the jury's ears," Scott said.

"What about the charges against John for breaking into Nolan's place? Anything new there?"

"Nope. Still low profile, but the trial will happen."

She grinned. "Will Lee's gambit work? I mean, do you think that Nolan will want to back off on the prosecution because of the tape of his conversation with Sarah?"

"I don't know. We have to be careful with that tape. I can't overtly threaten to use it, so we are just hoping the mere fact that Nolan knows it exists may dampen his desire to go after John."

"Joey! Look at your shirt." Lisa said. Scott looked at his son to see an enormous blob of tomato sauce sliding down Joey's shirt.

Joey looked down and then back at his mother. "Oh, oh," he managed and then grinned widely.

Scott couldn't help but smile. Being with these characters was the best thing in the world.

He smiled at Lisa.

"What?" she asked.

"Have I told you that you are beautiful, lately?"

"I don't think so, but don't hold back."

"You are more than beautiful, you are my dream girl."

"Still?"

"Yep. Now and forever."

"You know that words of love can be an aphrodisiac?"

"Is it working?"

Lisa flashed a big smile and said, "I believe it is."

Scott shook his head and said, "You still drive me crazy after all these years."

Katie frowned and shook her head. In tones that suggested she had been putting up with this for far too long, she asked, "Are you guys being all romantic again?"

Chapter Thirty

At 9:00, Judge Burke said, "You ready with your next witness, Mr. Graber?"

"Yes, your Honor. We call Dr. William Raymond to the stand." A portly man with a crew cut and an expensive suit took the stand. "Good morning, Doctor Raymond. Please tell the jury your profession."

"I am a psychiatrist in private practice in the Los Feliz area of Los Angeles. I treat patients and I am involved in forensic psychiatry."

"Have you testified as an expert, sir?"

"Yes, many times, both in deposition and in trials."

"How about in harassment cases?"

"Yes, sir. I have testified in a number of them."

"Did you, at my request, review treatment records in connection with this case?"

"I did."

"Did you also meet with Ms. Willis as part of your examination?"

"I did."

"Did you form an opinions concerning her emotional or medical condition?"

"Yes."

"Now, the treating psychologist, Dr. Spencer diagnosed severe depression and anxiety. Do you agree with that diagnosis?"

"No, sir, I do not."

"Do you have an opinion that a different diagnosis is more appropriate?"

"I do."

"What is your opinion?"

"I believe it is situational anxiety. Anxiety that results from a specific situation and her own guilt in connection with that situation. It is transient in nature and will have no long term effect. I believe that as soon as Ms. Willis finds new work, she will move on and be functional. That is not to say that situational anxiety is not significant, because it certainly can be. It's just that it is situational and when conditions change for the better, the anxiety is very likely to resolve in the near future."

"I have no further questions, your Honor," Graber said, satisfied.

"Mr. Winslow, cross-examination?"

"Yes, your Honor." Scott walked to the lectern and looked directly at Raymond, who smiled weakly. "Doctor Raymond, you reviewed the medical records provided by Dr. Spencer?"

"I did."

"Nothing in there about situational anxiety, right?"

"Correct. As I mentioned, I do not agree with her diagnosis."

"Right, you did mention that. Did you make any assumptions in arriving at your diagnosis?"

"Like what?"

"Like any at all. For instance, did you make the assumption that Ms. Willis had not endured a rape?"

"No, sir."

"Well, sir, a rape is a violent and brutal act, is it not?"

"It is."

"And you are aware that many who suffer through such horrific attacks have severe depression and anxiety, aren't you?"

Raymond reflected and then said, "Some do, yes."

"And precisely how did you conclude that Ms. Willis is not one of those persons?"

"That's my opinion."

"Well, let's think about the sources of your factual information. You reviewed Dr. Spencer's records?"

"Yes."

"And those told you that Dr. Spencer concluded Ms. Willis had been raped, isn't that correct?"

"Yes."

"And you met with Ms. Willis?"

"Yes."

"Just one time?"

"Correct."

"And you did not treat her, correct?"

"Correct."

"How long was your meeting?"

"About forty-five minutes."

"Did you take a history from her?"

"I did."

"And did she tell you she was raped by Mr. Nolan?"

"Yes."

"So, did you have any information that suggested that no rape occurred?"

He was quiet a moment and then said, "Only the letter I received from Mr. Graber stating that his client said no rape occurred."

"You did not come to a conclusion that there was no rape?"

"I didn't come to any conclusion about that."

Scott looked at Raymond with concern. "Isn't that important to a proper diagnosis?"

"No, I can just see her as she is now."

"And you did that in one visit of forty-five minutes?"

"Objection, your Honor, argumentative," Graber interjected.

"Overruled. The witness may answer."

"Yes."

"And finally, sir, how much do you charge for your time?"

"Six hundred dollars per hour."

"Any minimum for court appearances?"

"Yes."

"What is that minimum?"

"Five thousand dollars."

Scott nodded and said, "I have nothing further of this witness, your Honor."

"Redirect, Mr. Graber?"

"Yes, your Honor," Graber replied. He stood up at counsel table and asked, "Dr. Raymond, were you made aware of the facts alleged by Ms. Willis at the time you saw her?"

"Yes."

"And the opinions that you provide are with full knowledge of what she alleged?"

"Yes, that is correct."

"You were also aware that Mr. Nolan states that there was an affair and not a rape."

"Correct."

"Did you need to resolve that dispute to provide your opinions?"

"No, not at all and that's not my job. I examined Ms. Willis, looking at her condition as relayed to me by her and by the medical records I reviewed. My opinion is about her emotional condition, not about who is right with the story they tell."

"So why do you believe that the proper diagnosis is situational anxiety?"

"A number of reasons. Ms. Willis is very functional, socially and in the work environment. There is nothing that all of us do that she cannot do. She has suffered anxiety, but that will change as soon as she returns to work and resumes a normal life.

She will put this episode behind her and move forward without limitation."

"Thank you, doctor. I have no further questions."

"Mr. Winslow," Judge Burke said, "anything further?"

"Yes, your Honor." Scott stood at gave the witness a perplexed look. "So you are telling us that your opinions are the same whether Ms. Willis simply had an affair or whether she was raped? It makes no difference to her emotional condition?"

"I'm just saying I looked at her condition and based my opinions on what I saw."

"Really. So the history a patient provides about whether they were raped or fooled around on their spouse makes no difference?"

"Objection, your Honor, asked and answered," Graber interjected.

"Overruled."

"You have the question in mind, sir?" Scott asked.

"Yes."

"And your answer is?"

"I wouldn't say it makes no difference, but in the end analysis, what is really important is to consider the patient's emotional status."

"And do you believe that women who suffer a violent rape always promptly move past the situation and have no residual?"

"Not always, no."

"In many instances, sir, rape has a lifelong impact on the lives of victims, isn't that true?"

"Yes."

"And in this case, you provide your opinion based upon one short visit with Ms. Willis, and the review of Dr. Spencer's opinions that do not agree with yours?"

"Yes, and years of experience,"

"And without even reaching a conclusion as to whether Ms. Willis was raped or had an affair?"

"Yes."

Scott shook his head, disapprovingly. "I have nothing further, you Honor."

"Mr. Graber?"

"Nothing further, your Honor."

"Dr. Raymond, you may step down," Judge Burke said. "Ladies and gentlemen, we will now take a fifteen minute break. When we return, the attorneys will make their closing arguments. When that is completed, I will instruct you on the applicable law and the case will be given to you for deliberation so that you may reach a verdict."

* * *

When everyone was back in the courtroom and there was an electric quiet in the room. Judge Burke looked at Scott and said, "Mr. Winslow, you may proceed with your closing argument."

Scott stood and walked closer to the jury, but not so close as to invade their personal space. That was one of the many things the movies always got wrong. Lawyers don't lean into the jury box and hover over the seated jurors for dramatic effect.

He smiled and said, "Thank you, ladies and gentlemen for having given the evidence your careful attention throughout. And now, you have the hard work of reaching a verdict. Let's start with the fact that there are two stories that are irreconcilable. Ms. Willis told you about a course of sexual harassment and a rape that occurred on a business trip. Mr. Nolan told you that there was never any kind of harassment and simply a one night affair. You are the judges of the credibility of the witnesses and the evidence. Let's consider some of the critical evidence that I believe tells the story.

Ms. Willis told us about specific words and conduct. He told her how hot she was. He told her how lucky her husband was to be going to bed with her. He said that he wanted to have sex with her. He regularly stared at her breasts. You heard Ms. Willis.

Is she someone who endured all of this, or is she here making that up? I think the answer is clear." Scott paused and then said, "Under oath, Mr. Nolan testified that he never did anything like that and never harassed anyone. Well, think about what he did to Margo Traynor. He made it clear he wanted to have sex with her, he put his hand on her knee during a meeting, and then had others leave and slid his hand up her skirt to her crotch. She got no help from human resources so she went to Nolan and he told her that they were going to have sex and if she complained, her job was gone. You heard and observed Ms. Traynor, and just how credibly she came across.

Let's talk about the evidence surrounding the trip to Seattle. Nolan wanted Ms. Willis there. At the last minute she was told that he couldn't make the meeting he was scheduled to attend and she had to do it. You never heard, during the course of this trial, why Mr. Nolan couldn't make that meeting, but Ms. Willis went because her boss said she needed to cover the meeting for him. Then he asked her to meet in the hotel lounge. Under the pretext of picking up documents to review, he had her stop by his room, and then he pinned her to the wall and forced a kiss on her. She ran out of his room extremely distressed, and went directly to her room. She started getting ready for bed, and then finds Nolan pounding on her door, saying he wants to apologize in person. She says, 'tomorrow—let's talk tomorrow.' But he is insistent and, ultimately, she lets him into her room to apologize. What follows is the most horrific nightmare of her life. A violent attack that no woman should ever suffer."

Scott gestured with arms open in front of him. "That's what really happened. What's the cover story? A one night affair. Mr. Nolan told you that they had a voluntary affair. He can't tell you why they happened to go from his room to hers, but, according to him, he walked with her to her room. Is that true? Not even a little bit. You'll remember that we found a hotel employee who saw Nolan alone, pounding on her door.

Ms. Willis was a devoted and hardworking manager with a good track record at Ellison. Suddenly, after reporting harassment and rape, Nolan fired her. At first it was for some undefined performance problem supported by no documents and no statements to anyone. Then it was because he has to be able to communicate closely with those who report to him and she couldn't do that." Scott shook his head, as if baffled by it all. "She had temporarily sought to communicate through human resources with respect to a report she prepared on a project because he raped her and she couldn't deal with him." Scott pushed a hand through his hair and said, "It was incredibly brave that she kept trying to work given what she had just been through. And the Director of Human Resources said 'yes.' He approved her reporting through HR on this project and then Mr. Nolan fired her, purportedly for that reason. The real reason for the firing was evident. She had complained about the harassment and the rape, and he fired her for it. Just the way he threatened Margo Traynor with termination, if she complained."

All eyes were on Scott as he spoke. A couple of the jurors seemed emotionally affected. A couple of others were nodding. "Ladies and gentleman, Mr. Nolan is a corporate CEO of one of a major corporation. He is very powerful and he is used to being able to do whatever he wants. What happened to Ms. Willis is a massive abuse of that power. Now, this is not the punitive damage phase of the trial, so you cannot yet consider damages to punish Nolan and Ellison, but you are to provide compensation for all emotional and monetary damages that Ms. Willis suffered. Economic losses are pretty easy because we know Ms. Willis made $180,000 per year and her benefits were worth another 20% or $36,000. So those losses are about $216,000 per year since her termination and for a reasonable period into the future.

The economic losses are the most minor part of her injury. Money is inadequate because you cannot give back the peace of mind, the security, the confidence, the view of life that was taken away, but it is the only way our legal system can address grievous wrongs. There is no amount of money that can compensate for what Mr. Nolan has done to Ms. Willis. For him, it is one more day of being in power. For her, it is a personal violation that will never go away. An intimate attack of horrific violence that she lives with every day and always will. Depression, anxiety, recurrent nightmares, and destruction of self-confidence built over a lifetime. Think about living with the fallout from this attack every day. Every morning when you wake up and every night when you go to bed. Every time you are alone on a street. Every time it is a little too dark. The terror of this night is never far away, and it never will be. What can possibly compensate for this? You are charged with that decision and we have faith in you to make a fair and just decision that will properly compensate Ms. Willis. I suggest to you that five million dollars is not enough, but you tell all of us the right amount to compensate Ms. Willis for what was done to her. This is about fairness and justice. It is about doing the right thing to compensate for the lifelong damage wrought by this abhorrent conduct."

Scott took a breath and a short pause, then he said, "Thank you ladies and gentlemen. Thank you on behalf of Ms. Willis for your careful attention. We have faith in you."

* * *

"Mr. Graber," Judge Burke said, "Your closing argument."

"Yes, your Honor," Graber said, as he stood and walked toward the jury, stopping at the lectern. "Ladies and gentlemen, I want to thank you for the many days of careful attention you have given all of us. Mr. Winslow tells a good story, but as the Court will tell you in jury instruction, the argument of counsel is not evidence. It's simply our perception of what the evidence has shown." Graber looked at the faces of the jurors and said, "I want you to consider for a moment what it is to be falsely accused of something like a rape, because that is exactly what happened here. Ellison is a deep pocket in the eyes of many people, which makes them a target and anyone can file a lawsuit against anyone for anything.

"Consider that Ms. Willis told no one of any harassment at any time before the Seattle trip. She was a manager. She knew that Ellison policy required any form of harassment to be reported immediately. She was required to carry out those policies where her subordinates were concerned. No one witnessed anything she complained about and she never complained about any of it. Why not? They even tried to make something nefarious out of Mr. Nolan asking a manager to attend a meeting that he couldn't make because he had been called to another." He shook his head and said, "Ask yourself why nothing is reported for days after the Seattle trip. Ms. Willis never told anyone before the trip about any alleged sexual harassment although it was purportedly going on for some time. Not anyone at work, not anyone anywhere. Why is that?" He considered the faces of the jurors as he said, "Because it never happened."

"On a night in Seattle, after they had attended separate meetings, Mr. Nolan and Ms. Willis had drinks in the bar. They talked freely about work and other things, they flirted and they both made a decision to go upstairs together. They had an intimate night together that they were not supposed to have because they were both married. Willis did not want to deal with the realities of her decision, so she concocted a story of rape. Alleged rape by someone who had been good to her and whom she liked, right up until she came to terms with having to tell her husband about the affair. Instead, she hid and then she made up this terrible story. Nonetheless, her claims were fully and thoroughly investigated by someone with no horse in the race. And that experienced investigator found that there wasn't credible evidence to sustain what Ms. Willis claimed." Graber shook his head, "There are times when companies need to be held accountable and there are times when there are abuses of power. This case is neither of those situations. This case is about someone who created a false case, contrary to the conclusions of a thorough investigation, rather than face the consequences of her own actions. You heard from Dr. Raymond, an experienced psychiatrist, that Ms. Willis' emotional condition is situational anxiety, which is not a long term condition. More importantly, in this case, ladies and gentlemen, you must return a defense verdict. You must tell the plaintiff that what she has done here is not acceptable and that she can't profit from her own inability to deal with a situation she created. We have faith in your ability to do the right thing, ladies and gentlemen. And the right thing is to send a strong message that Ms. Willis must be accountable for her own actions. You must return a defense verdict."

* * *

"Mr Winslow, your rebuttal argument."

"Yes. Thank you, you Honor."

Scott stood and walked over to the jury. He regarded the panel thoughtfully and then said,

"I get one final opportunity to speak with you because we have the burden of proof in this matter." He paused and then said, "You know, I listened carefully to the evidence and to Mr. Graber's closing argument, I can't help noticing that there was a great deal of evidence that he simply avoided. He didn't explain how his client could be telling the truth about never harassing anyone when not one, but two, very credible woman told you of all the specific acts and conduct he engaged in. Where was the explanation that you needed to hear? And where was the defense explanation of the unrefuted testimony from Jason Chambers, that he saw Nolan all alone, pounding on Ms. Willis' hotel room door? He told you that he walked with Ms. Willis to her room and they walked in together, but that never happened? You learned about Nolan pounding on the door from

Ms. Willis. The accuracy of her testimony is confirmed by hotel employee, Jason Chambers, who saw Nolan pounding on the door as he walked down the hallway from the elevator on his way to deliver food." Scott shrugged and said, "So, where was the explanation for any of this evidence?"

Scott leaned forward on the lectern, and said softly, as if sharing a secret. "You know, ladies and gentlemen, the Court will instruct you that you are to decide this case based only on the evidence you have seen and the law. But you are not required to leave your common sense at the front door when you enter this building. In this case, there is a large quantity of evidence, unexplained by the defense, which makes clear that the harassment and the rape occurred and that the defendants are doing their best to hide from accountability for this abuse of power. Please don't let them do that. Hold them fully accountable for the actions of the CEO at the top of this company and the permanent damage and injury that has been inflicted. Thank you, ladies and gentlemen," Scott concluded and then returned to his seat.

There was a momentary quiet in the courtroom, and then Judge Burke said, "We will now take a late lunch and let you calm down after all that excitement." There was nervous laughter from the jury. Judge Burke continued, "When we return, I will instruct you on the law that governs this case and then you will begin your deliberations." She smiled and said, "And don't forget my regular admonitions to you. You are not to discuss this case with anyone including each other, even though we are now getting close to the time for deliberations. I will see you all back here in forty-five minutes and you will hear the instructions needed for your deliberations."

* * *

Scott and Sarah sat at the counsel table, as Judge Burke read jury instructions covering harassment, sexual battery and retaliatory termination for raising complaints of harassment or discrimination. She went through the elements required for each claim. She gave other instructions telling the jurors that it was for them to decide whether the requirements of each claim had been satisfied, that they were to determine the credibility of all witnesses and that if they found a witness to be without credibility, that witness' testimony could be disregarded or given the weight they felt it deserved. It took one hour and twenty minutes to read all of the court-authorized instructions to the jury. Judge Burke then said, "You will now retire for your deliberations. Your first task is to select your foreperson, who will speak for the jury. Then you will decide each of the claims presented to you. You will have the instructions that I have given you in written form so that you may consult them if desired. If there are questions during your deliberations, the foreperson will write the question and give it to the bailiff, who will bring it to my attention. I will then consult with counsel for the parties and we will give you an answer to the question. It is now 3:15 p.m. and you will begin your deliberations and go until 5:00 p.m. Each day you will begin at 8:45 p.m. and go until 5:00 p.m. with a lunch break, until you reach your verdict. Thank you ladies and gentlemen, please follow the bailiff to the jury room and get started.

After the jury was escorted from the courtroom, Judge Burke looked at counsel and said, "We are off and running. Good luck to everyone. If you elect not to wait around the courthouse, make sure we have the phone number where you can be reached. You will have thirty minutes to get here from the time we call you. If you are not present at that time, we will take the verdict without you. Both counsel, thanks for doing a good, respectful job in trying your case."

Chapter Thirty-One

The wide hallways outside the courtrooms were furnished with marble benches that ran the length of each wall; places where people gathered to wait for their cases, where witnesses who couldn't enter until called sat nervously, where lawyers got a last minute look at their files before hearings, or waited nervously while juries deliberated the fate of their clients and passed judgment on the results of two or three years of work.

As soon as the jury began deliberations, Scott and Sarah joined John, Angie and Margo, all of whom waited outside. There were hugs of support and sighs of relief now that it was in the hands of the jury. Sarah felt that she had been heard, and whatever happened from here, she was prepared to live with the result. They walked to the courthouse coffee shop, and shared each other's company, as they suppressed the nervousness that waiting brings. They were all seated outside the courtroom when the jurors paraded out at 5:20 p.m. Mike Graber sat on the bench on the other side of the entry door as the jurors exited. As everyone expected, it was too soon for a verdict. After the jurors had disappeared onto the elevators to make their escape for the day, the bailiff stepped outside and said, "Counsel, the judge wants to see you briefly." Scott and Mike Graber stepped inside and walked to the counsel table, while Sarah waited in the audience portion of the court.

Judge Burke emerged from Chambers without her robe and said, "I thought you might like to know that they notified us that Juror #3, Madeline Neuman was chosen as their foreperson."

Scott nodded and said, "Thanks, your Honor."

"Yes, thanks for the update," Graber added.

"Okay, counsel, we will give you thirty minutes if there is a verdict or a question."

"Thanks, your Honor," both attorneys said and walked from the courtroom.

As they made their way out of the building, Sarah asked, "Are you surprised by the foreperson they chose?"

"No, not really. Ms. Neuman was a force of personality, and runs a business. She's one of three I would have thought most likely to be foreperson."

Sarah said, "Well, whatever happens, it's now in their hands. I think I will come back in the morning and sit outside."

"I'll be back after 2:00 p.m. tomorrow, unless I'm called in sooner. Save me a spot next to you on our favorite bench."

"I will," she said. Looks like I'll have company until then. John, Angie and Margo will all be back to help me wait." She looked at Scott a moment and then threw her arms around him. "I know I said this before, but thank you."

He smiled and said, "You are a terrific person, Sarah. I'm really glad I got to know you." They parted company and he watched her walk to her car, feeling good; the way you do when you found a friend that you want to keep.

* * *

Scott was back in the office at 7:00 a.m. He was returning emails and working with Donna to go over discovery responses that were due. Trials were fun and exciting, but they were also incredibly demanding. He worked every night for the next day of testimony and slept little. Meanwhile, all the work he didn't have time to do piled up back at the office.

Nikki's voice said, "Lee on line 1."

"Hi, Lee."

"Morning Scott. Any word from the jury yet?"

"No, nothing yet."

"Good news, right?"

"Yeah, I think so. Typically, early verdicts are for the defense because they don't have to discuss damages if they don't find any liability."

"I have a good feeling," Lee said.

"Well, hang on tight to it, because I'm just nervous. My good vibe machine is in neutral," Scott replied.

"Melissa and I are going to visit Sarah and John tonight. We figured we could add a little friendship, and some light conversation to a nervous time."

"Great idea," Scott said. "I'm sure that they will be glad to see you." He paused and said, "You know, you sound like you're still on the committed relationship path, my friend."

"I do, don't I?" He chuckled. "What can I say? Melissa is an amazing woman."

"Yep, you're hooked."

They both laughed and then Lee said, "On a work related topic, my research is complete, and I have everything I need for the packet. When do I deliver it?"

"Let's wait until the verdict comes in, and then you can capture their full attention."

"I think what I have will definitely do that," Lee said. "Speaking of attention grabbers, did you see the Times article about the Willis case today?"

"Yeah," Scott said. "Not bad."

"What words do they use? Oh yeah, the epic battle being waged against one of the most powerful companies in the country. They also got a lot of the facts right."

"They did," Scott replied. "A pretty good article."

"Call me when you hear from the court. If I'm not tied up in some inescapable situation, I want to come down to hear the verdict, too."

"You got it. Thanks for all your help."

"I've loved every minute of it," Lee said. "Talk to you later."

* * *

Sarah spent her morning talking to John, Angie and Margo. Something about being around friends helped deal with frayed nerves. The jury left their deliberations for lunch at 12:15 p.m., and returned at 1:30 p.m., disappearing into the jury room without fanfare. The afternoon in the courthouse hallway was eerily quiet. The jurors came out for a brief afternoon break with determined and sometimes intense expressions painting their faces. Scott arrived at shortly after 2:00 p.m., exchanged greetings with the group, and found a spot on the bench between John and Angie.

At 4:30 p.m., Margo gave Sarah a hug. "I have to leave tonight, because I have to be back to work in the morning. Will you call me when there is a verdict? I am on pins and needles, just like you."

"I will, Margo. I promise." She took her new friend by the hand and said, "Thank you so much. However this comes out, I couldn't have gone this far without this amazing group."

"I need to thank you, too." Margo replied. "I needed to do this. I needed to stand up and face what he did to me. And just maybe, there is some accountability for both of us."

The women hugged one more time, and then Margo said goodbye to each of them and slowly walked down the hall, as if going slow might allow her to hear the announcement of a verdict before she got to the elevator.

"She's pretty special," Angie whispered to Sarah.

Sarah nodded. "I am surrounded by special people," she replied.

Moments later, Melissa exited one of the elevators and came walking towards them. "Any verdict?" she asked.

Sarah shook her head. "Not yet. But, thank you for coming."

"I just wanted to keep you company while you waited. Looks like I'm not the only one who had that thought."

Sarah introduced her to Angie, and she offered greetings to John and Scott. She sat down on the bench between Scott and John, and sought updates about the process. At that moment, Sarah's phone rang and she saw an unfamiliar number. She hit a button and said "Sarah Willis."

"Ms. Willis, we have yet to meet. My name is Vince Harper with Diversified Development." It didn't register at first, but then he added, "Melissa Carter came to work for us a few weeks ago."

"Oh, yes. Of course. Melissa loves the job and has said great things about working with you."

"Well, that's good to know, thanks. The reason I called you is that I am in the final throws of my interviews for the Vice President of Finance position. I have two finalists who are very impressive, but I regularly hear great things about you from Melissa. So much so, that she has convinced me that I shouldn't make a final decision without meeting with you. That is, if you are still looking for a suitable position."

"I would love to meet with you, Mr. Harper."

"Can you make it this afternoon? Maybe 6:00 p.m.?"

She checked her watched and saw that it was already 4:45 p.m. "Is there any way we can make it a little later? I can't leave for another hour, and at this time of day it will take another hour to get to you."

"That's not a problem," he replied. "How about 7:00 p.m.?"

"Yes, sir, I'll be there." He gave her the address, although she already knew the building from conversation with Melissa. She hung up, feeling excited and nervous, and wanting desperately to move forward. She looked up and saw Scott walking towards her. As he sat down next to her she excitedly said, "I just got a job interview for late this afternoon."

* * *

At just after 5:00 p.m., the bailiff stepped out into the hallway to see who was waiting. He saw Scott and said, "We have a jury question. The judge will go over it with you as soon as Mr. Graber gets here."

"Okay, thanks," Scott said, feeling the excitement, and the anxiety, of the announcement. You never knew what to expect with jury questions. It was not the verdict that everyone was waiting for, but sometimes jury questions tipped where they were headed.

It was 5:20 p.m., when Mike Graber arrived in the hallway, and he and Scott walked into the courtroom together. The judge had the court reporter at the ready. As they approached the counsel tables, Judge Burke said, "Good afternoon, gentlemen." She looked at the note in her hand and said, "So, here is the question that we received. 'We want to confirm that we do not need the same number of jurors for whether there is liability and to determine the amount of damages. If we get to nine jurors for each, even if they are not the same nine, can announce a verdict.' It is signed Madeline Neuman, foreperson." Judge Burke looked at the attorneys and then said, "My intended answer is: Yes, as long as you have at least nine votes for each finding, it does not matter if there is the same number and it does not matter if they are the same jurors—as long as there is nine or more. Do you agree with that answer?"

"Yes, your Honor," Scott said.

"I agree, your Honor," Graber replied.

"Okay, counsel. I will give them the answer and let them leave for the day. Maybe tomorrow we get a verdict."

The bailiff delivered the Judge's written answer to the jury. Scott and Graber waited in the courtroom until the jury was released and walked from the jury room into the courtroom and then down the hallway toward the elevators. At that point, Graber said, "I have an offer of a million to settle the case with complete release and confidentiality provisions."

"I'll relay it to my client tonight and call you tomorrow morning," Scott said.

"Will you recommend it?" Graber asked.

"No. I would have before trial, but not now. But it is Ms. Willis' call, so I'll talk to her and let you know."

Graber nodded and said, "Okay, talk to you in the morning."

Scott was smiling as he left the courtroom. The fact that they were thinking about the votes needed on each issue might mean that they had found liability and were contemplating damages. If they had nine who favored the defense, there would be no reason to consider what it takes for each finding. He walked over to Sarah to tell her the latest.

* * *

Sarah arrived at the offices of Diversified Development at 6:55 p.m. and found that a receptionist was still on duty. Sarah carried a small file containing resumes and commendations that she kept in her car so that it was ready when the opportunity arose. She looked around the dramatic circular lobby, and then sat on a couch positioned to take in the city views. Five minutes later, a distinguished looking man with salt and pepper hair emerged and walked over to her.

"Good afternoon, Sarah. I am Vince Harper."

"Good to meet you Vince."

He smiled and said, "Let's talk in my office."

She followed him past the receptionist and down a wide hallway to a large office in the corner of the building. The two walls of windows presented panoramic views all around. His desk was placed where the windows came together and across the room was the conference table that seated eight. "Let's sit here," Harper said, taking a chair at the end of the conference table.

Sarah sat in the chair next to his and said, "Thanks for seeing me."

He smiled and said, "I've heard many good things about you. Melissa is a major fan of yours. Now that I've seen how talented she is, I figured that I better talk to someone who has that kind of an effect on subordinates."

"She's a dedicated employee and a great person," Sarah said.

"Well, let me get a look at anything that you want me to see," Harper said, getting down to business.

"Sure," she replied and handed him the file that had her resume on top and a variety of commendation letters and awards underneath.

Harper silently studied the file for a time, periodically turning pages. Then he looked up at her and said, "You handled financials from up to nineteen subsidiaries at the same time?"

"Yes, sir," she responded. She smiled and said, "Just like herding cats."

He laughed and said, "Don't I know it." He sat back in his chair and looked at her a moment, and then he said, "How are you at telling me exactly what you think?"

"Good. I don't hesitate to share my thoughts, but I will carry out a decision once it is made."

He nodded. "So I've got, as of this week, one more subsidiary for a total of fourteen. We have private investors and funds that invest. We have various types of projects in development at all times. We have shopping centers, residential communities, office buildings and a couple of office parks. So, the cats you have to herd are all over the country, with income and tax implications for all of them."

She nodded, and then asked, "Does the job I am applying for oversee all financials, including revenue, real estate and sales taxes, development of reporting plans within the subsidiaries? I assume part of the job is assuring that each of the departments adheres to cost and budget structures, is that right?"

He smiled. "You've got it. The duties also include working financial planning and development with me. I also need you to get out there and visit the top brass in each of the subsidiaries once a year, and maybe more often, when there are issues." He drew a breath. "This position reports to me and I am extremely busy. So, I need an executive who can run with everything we need to be on top of and keep me in the loop with respect to key decisions and anything consequential. How does that all sound?"

"It sounds like a position I'm well-suited to handle," Sarah said, surprised by the emergence of a level of self-confidence she hadn't felt in a while.

Harper looked over her resume and commendations again and then said, "Well," he said, "I think maybe you're right. It looks like you have been doing these same duties for Ellison." He paused, and then added, "And I know that you would have at least one subordinate you would have selected yourself."

"That's for sure," she replied.

He handed her a one page document. "Here are proposed employment terms. Salary, 401K and other benefits as listed. After one year, there is the possibility of stock options in amounts that are performance based. We like our executives to have an interest in the company. When you're an owner, you tend to give it everything you've got."

"Makes sense," she said. "I like the proposed terms."

"How's the case?" he asked, changing the subject rather abruptly.

"The jury is currently deliberating."

He nodded and asked, "So when would you be available?"

"Monday morning."

"What if the jury isn't back?"

"I'll be here anyway and just go back to the courthouse when the verdict is announced."

He nodded. Harper was quiet a moment and then said, "I'm sorry for what you had to endure over there. That should never happen at any company."

Sarah was not sure what her expression gave away, but she tried to contain the emotion, and the gratitude she felt for his acknowledgment of what she went through. She nodded and said, "You're right. It should never happen." She took a moment and then said, "I have always loved being busy and the challenge of what I do. I know you have other contenders, but I think I am what you need and I would very much like to work with you, Vince."

He smiled and said, "Okay, Sarah. Thank you for coming. You are one of my finalists, and I will decide in the next day or two. Either way, I will call you." He stood and she followed his lead. "Come with me a moment," he said. She followed him to the office next door to his. He opened the door and said, "This would be your new center of operations," he said.

She stepped in to see a large office with a conversation area on one end, consisting of a coffee table between two couches and winged chairs on either end. At the other end of the office was a large desk and credenza behind it. There was also a second credenza that afforded another surface for documents awaiting attention. There were two stacks of documents already awaiting the lucky winner of this office. "Looks like home," she said.

"Good. I would want you close because in addition to a couple of meetings a week to go over everything pending, I want us to be able to have impromptu meetings whenever we need them. Next door to you is a large conference room that seats eighteen, which you and I share. When you have subsidiary reps in, outsiders or your own staff, it's easy access. First come, first reserved between you and me. There are a couple of other conference rooms on the floor if this one is booked."

"Sounds perfect," Sarah said. They shook hands and she said, "It has been a pleasure to meet you, Vince."

"Yeah, you too, Sarah. I'll be in touch."

* * *

Scott met Sarah at 9:00 a.m. and they took seats in the hallway outside the courtroom. Last evening's jury question made everyone think the verdict would be coming soon, so all had gathered. Mike Graber and Bob Berg stood down the hall drinking coffee and talking.

After Scott and Sarah spoke for a few minutes, Scott approached Mike Graber. "Mike, you have a minute?"

"Yes, sure."

Graber left Berg and took a walk down the hall with Scott. Scott said, "We have considered it and we are declining your settlement offer."

Graber nodded. "Okay, your call to make." He paused and said, "I don't know that I could, but if I could talk them into one million one hundred thousand with a confidentiality provision, would your client accept it?"

"No. I think we will wait for the jury, but if that becomes an offer, I will naturally relay it to Ms. Willis." He reflected a moment and added, "Just so you know, we are not doing anything with a confidentiality provision at this point. All of this is out there in the public record. We are not precluding our ability to address it."

Scott walked back to Sarah and said, "Offer declined."

She nodded and said, "Do you think we are making a mistake? I mean, the jury could come in with a defense verdict, right?"

"They could find for the defense, so we are taking that chance. Or, they might find for us and give us less."

She was thoughtful for a moment and then said, "I felt like this jury really listened to me and to you. I already feel like we've taken a stand to hold Nolan and Ellison accountable, however it comes out. Let's wait and see what they do."

Scott nodded, and said, "I'm with you. Hard calls to make when the offers get to seven figures, but let's hold on." He reflected a moment and then said, "How did it go last night?"

"The interview?"

"Yeah, did you like them?"

"I did. I liked Vince Harper. He hired Melissa and he would be my new boss."

"And you would be Melissa's boss again?"

"That's right."

"There's a certain symmetry to that. I like it."

"Me, too, but I don't have the job yet." She gave a shrug and said, "He told me that I was one of the finalists and he'd get back to me today or tomorrow."

"You're a shoe in," Scott replied. "If this guy knows what he's doing, he'll bring you on board."

"You sound pretty confident."

"Of course, I know who you are."

Scott's phone rang and he punched a button. "Hi Donna. Yeah, okay. I'll be back in the office shortly. Keep the emergencies under control and away from other files until I get there."

"Will I see you this afternoon?" Sarah asked.

"I'll be back to warm this bench about 2:00 this afternoon, unless the clerk calls me sooner."

"I'll save your spot," she said. "And thanks for the kind words about the job."

He shrugged. "They're not just kind words. This guy is nuts if he doesn't hire you."

She smiled and shook her head as he walked down the hallway.

Chapter Thirty-Two

Scott met with Donna in the conference room, surrounded by the files that required immediate attention. He reviewed proposed discovery responses on three cases and helped her draft discovery to the other side on four others. They finalized a new whistleblower lawsuit for filing and started drafting another age discrimination complaint. They worked through until almost 2:00 p.m. with stops only to refill coffee cups.

Nikki walked in and said, "I knew you'd never get out of here for lunch, so I ordered turkey sandwiches for both of you." She handed them brown bags and said, "Let Donna and I know as soon as you hear something."

"Thanks, Nikki. I sure will." He turned to Donna and said, "Can you run with this stuff so that we can get everything out tomorrow?"

"Yeah, don't worry about it. We will make all the changes and have it all ready for signature when you can get back in here. Good luck!"

He ran out the door and climbed in the car, eating the sandwich as he drove. He was about half way to the courthouse when his phone rang. He recognized the incoming number. It was Judge Burke's department. "This is going to be it," he said aloud. He hit a button on the steering wheel and said, "Scott Winslow."

"Mr. Winslow, this is Denise Fletcher, Judge Burke's clerk."

"Yes, Ms. Fletcher."

"We have a verdict."

Scott said, "Okay, I'm on the way. I should be there within twenty minutes."

Scott parked quickly and almost ran from the structure to the courthouse, the line at the metal detector taking longer than he would have liked. He took the elevator to the fourth floor and walked rapidly down the hall to see Sarah excitedly waving a hand at him. John stood beside her looking worried.

As he reached the door, he stepped inside and made eye contact with Graber. They shared a knowing 'this is it,' expression and took their seats at the counsel table. Nolan came in and sat down next to Graber. Judge Burke stepped into the courtroom in her robe and asked the room, "Everybody ready to go?"

"Yes, your Honor, came from both tables."

"Mr. Bailiff, please bring the jury in."

The twelve jurors walked in from the jury room and took their assigned seats in the box. Scott and Sarah watched there expressions to see if there was any tell. They were stoic and impossible to read, right until they sat down. Then the foreperson, Madeline Neuman, looked in Sarah's direction and gave her a slight smile. Scott thought it might be good news, but didn't want to read too much into it.

Judge Burke looked at the panel and asked, "Ladies and gentlemen, have you reached a verdict?"

The foreperson, Madeline Neuman, stood holding a document that contained the answers that both sides were simultaneously desperate to hear and afraid of hearing. She replied, "Yes, your Honor."

"Mr. Bailiff, will you please bring me that verdict form?"

The bailiff took the document to the judge and walked back to his seat, as she carefully reviewed the document. Ms. Neuman sat down and waited.

Judge Burke said, "I will now read the verdict."

"We the jury in the matter of Sarah Willis v. James Nolan and Ellison Corporation find as follows:

On the claim of harassment, we find for plaintiff and award the amount of $300,000.

On the claim of sexual battery, we find for plaintiff in the amount of $6,000,000.

On the claim of retaliatory termination, we find for plaintiff and award damages in the amount of $1,500,000."

The impact of the verdict created a sudden vacuum. The air was gone from the room. Sarah and Scott hugged and tried to contain their excitement. Sarah looked to the jury with her hands together in front of her as if in prayer and mouthed "Thank you," to the members of the jury. She got several smiles and a couple of nods.

At the other table, Graber and Nolan were silent, trying to contemplate the scope of what had just happened. They lost it all, bigger than they believed possible."

"Do counsel want the jury polled?" Judge Burke asked.

"Yes," Graber said, finding the words to speak through a veil of shock.

One by one, Judge Burke asked the jurors if the each verdict was their personal verdict. All twelve said "yes" on each of the liability findings. All twelve said "yes" as to the $300,000 verdict for harassment and the $1,500,000 verdict for the retaliatory termination. Ten of the twelve jurors said the $6,000,000 was their verdict on the sexual battery claim, two said it was not their verdict. Judge Burke then said, "This court will be dark tomorrow as there are other matters that I must address, but we will return Monday morning at 9:00 a.m. You will hear brief argument from counsel and then you will deliberate on the punitive damages issue. Have a good three day weekend and we will see you Monday morning."

The attorneys and their clients sat while the jurors filed out of the room. When they were gone, Judge Burke looked at the parties and said, "Counsel, argument for the punitive damage phase begins promptly at 9:00 a.m., Monday, unless you figure out how to settle this case between now and Monday morning."

Sarah found herself crying as she hugged John. "This is so amazing," she said. "Part of me just never believed vindication was possible. I thought Nolan would get away with it again."

John held her tight and said, "I know what you mean. This is far better than trying to beat the guy to a pulp." They laughed, but neither had forgotten that John still faced charges.

As they walked from the courtroom, Graber approached Scott and said, "Congratulations." They shook hands and then he said, "Let's meet tomorrow afternoon to see if we can get this settled."

"Okay," Scott said. "How about 2:00?"

"That will work. Your office?"

"Sure. See you then."

Graber nodded and walked away.

Scott looked back at Sarah and John, who were walking a few feet behind. He had his arm around her and she had a look of contentment on her face that he had never seen before. He looked back again and John gave him a thumbs up. It was quite a day.

* * *

At 2:00 p.m., on Friday afternoon, Nikki escorted James Nolan and Michael Graber, along with senior board member Mark Dixon into the large conference room. She pointed out coffee, soda and water that had been set up and left them.

Within a few minutes, Scott, Sarah and John entered the room and sat across the table from the three men. There was a moment of awkward quiet, and then Scott said, "Mike, do you want to start off with your thoughts?"

He nodded, "Well, we are here to see if we can get the case resolved. We think the verdict is excessive and we believe mistakes were made with the evidence and instructions that prejudiced our position in the case, but we'd like to get it settled, if we can."

"Just so that our position is also on the table," Scott said, we do not believe there is error and we believe that the numbers will grow considerably in phase two of the trial." He paused and said, "So, what are you proposing?"

"We propose to pay three million dollars to resolve the case. Payment within twenty days, naturally a normal release and confidentiality provisions."

Scott looked at each of the men across the table and then he said, "You are asking us to take less than half of the phase one award. That makes no sense. Secondly, there will be no confidentiality provision. This case has gone all the way through trial. All of it is out there for the world to see. We are not going to agree to slap a veil of secrecy around it now."

Mark Dixon spoke up for the first time. "I understand your points, Mr. Winslow. I want you to know that I am here with certain authority from the Board of Directors to get this case resolved. Now, I don't know that we can get this settled, but if we can it's better for everybody to move forward without another year in the court of appeals. I'm told that's what the process involves, am I right about that?"

"Yes," Graber said. "That's about right."

Dixon nodded and then looked directly at Scott. "What is it that you want in order to resolve this case, Mr. Winslow?"

"We will agree to settle the case for the phase 1 verdict."

"You need to give us a little more room, Mr. Winslow. The full verdict does not sound reasonable and we cannot agree."

Scott nodded. "Mr. Dixon, what we are discussing is not the full verdict. I think that there is a good chance that the punitive damages verdict will well exceed the numbers of the phase 1 verdict. We will reduce our demand to six million dollars if it gets done today."

"Let us have some time to talk, if you would."

"Yes, of course," Scott said, and Scott, Sarah and John left the room.

In Scott's office, Sarah said, "I would like to make a deal and end this today. I got my vindication from the jury and I would like to see if I can put all of this behind me and try to move forward."

"I understand," Scott said. "Let's see where we get the number by late this afternoon."

* * *

At 4:30 p.m. everyone was still there. Dixon and Graber did all the talking during the discussions. They came up to 3.3 million and then 3.5 million. Both offers were rejected and Scott, Sarah and John were back in Scott's office when Sarah's phone rang.

She looked at the number and answered excitedly, "Good afternoon, Vince."

"Good afternoon, Sarah. You are my first choice, so welcome to the Diversified Development management team."

"Thank you, Vince. That is fantastic news."

"I trust you can still be here Monday?"

"Yes, although it could be late Monday, as there is a final hearing."

"That's fine," Harper said. "The sooner the better, so that you can get you familiar with the subsidiary madness around here."

"Perfect," she said. "I'm really looking forward to working with you."

"Me, too, Sarah. See you Monday."

Her face lit up. She looked at John and then at Scott, grinning widely. "I got it."

John stood and they shared a hug. "Wonderful, sweetheart."

"I told you," Scott said, "he had to hire you unless he was crazy." He smiled and gave Sarah a hug. "Congratulations."

Donna buzzed and said, "The Ellison team is ready for you, and Lee is here."

"Got it. Take Lee to my office and tell him I'll call him in shortly." Scott replied.

"Shall do," Donna said, and they hung up.

Sarah looked at Scott and said, "More than ever, I want to put this away. If they get to four million, let's get the case settled."

Scott nodded, "Okay, but once we get there, give me a little room to test the waters."

Scott, Sarah and John walked into the conference room at 6:00 p.m. and sat down. "Well, where are we?" Scott asked.

Graber said, "We have five million to settle the case today."

There was quiet for a time and then Scott said, "We would like to get it resolved today as well. We will come down to 5.5 million to get this done."

Graber shook his head and said, "I don't know that we can go higher, Scott."

Dixon spoke up and said, "Consider it done."

"So we have an agreement?" Scott asked.

"Yes," Dixon replied.

"No confidentiality provisions," Scott said.

Graber nodded and said, "Just full release of the company and its management and Mr. Nolan. I will send you the proposed release over the weekend."

"That is agreed," Scott said. "It needs to be signed before we appear in court Monday morning."

"Anything else?" Dixon asked.

"One more thing," Scott said. He picked up the conference phone and said, "Donna, can you have Lee step into the room?"

A moment later, Lee walked into the conference room carrying a thick envelope. "Lee, I think you've met Michael Graber."

"I have, yes. Hello, Mr. Graber."

"Hello, Mr. Henry," Graber said, sounding curious about Lee's presence.

"This is Jim Nolan and Mark Dixon."

"Good afternoon," Lee said. He added, "Hi, Sarah." He gave her a smile, as he took a seat next to her.

"What is he doing here?" Nolan asked, sounding alarmed.

Scott said, "Go ahead, Lee."

Lee was about to speak, but Sarah raised a palm in his direction, signaling that he should wait. She looked directly at James Nolan and said, "The settlement is done, and the case is over, but I want you to acknowledge what you did, Jim. It turned my life upside down, and I need you to own it." She looked directly at Nolan, and then added, "I will not use it, or tell others that you admitted it, this is just for me." She watched his expression and waited. If he acknowledged what he had done to her, she would ask Lee to end this meeting and destroy the material in the envelope.

All eyes fixed on Nolan. The period of quiet grew longer and finally, Nolan said, "I have nothing to say."

Sarah sat back in her chair shaking her head. Scott nodded in Lee's direction and he handed the envelope to Nolan.

"What's this?" Nolan asked angrily.

"Open it," Lee said. "Read the document on top. All of the other documents provide back-up for what's in the first."

Nolan looked angry as he opened the envelope. He pulled out the top document and then he and Graber began reading the under oath declaration of Greg Munson. Suddenly, Nolan looked stricken and he yelled, "How did you get this?"

"I met with Mr. Munson," Lee said evenly.

"You son of a bitch," Nolan screamed. He looked at Scott and exploded, "This whole deal is off." He stood to leave.

Graber stood, but Dixon didn't move. There was a prolonged silence and then Dixon said, "No, the deal is not off Jim, now sit down." Dixon turned his attention back to Lee and said, "Tell the rest of us what this is, Mr. Henry."

"This is an affidavit identifying the specifics of Mr. Nolan's insider trading. It was the reason for his sudden meeting in Seattle the night of the rape. With information he got that night, Mr. Nolan made a great deal of money through the broker who signed this affidavit, using inside information to dump stock just days before the failure of an anticipated acquisition became public."

"You're accusing Jim of insider trading?" Dixon asked, incredulously.

"Not accusing, sir," Lee replied. "Presenting the proof. Please, take the time to review the documents and I believe your questions will be answered."

"Is this some form of blackmail to prevent Mr. Nolan from testifying that you and Mr. Willis broke into his house and caused him injury?" Dixon asked with concern.

"No, sir. This is no blackmail of any kind. These documents are proof of financial crimes by Mr. Nolan. I am delivering copies of these documents to the federal agencies that regulate and investigate insider trading, including the Department of Justice, the Securities and Exchange Commission and FINRA's Office of Fraud Detection and Market Intelligence." He paused a moment and said, "You and Ellison's Board should review these documents, Mr. Dixon. There are serious violations of federal law documented in these materials that may be a problem for you and your stockholders."

Nolan was shaking with an intense anger. His face had become red. He yelled, "You son of a bitch. You will not walk away from this."

Dixon looked at Nolan and said, "Jim, look at what has been presented and consider whether this is a good time to be threatening others."

"I will see you and her husband in jail for your attack on me at my residence, Nolan yelled." Lee shrugged, but said nothing. His lack of emotional reaction seemed to infuriate Nolan even further. "I will get you for this."

Scott said, "Don't make threats in my office, sir. If you cannot control yourself, it's time to leave."

Nolan pounded the table with a fist. Lee and Scott both stood.

Dixon said, "It's time to go." He stood and moved toward the door. Graber followed, but Nolan didn't move. "Now, Jim. Right now," Dixon repeated.

Nolan stood and glared at Lee, who stared back at him un-flinchingly. "I believe it is time for you to go, Mr. Nolan," Lee said evenly.

Nolan hesitated a moment, and then followed Dixon out the door without looking back.

Chapter Thirty-Three

On Monday morning, Scott and Sarah were back in the court-room once again, this time with Mark Dixon accompanying Michael Graber on behalf of Ellison.

"The clerk informs me that the parties have reached a settle-ment in connection with this matter," Judge Burke said.

"Yes, your Honor," Scott said, and Graber echoed.

"Do we need to put the settlement on the record this morn-ing?"

"No, your Honor," Scott said. "We negotiated the settlement agreement, and it was fully signed yesterday."

"Well, you are all to be commended on achieving a resolution of the matter," Judge Burke said, nodding. "Mr. Bailiff, please put the jury in the box."

The Sheriff's Deputy gave a nod and made his way to the jury room. In a few moments, he was followed into the courtroom by the jurors, who took their seats in the box.

Judge Burke turned toward the jury and said, "Ladies and gen-tlemen, based upon your hard work in hearing the evidence and reaching your verdict in phase one of the trial, the parties have been able to reach an agreement to settle the case. I want to thank you all for your devoted service, and for working so hard to come to your decisions. In our legal system, your role is crit-ical to achieving justice." She smiled and added, "Now that it's all over, you can speak about the case, and you can talk to the attorneys and answer questions they have if you would like to do so. That is a matter of choice, however, not obligation. Thank you, again, ladies and gentlemen. This jury is dismissed and you have completed your service."

Scott approached the foreperson and another juror to find out what had swayed the verdict. They said that the jury believed Sarah, and Margo Traynor, but they did not believe Nolan. They also told Scott that of the two jurors who did not agree with the verdict amount, one of them thought the number should be three million dollars and the other thought the number should be ten million.

* * *

At 11:00 a.m., Sarah walked into Vince Harper's office. He offered her a big grin and shook her hand. "Welcome to Diversified," he said. "Get settled in and we'll talk again midafternoon. I put a couple of large files on your desk to get you acquainted with the structure. One file details management structure here and at each of the subsidiaries, showing reporting relationships. The other shows projects underway and critical milestone dates for each."

"Perfect," Sarah said, "I'll start getting familiar with all of it right away."

"I hope you want to be busy. We are up to our ears around here, and every new acquisition increases the workload."

"That's exactly what I like," Sarah said. "Just this side of impossible suits me fine."

Vince hesitated a moment, and then asked, "I saw a news release on line. Looks like your case came out okay," he said, smiling.

"It did."

"Outstanding." He smiled and shook her hand. "Glad to have you on board, Sarah."

Sarah moved next door to her new office and began reviewing the materials that awaited. About fifteen minutes later, Melissa knocked on the open door. "Hi chief," she said, grinning, just like their earlier days at Ellison.

"Hi, Melissa. Come in."

Melissa met Sarah half way across the office, and they shared a hug, as if they were friends reuniting after years apart. "I'm so glad you're here," Melissa said, smiling. They sat down, and then she added, "Congratulations on the case. Lee brought me up to date."

Sarah grinned. "Your guy is one tough cookie," she said, shaking her head. "I believe that he would go toe to toe with anyone."

"Yep, and he's also the most amazing guy in the world."

Sarah grinned and said, "Love is in the air. You make a great couple." She paused a moment, and then said, "Thank you for recommending me to Vince Harper. You made it possible for me to break through the Ellison barrier."

"Well, it's good for me, too," Melissa replied. "You're the best boss I ever had, and I'm glad to have you back." She paused and added, "You're going to like Vince, too. He is absorbed eighty hours a week, but he's a great person."

"So, where do I find you?" Sarah asked.

"Third office down the hall."

"And the other three that report to me?"

"All on this floor, in the next four offices after the conference room next to yours."

Sarah nodded and said, "Okay. I'll set up an initial meeting with the entire group later today, so that I can meet the team."

"Great," Melissa replied, standing up to go. Before she walked to the door, she said, "This is a great moment." She walked around the desk and the two women shared another hug.

"Thanks for standing by me through all of it, Melissa. I will never forget what you did."

Melissa nodded, and then said, "Friends are the ones who are still around when the world turns ugly. It sounds like a greeting card, or a fortune cookie, but it's really true."

Sarah nodded, "And I feel like I've had the best friends a woman could have. I'll see you tonight at the celebration, right?"

"I can hardly wait," she said, grinning.

After Melissa left the room, Sarah stood and looked out at the city view outside her window. She was so glad to be back to work. All that James Nolan did seemed like it was in another time and place, entirely disconnected from this new world of friends. Maybe, sometime soon, the nightmares and the fear would fade away. For the first time in a long time, Sarah believed anything was possible. The settlement in the wake of the jury's verdict was great, but the best thing about the trial was the jury knew she wasn't lying—they believed in her. They told Nolan that what he did was not okay and helped her return closer to a normalcy she had long forgotten. She decided to call Margo Traynor and thank her for her courage. Together, they made a stand that mattered. Sarah sat down at her new desk and opened a file, smiling, as she began to review a real estate subsidiary's financial statements.

Chapter Thirty-Four

They occupied a private banquet room at Sergio's Florentine. With the glass doors closed and draped, they were in a private world of friendship. Sarah raised her glass and said, "To my dear and amazing friends. Thank you all so much for always being there for me, for believing in me, and for helping find justice." She was choked up as she said, "I will never forget all you have done for me. Angie, you pulled me through when I might not have made it. John, you stood beside me and never wavered in your faith in me. Scott, the legal journey was amazing, and you never doubted me. And I know that Lisa was pushing for me all the way, as well. Lee, thanks for all you did, including jumping in to intervene in prevent John's attempt to take down Nolan." She turned to Melissa, seated next to her and said, "Melissa, you stood beside me at Ellison when all support was gone, and then helped me find my new career at Diversified." She was fighting tears as she added, "I love you all, and I know that I will never be able to pay you all back for everything you've done for me. Thank you so much."

John stood and said, "Sarah's right. I owe Lee and Scott a great deal for saving me from what I might have done to Nolan. I know if it weren't for you two, I could be facing many years in prison, rather than six months or a year. I will be forever grateful."

Additional champagne was poured and shrimp salad was delivered. Scott smiled at Lisa and she leaned over and gave him a kiss. "These are good friends," she whispered. "We will hang on to this group."

"Yeah," Scott said. "They are incredible people."

Lee caught Scott's eye and raised his glass. "Nice work, buddy," he said, softly.

Scott said, "You too. Thanks for bringing home the evidence that made it all come together."

* * *

Five days after the settlement, an article hit the business section of the Los Angeles Times. The headline, posted on line the evening before, was "Ellison Company separates from CEO, James Nolan." The article contained only a single quote from Mark Dixon of the Ellison Board. He stated that "The Ellison Board and Mr. Nolan had different visions for the Company."

Lee smiled. 'Different visions' was an interesting euphemism for this guy raped a subordinate, cost the company a fortune, and engaged in insider trading along the way. Even then, it was likely that Nolan left with a substantial severance package. That seemed to be the way of the contemporary business world. Top executives are paid four hundred times the wage of the average worker, and then paid off with a massive severance when they screw up and cost the company millions.

Lee started work on a new project, going where most others couldn't, to get information he shouldn't have. He used codes that he had obtained to access separate corporate intranets, to research the email of fifteen executives in competing companies to find out who was feeding proprietary information to a competitor. He decided that the best way to narrow the field was to examine all of the email accounts of each of these executives. Once he saw who they communicated with, he felt he could determine who was on more than one team.

His phone rang and he hit a button. "Lee Henry."

"Good morning, Mr. Henry, this is Preston Talbot. I am an investigator with the SEC. We received the materials that you provided with respect to the activities of Mr. Nolan and I have been assigned to this matter."

"Yes, Mr. Talbot. How can I help you?"

"You obtained a signed affidavit from broker, Greg Munson, right?"

"Yes, that's right."

"So, the first thing I'm wondering is how you got him to sign such a declaration. What he attests to implicates his own license as well as the actions of Mr. Nolan, so this is not something that most brokers would do."

Lee smiled and said, "Well, sir, I do my best to be persuasive. Maybe I got through to his conscience, and he felt the need to come clean."

"Yeah, maybe," Talbot said, sounding unconvinced. "Anything you can add to that answer?"

"No, not that comes to mind," Lee said.

"I see. Well, how about other clients of Munson?"

"In what respect?" Lee asked, sounding as innocent as possible.

Talbot replied, "Often when a broker trades on inside information for one client, they do it for others as well. So, we'd like to know what you can tell us about what he did for his other clients."

"I'm sorry," Lee said, "I don't have any information about that."

"Your only interest was Mr. Nolan?"

"Yes, that's right. I'm an investigator who was hired to obtain information about Nolan. When I obtained the information that let me know what Mr. Munson was doing, I felt like it was my duty to alert the proper authorities."

"You got this guy to admit under oath that he was engaging in insider trading on behalf of Mr. Nolan, but there was no discussion about what he was doing for others?"

Lee smiled. This guy knew the right questions. "I'm sorry, I just have no information about what else he was doing."

There was quiet for a moment and then Talbot said, "I'll probably get back to you as the investigation proceeds."

"Feel free," Lee said. "I'm happy to help any way that I can."

Talbot said, "Great," but he clearly got the idea that there were limits on how helpful Lee was going to be when it came to anyone other than Nolan.

* * *

The day before he was to attend a preliminary hearing on the charges, Lee met with Barry Corbin to prepare. When he arrived, he was escorted into a conference room where Barry waited with a big grin on his face.

"What?" Lee asked.

"Your case is over."

"Really?" Lee asked. "Why?"

The District Attorney agreed that you were simply there to do a good deed in preventing John Willis from doing damage and you shouldn't be charged."

"Great news," Lee replied.

"Yeah, it also didn't hurt that Tyler Cornell and a number of his cronies know you from times you've testified, and think you're a good guy."

"Well, if that's all it took, I could have told them I was a good guy before this got started."

Corbin laughed. He shook Lee's hand and said, "Congratulations, man. It turns out that we have nothing to prepare for this afternoon."

Lee smiled and then said, "What about John Willis?"

"His case isn't going away, but I'm trying to make a deal for him."

"He's not any kind of a criminal. He came after a scumbag who raped his wife."

Corbin nodded. "I think you're absolutely right and I'm working to get that message across to the D.A."

"I will testify for John. He wasn't going to kill Nolan, he was just trying let the son of a bitch know what it's like to be really scared. And who can blame him after what Nolan did to Sarah?"

"I get it. I might want to get some revenge myself in that situation. The problem is, breaking and entering, as well assault and battery, are still violations of law. We have to hope that a jury won't want to find him guilty under all the circumstances, but it is a crapshoot. They may or may not consider John's actions justified, but they will not get a jury instruction that says his conduct is legally justified. I mean, the attack was long over, so there is no reasonable claim of self-defense or defense of others."

"Yeah, I understand," Lee said. "The conduct may not be legally justified, but it's justified in my mind. If someone I loved was raped, you can bet I'd go after the scumbag who did it."

"And then you'd be just where John is," Corbin said, shrugging. "I'll do my best to get him a good deal and keep this away from trial. Hopefully, the other side will see their vulnerability and feel like resolving it before trial is a good idea."

"What's a good deal?" Lee asked.

"Because it's a first offense, maybe six months to a year. There is a remote shot at a couple of years of probation, but I doubt it, particularly given how hard the victim will be pushing for his own form of justice."

Lee shook his head. "It's hard for me to stomach the idea of Nolan as any kind of a victim. He's the perp, not John."

"I understand," Corbin said, "but the facts are that John broke into the guy's house, smacked him around, and scared the shit out of him with a large knife."

"Is karma a defense? I'm pretty sure the universe wanted that asshole to pay a price for what he did to Sarah."

"One day he'll pick up that tab, just not today," Corbin said. "Hang on to that thought."

Chapter Thirty-Five

Six friends gathered for an afternoon barbecue at Scott and Lisa's house in Thousand Oaks. Scott stood at the barbecue, gauging the temperature and preparing to cook salmon. He smiled, watching Lee and John play catch with Joey. Joey had become one of the most accurate pitchers in the league among all of the nine and ten year olds. Lee bent down like a catcher and watched Joey hurl the ball over a make believe plate, while John called balls and strikes.

On the back steps, Katy was delivering her confident thoughts on some unknown topic, as Lisa and Melissa listened intently.

Sarah walked over to Scott and said, "You look pretty good in the role of the back yard cook."

"It's all natural talent. I've never had a lesson," he replied.

"Oh, oh," she said. "Should I worry about dinner?"

"Nope, it's guaranteed to be great or your money back."

She laughed, and then said, "There's something I need to tell you, Scott," her voice taking on a serious tone.

"Sure," he replied, smiling. "What is it?"

"I contacted Nolan this week."

He stopped looking at the barbecue, and looked directly at her with shock in his eyes. "You did? Why?"

She nodded and said, "We made a deal."

"You did what?" Scott asked, startled. "Let's sit for a minute," he said.

They sat down in two of the six chairs around the fire table. "Tell me," he said, regarding her attentively.

She said, "I couldn't allow John to go to prison. Not for a year, and not even for a day. John was there for me when I was at my most fragile, and he never doubted me. He is a hero of mine–along with the rest of you who are here." Scott waited without speaking, while she drew a deep breath to keep her emotion in check. Then she said, "We agreed that I would tell the prosecutors that I did not want to go through another trial, and that I didn't want to pursue a criminal case against Nolan, and in return, he agreed to tell prosecutors that he did not want to pursue any charges against John, and would not testify against him if the case continued."

Scott digested that for a moment, and then said, "What about the insider trading stuff?"

She shook her head and said, "I told him that he's on his own with all of that."

Scott shook his head and said, "Wow."

"Yeah," she replied, "I know."

"Does John know?" Scott asked.

"Yeah, I told him last night."

"How did he take it?"

"He said that I shouldn't have done anything that would help that dirtbag, and that he needs to spend time in a cell." She shook her head and then added, "But, I know John's relieved that he's not going to face prison."

He smiled, and then said, "I have to tell you that I think you have been amazing through all of this. You are an incredibly courageous woman, and a personal hero of mine." She wore a concerned, faraway expression. "What are you thinking?" he asked.

"Maybe it's not fair for me to tell you this, but I have been thinking that without the prosecution going forward, he might do it again."

Scott considered for a moment, and then replied, "I'd like to think that losing his career and getting hit with a big money judgment, may be a deterrent, but the truth is that these are character issues."

She nodded, and then spoke softly. "What I am about to tell you is something that, after today, I will deny I ever said."

Scott looked at her questioningly. "Okay, what is it that you never told me?"

She drew a breath and said, "People have accidents all the time. Margo Traynor and I discussed that. Sometimes people who deserve accidents." She smiled and added, "I also mentioned that fact to Lee, and he seemed to agree that accidents can happen. He says it is surprisingly common."

Scott's eyes flew open wide. He reflected a moment and said, "I hope nothing like that ever happens. I'm an officer of the court, and I can't support vigilantism, or accident voodoo, or whatever the hell we are obliquely talking about here." He shook his head and added, "John already tried the revenge card, remember?"

"Yeah, he was brave, but he made some mistakes," she agreed. "But if Nolan victimizes someone else, something has to be done. And I can't help but think that Lee could…" She let the words trail off, but the message was clear.

"No way, Sarah," Scott said, "the something that would have to be done is prosecution."

"You're probably right," she said, with a smile, but there was something in her eyes that said nothing was foreclosed.

Dear reader,

We hope you enjoyed reading *Personal Violation*. Please take a moment to leave a review, even if it's a short one. Your opinion is important to us.

Discover more books by David P. Warren at https://www.nextchapter.pub/authors/author-david-warren

Want to know when one of our books is free or discounted? Join the newsletter at http://eepurl.com/bqqB3H

Best regards,

David P. Warren and the Next Chapter Team

You could also like:

Altering Destiny by David P. Warren

To read first chapter for free, head to:
https://www.nextchaptcr.pub/books/altering-destiny-psychological-thriller

About the Author

I am a 39 year attorney with a passion for writing thrillers. My most recent book is 'Imploded Lives,' (2018), focusing on the lives of several people who are about to become hostages in one of the most remarkable bank robberies of our time, and the perpetrators, who will take hostages, and manage to completely disappear, leaving puzzled detectives and FBI agents with no idea how they or the money disappeared. My immediately previous book is the legal thriller 'The Whistleblower Onslaught' (2017), the story of an executive in the energy industry fired for complaints about the company's unsafe conditions in its mines. An explosion in a mine, resulting in one dead and three injured. A lawsuit that gives you a good look at the legal system and a company hiding the truth. Bribery and blackmail to protect corporate secrets and someone who will do anything to stop the lawsuit from reaching trial. I previously wrote 'Altering Destiny' the story of a young woman's flight with found money and something deadly she does not know she had, and 'Sealing Fate', about a newly elected congressman whose affair leads to blackmail and murder. I love characters who are compelling and plots that take you to the unexpected. I am already underway on the next book. Thank you all for your kind words and support. I will do my very best to keep you entertained with interesting characters and plot twists. Thank you to all of my fans and supporters! My website is DavidPWarren.com

Books by the Author

- Scott Winslow Legal Mysteries

    - The Whistleblower Onslaught
    - Personal Violation

- Altering Destiny

- Imploded Lives

- Sealing Fate

Lightning Source UK Ltd.
Milton Keynes UK
UKHW011235091120
373077UK00006B/974

9 781034 004257